Of What Stars Sing

Nathan Bressler

Copyright © 2025 Nathan Bressler

All rights reserved.

ISBN: 9798267893473

DISCLAIMER

Dear Reader,

Within this novel, you will discover both Biblical truth and elements of Scriptural fantasy. In writing I have employed a Christ-centric creative process, inspired by the Holy Bible, my own faith journey with Jesus, and my love of the science fiction genre. I would like to make clear that this is a work of worship towards my Creator, but it is also a work of fiction. You will encounter ideas that, while steeped in the Word of God, are inventive extrapolations from the world that God has made. I have had some fun with speculative ideas about the cosmos, but the firm and complete truth of our Lord is to be found only in the pages of the Bible. Thank you!

Nathan Bressler

CONTENTS

	Acknowledgments	i
1	Approach unto Archway	1
2	Resisting on Luna Side	13
3	Rejection and Rock Bottom	22
4	Embers in the Ashes	30
5	Repentance in Part	40
6	A Notion of Purpose	49
7	Warming Up	59
8	The Breath Before the Plunge	69
9	Into the Wild Black Yonder	85
10	Settling Into the Interstellar	94
11	Impressive Dodging	103
12	The Preexistence of Cultivation	112
13	A Toiseean Encounter	126
14	Introductions All Around	142
15	Founding Day	153
16	Preaching to the Choir	167
17	Hearts Laid Bare	183
18	A Prophet in His Hometown	200
19	Hills and Valleys	216
20	Catalysts	231
21	A Strand of Three Cords	243

ACKNOWLEDGMENTS

There could be no adequate words to express my deepest appreciation for my Lord and Savior, Jesus the Christ. His immeasurable creation has inspired me to write and create all on my own, wrapped up in worshipful response as I am beholden to the wonder of His world.

I also would be remiss not to thank Melissa, my stalwart support, who encouraged this endeavor onward as only a truly loving wife could.

CHAPTER 1
APPROACH UNTO ARCHWAY

Ugh, Jesse thought, smacking his mouth. The dry air of these transport shuttles always left a stale taste in his mouth, especially if he slept with his mouth open. He always tried not to because of it. He knew that taste would last until he had something more substantial to eat or drink than water and the absolute last thing he wanted was the recirculated water of the shuttle tap sitting in front of him, but it would at least remove the dryness so he swigged.

The sterile environment of the earth-to-station shuttle isn't the most comfortable. Then again, it's not supposed to be. Public transport is utilitarian, and any time they try to pretend it could be luxurious, they only seem to be fooling themselves. Inflight entertainment, travel pillows and snacks can only improve the shuttle ride so much. Everyone's comfort tolerance is honestly somewhere between how long one is willing to rub elbows with another unfamiliar human and the astronomical price of a private launch pod. But the 6 hour flight could also be much faster, as long as the passengers don't mind a completely vertical take-off or pulling 5 G's for much of the ride. There's no doubt it would be fine and dandy for families of small children.

It's not piss, he thought as he drank his water pouch, trying to convince himself to ignore facts he wished he didn't know. Yet he still couldn't stop his imagination from picturing the scene: The little tike in the back, bouncing in his seat, barely containing his pressing need. His mother, sighing annoyingly that this is the third time in the flight she's had to excuse herself by the also annoyed gentleman in her row to escort her son to the toilet. She really shouldn't have allowed him to drink the whole soda, but she knew the mistake she was making when she made it. She was tired and worn out and at the time she just wanted to say 'yes' instead of 'no' for once. Once in the tiny closet of a bathroom, she would have to help stabilize him especially through the turbulence, but by now it was a game to the boy. Seeing how close he could get the stream to the edge of the rim without it splashing over the seat. Jesse could trace it all from there, passing through various pipes and hoses along the underbelly of the fuselage. Forced through this filter here, cooked under UV light there, and chemically treated before dumping into the potable water holding tank at the end. He could even visualize himself from the third person, requesting the water as she passed by. And that's when the flight attendant would have pressed the tap, holding the fitting tight till she filled his pouch with "fresh, clean" and slightly chilled recycled water.

So before he drank, he had to open his eyes to be sure it wasn't yellow. He peeked and blinked until he saw clearly. Forcing his eyes to see nothing but clear liquid still didn't convince his mind, and so a single sip was all he could muster. He laid his head back against the headrest and tried turning to face the other side, but by now he was awake. He had learned long ago that the hours of these shuttle runs passed much faster when you were unconscious. However, he has now found himself outside of that comfort window that we all strive to remain in when we wake up a bit earlier than we had wanted to. He had to admit to himself that there would be no more snoozing on this flight, so he adjusted himself in his seat and assessed his surroundings again.

The first thing he noticed was gravity. He still felt the conscious weight of his body, so that meant the slow ascent off of the planet wasn't yet through even the lowest levels of the atmosphere. However, glancing out the porthole window to his left, the curvature of the earth was becoming more apparent. The blue of the horizon was slowly being left behind, replaced by the blackness of space. It really *was* pretty. A realization he barely notices now as usual as it is for him. Adventures into the vastness, however incredible, lose their wonder after a couple dozen ventures. The young couple in the row ahead of him jostled for peeks at the stirring view, and for a moment he was jealous. The first reason was because she was beautiful, but the second was a brief longing for the excitement of the view to be new again.

"Did you know the first explorers thought the earth was flat?" His father quipped. He had noticed that his young son Jesse was enraptured by the view out the shuttle window, and he wanted to be a part of the moment. He had leaned forward, across his wife's lap who sat in the middle.

"No, they didn't", his mother corrected him.

"Sure they did! Even into the 21st century some thought that!"

"Then why did Columbus call the native people of America 'Indians'?", she quipped.

"Probably because he asked what they're names were." He smiled and rested back against his chair. His father had known that she was correct, but he had wanted his ploy to continue. At this age, Jesse sometimes couldn't tell if his mother was aware of his father's antics or whether she honestly believed he was a simpleton. Her even toned demeanor was a constant combatant to his father's jests. But they seemed to still love each other through it all, which is the comfort that Jesse took the most notice of.

His mother leaned into Jesse's shoulder as she followed his fascination with the spectacular scene outside the shuttlecraft. "Pretty amazing that God made all that and still thought about me and you, huh?"

"Yeah" Jesse responded, somewhat absentmindedly. He wasn't really thinking of it at the time, and even now his thoughts were more abstract doubt than developed logic. *How could He have made all this?* At 9 he was encountering a lot of ideas lately that seemed to contradict what his parents had always told him. Especially in textbooks at school, what with the millions of years of animal evolution and billions of years of cosmological development. He hadn't really considered it deeply yet, he was still too enamored with the wonder of it all, but it was starting to grab his attention in ways he wouldn't realize till he left home: Maybe God wasn't what his parents had told him. After all, heaven was supposed to be up here and so far they hadn't flown anywhere close to it.

◆ . + . ◆ . + . ◆

And there it was. He was expecting it. The slow onset of the feeling that his inflight meal was wanting to make a second appearance. The weight of the world was drifting slowly away as the shuttle climbed higher and the feeling of gravity was becoming less and less of a burden.

DONGGGG!

The harness sign illuminated on the front wall of the shuttle and the hologram spokeswoman coalesced into life in front of the passengers. She glowed from head to, well, waist since that was all that she was. She was radiating with an inner light of the projectors and was definitely not lifelike in definition. More hazy around the edges, as if an old color photo was brought to life.

"As you can see out your windows, we are continuing our climb out of the Earth's atmosphere. To avoid any injuries, I must now ask you to please secure yourselves in your seats. Those of you with children, please secure yourself first before securing the harness of your child. If you need any assistance, press the call button on the seat in front of you. Thank you for your attention!"

Activity around the shuttle was always mildly chaotic at this point. The sound of clinks and clacks of passengers jostling and wrestling with the unfamiliar buckles around their shoulders and laps. The inexperienced of them either giggling or vomiting as they slowly begin to gently drift up from their seats. Folks grasping at their personal items or remaining snacks and drinks as they attempt to escape the clutches of their owners. The flight attendants literally flew down the aisles, harnessed to zip lines that run from the back of the shuttle passenger cabin to the front. Jesse felt as if he was an expert around these amateurs as he casually pressed his water against its Velcro holder to make sure it was secure, causing the liquid inside to bubble and churn similar to the water under a wave.

"Will you hold this a minute?" The lady next to him asked, pressing a book to his chest.

"Ya, go ahead." Jesse replied. He grabbed the book, and leaned a bit to his left against the bulkhead to give her space to adjust. She fidgeted with the harness straps for a few seconds until she found the right fold for her arm to go under. Then she easily matched the other side to her shoulder and snapped them together across her chest, where she worked on finding the other end of her lap belt.

Jesse glanced down at the title of the book she asked him to hold. *Into the Wild Black Yonder* was the title, with a simple image of tiny stars dotting the jet black cover. Jesse smirked, humored by the fact that of course this lady had a book. She matched the stereotype of someone who would carry one.

Paper bound books were increasingly rare these days, as digitized media was so much cheaper, easier and contained every novel ever written. But this woman carried the proud look of someone who blatantly defied the convenience of those facts. She wore glasses, a dead giveaway that someone is resistant to modern eye enhancements. Plus she was wearing pants. Not that pants in and of themselves demands that someone is old fashioned, but these definitely did. Tan cargo pants, with the nooks, hooks and pockets on the sides, ready for anything. And that's what struck him about her. She was ready. Absolutely eager in appearance and also in the demeanor of her eyes. Eager to experience what others are trying to avoid. She's the opposite of most of the people who are casually lost in the comforts of the digital and visual. She wants to get her hands dirty.

But that didn't deter him from wanting to interject a difference of opinion. As she settled, she gave him an expectant look that said 'I'm ready' and Jesse handed her back her novel.

"You know, there's much easier ways to discover the Black Yonder now." He commented.

"You mean those tabs?" She said and pointed to Jesse's tablet tucked into the zipper in front of him. She already knew where he was going with this. She actually carried books publicly in hopes of having these conversations, as folks like this normally do. Eager to persuade the less enlightened. "They just aren't the same."

"Ya I know, that's kind of the point. Where did you even find a book like that anyways? Had to have cost a fortune."

"Oh, this is one of my old favorites. My parents actually owned a bookstore back in the day."

"I bet that was lucrative." Jesse remarked. Books, especially ones in as good of condition as the one she held, could still be had but for a steep price.

She laughed at the notion. "Actually, quite the opposite. Not many enjoy books anymore, much less want to pay what they are worth."

"Ya, and see, that's what I was getting at. Your parents' entire bookstore, hell, ALL the books in the world can fit right here." Jesse made his point by tapping on the small screen built into the seat in front of him.

"Well, you're not wrong." She sighed, actually looking at the screen longingly. Jesse took it as a sign of defeat, but in reality she was considering what the world would be like if her parents' store hadn't closed. Her mind even took it a step further and pondered lovingly at the idea that she could keep it as easily in her pocket as a tab. But before the flood of memories took her away along with her thoughts, she held out the novel to him again.

"But here, smell this."

Jesse was caught so off guard, and his snort so abrupt, the young couple in front of him ceased their stargazing for a split second to shoot him an inquisitive look. Jesse took no notice and accepted the novel again from her hand.

"You want me to smell it?"

"Yes." She said, firmly and with a nod.

"Why?" Jesse was a bit lost on where she was going with this.

"I want you to understand why I carry a book instead of a tablet." She insisted. A half beat later Jesse shrugged and consented.

"Ok." As he casually brought the book up to his face, she immediately reached out and pulled his hand back down to his lap.

"No, no, no. Not like that." Jesse was beginning to wish he had a different seatmate. "I want you to *experience* it." she said.

She centered herself in her seat, sat up straight and held her hands in her lap. "Sit like this."

Jesse, again confused at what point this was going to make any sense at all, politely obliged. He shuffled himself to sit upright, making sure to copy her exactly so that she had no reason to claim he'd done it wrong. His feet were straight and flat to the smooth shuttle floor. His knees slightly apart and in line with his hips. His back nestled into the lackluster lumbar support of the commercial grade seat. And finally, he placed the novel in his lap, closed and poised with the cover facing up, his hands grasping either side evenly.

"Now open it. Just page it open to the middle of the book."

Jesse followed the command and looked at her, awaiting the next instruction.

"Close your eyes, bring it open and up to your face. Let your nose rest on the pages, and breathe in deep and slow."

It would be a lie to say that Jesse wasn't a tad curious at this point, even if he didn't want to let her on. So he gave her a quick skeptical glance, but then closed his eyes. He breathed once, and then brought the novel to his nose, and he breathed in again.

✦ . ✦ . ✦ . ✦ . ✦

Must. A touch of damp must. The scent of rain had always confused him as a boy. Mostly because the water itself didn't smell. Oh there were plenty of odors *in* water and none of them did he recall to be appealing. Especially those that emanate from the cattle tank in the back pasture. There was also the scent of the heavy mineral twinge of the water from the well, metallic almost with a slight tartness. But the after rain must smell had always been a mystery to him. It was deep and weighty, earthy with a touch of sweetness. A sweetness he couldn't describe or else it would drift away at the effort.

It was mostly that the smell signaled the end of the rain, which was his favorite part. Not only did it mean he could go outside again without his mother's chastisement, but the transition itself was intriguing to him. Watching the rain slowly end, the clouds move on, and the streaks of sunlight breaking through the grey. That was his favorite.

Here he found himself again. In a moment that was captured through a passing glance. Jesse wasn't trying to think of home, but here it came anyway.

✦ . ⁺ . ✦ . ⁺ . ✦

In actuality, Jesse didn't remember all of this fondly when his nostrils absorbed the microfibers of the pages in the old novel and translated the information to his brain. That's probably why he initially gave the distinct impression of being unimpressed. But as unimpressed as he was, he did decide to take a second smell, although he couldn't have told you why. Something compelled him, regardless of the pain of memory.

"Do you see?" She leaned her head back slightly, looking slightly down on him as if she expected some grand revelation to come across his face as he lowered the book back to his lap.

"I don't *see* anything. I was smelling it." He said smartly and offered the novel back.

"You didn't see anything?" She took the novel from him and stashed it in the zippered pocket of the seat in front of her. Slightly perturbed at his melancholy response. "I'm not sure if I believe you."

"You asked me to smell it. It smells… I dunno, like an old book I guess?"

"But I asked if you saw anything." She insisted.

Jesse, now annoyingly confused, "How am I supposed to see something when I'm sniffing through the pages? You even had me close my eyes!"

"Yes, so you could *see* better!"

Jesse shook his head and half laughed to himself. "Look, I obviously don't get what point you're trying to make here, so why don't you just tell me?"

"Son, you don't need your eyes to see what books show you. Yes, sure you can read the same words from the 'pages' of your tablet," She made the air quotes to go along with her point. Then she shuffled slightly forward in her seat, attempting to contain the excitement to practice her speech. "But when you fold the soft paper pages in your hands, delicately turning them as you graze the chapters, you feel something more than the words that are written. When you hold the novel in your hands, the sheer and slight yet potent weight of its volume insists that you measure its lines carefully. Or even when you draw in the scent of the pages themselves, you begin to notice that much like yourself, the novel itself ages, weathers and changes with time." She rests her head against the seat's headrest. "It is life itself."

"Hmmph." Jesse paused to consider her words. Eloquent, sure, but they seemed a bit fantastical to him. He had a knee-jerk skepticism to them that was tied to his already determined bias. He fought against it for a second, but decided he didn't want to anymore.

"So you would describe books as if they are alive?"

"Some of them are."

"I'm sorry but by definition of bookmaking, that's false. Aren't they made of paper? Dead trees?"

She blinked slowly as she looked at him and… read him like a book, pun intended. She could tell by his response he didn't want to admit to what he experienced. It was the usual response when she is given the polite time by strangers to engage over the novels she carried. Obviously she hoped that this time it would be different, but she hadn't gotten her hopes up too high. She'd been hurt before by the rejection of strangers who simply chose to not understand her, and she wasn't going to give in to that hurt again.

"I guess we will just have to agree to disagree."

By this point in the shuttle's journey, Archway Station was looming into view out the port window. The far and away most impressive engineering marvel that humanity had ever constructed never ceased to inspire awe in even its most regular visitors, and so Jesse's sudden rapt attention to the approaching station outside was a convenient excuse to bow out of the conversation. She noticed his retreat but didn't press the matter. She was intrigued as well.

Archway had been constructed piece by piece over two centuries of determined labor and devoted construction. Nearly every country on the planet came together to aid in some way in its construction, but to hope they could accomplish the task peaceably was a pipe dream. Constant delays of bickering and jostling for control plagued the beginning decades. Wars of words were fought throughout the congresses and assemblies. Presidents, tyrants and every leader in between made promises of amicability that they either never could nor ever would keep, and so progress ground to a halt. Each space faring nation then started to split off and design their own space port of some kind (if they hadn't had a small research station already) where each country claimed their own "sovereign space" above their respective lands on earth. A new space race birthed with as much fear and haste as the original. The hostility grew and it wasn't until the advent of the Slingshot Gateway and the Singularity Drive that the focus was shifted from climbing on top of each other, to climbing to the top with each other. The far reaches of the cosmos were opened anew, and a fresh perspective rained upon the Earth. One of these technologies developed out of the Western world and one of them out of the East. Each of them offered the missing pieces to the puzzle of interstellar space travel and thus forced the countries of the planet to unite, at least until the common enemy in the angst of uncomfortable collaboration was bested. The dream of Archway Station, a singularity powered, ambassador governed, starcraft constructing, orbiting city could finally be realized.

The impressive structure resembles two pearlescent, four sided pyramids, their tips facing away from each other and pressed close together at their broad bases making a brutalist looking glossy diamond, resting on its side. Its surface is covered by slick, white glazed panels that glisten in the sunlight, sharp and lined with reflective amber lights, dotted with portholes and multilayered viewing windows. At the center of where the base of the pyramids meet is a half mile gap separating the two, held together by four thick connecting beams at each corner. This is the spaceport of the station, the destination of the shuttle that Jesse is heading towards. The simplistic beauty and smooth, crisp pearly white lines of the outer shell of Archway ends here quite abruptly as industry, commercial and transport traffic does not demand such elegance. Purpose and efficiency take precedence in design matters at the center, unfortunately advertisement as well, which makes the glow coming from the middle of Archway's center gap alive with flashes of lasers and dances of multi spectrum light rays. Floating metal rings of green and red extend out on all four sides, denoting the approaching and departing lanes of shuttle and transport traffic, keeping them clear of the casual and personal spacecraft that zip this way and that. And as mentioned previously, Archway Station is made possible by its dual singularity drives; obviously present as large pearly white orbs, studded with white operational lights which hang, barely connected to the station by long white conduit lines that extend out for nearly a ¼ of a mile at either end. In its entirety, the station itself was roughly 2 ½ miles wide at its base and a total of nearly 7 miles long.

"So what brings you to Archway, Mr...?" Jesse had almost forgotten she was there, or at least he wanted to.

"Work." Jesse didn't turn around to face her.

"Oh, what line of work are you in?" She asked. She was apparently missing the social cues.

"Lunar." He sighed. He wasn't thrilled to say it and less thrilled that she asked.

"Oh so you're a miner? Must be in management. You don't have the build for it."

"Ha, wow, thanks." His sarcasm was getting thicker by the minute.

"That was meant as a compliment. Not that there's wrong in being a rock-grunt, but those men have a certain... timbre to their appearance. I don't hear that in you." Her way of speaking was amusing to some, and for some reason frustrating to others. She liked to express herself in ways not usual to the norm.

Jesse, who definitely still regretted not being able to fall back asleep, was trying to be frustrated and so far it was working. "I'm going looking for work, so I might yet be a grunt. Then you'll have to admit that I am one whether or not you get the sense of it."

"And I absolutely will! I actually enjoy being wrong. Helps me know how to be right." She was going to try and win him over regardless of his attitude. There was something in him that she could tell he couldn't see yet. And honestly on her end, she couldn't define it either. Maybe it was only her natural want to mother others, or sympathy for his pitiful runaway disposition, but either way she was going to pursue it.

She fetched the novel and held it in her lap again. "Do you know what I love about this book?" She flashed him the cover again in case he had forgotten. He definitely had. He glanced at it again: *Into the Wild Black Yonder.*

"The smell?" The sarcasm was made softer with humor.

She laughed at his wit and smiled through her words. "No, no. Although truly, yes!" She sighed and collected herself.

"No, what I love about this book is it reminds me of the wonder that is the cosmos. Have you ever read it?"

He shook his head.

"It's a marvelous title. A pretty quick and easy read, too. But the imagery and imagination is intoxicating. It's innocent in its admiration and yearning for the adventure of space exploration, but it was written over a hundred years ago, back when that was only fantasy. Now that that opportunity is at our doorstep, it refreshes and invigorates me. It's as if I can bring along and share all the discoveries of today with the characters of the past. That we are united across time and space, humanity striding into the future together."

She was beaming again, and Jesse was finally understanding why. The cargo pants, the adventure novel, the sunny disposition at the mention of the infinite beyond. It made sense now.

"You're going to be a colonizer aren't you?" He asked, but it was more like pronouncing judgement.

"As a matter of fact, I am already. I'm the Director of New Foundations at Venture."

Venture Colonies was the largest and proudest of the relatively new companies, enterprisingly dedicated to the spreading of humanity to the stars. As mentioned previously, only one half of the missing puzzle that brought the world to unite under the mission of Archway Station was the discovery of singularity drives. The other was the creation of the Slingshot Gateway which opened up the possibility of reaching those stars, literally. When before the only option was to slowly cruise for 6 months to barely reach the furthest planet in our own system, Neptune, suddenly reaching destinations within 10 lightyears was possible. After further development of the technology another 50 lightyears of distance was possible till finally today, nearly 100.

"My name is Junia Fresco." She extended her hand.

Jesse took it. "Jesse."

"Jesse, have you ever thought of colony work? I only ask as it seems you haven't landed a lasting career yet, since you're looking for work on the moon."

And here comes the recruitment pitch, he thought to himself. "No, colony work isn't for me." She hadn't let go of his hand yet. She was trying to keep him engaged as long as possible.

"Why not? What are you hoping to find out there in the lunar mines?"

"A paycheck." He tried to withdraw his hand from this awkward shake. She gripped a bit tighter for a half second before she let go of his hand, as if to indicate that she was letting go, but it was *her* choice to let go.

"That's a far way to go for a simple paycheck. You could get that back on Earth as well."

"Ya, but the Moon isn't as crowded."

DONGGGG!

The shuttle cabin announcement tone echoed softly through the air again. The holographic attendant flickered into life once more at the front, a few rows ahead of them.

"Ladies and gentlemen, we are commencing our final approach to Archway Station and will be arriving in a few minutes." The voice of the hologram was sweet and pacifying. It was also sweet music to Jesse's ears because it meant the end of the 6-hour journey, where only the last 30 minutes felt long. He began to shuffle in his seat, looking around and pretending it took all his focus to gather his small satchel, tablet and water pouch.

Junia allowed him to retreat yet again, knowing she had a few more minutes while offloading the shuttle to press the issue a final time. She knew she was annoying him, but still. Her perception let her know that she shouldn't give up so easily on this one. Something encouraged her from deep inside to ensure he knew he had other options than just to escape to the moon.

Rhythmically passing the port windows of the shuttle were the bright green approach lights of the Archway Station arrivals port; Quickly swathing the cabin from front to back in emerald glow. Sharp eyed individuals could spot an occasional maintenance bot clinging to separate free floating approach rings, seeming like robotic houseflies in space. They had 6 arms, with separate pocket knife like attachments to dispense for various repair duties around the station's port.

The actual physical flight attendants drifted down the aisles, zipping by on their cables. This time they collected various trash items and encouraged the passengers to secure their possessions. As they went, stopping to correct passengers who were overly enjoying themselves and had not yet strapped themselves in, their electronic counterpart continued at the front.

"As we approach Luna Side arrival, please prepare yourself and your belongings for entry into gravity. The captain will soon begin rotation to align us for proper orientation." The hologram motioned to her left, indicating that the shuttle will be rotating so that the bottom of the spacecraft is towards the Moon. Artificial gravity is created by any vessel or station powered by a singularity drive. Due to the gravitational forces of the dual drives on Archway Station, "up" depends on your perspective while on board: The pyramid with its point towards the Moon, called Luna Side, or the pyramid with its point towards the Earth, called Terra Side. From both perspectives, the spaceport in the middle of Archway Station is "up".

As the shuttle began to rotate, all the stars were now lost, swallowed up by the girth of the massive station, now only reflecting the bright unfiltered sunlight from its pearlescent walls. It really is a gorgeous sight to behold, especially remembering that this marvel of human achievement was nearly the cause of global war. It's a testament to what beauty can come from the union of a body of people.

"We will be entering gravity in 5... 4... 3... 2... 1..." The view felt interrupted too soon as shadow enveloped the shuttle when it cruised into port space. The returning weight of gravity was instantly felt by all, and as usual a few items clinked upon the glossy floor of the shuttlecraft. The spacecraft itself groaned and creaked along with a few heavy breaths here or there from the passengers, a sign that everyone and everything was now reminded of the various physical burdens they carry.

The pearly white beauty of the outer station hull was now replaced by the exposed dirty grey pipes, tanks and towers of machinery that must be present to run the spaceport. These are highlighted or covered up by the sharp and demanding lights and adverts of commercial trade. Various colors, shapes and sizes, as well as languages and symbols lined the tops and bottoms of every available space a sign could fit on the entry ports. English, Mandarin, Spanish and Hindi; as long as you spoke one of those languages (and honestly most people today could speak enough to get around with them all) you could at least decipher your way around any of the businesses on the station. A first time visitor of Archway would instantly get the impression that this was a melting pot of diversity, but as with many cities on Earth, cultural segregation naturally divides us to sections when living among one another. There was a "Chinatown", a "little Mexico", an "American quarter" and the like where each of these advertisements beckoned travelers, vying to convince them they had the superior service or products. With all their flash and lights, one could argue whether or not the advertisements themselves made the industrial equipment, storage vats, antenna and transport tubes prettier or uglier. However, although the necessary nexus of what made Archway Station even sustainably possible, the call of attention the spaceport demanded hid the fact that it was not the station's crown jewel. Not by a longshot.

The shuttle slowed and decelerated, which was a sensation that most passengers have forgotten by now. Traveling from the weightlessness of space so abruptly back to the drag of gravity was always caught by surprise. Many passengers, including both Jesse and Junia placed their hands on the back of the seats ahead of them, bracing against the braking rockets of the shuttle. In actuality, due to the distance from either of the station's singularity drives, the spaceport itself was only about 7/8ths of Earth's gravity. If you weigh around 180 lbs. on Earth, you actually only weighed just shy of 160 lbs. in Archways spaceport. This obviously assisted with commerce and trade of large products and goods, as well as giving the average dock worker no end of "miracle weight loss" joking material. Conversely on the lower levels of either pyramid, the ones closest to the singularities, the average person weighed 20 lbs. more. This meant that usually those who had no other choice resided, worked or visited the lower decks.

As the shuttle gently lowered, the wing tips tilted back and forth, delicately dancing in slow motion as the pilot eased the shuttle now straight down to its awaiting platform. With a soft bump, the feet of the landing skids rested on the floor. Once the shuttle was confirmed secured to the platform, it began to elevator down and airlock doors started to slide to a close overhead. Orange warning lights circled outside the shuttles port windows, and the glow of the overwhelming beacons of advertisement dimmed as the landing platform airlock closed overhead.

The flight attendants unbuckled their shoulder harnesses and stood from their jump seats, which also indicated to the eager passengers they were free to do the same. The attendants awaited for the security locks of the port boarding tunnel to engage against the shuttles passenger doors, and with a loud *CLACK & SCHINK* the confirmation light illuminated green. With a slight heave, the attendant disengaged the door lock and pushed open the hatch.

CHAPTER 2
RESISTING ON LUNA SIDE

The extendable gangway hissed loudly against the side of the shuttle, pressed down firmly and tightly with its vacuum grip. Noise was the reminder of atmosphere, and its dismissal was a reminder of the dangerous vacuum of space, so noise had always provided Jesse with comfort. Space travel was as common as a drive down the road nowadays, but despite his best efforts to leave earth whenever he could, he still would rather dirt beneath his feet than steel and nothingness. The notion that he couldn't go outside whenever he pleased was disappointing.

Junia had made her way ahead of him, shuffled between a few passengers down the stretched hall of the gangway. It seemed to the exiting passengers that they were walking through an enormous spring looking at the sides of the extendable hall. Descending slowly down the ramp, the spring ended at the terminal door, open and ready to receive them with their first smatterings of food, drink and merchandise. Here is where the hustle and bustle of the Luna Side terminal began. Travelers and workers gathering and scattering. If there were a viewable timelapse recording of the masses, one could observe the various patterns of movement and determine there was not much difference between ants in a colony and these people on Archway. Junia fought against the flow and found a niche off the end of the gangway. There she turned and waited.

Jesse tried to look beyond her, but their eyes met and she smiled. She noticed that he noticed her, and therefore the only polite way out of this final conversation for him was to hear her out one last time. And he couldn't help but be polite, at least at first. *Do unto others as you would have them do unto you.* It was how he was raised.

"You know what the worst part about those shuttle rides is?" She smirked, her response ready no matter what he was going to say.

His thoughts went a different direction than his mouth did, "The slow march of time?"

"The air! Oh, don't get me wrong, I'm very thankful for it compared to the alternative, but every breath no matter how deep, feels stuffy. I always make sure I have time for a stop at the gardens when I get back. Care to join me?"

He hesitated, grasping for the out. Jesse had nowhere pressing to be yet, so his eyes scanned the shops and restaurants nestled into this end of the arrivals terminal.

Junia's keen perception assisted her yet again. "I'll buy you a drink?"

He had thrown away his water pouch on the way off the shuttle. He couldn't bear the thought of its journey any more, no matter how thirsty he was. And the air was still just as dry and circulated here in the terminal as it was on the spacecraft, if not worse due to the amount of exhaling humans, so he was definitely thirsty. Jesse was also dangerously low on funds, so he was definitely in need of her to buy it. He braced his resolve and swallowed his desire to escape for a while.

"Ya, fine. Sounds good."

"Terrific! I know a great place. Follow me!"

She turned and led on with confidence, weaving between the passing travelers of the terminal. She didn't look back to ensure he followed. She considered it a test of his character.

The gardens that Junia referred to were the station sponsored botanical gardens located on both Terra and Luna Side on the levels just below the spaceports. With the lower gravity away from the singularities the plants tended to grow both thinner and taller than on earth, allowing more to be packed into this limited space station area. The space provided was really rather large in terms of territory allotted on the station. The areas on either side of the station at this point were at their widest, so both Luna and Terra Gardens were 2 square miles (or just over 1200 acres) of lush flora. Most of the garden was managed by various commercial exploits to ensure that Archway Station was as self-sustaining as possible. It's much more cost effective to grow your own food than to import it from Earth.

But where Junia was leading Jesse was a section of Luna Garden of smaller plots, managed by individual families for their own private use or sale. Although here the sunlight was reflected by the large, intensely focused mirrors on the high ceiling and thus artificial, these had the feel of the private backyard gardens of Earth. Each ¼ acre plot was even separated by cute, 3 foot white picket fences, and each entrance was a small, gated arbor. Most horticulturists had encouraged various vines and climbing plants to grow and adorn the gates, and walking among the Homestead Plots (as they were called) invited many sights and smells of home on the planet below.

Trumpet Vine, Crawling Rose, Boston Cucumber, Kajari Melon. Jesse could name quite a few of the varieties he could see on the arbor gates from the graveled pathway along the Homestead Plots. The smells that drifted across the fence lines were a welcome change from the stale air of the station as well: *Juniper,*

Rosemary, Lavender... and a floral bouquet that he couldn't quite place. It was such a mixture of sweet flowers and fresh, clean air that it overwhelmed the senses, but in a pleasant way. He breathed deep and savored the fresh oxygen.

"Here we are." Junia had led him straight to a small shack of a shop in the middle of the Homestead Plots. Whoever it was that operated this shop had an entrepreneurial spirit and utilized their "land" to open a beverage stand, selling homegrown and crafted drinks. "Grab a seat will you? I'll get the drinks."

Jesse found a 2 top barista style set up along the side wall of the shack, contained by a rough-cut post and rail fence. *There's no way this is real wood*, he thought and tapped his fingernail along the shiplap siding. Yep, sure enough the exterior was definitely steel that had been pressed, painted and stained to resemble a soft look of rough-cut wood siding. As was the table. And the chairs. And the fence. But the large Red Oak tree that stood to the right of the shack, looming with awkwardly thin branches and a not-so-broad trunk, was definitely real. He could tell by the many acorns it was dropping all over the flagstone and gravel courtyard where the drink shack stood. Its plentiful broad leaves shaded much of the seating area where Jesse had chosen. The lower gravity of the Luna Side Garden caused the tree to grow abnormally thin, and yet it still looked just as sturdy and resilient as an oak ever has.

As he swatted away a couple of lingering bees from the drink stains on the table, he could have been fooled to believe he was on Earth. As long as you didn't look for the horizon because all you would see are the tall, mirrored windows of the Archway wall, topped with gaudy ventilation ducts for air circulation. But that ventilation system did simulate a bit of a breeze, cooling the moisture heavy air and shuffling the leaves over his head. All of the scenery was beginning to make him just enough homesick that he decided to keep his gaze low.

Before too long Junia returned with a couple jars in hand. Each had hand chiseled ice, a couple white and yellow honeysuckle flowers and a pastel lemon straw. She placed them on the table, one for her and one for Jesse. Then she produced a pop-cap bottle from her back pocket containing a slightly foggy but mostly clear liquid with a few rice-looking grains at the bottom.

"It's Honeysuckle Kefir. A great way to appreciate the scenery." She flicked the bottle open with her thumb. It fizzled right away but yielded before cresting the bottle. She let the carbonation die a bit and then poured it over the ice. The cubes clinked against the glass and the beverage hissed. Jesse was watching the small bubbles pop and spit at the top of his drink when she spoke.

"So Jesse," She set the bottle on the table and the kefir grains settled to the bottom. "Where are you from? Do you have any family?"

"Carolina." He sipped on the kefir, which was delightfully refreshing. "My folks and my sister have a house there still."

"Oh, what part?"

"Near Asheboro. They have a bit of a farm there. A few acres. They've been homesteaders for most of my life."

"Oh, so a lot of this is fairly familiar to you?" She motions her hand to the vast greenery of the Luna Side Garden.

"Ya, quite a bit." He looked around, gathering his surroundings again. .

"My family is from Boulder. That's where I left my husband. We had always loved following life where it leads us. It's what keeps tomorrow so thrilling."

"You left him in Colorado? Why did you leave him there?"

She smiled, but with a twinge of pain in her eyes. "Well, he was sleeping so peacefully I just couldn't bear to wake him." She looked down at her kefir and swirled it. It struck her odd that she would feel so exposed to him at this moment when she had already been so incessantly outgoing. But it is always awkward to mention the recently deceased.

"He passed on a couple months ago."

"Oh, I'm sorry." There was a slight pause. Whether he decided to open his mouth to speak or not, he did find it easy to be around her. When the pause was too long and he didn't know what to say, he just blurted out: "I lost my brother too."

"Where is it you're going?" Jesse asked.

"*In all your ways acknowledge Him, and He will direct your steps.*" Stephen replied, shoving his socks even deeper into the already overstuffed bag. There were still yet a few more clothes to get in there, somehow.

Jesse's teenage face perplexed and cocked sideways. "What?"

"Proverbs 3:6! What do you mean, 'what?'" Stephen, a strapping young man with a thin chin beard, beamed with life. From youth Jesse had always felt enamored with his older brother. Not hoping that he would be as strong, tall and brave as him one day, although, yes, those were his thoughts as a boy. Now what mostly grabbed his attention with apprehension and jealousy was his zeal for life. His *called* life.

"Ya, ok, but *where* are you going? Where do those steps go?"

"Beats me, bro. I'm going to start in Chicago and follow the Lord from there."

Stephen was leaving on a solo mission. As he put it, the Lord had put on his heart to reach the lost in America and the way that he had figured it, you might as well start out with the place that you know needs more Jesus than anywhere else. Stephen had often called it his "Nineveh."

"Can't you follow the Lord here? There's loads of lost people here too."

Stephen was now fighting his bag with two hands; one holding the bag closed and the other yanking hard on the zipper. "Why do you think you're staying here?" Stephen managed to get out with gritted teeth.

Jesse huffed and strode in from the doorway, shouldered into his brother and drove his knee down on top of the bag. He leaned his body weight onto the clothes to compress them down enough for Stephen to finally close the zipper.

"I'm just sayin' you don't have to go." Jesse stood back up straight and folded his arms. "Mom and dad don't know everything, you know."

Stephen wiped the long hair from his face and rested his hands on his hips. This was his manneristic stance when he stood. A sort of proud pose. The sort of pose that a self-confident person would take when a matter had been decided and decided well.

"I'm not going because of them. I told you, Jesse, Jesus told me this is what I'm supposed to do. This is the life He is calling me to. I'm following Him."

◆ ✛ ◆ ✛ ◆

Jesse realized they both had been quiet for a while, both lost in memory at the same time. The moment was too heavy for him and he didn't want to air it out with a stranger but again Junia's words seemed to coax things he was running from to the surface. She hadn't even meant to. He shifted the conversation away before it was pursued any further.

"Thank you for this by the way." He held up his glass. He had already drunk half of it.

Without skipping a beat, she said, "To the too soon dearly departed!" And with that she quickly tapped her glass with his and they swigged. Apparently, she was eager to avoid the trip down memory lane too, but her smile returned as soon as she had swallowed.

"Is that why you're looking for work at the lunar mines?"

"What, because my brother died?" *Damn she's forward,* Jesse thought. For that she deserved to only hear half the truth, he had decided. "No, it's 'cause I told you, I needed the money."

"And a career on the desolate moon is where you wanna make that money, huh?"

"It does pay well. It's not like I'm going to live there forever," he defended.

"Oh, no doubt. No doubt. But is that where you want to *live*?"

He didn't follow right away. "Umm… yes? I have to live where I work, Junia."

"No no no, Jesse, what I'm asking is that where you *want* to live? *How* you want to live? *Why* you want to live?" She was leaning forward again, that feeling in the pit of her stomach eager to share what wisdom she had on the subject. She desperately wanted him to understand.

"It could end up being a career, I guess, ya."

"And that's what you were made for? Is that what you would say?"

He furrowed his brow. He'd heard that before and he didn't like defending his choice all over again. "I've got to eat! And pay for things… for stuff like this!" He patted the table to make his point, perhaps a bit firmer than he meant to. But he was getting angry, and he didn't mind if she jumped when the glasses rattled.

She backed off, but only in demeanor. "Jesse, dear, I'm not trying to upset you." She hesitated, collecting her thoughts for a different approach. "I'm trying to understand you."

"So you can recruit me for Venture?"

"No, because I honestly don't understand working for a paycheck. I never have."

He laughed at the absurdity of it. "You mean you don't get paid?" He poised his hands on the table and braced his elbows, acting as if he was going to have to get up and sprint at any moment. "Do you not have money to pay for this? Are we going to have to run?"

"Don't be silly, of course I get paid! But Jesse, I would do this even if I didn't. It's as if…" She grasped for the right words, fully trusting that they would come to her as they always have. "As if I had been designed to do this. I'm living my fulfilled purpose for being. I'm talking to you now because I want you to realize that too."

"Ya, 'He has a plan', huh?" Jesse rested back in his chair. He thought he had left his parents behind on earth. Turns out they were with him here too.

Junia had missed who Jesse was referring to, but at least she could hear in his answer that he had a concept of what she was saying. She spoke the truth without even knowing Who's truth it was.

"Jesse, I've always had a tender heart for people. I can see things in them that sometimes they can't, or even won't, see in themselves. I said it on the shuttle, you don't feel like a miner."

"You said I didn't have the timbre of it. You couldn't *hear* that in me. Are you saying you're getting another sixth sense about it? Is this where you *taste* that I don't have the flavor or something?" The full blown smart aleck was just him being rude now to get her to back off.

She put her hand on the table, gently placing her fingertips across his. She wanted this to have as much of an impact as she could. She could tell her opportunity was closing fast.

"I don't know you well, but I know you well enough to know you're lost. Forget about the moon, and forget about Venture. I'm not trying to convince you to escape even further away."

He stared at her with jaded eyes, but he didn't move his hand. She understood that meant she had a little more time.

"I want you to live, Jesse. I want you to live as you were meant to." Her eyes became glossy. It was Jesse's turn to speak truth that he didn't know he knew.

"Who are you talking to?" His eyes narrowed as he tried to discern the glimpse he saw. "You don't even know me… why do you care that I live my 'purpose' in life?" For the first time in this conversation, he could sense he wasn't the only one she was speaking to, but there was no one else at the table.

Junia took a breath. "My son." She caught herself and quickly corrected before he clued in. "Jesse, my son. Life is there to be fulfilled, to have it abundantly. It's not to simply have a job to pay to be alive. Work, buy, work, buy, work, buy then die. That isn't living."

"Then what is living?" Jesse leaned forward over the table between them. He wanted to be as clear as possible when he spoke his peace. "Junia, It's not like I don't have things that I wanna do. I have wants and dreams and stuff. But those things can't be had by simply *living* a life, right? They cost money! Life costs money! I'm wanting to work a job so that I *can* pay for my life. What don't you understand about that?" He opened his hands with palms up, offering the only explanation he could think of for his actions, but they were good enough for him. Jesse was done. He had closed and locked the door.

"You are right, Jesse. Life does cost." She sat back. Her eyes lowered to the table. She smirked in sad satisfaction. "I suppose like you said, it just depends on what you want to buy, and how you want to pay for it."

She had tried and seemingly failed at justifying her living full of life outlook yet again. Junia found herself a bit more hurt by this one. Every runaway or vagrant that she encounters has usually two reasons for their flight; pain and turmoil. Jesse definitely had both. And yet, unlike the others, instead of beating down her door at Venture to run away as far as they could, this one was avoiding it completely. He must have been hanging onto something in his past still. A hurt or an anger that demanded that he disobeyed and stayed near instead of escaping completely. Perhaps that's what made her so attached from the beginning. Jesse needed the same kind of encouragement to let go and chase after life as Leonard did. But she didn't know him as well as she knew her son.

There were a few moments of quiet now. Both of them had spoken and made themselves understood, but neither was heard. At least not the way they wanted to be heard.

It was fitting of the mood that the reflected sunlight began to fade, and fade quickly. Archway station is fixed in geosynchronous orbit above the Earth, approximately 28,000 miles above Point Nemo in the Pacific, so its day/night cycle is technically the same 24 hour period of the Earth. However, the sun doesn't set on the station. There is no curvature of the sky, nor is there an atmosphere to refract and beautify the sun's rays as they diminish in the sky. The sun's light is there, then dims for a few minutes as the planet blocks the star, then the sun's light goes out. In Luna Garden, the solar mirrors that stream down the sun's rays now act as starfield reflectors in the ceiling, so although backward, the same stars and constellations could be seen as if they are from the planet's surface.

With the coming of the dusk, Jesse could tell that the conversation was over but that Junia seemed content to enjoy the evening at the kefir bar, so he pushed back his chair and stood.

"Thank you for the drink, but I'm gonna get going."

"Good bye, Jesse." She extended her hand. He took it, and noticed that he was getting cold. He could tell because her hand was so warm. "I very much pray that you find your life on the moon."

He nodded, and especially because he was eager to end goodbyes as soon as possible, he quickly turned. He walked out of the shade of the oak tree, back down the gravel path towards the transport tubes. Jesse felt instant relief to be back on his own again and with his life heading the way that he knew as the right direction. At least he hoped it was the right direction. Honestly, he hadn't thought it through but of course Jesse wouldn't let himself see that yet. He adjusted his satchel over his shoulder so it wouldn't bang his knees as he walked, and put his hands in his pockets, thinking back on his encounter and drinks. Junia, although definitely genuine, was being a tad forward and starkly opinionated. He reflected upon their conversation as he crunched the gravel pathway.

Why wouldn't she understand? Could she not understand?

He had encountered the same unwillingness in his parents. They seemed to him as unyielding and especially dismissive of his objections. Jesse had lost his temper last they talked a few weeks ago, which he still regarded as their fault and not his own. He shook his head so that the thought would leave his mind. He did not want to deal with that right now. It was his first night on the station and he needed to find a place to sleep.

His scratchy gravel steps transitioned in the blink of an eye to the click clack of Archways panel flooring. The reflected stars and moonlight switched to canned recessed lights. And unfortunately, the rich, floral oxygenated air was left behind as the lift doors slid to a close. Jesse hesitated and thought for a second, staring at the location buttons, trying to remember what level the affordable hostels were on. He had a vague recommendation from a friend that he was going off of, and so he selected a humble floor near the point of the station.

The transport tubes of Archway station were many and plentiful, one of the best designed public transport systems ever built, actually. There was hardly ever a wait for a lift to another level. This was due to their slow-lane / fast-lane approach and departure from each level, their comfortable and yet surprisingly high speed, and the fact that they could move both vertically and horizontally.

Jesse's tube journeyed non-stop on his way to Lower Luna Point. The colossal size of Archway Station was minimized into a single 2-minute tube ride as Jesse's destination was close to the "bottom" of the pyramid, a distance of around 2 miles from the gardens. Jesse felt the effects of the change in gravity the most in his thighs as they flexed a bit firmer to accommodate his increasing weight. His breathing was becoming a bit labored and heavy, a feeling that reminded him of climbing to the top of a mountain, but with a toddler standing on your chest. Once the transport tube coasted to a halt, he now weighed about 15 lbs more than he did at the beginning of his journey down due to the closer proximity of the singularity drive on this end of Archway.

The transport tubes slid open and immediately a first time visitor could tell why the locals took to calling Lower Luna Point, "Low Point". The same architecture, paneling, lighting and support structures provided the backbone of every level on the station, but due to certain local influences, that new and glossy backbone may or may not stay as pristine. As was mentioned previously, due to the increase in gravitational pull on the lower levels most attempt to avoid the areas. This fact drives up the cost in the upper levels of the station, and down in the lower levels. And with lower cost, comes lower expectations.

With the amenities that Archway offers, Low Point is definitely not the squalor you would expect from an impoverished area on Earth, but along the main strip of the level, so called "the Dragway", a thin haze of smoke lingers. Smoking is forbidden in nearly all of the station's levels, but is overlooked the further you descend.

The Dragway is one of the "town centers" of the Station, which are central points in the residential sections that have elevated ceilings to allow for structures as tall as 3 stories to be erected. Its purpose, similar to the gardens, is to provide a bit more of the feeling of home to the residents as the grey paneling and low ceiling recessed lighting gives many a sense of entrapment and depression after a time. But what the Dragway does offer is a bit too close to home for most.

Tattoo parlors, cheap dive bars, high interest lenders and convenience grocers line much of the small city blocks. Many of the poverty stricken have higher priorities than cleanliness and so litter collects, mostly into piles in the corners. Down this far Low Point is only ½ mile across in every direction, and so each shop and stall feels cramped. Not everyone who comes to Archway is as successful as they hoped and so some poor souls sleep in the nooks and crannies of the aisle, building makeshift "pods" out of whatever scrap building material is available. The smell of a mixture of freshly oiled street food wafts through the air, sizzling at each stall where the high heat keeps likely contaminants at bay.

The people who live here are the true melting pot of the station. Hindi, Mandarin and English words are thrown this way and that. The cultures of Earth are mixed together in a jumbled mess that rearranges almost daily. Thankfully, violence is not usually a problem in Low Point, mostly due to the fact that many of those who reside here have a hard enough time as it is. Their frustrations are taken out on those who work and live above them in the high levels of Archway. But Jesse stuck to the middle of the wide aisle, B lining his way to a tall, 3 floored building on the far side of Dragway. He felt exposed and out of place. He grew up outside of cities and so everything about them always felt too close, too space invading. Even though he could feel eyes on himself, he made sure to keep his eyes focused on where he was going. He could just make out the sign from the middle of Low Point, "Brigg's Youth Hostel", where he was told he could rent a personal pod for the night for cheaper than anywhere else.

When Jesse reached the door, the steel from the sliding handle felt greasy on his fingers. He wiped his hand on his chest and went inside the hostel lobby.

CHAPTER 3
REJECTION AND ROCK BOTTOM

He entered his personal pod, and slid the door shut. The fidgety locking mechanism *seemed like* it might have worked, but the way the knob jostled so loosely didn't fill him with too much confidence. Jesse figured he might be sleeping with his face towards the door tonight, to be ready incase of intrusion.

The same greasy slick feeling stuck to his fingers after shutting this door too. At least, unlike the front door downstairs, the grey white of the door and the wall paneling of his rented pod had some streak marks where an apparent attempt was made at cleaning. He took stock of his private spot for the night, looking for a place to set his satchel and tablet.

It was an uncomfortably quaint but efficient use of the space available. Couldn't have been more than 50 square feet. Above him to his right was the bunk, a small, lofted bed that he nearly hit his head on as he turned around. Below it was a shallow sink (more recirculated water!) and some counter space with a single built in, plasticky looking seat. On the left was the pod's viewscreen and an empty thin, recessed closet. There was no bathroom in the pod itself, that was a communal unit down the hallway. Jesse had the half serious thought of using the sink if it was absolutely necessary. The pod was already putting him slightly on edge due to its claustrophobic nature, but he was able to keep his anxiety at bay due to his thankfulness of at least having his own private space.

Jesse threw his satchel off his shoulder on the counter and opened it. He shuffled his meager possessions around till he discovered the last food bar he had. The label read "chicken spaghetti". Jesse ripped it open and switched on the sink. He hesitated for a moment before filling the package with the water, remembering where it came from, but decided he wouldn't enjoy eating the bar cold and stiff. He filled the package with water and turned off the sink. He sat down and used his tablet to login to his comms account, careful not to spill the now activated and steaming pouch of hot food in his hands.

The only unopened new message was the one he had received from his mom

5 days earlier. He scrolled past it to open the link for another message from Mitchell and Son Lunar Materials. Jesse slurped a bit of the hot chicken spaghetti and re-read the message again:

Thank you for your interest in a position within Mitchell and Son Lunar Materials! We regret to inform you that your application for employment has been denied. This is due to your application not matching the requirements of the position available. We wish you the best of luck in your future endeavors!

Jesse had applied for the advertised "always hiring" position of Resource Collections Technician, AKA a "rock-grunt" in the mines. *That's gotta be a mistake,* he reassured himself. *They say in the advert that they are always hiring. I'm just wanting to be a grunt!* Tomorrow he was planning on making a visit to the Mitchell and Sons General Office to rectify it. So he cast his tablet aside, allowing that to be a worry for the morning. He slurped down the last of his evening meal, and flicked on the pod's viewscreen before turning out the lights. His eyes grew heavy after a time and he didn't notice when he dozed off to sleep.

◆ . ⁺ . ◆ . ⁺ . ◆

He opened his eyes, but did he? Looking around there was nothing but black. But It did seem to move and swirl, and he could just make out differences in waves of jet black vs satin black. As if the void itself was rippling in waves of gloss and matte. It swirled in places and undulated like the sea in others. The black was deep and soupy, but nothingness.

But as he reached out forwards he did notice that he had hands, he could see them bright as day, reaching out with fingers stretched to touch that which was beyond grasp. Looking down he had feet too, but shockingly the void was not empty below him.

The Earth, seen fully spherical, rotating slowly below him was here too. But it was grey, various tones of grey, completely devoid of its bright blues, greens and tans. From Jesse's perspective, the Earth felt lifeless. He had no reason to know, but he intuitively knew it was dead. Not lifeless, as he could still envision mankind and the animals moving about the planet, oblivious of his floating body miles above the surface. But the Earth was dead to him. There was no life for Jesse there.

As he felt the hot tears of frustration, depression and anger welling up behind his eyes, he suddenly heard a whisper of a voice inside his head.

Come, find me here.

His head shot up, looking this way and that, scanning the dancing black void for the source of the voice. There was nothing. No indication of anything in the darkness.

Jesse.

Suddenly, he could pinpoint exactly the direction of the voice. Jesse's eyes zeroed in on a far point slightly over his head. One fixed pinpoint of light, alone but brilliant in the black.

Jesse, come, find me here.

The light was small, insignificant, lost in the infinite. But to Jesse in that moment, it was an oasis of color. Rays of gold, hues of purple, chills of blue, fire of red… each color of the rainbow was emitted from this tiny speck of life. Jesse was fixated on it, listening intensely for another breath of the soft and deep whisper he had heard. Now, instead of attempting to breach the void, he reached out towards the light.

✦. ✢ .✦. ✢ .✦

CRAAACK BOOOOMMMMMMMM! Jesse shot up from sleep so fast he knocked his head against the bunk of the bed above him. The crash of lightning lit up his room and the thunder reverberated through the walls, slowly rolling away in intensity. It was storming and raining pretty good outside, or at least for a few seconds that's what he thought. He realized after a few glances around the tight pod he had slept with the viewscreen switched to the ambient weather channel.

The stark awakening had chased away the memory of any dreams he had had. Jesse had the vague notion that it was a good one, so he felt a mild case of regret to have awoken from it, even if he couldn't remember exactly what it was. He glanced at the time on his wristwatch. It was 9:32 in the morning. He had to check out by 10, so he lifted his now aching back off the plastic seat and gathered his socks and shoes. He regretted not caring enough to move to the bed in the middle of the night. Jesse had a last pair of clean clothes to change into before he had to worry about laundry, so he half dazedly put them on.

Jesse paid for his pod, leaving a miniscule amount of funds in his account. As he left and re-entered the center of the Dragway, the hustle and bustle of the morning was not very different from the night before. The sights, the sounds, the smells, all were the same aside from the very real sun rising very artificially reflected on the ceiling. His hopes of earning a living wage were dependent on convincing Mitchell and Sons that they should accept his application, but walking by the vagrants, he wondered if tonight, that would be his fate.

Re-entering the transport tubes from yesterday, he pressed the Mid-Luna Plaza button. He glanced at the location screen to make sure he was heading in the right direction, looking through the titles of businesses which were headquartered at Mid-Luna town center. Flashing on the location screen of the tube was the station wide announcement that Archway was beginning its relocation to Moon Apogee.

Aside from the marvel that Archway Station was in and of itself, there was also the well-engineered idea that the station would not remain stationary. Space travel by conventional rocket, thrusters and the like still require fuel, and lots of it. Once established colonies took root on the moon, there was the problem of getting there and back cheaply. There was great profit to be had in the ores and shipyard docks of the lunar colonies but travel back to Earth was expensive and time consuming. As the dream of Archway became a reality, one genius level engineer proposed the idea that the station itself could ferry passengers and cargo back and forth, and so the original idea of a single singularity station was scrapped for the dual design that exists today. About every 7 1/2 days, Archway station fires up of its alternate singularity drives and relocates to close proximity of either the Moon or Earth, depending on where the Moon is in its 30 day orbit of the planet. When the station is close to Earth, Archway is in its Perigee orbit, when near the Moon, it is in its Apogee orbit. And of course, all of this is done while still in geosynchronous location above Point Nemo in the Pacific Ocean. Viewed from Earth, depending on its proximity, the station appears as either a dot or as a tiny diamond in the same spot in the sky.

The slip doors of the transport tube closed and Jesse, along with a few others, were on their way back towards the middle of Archway. Mid-Luna Plaza was the business park nearly exactly in the middle of Luna Side, so the literal weight was being lifted off of Jesse's shoulders as they climbed. When the doors slid open upon their arrival, gravity in this part of the station was 98% of Earth gravity. He breathed normally again and stepped into the business park.

The slick and corporate feel of Mid-Luna Plaza felt right at home in the atmosphere of Archway's station design. Everything here was meant to complement the feel and sense of crisp and clean progress. The walkways were lit with glowing guidelines on the curbs of the buildings themselves, each a different hue of the business that operated there. Small electromagnetic scooters shot this way and that in the middle of the walkway "streets", gliding along effortlessly, contained by rows of yellow lights embedded in the floor. These scooters only operated above the magnets in the floors of these "highway" areas of the plaza and zipped their riders to destinations on the far side of the plaza much faster than walking. After all, from one side of the plaza to the other was a couple miles based on the width of Archway Station at this point.

The future was now, and each of the business fronts wanted you to know that they had the key to unlocking its potential. There was the headquarters of Luna Side Operations in the middle, the meeting place for half of all the ambassadors on board the station where they mostly squabbled but occasionally oversaw the daily management of Archway Station affairs. Venture Colonies had its newest offices in this section and so Jesse kept a sharp eye out for Junia. He didn't dislike her but also didn't want to run into her again. Especially for her to find out that he was literally begging for the job he already claimed to have. Various Earthly stock exchanges from New York, Nairobi, Beijing and Munich stood tall and imposing, facing each other at diagonal corners. Humorously, each building was obviously vying in style and design to be the most noticed by the public, symbolic considering their want to be the economic focus of the people. And then off a side pathway, there were the Lunar based companies: Moon Hearth Colonies, Lunar Crafters & Research, and the biggest of the mining operations, Mitchell and Son's Lunar Materials. As Jesse approached the door and saw his reflection in the glass, the thought finally occurred to him to consider his appearance. He stopped, brushed his hands across his hair, pressing down a small cowlick in the back. Thankfully he had the good sense to save his last clean shirt as a button down, even if it was by accident. He dropped his satchel for a moment to tuck it in his waist, breathed out slowly, and opened the door to the lobby.

In each of the back corners of the entrance lobby stood monumental Moon rock samples, black and worn down on the edges where numerous curious hands had touched them. A line of a few waiting room chairs crowded around a steel coffee table, and there was a single, small receptionist desk directly ahead in line with the entrance door. Behind the sleek and backlit desk was the digitally locked door to the executive offices beyond, where Jesse found his eyes focused. So much so that he was almost startled by the greeting of the woman who sat in front of him.

"Hello, welcome to Mitchell and Son's, how may I help you today?"

"Ya, hello, I applied for a job and I wanted to follow up on the response I received." Jesse tried to be as professional as possible, but he had never worked in the corporate world. He hoped his pretense was close enough.

She either bought it, or was simply consistent with everybody who walked in. Her eyes matched the surface level enthusiasm found in the best waitresses. "I see! What position was it that you applied for?"

"Umm, Resource Collections Technician."

"Ahhh." Her tone changed a bit to slightly more demeaning. "This isn't the office for those applications. That office is actually located on Luna Side Docks. Would you like directions?"

"Ya, I know, but I was kind of hoping I could talk to someone here about it."

She was no longer looking him in the eye, and her focus was diverted to the viewscreen in front of her. "So, you receive a response to your application?"

"Yes, I did. That's what I wanted to discuss." He was getting nervous.

"It was a rejection, wasn't it?" Her response was cold and inattentive to Jesse.

"Yes, ma'am, but I believe that was a mistake."

"Here at Michell and Sons we use top of the line aptitude measures to ensure that each employee hired is a perfect fit for the position they take. This ensures not only the fulfilled contentment of every hire, but also maximum efficiency within the company dynamic." Her voice took on the sound of a voice recording, as if she had repeated this phrase many times. "If you were rejected, it was because you do not belong here at Mitchell and Sons."

Most, if not all major corporations used standardized aptitude tests to fill every position in the company. From the top executives all the way down to day laborers were assessed, sorted, cataloged and systematized to ensure each employee hired is 'fulfilled' in their jobs. Whether this was fair or not was vocalized by a minority of the public, namely Christians and other religious minorities that would claim it takes the place of divine design. Assigning the job based on these tests and designating who alone has the skills to do what flew in the face of God's purpose and mission for each individual. Some Christians would go so far to claim that sometimes the one most suited to perform a task or job doesn't mean they are the highest performer statistically, physically, mentally or educationally. They simply are the ones God chose because 'God looks at the heart'.

In this instance, Jesse would argue the aptitude test absolutely got his assessment wrong, not because God designed him for something else, but because Jesse simply believed it to be wrong.

"Umm... Look, Miss?"

"Stapleton."

"Miss Stapleton, could I please arrange an in-person interview? I know I have what it takes to do this. I just need someone to talk to. I can explain better!"

"Sir, as I said, our tests have rejected you as a candidate. I'm sorry, but I'm going to have to ask you to leave." Now she met his eyes with hers, however he did not like what he saw. They were as cold as ice.

As she was speaking, another woman entered the building. She was sharp and professional in appearance, walking with purpose and confidence. As Jesse turned to see her, he decided then and there that she must have some type of authority. He rushed upon her so fast that she took a self-defensive stance.

"Sir, SIR!" The receptionist called.

"Ma'am! I'm sorry, excuse me ma'am, I need to talk to someone about my application." Jesse's voice was getting desperate.

The executive sighed, relieved that this young man wasn't going to attack her and relaxed her pose in annoyance. "We here at Michell and Sons we use top of the line aptitude measures to ensure - "

"YES!" Jesse interrupted her monologue. "Yes, I'm sorry, yes, I know. But there has to be a mistake. Can you look?"

Insulted that she was interrupted, she huffed and tried to walk past her rude intruder. Jesse put his hands up and moved to his left to block her way.

"EXCUSE ME!" She looked past him to the desk. "Inform security that we have an aggressive intruder!"

"No! Please, no! All I want is a fair chance! I just want you to look at my application!"

"Sir, security is on there way -"

"PLEASE!" Jesse yelled, but didn't mean to. He closed his eyes slowly and released a much calmer, "Please."

She cocked her head slightly at the audacity of Jesse to interrupt her and then forcibly demand her assistance, but she did reluctantly pull her tablet out of her shoulder bag. "What's your name?"

"Jesse Heartshire."

"And the position you applied for?" She worked her tablet with speed. She wanted to get this over with.

Jesse was calming down. She was reluctant but she was hearing him. "Resource Collections Technician."

Upon hearing this the executive rolled her eyes and shot a look to the receptionist. A look that said, 'really? Why am I dealing with this?' Jesse noticed and lowered his head. He knew he was throwing a bit of a fit over a menial, entry level position, but it was vastly important to him even if it wasn't to them. But he had a feeling he already knew the answer.

After a few seconds that seemed to Jesse to be 5 minutes, the woman executive finally smiled and nodded, now fully understanding the situation she found herself in. She studied her findings for a moment.

"I believe I found you, Mr. Heartshire... And looking over your APT (your aptitude test), I can officially confirm that you are NOT employable here at Mitchell and Sons." She restashed her tablet in her shoulder bag and adjusted it. She stared at him uncaringly. "Does that conclude our business here?"

Jesse sighed, defeated and unable to think of how to fight the results anymore. "Yes... thank you."

She nodded in dismissal and continued her confident walk towards the office door. As she passed the receptionist, Jesse heard her say under her breath: "Please make sure this incident is logged."

He felt the sting of her words. He knew what that meant.

Most corporations and businesses access the same aptitude tests across all of their hiring practices. This includes character references, interview notes and incident reports. Having a company like Mitchell and Sons list this invasion of property and accosting of an executive to Jesse's aptitude results effectively blacklists him. Any reputable hiring manager wouldn't even consider his results, as these kinds of reports appear first on any application.

With nothing left to say or do, Jesse sauntered his way to the door. He tried to avoid looking at himself in his mirrored reflection in the glass as he pushed it open.

"Have a pleasant day!" The receptionist chimed as he passed through the doorway. He knew she was back in automaton mode as her tone indicated nothing of the uncomfortable situation that had just passed.

Jesse lowly glanced around Mid-Luna Plaza. All of the corporate and service professionals walking this way and that, going about their business as usual, not noticing or caring about his plight. His eyes caught the Venture Colonies sign in the distance. Its radiant green and gold logo beaming with welcome, but Jesse knew Junia would see the same report as anyone else. She probably wouldn't be interested in him now. Besides, the last thing he wanted to do was start over some new life on a distant planet. He didn't even care much about this one at the moment.

Glancing down at his wrist, he checked his on-body comms account through his watch. He scrolled past his missed message notification from his parents to discover what he already knew. He was only a few measly credits away from going broke. His stomach growled in protest of what his mind was comprehending: He needed money to eat. He needed money to sleep. He needed money to do everything he wanted in life, but now where was he going to get it? He could think of at least one option, but begging street vendors and seedy shop owners for day wages to sweep or clean so he could get a meal was heartbreaking. But what else could he do? Every other company on the station would view his APT profile and deny him any opportunity for sure. So he swallowed his pride, found his way back to the transport tubes and pressed the button for Low Point. He now fully understood why it was so aptly named.

CHAPTER 4
EMBERS IN THE ASHES

When the transport tube doors slid open, and the now familiar waves of oily and humid air hit his nostrils, Jesse couldn't help but consider this may forever be his home. He forced his eyes to graze on his surroundings, allowing the depression to seep into his mind through the grime of what his life was going to become. *I could probably use that nook as a bed for tonight,* he considered. *Maybe that barbecue stand would let me scrub the griddle for a few hours in exchange for a bite or two,* he pondered. With each progressive thought he forced himself lower and lower with self-pity. *It won't be so bad.* Jesse tried to lie to himself, but his heart didn't believe it.

The thought did cross his mind that he could simply return his mother's messages, and he would probably be on the next shuttle back to Earth. That would mean he would have to tolerate being around them again. He didn't know if he could do that right now. Jesse knew his parents very well and they would absolutely send him the credits to eat well and sleep comfortably before he left the station. But then he would have to begin a relationship with them again. He would have to succumb to their preaching again and to their perfect outlook on life. Jesse would have to grieve the loss of Stephen with them, their hope poking uncomfortably at his unforgiveness. No, it was still best to keep his parents at a distance. He figured he could tolerate this hardship a little longer.

In his look for credits, Jesse started with the most likely to want some help, and most likely to have something to give him. He thought that was probably a place with an actual storefront and not a simple stand, so he made his way inside the next food shop, a greasy southern soul food restaurant. Sales looked slow as the man in the cooking apron was out of the kitchen and wiping the empty tables.

"Hey, how's' it goin?" The man stopped cleaning and stood, eager for Jesse to let him know his order.

"Excuse me, sir. I was wondering if you had any jobs that needed to be done around here?"

Slightly frustrated that Jesse didn't read the room, the cook presented the clean table with his hands. "Does it look like I can pay anyone to help?"

Jesse nodded in understanding and ducked out of the store. The next shop was only a few steps away. It had the looks of a tattoo parlor or a bar. Jesse couldn't tell which as it wasn't a place he would have likely gone into without desperation driving him.

Inside were a few patrons sitting at one of the small tables, drinks and smokes in front of them. Jesse felt their judging eyes right away. He definitely didn't fit here. He opened his mouth to speak, didn't feel any words coming to him, and so turned right back out the door with his tail between his legs. He could hear them laughing as the door shut.

The next opportunity wasn't looking much better. A credit lender, and you can't borrow money without any collateral. Jesse decided to skip that one altogether. He thought maybe he would go out to the middle of the street to get more of a lay of the land and determine which places he should talk to first.

Standing in the thick midst of the Dragway, there wasn't much to see. This was already feeling hopeless as he couldn't make out who were patrons of establishments and who were down on their luck. Plus with so many people here on the streets already, what hope did Jesse have to find? Surely any jobs to be had would already be had. Might as well think about getting comfortable for the night at least. While he was debating in his mind as to which transient he would rather have as neighbors, his eye happened upon a symbol in the distance that he hadn't noticed in his visits to the Dragway yet.

Around the corner, partially obscured by the steam plume coming from a vendor's pot of rice, was a small red, circular hand drawn sign. Inside the circle was the shape of a Christian cross, the middle of which had the words *Neu Retter Church*.

The Neu Retter movement was a Christian movement that was birthed from an underground church deep in the German Black Forest countryside. It had been long since the followers of Christ were considered openly welcome and, in some cases, violently persecuted in much of the European Union, and so adherents of the faith either retreated to other parts of the globe or went into quiet hiding. Fortunately, as this story had developed over the course of Christian history, persecution has only ever made the church stouter and more devoted. This produced a deep appreciation for the salvation that Jesus provides, and the devoted German followers found new and intense comfort in that promise of glory-ridden future. This redirected focus on the future state of eternity with Christ over the persecution in their present day woes was what set their teaching apart, as well as inspiring new followers to consider *"für das Nächste leben"*, or *"living for the Next"*. This ignited many of the believers to burn passionately with purpose and mission in their faith, undeterred by their current circumstances. Incredibly, and with undoubted support of the Holy Spirit, the

Neu Retter movement began sending missionaries abroad despite their oppression. When one of their missionaries held a small meeting in Asheboro, North Carolina, a young, freshly married couple was introduced to this new fire and drive for purpose-driven life. Not many years later, they would welcome their second son to the world, and name him Jesse.

Normally, Jesse would have avoided the church, but things were looking more destitute than he originally thought. And despite his current disdain for his parents, the church was a welcome comfort that he was badly needing at the moment. He shuffled his way past a few patrons awaiting food and approached the entrance of the church. It was tucked in between two store fronts of a Chinese hotpot and an Indian curry restaurant, which created an odd stereo-affect smell as Jesse moved between them. The door of the church was loose and well used, and it freely swung in as Jesse pushed on it.

There was a short hallway that most likely led past the food establishments sitting and cooking areas, and then the church opened up. Jesse found himself in a quaint and dimly lit lobby area, with a welcoming sign directing attendees to two other entrances: the sanctuary for worship services on the left, and the church cafeteria to the right. Based on the worn traffic pattern in the carpet on the floor, the kitchen was the main draw of this church. There was also light and commotion emanating from that way, so Jesse continued on towards the kitchen.

Jesse's stomach growled a bit in anticipation as he approached the warm red lamps over the buffet style serving line. A few rough individuals were scooting down the line, pushing trays along with them, bowing their heads in humble nods towards the cafe workers on the other side. They were gracious but quiet in their appreciation for the food they were served. Anyone who has had to rely so heavily upon the kindness of others to simply live recognizes this particular feeling of shame. They couldn't blame the smiling and kind faces of the servers who were trying their best to be loving, but only their own consciences for this undeserved feeling of guilt. Jesse himself wasn't to that point of desperation yet, but he was hungry, and he felt an unfair amount of shame to ask for the same handout. He stood at the entrance way for a moment because of this. Jesse also wasn't coming for the free meal that he didn't even know was here. And he didn't really want to talk to anyone either. Honestly, he couldn't have told you why he came inside at all. Merely followed a longing for something familiar in a lost world.

"Are you in line?"

A gruff but soft voice asked him from just over his right shoulder. Startled slightly, Jesse shook his head "no" and stepped aside. The worn man nodded his head, passed Jesse and grabbed a tray. After he began scuttling down the line, this drew the attention of the first line worker to Jesse's idleness.

"Hey, brother! You're next!" He welcomed him forward with warmth in his baritone voice, and a friendly wave of his hand. "Come on up!"

"Oh, no it's fine… I was just looking around." Jesse was embarrassed. He didn't want to take the handout.

"Bah, nonsense! If you haven't noticed, we make plenty for everyone, and it ain't gonna eat itself! Come!"

Jesse sighed slightly and stepped up for a tray. The food did smell very good for being served in a church cafeteria. He didn't remember them always offering the choicest of selections. His newfound friend on the other side of the counter started building him a plate as he spoke.

"I dunno if I've seen you around the Dragway before. My name is Gus! What's yours?" His enthusiasm was as thick as his accent, but Jesse couldn't place where it was from. He wore a hair net over both the white hair on his head, and the white hair of his full beard.

"Jesse. And I haven't been here long." Jesse's eyes stayed on the plate that was being made for him. He also watched Gus' girth brush along the cafe trays as he sidestepped to each ladle. *He must sample his own serving trays a lot,* Jesse decided.

"Well welcome, young sir, to the jewel of the Dragway! Ha ha!" He followed Jesse's eyes to his plate. "You likin' everything that's going on here?" He lifted the plate slightly towards Jesse.

Jesse nodded in approval. "Ya, it looks great, thanks."

They continued their slow shuffle down the serving line as Gus ladled this and that. Seemed to be a lot of southern US food staple foods today. Various casseroles and steamed veggies from Luna Side Garden. Dragway Neu Retter Church maintained a few plots there, growing food for this aspect of ministry.

"You said you ain't been here long, so what brings you to Archway?" Gus' demeanor was disarming, but Jesse couldn't tell if it was genuine or not. He'd been around so many others who lived their lives in the church buildings and yet seemed so far from the Jesus they worshiped there. Those faithful seemed to put on the facade of love while in front of their God, but the glory diminished when they felt like He wasn't watching.

Instead, Jesse was looking around the facility while Gus talked. He had heard the question, and was ignoring him, but not because he was being rude. He was guarded, and Gus had been at this long enough that he knew when someone wasn't ready to admit they needed to chat.

"Alright then." He smiled to himself and said a short prayer, asking for spiritual insight.

Jesse chose not to take the water that was offered from a tap at the end, opting for a bottled soft drink instead. He held his tray, and navigated to the last table in the room, back in the corner. His meal was piled on his plate in healthy proportions of mashed potatoes, green beans, chicken fried steak and squash casserole. Jesse was glad for the lack of company due to his depression, but also now no one would judge him for diving headlong into his tray. He knew he was hungry, but at the sight and smell of actual food piled in front of him made him instantly ravenous. Jesse hadn't noticed or given it much thought, but it had been well over a month since he had eaten a home cooked meal. Before long, there were smears left where mountains of old comfort food had been before.

Jesse looked up at what had been written on the walls of the cafeteria. It was the usual Bible verses of encouragement that you would find in a Neu Retter church. Their trademark go-to in Scripture was Revelation 21:4, which was indented in broad, gold lettering across the entrance of the cafe: *He will wipe every tear from their eyes. There will be no more death, mourning, crying, or pain, for the old order of things has passed away.* Jesse had read those words many, many times before, but they happened upon him a bit differently now.

✦ . ⁺ . ✦ . ⁺ . ✦

His parents were crushed; it was obvious. They huddled together on the couch, clutching tissues between them, praying out loud when they felt they could breathe. They were crying out to God in their anguish, looking to Him for His comfort. Their love for Stephen was never in doubt by Jesse, and he knew that they felt the same deep, dark pain that he did at his loss. But Jesse was angry, and they were not. And that infuriated him all the more.

He had tried to be silent, to be the "good Christian" and to trust God's protection over his brother. After all, he was on mission, he was following after the calling of Jesus on his heart. Wasn't that supposed to mean that God would protect him? It's hard to be a missionary if you're dead, and Jesus couldn't possibly use death as a way of leading people to life.

"You know He did this right?" His voice was low and brooding.

"Jesse, please." His dad pleaded. He knew Jesse was frustrated, and he could see this confrontation coming, but he was powerless to stop it. "We can talk about this at another time."

"NO! God sent him to Chicago, God did this to him!"

"He was following where Jesus was leading him." His mother said softly and slowly as if she was trying to convince herself as well. She didn't look up as she was deeply grieved and was clinging to her faith in ways only the faithful know. It's all they can do.

"Following Him to his *death*. Robbing him of his life. Some loving God He is!"

"Jesse, it's going to be ok - " His dad reassured.

"It isn't though; it isn't going to be ok!" Jesse's cheeks were hot and wet with tears. "What's the point?! What good did he accomplish?! Dad, they even burned the mission to the ground! There's nothing left of the work he did!"

His father kissed his weeping wife's forehead, rubbed her shoulders and stood. He took a step towards his furious son with low, open arms. "We don't know that. His death had meaning."

"He stole Stephen from us! He called him away, and STOLE his life from us! And from him!"

"Your brother loved Jesus, Jesse. He gave his life willingly, loving God with it in return." His father took a breath. "We have to trust, now more than ever, that God is good."

That struck a nerve with Jesse, and in an instant his anger flipped from wanting to rip apart a distant and unreachable God, to ripping apart his present and exposed father. He lowered his forehead and glared against his father's sympathetic eyes.

"Do you want to know what I prayed for this morning? Do you want to know the Scripture verse I read today?" Jesse spun around, yanking his Bible off the armchair behind him. He paged open to where the book ribbon was keeping and held the book up, as if to preach. *"Ask and it will be given, seek and you shall find, knock and the door will be opened to you."*

He lowered the Scriptures for a moment. "Do you know what I asked for? For Stephen to come home alive! For divine protection over his life! Because - " He raised the Bible back to his face.

"Because *If you who are evil know how to give good gifts to your children, how much more will your Father give good gifts to those who ask of Him!*" Jesse's voice wavered in anger, adding emphasis and sarcasm to the verse with his tone of voice.

"Jesse, He works all things for the good of those who -"

"What kind of hellish *GOOD* is this?!" His mother quivered at his words. She was becoming more broken by the second. She was beginning to feel as if she was going to lose two sons today instead of just one. His father took a brave step towards the rage of his son.

"My son, we're all hurting right now, together."

"NO, no we're not in this together!" Jesse stepped away from his father, pointing an accusing finger. "No, you want to still worship this 'God' even though he is absolutely disgusting! Why are you praying to a sicko savior that calls this kind of evil good!"

"This isn't the end, son." His father reached for him. Jesse laughed and tore away.

"You know that's true! We've taught you that from the beginning!" His father pleaded. But His fathers voice fell on deaf ears as Jesse turned his back to him and began grabbing his coat off the hook by the front door. He threw it on in a fit.

"God is a terrible father. He punishes those who love him the most by slaughtering them when they follow too close." Jesse spat.

His father tried a couple more steps towards him, arms outstretched and eyes overflowing with hurt, love and tears. He approached the back of his son, "Jesse, God didn't do this -"

The fire in Jesse's eyes blazed, burning a hole in the door in front of him. "Is He in charge of this universe or not?"

His father was silent. The answer was of course, yes, but he knew anything he said in response was going to drive Jesse further away. He fought the urge to dive upon his son and hold him close. There was nothing else in the world he wanted to do more. To hold him, here.

"If you won't blame God for this, you're no better than He is." Jesse spun around. His eyes locked with his fathers, and he lashed out as hard as he knew how. "And if you're no better than He is, I don't want to be your son."

With that Jesse slammed the door on his father and strode out on his own.

✦ ✢ ✦ ✢ ✦

Gus was still keeping an eye on this new kid from his serving line. He had finished eating and was seemingly lost in thought, alone at a table in the back. Gus was excited as this was a new opportunity to love on someone, something that filled his life with purpose and meaning. But the Spirit was giving him the feeling that he needed to tread carefully with this one. This is a special kind of hurt that does not diminish easily, and that only prayer can help. However, Gus was hopeful as he did have his natural charisma to lean on, which had broken the stubborn and forlorn many a time before. He mentioned to the other volunteers that he was going to take a quick break, and he took off his apron, hanging it by the end of the bar as he rounded the serving line. He approached Jesse from the front but the young man didn't seem to notice him until he was right up to the table. The second Jesse caught sight of his approach to converse, he stood and began to gather his tray and utensils.

"Whoa, whoa, whoa! You just gonna dine and dash on me, bro?" Gus said.

Jesse grasped for an excuse. "Ya, I mean, it was great but I gotta go."

"Alright well here, lemme get your bill." Gus wiped out an electric tablet and started scratching it with his index finger.

"Wait, isn't this supposed to be a free meal?" Jesse suspected he might be kidding.

"Hmph, you'd like to think so, right?" Gus kept scribbling, and now Jesse wasn't so sure. His mind raced on what to do. He could run?

Gus held out the tablet, staring at Jesse with a look that threatened to take it, and take it seriously. Jesse sighed, knowing he had next to nothing to pay with and glanced at the screen. Gus had scribbled a note: <u>Cost</u> <u>of a Free Meal:</u> <u>5 Minutes of your time!</u>

Jesse huffed and half cracked a smile. He handed the tablet back to Gus, and they both sat down opposite each other at the same time. Gus slid Jesse's tray to the side, leaving nothing between them in the conversation, aside from Jesse's soda.

"Jesse, Jesse… where'd your parents get that name?" Gus inquired.

"It's biblical."

"Ya, the father of King David right?"

"Yes, sir."

"Your parents grow you up in church?"

"Yup. This one actually. Well, this denomination." Jesse was being more open already than he originally wanted to be.

"Hey, get outta here! Me too! So, what brings you to Archway?" The honest answer to Gus's question was still right at the heart of the matter, and Jesse didn't want to face it. He was running. Running to stay ahead of his anger, his doubts and his faith. His parents just happened to be the embodiment of it all.

Because he didn't want to answer that, he hung his head, muttering, "I dunno."

"Hmm. Ya I feel that too. I feel that too." Gus thought a second and then leaned forward. "Did you notice all these verses all over the walls?" He waved his hand around the room.

Jesse nodded.

"What about that one?" Gus pointed to the verse above the cafe serving line. It read: *He who has ears, let them hear.* "See when I painted all these verses, I put that one specifically above the serving line. Do you wanna guess why?"

The odd idea of mixing the sense of hearing with the sense of taste reminded him of Junia. Jesse shook his head no again.

"Because in my line of work, I've noticed a lot of folks come to Jesus looking for what they want from him, but they miss out on what he offers. Here we give folks a free meal, no cost, no questions asked - "

"No questions asked, huh? No cost?" Jesse answered, looking accusatory at Gus.

"Hey bro, I didn't make you sit down, did I?" Gus spoke with his hands a lot. He opened his arms at this point, insinuating that Jesse could make whatever choice he desired. "But we give folks a meal whenever they come in, and they think that's what they need because they're hungry. What they really need is a future of hope and promise."

"Ya," Jesse got annoyed at the notion of future hope. "well, what about when Jesus takes that too?"

Gus looked inquisitively at Jesse, "How do you mean?"

"God's promise of a life with him isn't always a hope and a future. When you give your life to him, what you're really doing is signing up for your death."

Gus's inquisitive look remained. He couldn't tell at the moment if they were about to get into a theological argument, where it appeared Jesse had already made up his mind, or if this was going to be a psychologist session, with Jesse on the proverbial couch. It actually felt as if it would be both.

Gus slowly answered. "So, then you already know?"

"Ya." Jesse answered. "I already know." But then a half beat later. "Know what?"

"That you have to die to follow Jesus." Gus put it simply.

"Exactly!" Jesse stated emphatically. "Then what is the point of living? What is the point of doing any of this?"

"It's the promise, Jesse. The promise of eternal life. That's what we're living for. What Paul said, 'to live is Christ and to die is gain.'"

"I dunno, Gus. Living to die? All this loss feels like losing to me. I don't feel like I'm gaining anything."

Gus was starting to clue into something. "What is it you've lost?" he asked delicately.

Jesse stared at him. He was trying to decide if he was ready or not to be direct. Gus was asking for it. So fine, he let him have it.

Jesse settled and leaned forward. "Gus, I grew up in church. I've prayed, read the Bible twice all the way through, my parents are missionaries." He was listing his credentials. Then he swallowed. "My brother was a missionary. He went to Chicago because he felt called to follow Jesus there. And that life that Jesus promises? That life ended there. They burned him. Him and his mission to the ground." His eyes were hot again.

Gus winced. "Oh dang, Jesse, I'm sorry, brother."

"My folks still have the audacity to worship the same Jesus that led my brother away to the slaughter. But not me!" He leaned back, arms crossed. "I won't. I refuse to waste my life dedicated to a God that rewards my loving devotion with fire."

Gus bowed his head and nodded slowly. He really did understand exactly where Jesse was coming from. All too well. He thought and after a moment, he spoke.

"I told you that I put that verse up there," he pointed to the one above the serving line again. "Because folks come to God expecting Him to give him what they want. I didn't do that just for everyone else."

Gus' eyes started to reveal an old hurt. "I didn't come to this floating white diamond in space by myself. I started this church as a mission with my wife. ... but as you know, not everyone wants to hear what God is talking about. As a matter of fact, this is the 3rd installment of Archway Neu Retter Church. And she was inside the last one when the men came to rob, kill and destroy." Gus turned to look at the verse above the line again.

"No, I repaint that verse above where I serve so that when I look up and wonder why, I'm forced to read it again."

Jesse was truly confused, the same confusion that drew him in wonderment to his brother. It just didn't make sense. "Why? Why do you still do this?"

"Because I learned that I can live my life one of two ways: angry or hopeful. I can be bitter, and believe me I was, or I can accept that death is a part of life."

"Would I have chosen differently when it came for my wife's time to pass on? Absolutely. There isn't a day I don't think of her. But we all die, Jesse. And I realized I can miss her terribly and hate God and hate the world. Or I can miss her terribly and I can truly hear what Jesus says when He speaks, and accept the hope that He offers for eternal life."

Jesse sighed and shook his head. He's heard this explanation before, and it made sense in his mind, but he couldn't accept it in his heart. He still felt so angry, so enraged at what true Christian living cost because it seemed to be astronomically expensive. Like an unattainable amount of wealth that one knows exists but has never seen. Like wrapping your head around the breadth of the cosmos. He rested his head on his hands, leaning his elbows on the table. Gus glanced back at the serving line, which was getting a bit backed up.

"You got somewhere to be?"

Jesse shook his head. Gus stood and grabbed Jesse's tray. "Tell ya what, you help me finish up here, and I'll get you a bed tonight. Deal?"

Jesse weighed his options. He wanted to be alone, and he wanted to hurt. But he was starting to realize that he was wanting it. Not that it was externally being heaped upon him, but that he was crowning himself with it. It was the cross he had to bear, but he was making it heavier than it needed to be.

Gus waited patiently for Jesse to size up his options, and patted him on the back when the lost young man decided to don an apron and help serve the people of the Dragway.

CHAPTER 5
REPENTANCE IN PART

This dream space felt familiar but he couldn't place why. Jesse was weightless, floating above the earth which was doused in grey. The beyond was starless and void, a shimmering and shifting black sea, undulating as the ocean. Then came the voice, and Jesse remembered why it felt like déjà vu.

Come, Jesse. Follow me.

He looked up into the blackness and there it was. The same pinpoint of brilliant light just as before, its rays dancing in radiant hues. Even without the beaconing of the voice, it was tantalizing to view and tempting to grasp. Although this time Jesse didn't want to reach for it.

It was his first instinct to reach, but Jesse was more aware of himself, his actions and his feelings this time. He simply drifted, and watched the glimmering star from his static position. He fought the urge to be curious, to desire to grasp at the light with all the strength his fingers had in them. But in his mind, it was pointless to try, so he didn't. The fact that it was unreachable was the excuse. So he just watched from a distance and waded in the ocean of black.

SHOVE!

Jesse lurched forward and almost lost his balance. He didn't realize that his floating position over the Earth was precarious, but based on his need to catch and right himself, apparently it was. Jesse cast his hands automatically away from his sides, balancing himself. Where did that push come from? There was nothing behind him.

SHOVE!

As he was looking, there it came again! It was as if someone were leaning their body weight into his lower back, moderately urging him forward. But forward to nothing! If Jesse were to lose his balance on the Earth, he would drift into the black and violent looking sea of nothing. His uneasy fear and desperation to not fall rose in his throat and he frantically looked about for any sign of the dangerous aggressor.

SHOVE!

This was the hardest push yet! It nearly felt as if a fist had hit his kidneys. His legs were wobbled at that impact, and Jesse knew that just one more like it would topple him over the non-existent edge. He instinctively looked around for something to grab hold of, to right himself and withstand the invisible force ramming him from behind. As he spun about in a panicked search, his eyes met eyes behind him. The invisible force shoving him from behind had appeared.

It was his dad, dressed just as he was when Jesse left. Jesse, both relieved to see the source of the shoving was familiar, was also instantly upset at who was doing it. His dad was smiling at him in the way he always did when he was joking around with his son, but obviously Jesse was in no mood. He had almost lost his balance and was angry.

"Dad?! What are you doing?! I almost fell!"

His dad didn't react nor say anything in response. Just simply smiled. Conscious Jesse would have been terrified at the eeriness of it, but this Jesse was only more annoyed.

"Are you crazy?!"

Still, dad smiled, his arms were poised, palms ready for another push. But this time Jesse was ready, and he somehow braced himself for impact while floating.

Suddenly soft, warm hands were on his face. They instantly disarmed him and gently beckoned his attention to his right. He relaxed and turned his face to match the gaze of his mother.

She held his face in her hands, which were comforting and reassuring. She smiled with her lips and her eyes, filling Jesse instantly with the confidence that he was loved unconditionally. He felt safe and secure, so he softened and let down his guard. Being beheld by her pacified him as only a mother's touch can.

SHOVE!

The impact to Jesse's chest felt deep. The punch of his father's hands coupled with the betrayal of his mother's clasp hurt to a point beyond pain. He fell, back first, and watched in slow motion the grins of his parents slip away from him. Jesse was yelling, anger and treachery spewed from his mouth, although in the vacuum of space there was no sound. This made him all the more furious, for the ones charged by God with protecting him, had just thrust him into the abyss.

Jesse awoke with a jump and a gasp. He'd had dreams before, but this one felt different. It was vivid in ways his normal dreams were drab by comparison. This one had a depth that he couldn't describe, other than to realize it meant something more.

Now he remembered the dream of the pinpoint light in the black void he'd had the previous day. He remembered that one had a feeling of awe and wonder juxtaposed with this one's feeling of nonchalance and betrayal. Jesse also was starting to grasp the gravity of the situation he was in. Was God calling to him? Is this what that felt like?

Before Stephen had left, he did claim quite firmly that Jesus had "called" him to the mission in Chicago. Jesse had no concept of what that meant. In all actuality, Jesse hesitated to even call himself a Christian most days. His belief in God was somewhat firm, but the desire to follow Him anywhere was missing. As he grew up, Jesse didn't see much point in it, and then after Stephen's death at the invitation of the Jesus he followed, Jesse was very against the idea of trusting God with his life. After all, look at where that ended up.

Jesse threw the blankets off his legs and swung over to the side of the bed. He stretched and wrung his back out as best he could. Jesse is not necessarily a tall man, but the cot that Gus had provided was still at least 3 inches too short for his frame. It was soft but gave a lot in the middle. Either the springs had worn out, or someone of Gus's stature had done a number on the bed frame. Halfway through the night, Jesse considered switching to one of the pews in the sanctuary of Archway New Retter Church but fell back asleep before he moved.

Gus had situated Jesse's cot in the church office just past the pulpit area of the church. There were no windows and so it was rather dark and shared a wall with the power transformers for Lower Luna Point, which generated a soothing hum. This caused Jesse to sleep well past the beginning of breakfast, but that just meant that he missed the rush. As he reached for his satchel, he noticed a ragged Bible sitting on top of it.

He picked it up, as it had a note on it. *For light reading, or for reading the Light.* It was obviously from Gus, as who else would have snuck in the office to put it there. It was used, worn on the edges and some of the pages were dog eared. The leather on the outside was soft and marked with various pens, scrapes or creases. This had to be Gus's old Bible. He opened it to see if his suspicions were correct, but the inside cover read: *If lost, please return to: JESUS!* Jesse smirked at the play on words of the clever author. He tucked the small volume in the top fold of his satchel, where it barely fit, but it fit snuggly.

Jesse got up and absent mindedly folded the sheets and blanket he was given. Regardless of his rebellion, politeness was so ingrained in him he couldn't help it. It was automatic. Afterwards he shouldered his satchel and made his way through the sanctuary.

As Jesse left the office, he was turned and shutting the door when he heard a jovial voice behind him.

"Look who's up!" Gus strode towards Jesse wielding a small plate of some kind of sausage and egg mixture, along with a couple steaming cups of coffee. By the rich smell of the earthy aroma wafting from the mug, it was real coffee too. Jesse's mouth began watering instantly.

"I was gonna coax you up and at 'em with this plate of fixin's. You like coffee?" He offered the mug to Jesse as the young man took off his satchel and laid it on the pew next to him. Jesse grabbed the mug with one hand and steadied its full contents with the other. Gus waited patiently with his plate, watching Jesse enjoy the first sip with pride. "Yaaa that's my own private stash, so enjoy!"

Jesse sat down next to his satchel, and Gus handed him the plate of breakfast with a fork and napkin tucked underneath. Gus sat in the pew diagonally from him. All the pews in the traditional Neu Retter Church were facing the center of the room. This encourages conversation and participation within the congregants.

"I actually have a few arabica coffee plants up in the Luna Garden, tucked in the back of our plots. I pick 'em and then I roast 'em in the oven down here."

"Wow, thanks. It's really good." Jesse had never had freshly roasted coffee before. He now knew he would never fully enjoy anything less ever again. He set it down and started on his eggs and sausage. It looked like some kind of chorizo.

"How'd you sleep?"

"Hphm - " His mouth was full of delicious morning goodness. He held up a finger while he chewed. Gus waived his hand as an "ok" and sipped from his mug. The sausage was a little spicier than Jesse expected, so he sipped on the hot coffee, which was no help at all.

"It was a bit short... but it was dark. And the humming of whatever is on the other side of that wall was nice." Jesse pointed with his fork. Gus knew exactly what he meant.

"Isn't that right?! If I told you I was hardly ever in that office, would you be surprised?" Gus grinned and Jesse shook his head with another mouthful. "I'd never get any work done, I tell ya. Too much dark and with all the white noise? Shoo, I'd pass right out."

Jesse took another bite of his food. He wanted to ask Gus about his dream, but didn't know how to bring it up without sounding crazy. Jesse trusted that out of anyone, Gus would probably understand. But it's not everyday you want to accuse God of giving you a dream. He went about it indirectly instead.

"Gus," Jesse said. "How do you know that Jesus is calling you? What does that feel like?"

"Well let's see..." Gus took a sip and leaned back in the pew. He tried to hide his excitement for Jesse to be asking these kinds of questions, but his giveaway grin never left his face.

"I suppose it sounds different for everyone. I mean, *if* it sounds like anything at all." Gus looked over at Jesse and narrowed his eyes. "Why do you ask?"

Jesse shrugged as he had another bite of the sausage and eggs in his mouth already. It was almost gone so his bashful excuse for thought and speech was wearing thin.

"I know I'm called to be here, I can tell you that much."

Jesse was a little confused. "You feel called to here?" His voice sounded a bit demeaning.

Gus picked up on it and played a bit at being offended. "Ya, why, what's wrong with it?"

"Nothing! Nothing. It's just, I dunno, isn't this a little... minor?"

Gus roared with laughter. "Are you saying I'm small time?!" He reached forward and grabbed at the coffee and plate in Jesse's hands. "Gimme that back! You're done here!" Jesse swerved his hands this way and that, dodging the flailing arms of Gus. After a few swipes, Gus sat back a little winded. "Na, man, you know how to charm don't you?"

"I wasn't trying to do that!" Jesse smiled in his defense, then he got serious again. "No, what I mean is, when my brother, Stephen, was called he went off and started a mission in Chicago. Like, it was a big deal. Then my parents were lead missionaries in various cities all over." Jesse had finished and set his plate aside, leaning forward with his coffee in both hands. "I thought being called was a big deal."

"It is!" Gus reassured him. "It ain't a small matter, getting called by Jesus to get to work. But Jesse, not everyone is called to the same thing. Not everyone starts a mission in a dangerous city from scratch. Most of the time, just obeying where the Spirit leads you is responding to the call."

Jesse nodded his head in understanding, his eyes were on Gus but now focused on a spot on the floor in front of him. He paused for a moment, then decided he trusted Gus enough to ask.

"And God can use dreams to call people right?"

"You've read the Bible, haven't you? Can't you tell me?" Gus responded with leading questions of his own.

"Ya, but... it's been a while." Jesse just wanted Gus to tell him that his feelings were correct. He thought for sure God could, but he wanted external confirmation.

"Yes, Jesse." Gus was now serious as well. "God can use anything to speak to *his* people." Gus had put an emphasis on the word *his* when he spoke. He wanted to drive the point home that regardless of how Jesse felt about God, that God did not change how He felt about him. He cocked his head slightly sideways. "Something you wanna tell me?"

Jesse took a deep breath. "Ya. I had a dream last night, and it was definitely something. It just felt... different. Deeper, and more tangible than anything I'd dreamt before."

"Really? Tell me more." Gus was very interested.

"It was just me. Floating in space over the earth. The earth was dead to me though. It felt like there was no life there, but just specifically no life for me. Then there was a voice calling my name. I could hear it in my head but not hear it out loud... you know what I mean? Like, it was a voice, but not audible."

"Ya, I think so." Gus's intrigue was palpable.

"But, anyways, then I felt someone push me from behind. When I looked it was my mom and dad, shoving me. Trying to shove me off the planet towards this small point of light. The light was the only thing in color in my dream, too. Lots of color for something so small. Then, I woke up when I fell off of... I mean, I was floating, but now I was falling down. Then I woke up."

Gus was stroking his beard, looking inquisitive. "Hmmm. And you heard a voice?"

"Ya, saying: 'Come, Jesse. Follow me'."

"Did you want to follow the voice?"

Jesse adjusted himself in the pew. "I mean, ya, I kind of wanted to. But I didn't in my dream. The light was so far away I didn't reach for it. I just sorta watched."

Gus turned around and grabbed one of the church's worn Bibles from the back of the pew cubby. "Can I show you a verse?" He opened it and started paging through. Jesse followed suit and took the Bible he had been gifted in the night from his satchel.

Jesse took out the Scriptures and settled the open pages on his lap. He really wanted to know what this was all about, even if he was skeptical and unsure. He still wanted to believe, even when he fought it. Gus sat back again and sipped.

"Turn to the Gospel of Matthew. Chapter 7, verse 7."

Jesse hesitated for a split second, but then followed the command. The last time he looked at that verse was not a pleasant moment for him. He tried to diminish the thoughts about what he had said to his parents as he turned the soft, worn pages. He stopped, and Gus motioned to him to read it, and so Jesse put his finger to the verse as he read out loud:

"Ask and it will be given, seek and you will find, knock and the door will be opened to you."

"Jesse, do you know what this verse means?"

"Ya, I thought I did." Jesse said with a bit of heavy heart.

"Jesus wants us to invest our hearts in him. This is a promise that if you do, you will find God in what is given in return." Gus laid it out simply for him.

"But what about when you ask and the answer is no? Or there's no answer at all?"

Gus nodded and scratched his head a moment. "Ya, there can be a bit of fogginess there sometimes, can't there?" Then Gus got a little inspiration from some external source. It was imperceptible to him aside from the insistence in his mind that he needed to make a precise statement. "I mean, for one thing, I can't ask God to give me a gift that was already given to Him."

At that statement, Jesse's heart skipped a beat. He caught his breath quickly afterwards, and was attempting to stay calm on the surface, but his mind began to ignite with epiphany. Had he misunderstood this principle all this time? When he demanded for his brother's life to be spared, was he actually behaving as a spoiled child who wanted to play with someone else's toy? Very quickly his stored up anger was transforming to unrepentant guilt. He sipped on his empty coffee mug to try to hide and control his composure.

Gus, although not privy to Jesse's internal monologue, could perceive that he touched on something with his astute statement. He checked his watch and sighed, realizing the time meant he had to move onto his other duties of the day. But watching whatever it was wave over the young man across from him gave him a sense that his purpose was accomplished here. Gus felt assurance that he could move on from the conversation. He shot down the last drips of his now cold coffee.

"Jesse, I do apologize, brother, but I have some things to take care of this morning. You're absolutely welcome to stay here for the day if you want to, but just let me know what's goin' on, ok?"

"Ya, ok. I will." Jesse's comment back was a bit distant. He was still captive in thought. Gus stood and loomed over him.

"Do you mind if I pray over our day?"

Jesse shook his head and bowed. Gus's hand felt warm and heavy on his shoulder. It was still obviously customary to close your eyes and concentrate on what was said during prayer, but Jesse's eyes stayed open. He tried to focus on Gus's baritone voice, agreeing with him on his petition to God. However, all Jesse could think about now was obeying the voice from his dream.

He had been wrong about his brother's calling, at least wrong about his understanding of it. Jesse had been considering it the wrong way. He was so lost when he couldn't see what Stephen was getting out of it, that he had never considered what Stephen was giving. He was giving God a gift. It wasn't a demand from God that Stephen go, it was an offering from his brother that Jesus had accepted. This thought now stirred new ideas in Jesse's head.

What would happen if I followed the call? He couldn't answer his own question to himself. But what was coming was an instant desire to act. To do something about the call. To answer in the only way he knew how, and to knock on a door that might be the only one left for him to open. He felt the need to find and talk to Junia.

Gus wrapped up his prayer and Jesse stood determinedly. His body was engulfed in a powerful hug from his host, who then walked him to the door. Jesse thanked him for the bed and breakfast, and stepped back again into the moist Dragway air. It really was incredible to remember that he was on Archway Station because looking around again at the shops and stalls, taking in the sights and smells, everything felt so earthy. He was so convinced as he set off away from the church that had a half thought that he would need to go to a shuttle depot to get to the Venture Colonies office. As his mind settled back to the reality of where he was, Jesse started for the transport tubes.

As he made his way to the transport tubes, a warning prevailed in his mind. *What about your APT scores? How are you going to explain those?* Jesse started to worry a little. Surely Junia would listen to his side of the story, unlike the ugly execs over at Mitchell and Sons. It was frustrating that so much of his life depended on the results of this single test but its creators had successfully lobbied and convinced the vast majority of its credibility. Opponents were the quiet minority, and forcibly so.

At quick glance he didn't see Junia's name listed in the interactive directory for Venture Colonies at Mid-Luna Plaza. A man walked up and pushed the call button for the tube. He had a sleek looking suit, and a name tag from the shady looking money lender on the far side of the Dragway, so Jesse figured he probably could answer his question.

"Hey, is the Venture Colonies in the plaza the only one here?"

"That's the new one." He was looking down at his tablet, seemingly too busy to answer him although he did anyway. "Their main office is on Terra."

Jesse thanked him and the man ever-so-slightly acknowledged him with an eyebrow raise. He turned back to the screen and swiped over to the Terra Side directory, the other side of the station whose tip points back to Earth. Venture Colonies had a much larger registry there, it felt as if a thousand names popped up on the screen.

Jesse paused, looking a tad forlorn at the screen. For the life of him, he could not remember Junia's last name, so he scanned the screen for her first name. There couldn't be too many 'Junia's', right?. After a few frustrating minutes, Jesse decided on a different tactic. He focused and remembered that her position was a director... something to do with founding's? Or finishes? He sorted the directory to 'positions' and scanned the directors names. This narrowed the field quite a bit and he happened across Junia Fresco, Director of New Foundations fairly quickly. And yes, she was officed out of Venture on Mid-Terra Plaza. Not long after Jesse selected the plaza on Terra Side a transport tube arrived, although this one was red on the exterior instead of the usual green. This was to indicate that it was a *gravimorphic* tube, complete with harnesses built into the seats and vacuum charged vomit receptacles on the handrails. Jesse climbed inside and chose his seat, clipping the harness across his chest and tightening it snuggly. The seats of these transport tubes all faced straight ahead instead of facing the doors, and they all had foot rests attached to the base of the chairs. After an announcement *BING* the doors slid shut and the tube took off.

The Grav Tubes were speedier than the regular Luna or Terra side tubes, and they only delivered passengers to the main lobbies or plazas of each side of the station. Soon after the transport left the depot, it started to pitch up, as if it was climbing a mountain. The tube picked up speed and Jesse could feel the acceleration pushing him into his seat, which was paired with an odd sensation as the gravity diminished the closer it got to the center of the station. Now the tube was going straight "up", heading for the middle of Archway, and Jesse and the other passengers were pressed into their seats as it felt that they were laying on their backs. As the Luna Gardens streamed by the window outside of the tube's windows, the external thrusters of the tube took over propulsion and the tube lurched forward with renewed vigor. The interior lights of the tube changed to a red hue and an automated voice cracked over the intercom:

Attention passengers, please prepare yourselves for transportation gravity reversal. Attention passengers, please prepare yourselves for transportation gravity reversal.

The lush green of the garden concluded as the transport tube entered into the area of the Lunar Side Docks. This tube was one of a few that transported passengers from Luna to Terra sides of Archway via the large white pillars that hold each station half together at their corners. As the tube climbed higher over the docks, Jesse could see out the window ahead of them that Terra Side Docks were getting closer and closer. He could also make out ahead that the tube was about to pass through five closely spaced, red lit rings. This was the final warning that gravity, which was getting so light now that Jesse's head was swimming, was about to reverse the opposite direction.

Attention! Gravity reversal! Attention! Gravity reversal! In 3… 2… 1!

Jesse could feel the now very light tug of "down" pulling him back into his seat start to flip in his stomach, giving him uncomfortable butterflies. It was beginning to feel like he would fall forward out of his seat, instead of feeling his weight pulling him to the chair. His seat clicked and whirred and began to spin so he tucked his feet quickly into the footrest. Automatically, all of the seats spun at the same time, rotating a complete 180 degrees precisely at the midpoint of where the Luna singularity drive gravity ended, and the Terra side gravity began. In a dizzying moment, up was becoming down and down becoming up. Within a few seconds, the rotation was complete, and the passengers of the tube were now traveling backwards. Instead of watching the Terra docks loom larger into view, Jesse was watching the Luna docks drift away. He now also felt the sensation of lying on his back in his seat again, instead of wanting to lurch forward. This part of the transport tube ride always relaxed him and made him want to close his eyes, and so he did. Jesse was still nervous about appealing his APT scores to Junia when he arrived. But he let the rocking of the tube and whooshing of the atmosphere returning lull him to a short doze. And short it was, as it only took five minutes from this point past Terra Gardens to arrive at Mid-Terra Plaza.

CHAPTER 6
A NOTION OF PURPOSE

    Mid-Terra Plaza was alive with activity. In a number of ways, the Terra side of Archway was close to identical to the Lunar side, with the same directional signage, same basic layout of levels and town centers. However, Terra Side had the reputation of being the "old" side of the station. Everything here was a bit more enriched with traditional Earth values and styles as compared to the more progressive themed Lunar Side. All of Archway was focused on advancing the future of humanity, but Terra Side always felt like it wanted to bring the past along with it whereas Lunar Side was ready to leave it behind.

    This was seen in the design cues of the Terra Side Operations building, towering in the middle of the plaza with its Greek marble columns and trusses. All of the main walkways that surrounded it were cobblestone, which gave a pleasant click-clack echo to every heel and toe that passed. The windows of the store fronts and businesses here had crystal clear glass in their panes instead of the slightly opaque gloss of clear polymer. These glass windows could not display information and advertisements digitally like their enhanced polymer cousins, so most storefronts communicated information on the glass via printed paper. Of course there were still the usual clues that gave away the fact they were in space, such as the same recessed lighting, trash collecting robots and stale recirculated air. Jesse's taste buds would enjoy a stroll through the gardens again.

    It was approaching lunchtime, and that meant that all of the personnel of the plaza were out and about. Chatting here and there in couples or bunches, moving from purposeful business conversation to casual chit-chat. Some had jumped onto their scooters and were shooting down the "highways" in the middle, obviously aiming for a lunch destination a bit further than they cared to walk. Unlike Lunar Side, many of the scooters here were not individual transport, but rickshaw style hired taxis, with the driver up front and a bench seat for at least two on the back.

Jesse already felt out of place, but it had been a few days since his last shower, and now he was also painfully aware he had been wearing the same clothes for the past two days. As he swam through the various pockets of executives and administrators, he was keeping his eyes to the horizon, looking for the Venture Colonies sign. He didn't notice many of the people going by perceiving his stench nor did he catch anyone taking offense to his appearance, but he felt watched all the same and he wanted to ignore that as much as he could. There were shops and stalls here of various clothing providers, but Jesse knew his pockets were not near deep enough for that at the moment. He did consider if Junia would reject his plea based upon his current state and apparel, but his outerwear did look the part of a poor and dirty colonist, so he figured he had that going for him.

Down the next cobbled walkway, Jesse noticed a street was named *Colony Way* which matched with the local clientele that suddenly took on appearances similar to his current predicament. More and more of the rabble around him were too shabby to be regulars to Mid-Terra Plaza. This was due to the colony companies attracting folks that had not much to look forward to here in this system, so they figured they would try their luck at another. Begin fresh on a brand-new planet. When Jesse turned the corner, he could see the Venture Colonies sign, large and broad, a silhouetted forest green hawk amid a golden background across the building at the end of the street, so he started his way down.

On either side of the walkway were the other startup colony companies. Space travel and exploration had long been a primarily private enterprise, however nearly every country on the planet had their hands in sponsoring various voyages throughout the Solar System and now beyond. The sponsors behind the trips would enter into contracts with the starships who would carry the actual mission out, each of them investing in either time or money in hopes of the grandest of returns of exclusive rights to an entire planet. Colony companies would broker the deals, sort, hire and train the personnel, and establish the foundations necessary to successfully launch these endeavours. The major players were Ming Enterprises, New Capital Worlds, Intrepido Explorar, and of course Venture Colonies, along with some other smaller startups that are working towards their first effort to the stars.

The hopefuls lining the walkway, waiting in line to enter each company's consideration forums, were more numerous than normal. This was due to Archway station moving to apogee, its closer orbit to the moon, where on the far side was the slingshot gateway and the lunar starship docks. This is where the massive HomeMaker starships were built and launched to the distant star systems. While Archway is close to the moon is when the colony missions launch.

Jesse worked his way to the entrance of Venture Colonies, where most of the folks waiting looked a bit more upscale and put together than the other hirelings. Venture had the reputation of being "the" premiere colony production company and so they attracted the best of the best to their efforts. Upon entering the building's lobby, all of the colonizers were filing into double doors to his left, entering below a sign that read DEPARTURES. They each had their own matching tablets and Venture duffels and backpacks, so these were persons already assigned to an upcoming launch. Indeed, below the DEPARTURES sign was a digital readout that read: *Gliese 1061 t-minus 4:16:23:00*. With every passing second the time was counting down, and based on the time remaining, they were leaving in just over four days.

Aside from the mass of people entering the double doors, the lobby was relatively calm and open. The reception desk was manned by two, tucked into the right side of the lobby wall. There were temporary stanchions protecting the dual elevators beyond that, with a light security guard stationed on a stool in between them. He looked relaxed but capable of handling any minor disturbance. The back wall had hoisted a large viewscreen high, displaying various facts and brag points that Venture used to attract hopefuls. Greenery surrounded the viewscreen, lush with life of ivy and climbing vines. Jesse identified honeysuckle among the vines and craved the sweet Keifer Junia had shared with him.

"Hello! Can I help you?" A voice called to Jesse from the reception desk. He must have looked lost.

Jesse approached with a smile. "Hi! Yes, I'm here to see Junia Fresco."

The gentleman worked the screen in front of him on the other side of the desk. "I see. Do you have an appointment?"

"No, I don't, but she knows me." Jesse went with an appeal to their shared camaraderie. "We're friends."

"I understand. Unfortunately, she is especially busy today with the onboarding process and all that entails." He motioned with his eyes to those entering the departure doors. "Perhaps you could come back another day?"

"Actually, it's kind of important." Jesse insisted. "Is there any way you could just mention to her that I'm here?"

"I can send her a message for you, and you're welcome to wait for a few minutes, but that's all I can do." The receptionists here at Venture were much more friendly and helpful than the ones at Mitchell and Sons. "What's your name?"

"Jesse Heartshire. But she just knows me as Jesse." Jesse realized he never gave Junia his last name. Hopefully she remembers him.

The receptionist worked the screen and assured Jesse. "Ok, I've sent her a message. You're welcome to wait here in the lobby to see if she responds." He motioned to the chairs around the greened screen. As Jesse settled in, he noticed that there was a koi pond in the middle instead of a coffee table. The large golden orange fish paddled gracefully, nibbling at the water lilies and the algae growing along the rocks. Jesse turned his attention to the large screen while he waited.

Welcome to Venture Colonies! The leader in all exo-development endeavours in the Solar

System, and beyond! There was a blonde woman in the bottom corner, motioning to the changing images of Olympus, Venture's most successful colony to date on Mars, home to over 28,000 people. The Martian colony looked as if giant bubbles had landed on the planet's surface and the people had simply moved in. The scenes were depicted in an appealing way, but Jesse thought to himself it looked nightmarish. No greenery, no forests, just red rock and recirculated water. He cringed a bit inside at the thought of being stuck in a place like that.

Centauri, our shining star, has been successfully self-sustaining for the last 22 years, and stands as the definitive example of how colonization of the cosmos should be done. The red planet transitioned to the stars, zooming the camera to Venture's first interstellar colony on Proxima Centauri B. This planet was renamed simply to Centauri (considered an intergalactic right by the first permanent colonists) and has been the poster child example for every other colony attempt. It has grown from its initial population of 243 to nearly 500, and had been the first colony to successfully construct their own slingshot gateway, allowing residents and harvested materials to travel back to Earth.

We now reach further into the future than mankind has ever thought possible, touching multiple star systems, spreading hope and prosperity throughout the galaxy. A sweeping shot of the known universe panned across the screen, highlighting those stars where Venture had sent colonizers throughout the years since. There were 12 in total as Venture profited massively from the Centauri colony, and poured its new capital into a number of investments, expanding their partnerships with various private and governmental sponsors. This was more than all of the other colony companies combined.

We have high hopes and assured expectations that with the right sponsors, and partnerships with civilians like you, she pointed at the camera, right at Jesse, *we can build an exciting new universe, where home is wherever you make it!* The woman was unspecific about the hope she mentioned, but Jesse knew just like everyone else did. Colony work was not without risk, monumental risk.

HomeMaker starships are built to be as self-sufficient as possible; however they are primarily designed to be colony builders. It is compartmentalized, with some of the ship intended to land on a planet where it terraforms, creates instant habitats, and provides the means to mine materials. These materials would then be sent back to the orbital portion of the ship, which would establish communication with Earth, and begin constructing a return gateway. Without the ability to create their own slingshot gateway above the planet they arrive on, there is no possibility of returning to Earth. Also, due to the light-years of distance that these star systems are from Earth, it takes years for interplanetary communication to be established. It was mentioned that Centauri was so far the only colony to successfully construct a gateway, but in fact not even half of the other colonial efforts have even communicated that they have successfully been established. The next closest HomeMaker starship was sent to Tau Ceti over 15 years ago, and with that system being approximately 12 light-years from Earth, communication of at least a successful arrival should have been received by Venture. That message is 3 years past due.

"Mr. Heartshire?" The receptionist's voice called.

Jesse stood and made his way to the desk. "Yes?"

"Mrs. Fresco will see you now." He worked the screen and drew a digi-pass from a slot on the screen, then slid it to Jesse along the desktop. "This is your digi-pass for today. It expires in 1 hour, so if you need to stay longer, Mrs. Fresco will have to send approval to us here."

"Ok, great, thanks!" Jesse took the pass, warmed the temporary adhesive on the back with his hand, and stuck it to the front of his shirt.

"Mrs. Fresco's office is located on the 3rd level. You will need to exit the elevator there and proceed down the hall to your left. Her office is the 3rd on the left. Simply look for her name. Is there anything else I can help you with?"

"No, sir. Thank you." Jesse proceeded to the stanchions which automatically recognized his credentials from the digi-pass and slid aside. The security guard perked up, read his pass, and pressed the call button on the lift. It opened almost immediately.

"Have a good day." The guard mentioned to Jesse as he walked by. Jesse nodded and began tossing in his mind the possible objections and outcomes of his conversation with Junia. He practiced how he would respond to her undoubtable questions on his APT results. How he would explain himself if she mentioned the altercation with Mitchell and Sons. He wasn't exactly desperate for this job, and the sobering notion of leaving Earth and his family behind for years hadn't hit him yet. He knew in his head that if he was able to board a HomeMaker starship, there was a strong possibility he would never return, but the most pressing need on his heart right now was justifying himself in front of an authority figure. Jesse wanted redemption, and he had a good hunch that Junia would be his best shot at that.

The lift ride was well short of the time that Jesse needed to work through all of the possible scenarios in his head, but perhaps that was for the best. Overthinking these things does not always help and often hurts. He made his way down the left hallway, stopping at Junias' door. It was real wood, with a classical golden nameplate on the front, presented in printed script: Junia Fresco, Director of New Foundations. The name plate also had a small camera and speaker embedded on it. Jesse took a breath, straightened his hair and shirt as best he could, and knocked. The automatic announcer in the door read his digi-pass and he could hear this communicated on the inside of the door.

Jesse Heartshire requests your conference.

"Yes, let him in." Junia's voice responded. The door disengaged the lock and swung gently inward. A soft smell of sage drifted across the breeze of the opening door. Jesse stepped inside and into a comfortable space of carefully placed green plants among dark wooden shelves adorned with touches of what looked like museum pieces. Her desk was cluttered with some papers and a few digital tablets, each displaying what looked like passenger and equipment manifests. In front of that was a sitting area of 3 armchairs and a low table in the middle. On that low table was a steaming cup of tea, and an open APT test result. Jesse could make out his name at the top already. Junia was standing next to a large, golden spyglass in the corner, facing out the window, on which she rested her hand lightly. She smiled in greeting.

"Good afternoon, Jesse. I was curious to know if I would ever see you again and here you show up at my door." She motioned for Jesse to come inside and have a seat in the armchair in front of the table.

"Is that to keep an eye on your competitors?" He pointed at the spyglass. Jesse tried to make the meeting light from the start, considering the weight of the matter to attend to.

Junia chuckled and lightly stroked the spyglass. "Oh, this? No." She glanced down at it. "Actually, quite the contrary." She moved around the spyglass and took a seat in front of her tea and tablet.

"How have you been? When do you ship off for the Lunar mines?" She asked with an expectant look. It was obvious she knew the answer already.

"Ya, about that..." Jesse trailed off, embarrassed that he was so firm in his affirmation of his non-existent job opportunity. The excuses he was practicing failed to come to mind, so he grasped at technicality. "I really did plan on working there. I applied and everything, but -"

"But the aptitude revealed to them you weren't right for that kind of work, didn't it?"

"Ya. I tried to explain it." Jesse defended himself.

"I told you when I first met you the other day that you didn't give me the sense of a rock-grunt." Junia chided.

"Actually, you said I didn't have the timbre of it. I didn't sound like one." Jesse corrected.

"Nooo, I said you didn't *look* like you had the timbre of it. It was more of your, how should I say it, your color? Your aura? That's what I was keying in on. And it looks like I was right."

"Ya, I guess you were." Jesse still didn't like being figured out, especially when he was fuzzy on the details himself.

"So what are you doing now?"

This was what Jesse was eager to talk about. "I'm open to new opportunities. To new ventures." He cracked a smile at the play on words. She caught it and smiled back.

"Oh, are you now? Well, let's talk about that." She picked up her tablet and set it in her lap, sitting back in the chair and crossing her legs. She was in a bit more professional attire today, wearing a Lunar style business skirt, but she somehow still looked ready for adventure. Maybe it was just the surroundings and how at home she seemed in them.

"We're obviously going to have to talk about a few things. First, before we get to all this." She waved her tablet and put it back down in her lap to address him politely. "You seemed very opposed to colony work when we first talked, and so I'm curious as to the change of heart. It's definitely normal for Venture to accept those who are desperate, but I am not in the habit of welcoming colonists who… have no purpose among the stars." She leaned in to put it simply. "Why are you here?"

Jesse thought for a moment how to answer this. He wanted the right words, but he also wanted her to believe he was genuine, and usually genuineness takes its time. "After I was rejected at Mitchell, I was upset. I had to take a day to calm down and think through my next steps, and while I did I did some soul searching. Before that, I was not doing well with working on Earth, and then working on the Moon fell through, so I actually considered colony work for the first time, and it didn't seem that bad."

"It didn't seem that bad?"

"Ya, I mean, at first I was very against it. It's a big commitment and I wasn't ready. But now I feel like being rejected at places I wasn't meant to be, has forced me to see somewhere I *was* supposed to be." She was nodding at Jesse's words, following them and seemingly agreeing, so he kept it going. "It just sorta clicks now. It makes sense. And because of our connection the other day, I thought I could explain to you the best about what happened at Mitchell. Maybe you could overlook my APT."

She nodded in agreement, picked up her tea and sat back.

"I don't believe you." With that she adjusted more comfortably against the chair and sipped.

"Wait, what? Why?" Jesse was uneasy now. He was being truthful, just shallow.

"Jesse, in all of what you said, you gave me nothing specific as to why you are here now."

"But I just explained how having those doors closed on me made me realize this must be the reason I should be at Venture."

"No, all that tells me is Venture is your last resort. That's precisely why I *don't* want you here." Junia was much more resistant to him now, her attitude was offended at his offer to join. This confused and frustrated Jesse, especially considering how insistent she was at first meet.

"But, Junia… Mrs. Fresco. You were trying to convince me to join when we talked last." Jesse pressed.

"No, I encouraged you to find your purpose. I told you I would do this even if it meant getting no benefit. No money, no prestige, no title. I am exactly where I am supposed to be. That's what I want for you and anyone who joins Venture." Junia was firm.

"But this is where I am supposed to be!" Jesse pleaded. "I know it is! It has to be!"

"What causes you to say that?"

"Because!…" Jesse hesitated. She's going to think he's crazy. Isn't she? But what has he got to lose? As of right now, he's out. "Because I feel called. I feel called to the stars." He relaxed. The weight was off his shoulders, and he bore as much as he dared.

"I had a dream. Actually, I had two dreams. After my rejection. Junia, they were deep. I've never felt dreams like this before." He was looking at the table, making gestures with his hands. He didn't notice the smile creep back across her face. "A voice was beckoning me to follow, and there was nothing left for me on the Earth any more."

"Now, that is an interesting purpose to draw you to Venture." Junia was wanting to accept Jesse, but she couldn't without knowing that his heart was in it. Runaways usually only ever look for the first thing solid that they can grasp, and then they burn out fast. Junia couldn't take a chance on Jesse without trusting that he wasn't going to keep running. She picked back up her tablet.

"We have the reason you're here, which is the most important, so now let's deal with this." She scrolled on the tablet screen and spun it around to show Jesse the display. It was an incident report, coded in red. This usually designates when an applicant has displayed qualities that would disbar them from accredited business practices. Jesse's semi-aggressive run-in with the executive at Mitchell and Son's was front and center. The company used heavy words such as "accosted", "disrupted" and "emotional outburst" to describe the altercation. Rather unfair and unforgiving, which instantly riled Jesse's defenses.

"Hold on a minute, let me explain -" Jesse started but Junia interrupted and held her hand toward his face.

"Jesse. Wait. Can I tell you what I see here?" Her voice seemed reassuring, so he relented and bit his tongue.

"What I see is someone smart enough to go to the ones who can solve his problem, with no regard or care for his approach. That shows me determination, and an acute sense of right and wrong." Jesse was disarmed by her words. He blinked and listened. "I see someone who understands justice and will act when there is none. I see someone who will challenge authority when that authority needs to be questioned. Jesse, before I even study your aptitudes, I already want you in a Venture colony."

Jesse could feel his eyes tearing up, so he sniffed and wiped them before he cried. It was so relieving to have someone accept him, to listen to him and see him instead of analyzing his file. The relief was so great for his heart that at this moment he wouldn't have cared if she ultimately rejected his request for the colonies. A professional profiler saw him for who he was.

"With this, we can see where you might fit." She reviewed his APT profile a tad more, scrolling to his major characteristics. This took a few moments as Junia grazed the highlights of his scores. "You scored high in emotional intelligence... and cognitive dissonance! That's rather fitting for a man of your peculiarities!" Jesse smiled, not quite sure what that was but he thought it was positive. She made it seem like it was. "Ooo, rural data scrutiny! That's a predictable one for sure... and medicinal-horticultural agronomy! I must say, this makes a lot of sense for a homesteading Carolinian!" She thought for a moment and sat back in her chair, and she got a bit more serious in her tone.

"Jesse, a man of your skillset could be an asset to any colony excursion, and I'm going to send you along to our physiological testing department. But before we go any further... I can be direct with you?" Jesse nodded excitedly. "Are you running from your parents?" Jesse's mood diminished. He hung his head, shamefully recalling his outburst.

"Ya, we had a... falling out after my brother died."

Junia nodded in understanding, stood and crossed over to the window, her hand lightly resting on the golden spyglass. "Come here."

Jesse rose and approached the end of the spyglass. Through the window, he could now see that at the angle it was aimed, the glass looked past the other buildings on Colony Way. It was aimed above them, to an exposed Archway wall that revealed the stars beyond the Solar System.

"Look through here and tell me what you see." She patted the end of the spyglass gently.

Jesse obliged, leaning over to peer through the small eye piece. As his eye adjusted, he could see a number of small, distant stars through the glass. They seemed so far removed from where they were. Almost as if it wasn't real at all, but a painted backdrop. But, out of all the stars, one in the middle of the spyglass was the most eye-catching. It was red or gold, the color seemed to fluctuate every time he blinked, but it was easily brighter than all the others so that was probably what Junia wanted him to see.

"I see a few stars, but one in the middle is brighter than the others. It's very pretty."

Junia spoke softly, "Yes, that's the one. That's Tau Ceti. We sent an expedition there 15 years ago and are still waiting to hear back." She paused a second, then spoke again. "My son is with them."

Jesse didn't want to look through the glass anymore after that. He stood up and met eyes with Junia.

"Every day that that star is visible, I watch and wait. I miss Leonard so much, and I anticipate his HomeMaker's signal every day. But I do take comfort that before he left, I knew he was following his purpose. He was driven to the stars, and as a mother, I did what I could to encourage and fan that flame." Junia slid her hand down the spyglass and rested it on Jesse's. "Please make sure that before you go, you make peace with what you are running from. Heartache will still follow you to whatever distant star you run to."

Jesse nodded. He had been avoiding his parents' messages because he was angry. Now he was avoiding them because he felt guilty. There was no pressing need to resolve his feelings on the matter, but now with the potential years of interstellar travel, he was going to have to address them. "I will," he assured her.

"Good!" Junia grabbed another tablet from her desk, and worked it. She switched back to her professional tone to move past the uncomfortable wait of hearing from her son. "Are you free today?"

"Yes. For what?"

"I am scheduling your Venture exams for 2:30." She looked him up and down, then met his eyes. "Good thing for you that you'll need to redress in athletic attire for the tests! I'm re-upping your digi-pass for another 24 hours, and granting you access to the testing locker rooms. In there you will find vending units for some fresh clothes."

"Great, thanks!" Jesse walked back to his chair and picked up his satchel, throwing it over his shoulder. The flap flipped open for a moment as he was adjusting it, and the old Bible that Gus had given Jesse nearly fell out. Jesse grabbed it before it fell completely out, and he didn't feel her eyes on him as he shoved it back in. Junia had noticed, and she began to feel slightly nervous, but hid her emotion behind the work she was doing on the tablet.

"I am also granting you temporary access to the staff cafeteria. It's one level down at the end of the hall. Go have something to eat, but make sure it's light. Some of the tests are rigorous." Junia finished and set the tablet back on her desk.

"This is amazing, Junia. Thank you so much!" Jesse reached his hand out to shake hers. She took it, and held it, not letting Jesse break the handshake so quickly, just like before.

"You're welcome, Jesse." She pulled the handshake slightly closer to her. "And Jesse, be as honest as you can be in all of these exams. It's very important." Her voice was both warm and stern. In his freshly excited mood, Jesse didn't take much notice but smiled in reassurance. She smirked back and let go, again with the slight squeeze before releasing. Jesse turned and made his way out of her office.

CHAPTER 7
WARMING UP

Seven hours later, Jesse slumped back against the one sofa in the room as he awaited his final test in the Venture testing center. It was more of a loveseat than a sofa, short in both seat and back, with no armrests and a fabric very silky smooth. They said that they would call him in for the last exam at any moment, but he welcomed the wait. The tests were grueling to say the least. He welcomed the rest in this quiet room, even with its sharply pointed walls and springy floor. The last test was said to be the anechoic stress measurement, whatever that was. This was the first moment alone he had to consider everything since this morning, and so he began to muse on the latest happenings.

This room gives me the creeps. Looking around, the walls and ceiling seemed dangerous, jutting out at him in jagged, sharp angles, except that the points themselves were soft foam. His only light source was an electric lantern that they placed in the center of the room, a few feet from his loveseat perch. This cast epic shadows of all kinds of crisp contours, creating a clear distinction between the light and the dark.

I hope I passed the competency exams, Jesse thought. Venture is very thorough with their interview and examination techniques. Before they send anyone lightyears away from Earth, depending on them to effectively rebuild civilized society, they want to make sure these people are vetted, sorted and vetted again. Although Jesse finished his schooling, he was never very good at it. Mathematics, language arts, science… it was hard to stay focused on it all, especially when –

Wait, what was that? Jesse's line of thought was interrupted by movement out of the corner of his eye. Something seemed like it flashed in the far corner to his right. Was it a flash? More like the shadow moved. Like the dark lunged at the light and then retreated in the blink of an eye.

No, all was still. He didn't see any movement, and when he stood to get a better look, there was nothing that could have moved. Must have been his imagination. There was a high-pitched ringing that Jesse could just make out when he entered the room, that seemed like it was louder now. He paced for a moment, looking at the peaks and valleys of the walls. The ringing didn't seem to get louder or quieter from his movement, so Jesse couldn't discover its source. He stuck his finger in his ear and wrung it a couple times. That was it! The ringing was his own ears, singing their high pitch of hearing nothing. This was a quiet room! He sat back down.

I bet I aced the physical exam though. I could have probably ran longer. All of those interviewed for colony work are put through a number of physical challenges as well. Running a couple miles, holding heavy weight for minutes at a time, lifting, pulling, throwing, catching, etc. Nearly everything the Venture team could consider and measure, Jesse and the others endured. There was even a physical intelligence aspect, where they would examine participants willingness and knowledge around health education and –

THAT WAS IT AGAIN!

Jesse was sure of the movement of the shadows this time, and it wasn't in his peripheral vision but straight ahead of him. It seemed as if the dark reached for the lantern from the back side, hit it like a wave crashing upon a large rock wall, then retreated. Again, all of this Jesse saw, but he continued to question if he saw it at all. It was so quick but stretched. As if a second was switched to slow motion, lasting twice as long, then speeding back to normal.

Jesse stood to investigate but immediately sat back down. His head was swimming and dizzy. The ringing in his ears was starting to make his head hurt, so he reached to rub his temples.

SCHHHH! SCHHHH!

His eyes shot open. Each time he touched his temple with his fingers and slowly massaged, he could hear it! Not just the normal, smooth sound of skin sliding across skin, but it sounded in his head as if he was scratching sandpaper against wood. Rough, coarse sandpaper by the sound of it. He was fascinated by the fact. He did it slowly over and over as he could hear each microscopic imperfection on his face catch on the ridges of his fingertips. He looked down in wonder at his fingers. The tops and valleys of his fingerprint looked magnified in his vision. He could see them as mountains.

THUD, THUMP. THUD, THUMP.

His heart was pounding, literally the sounds of pounding, from his chest. He looked down at his chest. Jesse would have sworn on oath that he could see his shirt jump with each beat. *HOW AM I HEARING ALL OF THIS? WHAT IS GOING ON?!* Jesse's mind was becoming overstimulated by the sounds. It wasn't as if he could hear one thing over another, but that a cacophony of vibrations were crashing upon his ear drums all at once. He placed his hands over his ears.

WWWWOOOOSSHHHHHHHHHHHHHH!!!

"*Gah, what the hell!?*" Jesse's ears were suddenly flooded with static. It wasn't static however, but the sound of the blood being pumped through his hands, trapped when he clasped them over his ears. He was even shocked by the sound of his voice. It didn't travel. It felt as if it stopped right at his lips. He could hear it in his head, but could not make sense of his own vocal chords. Jesse stood.

SCHHHHHT! It sounded as if he had ripped himself off the loveseat with industrial Velcro, the smooth fabric gripping and tearing at the seat of his pants. Every sound of every fiber, Jesse could distinguish. It was as if a horrible superpower had bestowed itself upon him, and with every passing second, he desperately wanted to be normal again.

The shadows were now leaping at him. He backed his way to the center of the room, his back to the lantern, blocking the light. This was a mistake as he felt engulfed by the darkness, He could watch its tentacles at the edges of his vision wrapping around him towards the lantern. Jesse spun, and stared at the lantern.

SQUISH!!! SQUIRM!!! As he swung around, he felt his stomach twist and turn in uneasiness. He could hear his organs moving! When he spun and suddenly stopped, not only could he feel the shifting inside of himself, he could distinguish his stomach and intestines resettling in his abdomen.

SCHHHHH!!! THUD, THUMP!!! WOOOSH!! SQUISH!!! SCRATCH!!!

Jesse was drowning in noise. Every corner of the shadows dove at his face, their sharp angles slicing this way and that. There was no escaping, only embracing his demise. So he breathed.

WHOOOOO HAAAAAA!! WHOOOOO HAAAAA!!

And he blinked.

SLICK, SLAP!! SLICK, SLAP!!

He was panicking. He couldn't breathe as he felt everything around him growing closer and closer and louder and louder. His eyes darted around the room. Everything was moving. Everything was loud. Everything was dark. But then his eyes settled on the lantern, and he focused on the light. It was bright and watered his eyes to stare at it. But it was constant among the chaos. Its ambient, incandescent orange felt warm against the attacks of his mind. Jesse was still in audible hell, and every second dragged on for an hour. Still he was kept. Kept sane. Kept still. Kept by his focus on this simple lamp, a light in the loud black.

Moments as long as days passed, and in exactly twenty minutes from the time he first entered the room, the door was opened. He didn't notice that fluorescent white bathed half the room in outside exposure. And he shook for a moment when a gentle hand grasped him from behind by the shoulder.

"Time's up, son."

The man pulled Jesse up and took Jesse's arm to lead him out of the room. At first It was difficult for him to trust it was happening, but the instant that Jesse stepped foot back onto the clean, white tiled floor of the Venture testing center, his senses returned to normal. Similar to removing nitrous oxide from your nose, everything becomes clear again, and the hallucinations quit. He was able to walk on his own easily now, and when Jesse looked back at the open door to the Venture Anechoic Testing Chamber, everything in the room was back to normal, the spikes of the floor and walls were docile and the shadows no longer reached for him. The only sounds he could hear were the footsteps of himself and the technician walking down the corridor, now seeming eerily quiet from the eruption of sound just moments before. The technician walked him to the testing coordinators at a central desk in the middle of the lobby.

"This concludes your final examination, Mr. Heartshire." The woman in spectacles said to him as he approached.

"Did I pass?" Jesse asked, half jesting.

"It's not a pass or fail. We simply collect data and provide the analysis to our starship proctors." The humor seemed to be lost on her.

As it had been explained to Jesse at the beginning of the testing, each colonist hopeful is run through the same series of examinations to decide whether they are suitable for colonial life. Those tests look at a many number of factors, but basically divide into cognitive ability, physical prowess, spiritual health, and genetic diversity. Each one of these have their various subgroups and factors that are then measured and each applicant is given a score. These scores are then provided to all three entities that collectively oversee any colony exercise: Venture Colonies, the expedition sponsors, and the HomeMaker starship captain.

It had taken Jesse by surprise that he would have to undergo genetic testing, but then he realized that if he was living in a colony for the rest of his days, the selection of a spouse was going to be rather tight. Fortunately he was male, and each colony expedition crew was predominantly female on purpose. His options were going to be a bit more open, and in fact, Venture insists upon polygamy to increase the colony's growth rate. It was explained to him previously that he would actually be provided a list of "approved" women upon arrival at the colony that would fit with him both in personality and genetic benefit.

"Mrs. Fresco will see you now. I am sending her your results." The attending coordinator told Jesse.

"Now?" Jesse glanced down at his watch. "It's nearly 10. Are y'all even still open?" He glanced around the mostly empty assembling lobby of the testing center. There were still a couple other applicants in the room. *Have fun in that last one!* Jesse thought to himself.

"Yes, she has requested that we send you back as soon as you're finished. Mr. Cooper will escort you to the elevators." And with that, Mr. Cooper's grip on Jesse's arm was again guiding him down the hall. Jesse shook him off.

"It's ok, I can walk fine now." Jesse shot him an annoyed look. He didn't like being manhandled like that. Who would?

Mr. Cooper, the technician cued the lift with the call button. Jesse yawned and looked over at him.

"I guess Mrs. Fresco sees a lot of applicants, especially in apogee, huh?"

"Actually, no. This is the first time I know of." Mr. Cooper kept his eyes on the doors, waiting for them to open.

"Really?" Jesse was surprised.

"She's a director. They oversee the entire operation. I don't know if I've ever seen any of them take a direct interest in an applicant." Mr. Cooper's eyes shifted to Jesse's. "Don't screw it up, kid."

Jesse didn't even know what he did right, let alone how to not get it wrong. "Ya, right." he said. Why was Junia so interested in him? Did he score really well on his exams? Was there more in their conversations that she was seeing that he wasn't? The lift doors opened with a *BONG* and Jesse entered. Jesse pushed the button for the 3rd floor and Mr. Cooper nodded in dismissal as the doors shut.

When they reopened a few seconds later, the hallway was only dimly illuminated by Venture's office night lighting. Only every 5th light in the ceiling was on, giving the executive hallway an ominous and creepy feel. Jesse's footsteps were just as loud as they had been before, but with the lights out the footfalls felt much more exaggerated. He scanned the empty hallway with his eyes darting back and forth, although he walked confidently to Junia's door. He knocked and the door announced his arrival again.

Jesse Heartshire requests your conference.

"Yes, let him in!" Her voice was demanding and a touch impatient. The door opened, and hints of sage filled his nose yet again, but this time mixed with a bit of sandalwood and cedar. Her office was much darker, save a light on her desk and a wide base candle with 5 wicks that danced on the coffee table. Junia's large office windows overlooking Colony Way let in some ambient lighting from the street down below, and the stars artificially glowed in the "sky" above. She was sitting at her desk, pouring over a tablet in her hands. Undoubtedly scrolling through Jesse's fresh recruitment scores from the testing center.

"Please Jesse, come in. Have a seat. Give me just one second." She glanced up at him briefly, but then realized she was being rude, so she lowered her tablet for a moment. "I made you a cup of tea, it's there on the table. Give me one minute." She smirked at him and then went back to reviewing.

Jesse made himself comfortable in the chair he sat in earlier in the day. Before him was a steaming cup of what smelled like herbal tea. He lifted it and sniffed, but couldn't tell what kind it was. He took a very delicate sip as the mug was very hot on his lips. Chamomile? With honey and a touch of… is that spearmint? There was also a bitterness he couldn't place. It wasn't unpleasant though, and he sipped in the quiet for a few moments, feeling his eyes get heavy waiting in the dark.

He was halfway through his cup by the time Junia pushed back her desk chair and stood, still holding the tablet to her nose, and she picked up her own mug. Without looking, she made her way around her desk and sat across from Jesse in the other armchair. When her back settled into the seat, she laid the tablet down in her lap with a sigh.

"Well, that was a long day, huh?" She sipped her tea.

"Ya, have you ever taken those tests?"

"I'm not going to be a colonist anytime soon, so, no I haven't had the pleasure."

Jesse laughed a bit. "The pleasure? Those things are brutal." He sipped as well. "What kind of tea is this?"

"It's a mixture I make when I'm ready to wind down for the evening. Mugwort chamomile with a touch of honeymint."

"Honeymint? That's a new one."

"Yes, I found it at a dealer just last year -" She leaned forward and cut herself off. "I'm sorry Jesse, it's late and I should be explaining why I've asked you to come back." Her tone got serious. "I want to talk about your scores."

The inflection in her voice made Jesse's stomach drop. "Were they... bad?"

"Applicants' scores are neither good nor bad, Jesse, they simply help us understand who we are sending away to begin humanity all over again." She glanced down at the tablet in her hands again, then back at Jesse. "Your scores are... interesting. And concerning."

"Concerning?" Jesse leaned forward in his chair, anxious to hear what she had to say. Interesting he could live with, but concerning?

"Yes, so for the most part, you are a very healthy consideration. You've no major ailments, nor do you show any genetic signs for concern. Socially, you score well on the major metrics as well... but, Jesse... are you Neu Retterian?"

Jesse was taken aback. It was an exposing question, almost to directly ask someone what secrets they were hiding. What would his denomination of faith have to do with anything?

"Why do you ask?"

"In your family history you listed your parents, Benjamin and Deborah Heartshire, as missionaries in their primary occupation. You had told me they were homesteaders."

"Ya, they were missionaries before. Once my brother was born, they had settled in Carolina. What does that -"

"And then you mentioned to me when we talked earlier you felt 'called' to the stars recently. That a voice spoke to you in your dreams. Would you describe that voice as divine?"

Jesse was feeling attacked and not only without warning, he also didn't fully understand why. "What does it matter?"

"Please be honest with me, Jesse. This is important."

He felt more uncomfortable here than in the exams downstairs, but he swallowed and confessed. "Ya. I mean, I think so, I don't know for certain... but ya, I think God wanted me to come here. To see you." He tried an appeal that would rope her into the explanation. Make her feel included and less likely to be upset. Was she angry? He couldn't read her expression. It was direct and blank.

She thought a moment before speaking. "Jesse, Venture designs their expeditions with the intent of giving every colony a jumpstart at recreating human society. In all our best efforts, we attempt to do this without any defect present in our current culture. I'm not saying that your spiritual life is necessarily suspect, but in all of our applicants, those that have strong religious affiliations are weeded out. This is because Venture has determined that those who have strong faiths in a divine, tend to have their loyalties divided compared to the rest of the colonists. This has the potential to create disunity and can jeopardize the colony's objective as a whole."

Jesse considered her long explanation for a moment, puzzled that Junia had previously seemed to be on his side, but then threw up an unexpected roadblock. "So you're saying that because you think I'm a Christian, you're having second thoughts on sending me to a colony?"

"Are you a Christian?" Junia's face was still unchanged and direct. *What is this?*

He smiled as he thought about his answer and at the notion of the ridiculousness of this inquiry. He glanced about the room while he quickly thought, halfway chuckling to himself. *What did it matter? Should he lie and try to cover it up? Was he even still a believer anymore?*

"Jesse? Are you a Christian?"

A tad agitated, he threw up his hands briefly, then sighed. "Ya, I guess so."

"I need a yes or no."

Jesse was bothered now. He'd gone through all of this to be thrown out again over his faith? Maybe he should have just lied, but instead he admitted to the truth. The truth as best he could tell.

"Yes. Yes, I am."

Junia leaned back in her armchair. She narrowed her eyes at him and curled her lips slyly. "Do you know I knew that already?"

What kind of circular questioning is this? Jesse was getting very frustrated now. "Now, what does that mean? What are you getting at?"

"Based off of this:" She spun the tablet around in her lap and lifted it on the end so that Jesse could see what she was reviewing. It read *Anechoic Response* in bold font on the top. His score was listed below. It read *10/10 - Applicant showed particular resolve in maintaining sanity among chaotic increase.*

"You could tell I was a Christian just based on how I barely survived that hell hole?" Jesse wasn't believing it. *What did that have to do with anything?*

"There is nothing in that room other than you. The only torment that applicants suffer is from within as their own mind begins to go mad at being able to hear their own blood circulate and their organs move. Most can't handle the distress and then collapse after only a few minutes. Jesse, you out scored nearly every applicant we've ever had."

"I still don't see what me being a Christian has to do with this."

"Your faith in an external divine, something that gives you a solid purpose and focus outside of your own humanness, something that you believe is so concrete that nothing can shake it… Only Christians have shown this resolve. Only Christians have tested better than any other in this exam."

Junia sipped her tea. Jesse was flabbergasted. He wasn't thinking of Jesus when he was in the room. Even when things got horrifying, he was grasping at anything to escape. He fixated on the light in the center of the room because it was the only constant, unchanging point in the maelstrom. He simply focused on the light.

"Venture would say that Christians are a liability in colony life. That spiritual differences have divided and disrupted our society for generations, and therefore they are unwelcome to help rebirth humanity anew. I would disagree."

"But, Junia, I need to confess. I wasn't praying or anything."

"But you cued in on the light in the center of the room. You lost yourself in it."

"It was just a light though."

"Jesse, do you know how many other applicants have smashed that lantern trying to escape into the shadows? They actively destroyed their only source of light and embraced the abyss. That was their method of escape." Junia continued. "Whether you were conscious of it or not, your faith in that constant is what 'saved' you, to borrow Christian vernacular."

Jesse decided to turn it back on her for a moment. "Are you a Christian? Is that why you're so interested in me?"

Junia responded, "I understand that there is purpose to life. I see elements of design in the order of the world. And there are many beautiful things to marvel at in the universe." Her answer was an answer and yet not an answer at all. Junia had dodged around the question and he couldn't tell if she was unsure of her answer, or unwilling to answer. Jesse decided to leave it, as he wasn't the interviewer in this scenario.

"So, what now? Am I qualified or disqualified?"

"This is a big weekend for Venture. We're launching two different excursions. One to the Gliese system, which is to capacity. And one other, to the Toisee system, which is currently in need of a horticultural specialist." Junia worked her tablet and turned it to Jesse so he could view the display. The screen glowed from the center with deep crimson flames, emanating from the model of a red dwarf star. Above the star was the name Toisee, where the name of the system came from. Orbiting around it were 4 planets, each with varying hues of blues, greens, browns and reds.

"This system is 101 light years from Earth. It is by far the furthest colony expedition we, or any others, have ever attempted. We are hyper-charging the slingshot gateway to 105% capacity just in order to reach it."

Jesse attempted to read between the lines. "So anyone who goes, the chances of getting back are pretty slim to none?"

"No, the excursion has just as much of a chance at success as any other. The objectives remain the same: Establish a sustainable colony and construct a new slingshot gateway for the return journey. The danger is not in the distance, despite what our hearts tell us."

Junia turned the tablet back around to face her. "No, the danger for you in this is the fact that this is not an evangelistic mission, Jesse." She looked up to him. "Followers of Christ are specifically not welcome in any of the Venture colonies. Not officially, of course, but by practice. But in this particular excursion, you also have other cards stacked against you. You are familiar with C.D. Horizon?"

Who wasn't? Chao Daivi Horizon is the most influential political figure of the day, who rose to power following the purging of Christian influence in Europe. Particularly, against the evangelistic and missionary like those of the Neu Retter movement in Germany and elsewhere. She currently leads the European Union and is given credit for summoning the rallying cry to remove spiritual influence throughout all of the old world. Humanization was the popular motive for advancing mankind to the stars beyond, and those in power sought to leave 'ancient spiritual myths' behind. Their main purpose was to celebrate human achievement, the pinnacle of cosmic evolution, claiming our exploration of the universe was 'humanity returning to the stars from whence we came.'

"Jesse..." She collected herself, conflicted but determined to keep his options open. She was obviously wrestling with her professionalism, the wounds of her missing son, and her desire to see Jesse live out his purpose.

"I hesitate to even offer you this. But, how strong is your calling to the stars?"

Jesse shrugged. This was all still very new to him, divine conviction and all. "I don't know to be honest. I do know I felt very compelled to be here, today."

Junia continued. "President Horizon, she and the European Union are the primary sponsors of the expedition to Toisee. Her former President of State, Tristan Yale, is the HomeMaker's captain. To my understanding, their charter explicitly forbids an establishment of religion in the colony." She finished her tea and set the mug on the table. "You're going to have to deeply consider what environment this places you in, if you decide to follow your calling on this journey."

Jesse was definitely uneasy about this intimidating conversation with Junia, let alone the idea that he would have to hide his affiliation with his family and Neu Retter, no matter how removed he currently was. But he didn't know if he could ignore the way he felt any more, either. He wanted to find and talk to Gus again. He seemed to be a wise man.

"But for now, it's getting late. I apologize for putting all of this on you tonight, Jesse. This is a big decision, and most applicants have months before they depart. Given your current situation and considering the sense I got from you in our conversations, I concluded I would do you the favor of offering you this opportunity, even if it's hasty." Junia stood and lifted her tablet to her face. In the glow of the screen, he could see her eyes. They were bloodshot with conviction.

"You don't have anywhere to go tonight, do you?" She inquired.

Jesse considered for a moment returning to the church in Low Point, but answered, "No, not really." It was late and he didn't want to disturb Gus way back on the bottom of Luna Side.

Junia worked the tablet a second more. "I have assigned you full permissions as an active colony recruit. That entitles you to private quarters, cafeteria access and Venture issue clothing. The colonist barracks are on level 1, on the far side of corridor A." She lowered the tablet, quickly wiping away some moisture from below her eyes, feigning as if she had an itch.

Jesse stood and slung his satchel over his shoulder. He reached out to shake Junia's hand in appreciation. She clasped it warmly with both hands.

"Take your time to come to a decision." She said without letting go, as was her habit with handshakes Jesse noticed. "But don't take too long. The expedition for Toisee leaves at 0800 on Tuesday. I'll need your decision by tomorrow morning to make the appropriate arrangements. Goodnight, Jesse."

"Alright, thank you, Junia." Jesse turned and walked towards her door. As it opened for him when he approached, he turned to face her. She already had her back to him, with her arms across her chest, facing towards the golden spyglass and the stars outside Archway. He thought he would say something hopeful, but the words didn't come, so he left her office and continued down the eerie, dimly lit hallway to the lifts.

CHAPTER 8
THE BREATH BEFORE THE PLUNGE

Jesse's quarters tonight were a significant upgrade from the hostel he rented after his first day on Archway. They were sleek, modern arrangements, with no visible lightbulb but only embedded lighting strips tucked into every crease and crevice of the walls themselves. Where the floor met the wall, where the ceiling met the wall, where the walls met each other; every straight line was recessed and backlit into the creases. The surrounds themselves were polished white, with accents of forest green and gold to complement the Venture logo printed on the ceiling. The accommodation was not very large, but it still felt spacious enough to breathe in, even with an included sink, shower, toilet closet and dresser. Inside the dresser is where Jesse discovered the standard issue colony recruit uniform, so he used this opportunity to shower and change. Although it was midnight (Archway uses Earth Alaska Daylight Time as their standard, matching Point Nemo geo-orbit), Jesse found it difficult to sleep. A lot had happened, so he opted for a walk.

He exited out of a supplemental back door of Venture Colonies main offices, one that led directly to and from the colonist quarters in the hind end of the building. He wasn't overly surprised to find a few stragglers matching his uniform outside the building, milling about in small groups, smoking and conversing. But he wanted to be alone, so he ignored them and moseyed past. Fortunately, they paid him no attention either.

Jesse's footsteps on the cobbled walkway of Mid-Terra Plaza echoed the further he got from their conversations. Strolling the business neighborhood in the middle of the night felt as if someone had simply turned out the lights of the shop. Walking through housing developments in the night hours felt homey by comparison, where glows of life and rays of light were cast out into the dark, where passersby may have been outside but still felt touched by the warmth of family from within. Here, the plaza simply felt 'turned off', as if a switch was touched and power simply removed. It gave emotions of cold and sadness and caused Jesse to feel alone.

As he strolled, not lost in thought but lost in the heaviness of the decisions to be made, he glanced up at the reflected stars on the ceiling. He knew why he felt so alone here. Even with the added and very realistic aesthetics, it did not feel real. There was always the reminder that life on the station was an imitation of life, merely a copy of the life that existed elsewhere. Jesse wanted to feel the earth under his feet again at that moment. He could vividly recall the breezes in the summer nights on the homestead in Asheboro. He was feeling awfully sentimental for the comfort of his old way of life, where simply growing things was the main reason to exist. He knew he was ready to call home.

Colony Way wasn't but about ¾ mile removed from the outer wall of Archway Station. As Jesse approached the end of the cobbled pathway, the street opened up in a T-junction. To his left and right the street continued, but straight ahead was the growing and glowing besmirched surface of the Moon. As Archway was moving into apogee orbit, the Moon was visibly growing larger by the second. Many cafes and restaurants fronted this end of the plaza to take advantage of the changing and awe-inspiring views outside the station. On the right-side corner, there was a commemorative holo-booth. These were interstellar, three-dimensional holographic communication pods that connected to other holo-booths on Earth, the Moon and beyond. Anyone who had one, or used one, could enter the pod and chat with a 3D projected image of the users on the other end. Like most, Jesse's family had one in their living room.

It was late, but as any child knows, no matter the time, mom and dad will answer. He stepped inside which activated the pod. Behind him was the growing image of the Moon, which made this pod more of a spectacle. He dialed his home address and waited, rocking on his feet, not entirely sure of what he was going to say, but he knew he needed to say something.

DOOT DOOT!

DOOT DOOT!

DOOT DOOT!

Beep, BEEP! The sound indicated that the transmission was received, and a fuzzy, particlized image of his father, Ben, materialized in front of him.

"Hello? Yes?" His dad said, waiting a moment for Jesse's image to form on his end. "Jesse! Hello, son!" He leaned towards his left. "Deb! Debbie! It's Jesse! He's in the holo!"

"Jesse?!" He could hear his mom say from out of view. Her image quickly materialized from the left side of the pod.

"Hey Dad, hey Mom." Jesse waved a small bit, and sheepishly stood in front of his parents, already embarrassed to be seen by them again.

"Where are you?" His dad asked, then looking past his son, he questioned more specifically. "Are you on Archway?"

"Ya. Ya, I was looking for a job up here."

"Well praise Jesus you're ok! We've been so worried!" His mother was clutching her bathrobe. She desperately wanted to reach out to her son, but this was all she could do for now.

Jesse wanted to hug her too. "I'm ok, mom. I just needed to get away for a while."

His dad had his arm around Deb's shoulders. "Well, when do you think you'll be coming home?" He asked. His voice was soft and assuring, and they looked so relieved to see him well.

"I dunno yet." Jesse responded. That was a very loaded question that he didn't know how to answer, especially right now. So, he shoved his hands in his pockets.

Ben started trying to apologize, "Son, I'm sorry for what I did-"

"No!" Jesse interrupted. "No, no I'm sorry, dad. I know what you were trying to do now. I was just angry and I took that out on you." Jesse could feel his eyes getting hot and wet.

"Jesse, sweetheart, just come home and we can talk about it." His mom reassured. "We can schedule you a shuttle flight."

"No, I can't yet."

His parents were visibly disappointed. "But, Jesse, we should all be here for Stephen's celebration service." Deb had a coaxing tone to her voice. In true Neu Retter tradition, when members of the church passed on, the funeral services were jovial and celebratory. This was because the deceased was now with Jesus in eternity, living in glory. Due to life on Earth being so difficult, graduation to life everlasting was widely considered a happy occasion, and not a dismal one.

"Ya, and I know y'all aren't going to like this, but I might have something kinda big happening up here, too. I… I… " He hesitated on how to explain what he still had a hard time accepting. No matter how many times he said this out loud to people, he still didn't know if he trusted it himself.

"Son, we can always find you another job-" His dad began.

"No, dad, it's not just a job. I had a dream."

His parents perked up a little taller, interested to hear about their son's revelation.

"What kind of a dream?" His mom probed.

"I was on, well, floating above Earth. But Earth was dead, or dying, or… at least, dead to me. And everything was black. There was nothing around me. But then I heard a voice, a voice saying 'Come, follow me here.'" His mother clasped her hands to her mouth, but his dad simply stood with his agape. "So I reached for this star that I thought it was coming from, but it was too far so I gave up. But, then out of nowhere, you both show up and start pushing me from behind, trying to knock me off the Earth. And I fell, and woke up."

"Oh my God, Jesse!" His mom and dad were both visibly excited now, anticipating his conclusion.

"Ya, I mean, I don't know for certain or anything, but... but I think I feel called?" Jesse's face was unsure of what he was saying out loud. He had his own opinions, but he also looked to his parents for guidance on how to feel about this.

"Called to where?!" Ben asked, wanting to know what they should be excited about.

"I think I might be called... to leave. To leave on a colony ship."

"PRAISE GOD! PRAISE GOD!" His mother began screaming, raising her hands to the top of the pod. His father clapped his hands and bowed his head in prayer, exclaiming "Thank you, Jesus! Thank you, Lord!"

This was not the response that Jesse expected at all. He was startled by his mother's sudden outburst, but then watching them praise God so exuberantly at the mention of him leaving? His confusion and anger and frustration at his parents' faith came back quickly. It hurt his heart to watch them excited that he was leaving.

"What the hell?!" His parents toned it down and beamed at him, proudly. "What the hell are you doing? I just said I was going to leave! On a colony ship!" Jesse was furious. "Mom, dad, I might not ever come back!"

"Oh, son, my son Jesse." His dad pleaded, his hands outstretched to him holographically. "We aren't happy that you're leaving!"

"No!" His mother tried to explain. "No we love you, and we love that God has decided to use you in such a life changing way! We are so proud of you!"

Jesse blinked.

"We're happy *for* you! Jesse, you don't understand what it feels like to hear that your son is following Jesus in such a bold way!" His dad tried to explain. His mother was nodding vigorously.

"Yes! Jesse, sweetheart, this is an answered prayer for us!"

"I can't believe you! I can't believe I just told you I'm going to be gone, probably forever, and you're happy." He reached over to the pod controls. He wanted to slam the door in their face again, but cutting off the transmission was the best he could do.

"Jesse, no, please-" Ben reached for his son's hand as Jesse pressed the terminate holo button. Jesse stormed out of the holo-booth, slamming his heels down on the cobbled walkway. The pod chimed DOOT, DOOT with an incoming call. Obviously, his folks were trying to re-establish the connection, but Jesse wasn't interested. How dare they!? How dare they celebrate his brother's death and then leap for joy at the fact that their other son will most likely never come home. As tears of frustrated rage streaked down Jesse's face, he headed straight back to the barracks. This time some of the milling about colonist recruits noticed. Hard to miss a young man weeping, speed walking by hoping that they could move so fast no one could see. Jesse didn't really care though. He crashed into the bunk of his quarters and fell asleep nearly instantly.

◆ . ✛ . ◆ . ✛ . ◆

He was falling. Back first, looking up at his parents standing on the greyscale earth. They smiled and waved as Jesse fell in the abyss. He yelled curses and spewed venom at them as he fell, but his words were silent in the vacuum. Regardless of the fit he threw, Ben and Deb Heartshire watched their son fall away from the Earth with warm grins on their faces, waving farewell to their son.

Jesse was falling so in a short time he could no longer see them, just the grey Earth getting smaller and smaller in the undulating black. He twisted and spun himself around, looking down to where he would eventually land. There was nothing below him. He was falling, and falling forever by the look of things, into infinite nothingness. However, there were objects coming towards him awfully fast. Stationary objects that if he were able to grab them, he could save himself from demise.

Quickly, one was approaching that would just pass by his left side. Jesse strained, gritting his teeth and stretched his left arm out as far as he could. As it approached, he could see he was reaching for a lunar miner? The ridiculousness of this miner floating out in the nothing was beyond Jesse at the moment, and so Jesse called out to him. The miner turned and saw Jesse falling towards him. All he had to do was reach out his hand, and Jesse could grab him as he passed. But he didn't. Time slowed for a half second and the rock-grunt merely watched him pass by. Jesse felt the pit of his stomach drop in his continued freefall as the miner disappeared into the distance.

Looking down in his fall once more, he turned to see another object approaching. This time, the figure was on his left. This individual Jesse recognized right away based on their shape. Gus was coming up fast as Jesse fell. He yelled out into the vacuum, and although he made no sound, Gus heard him. He turned upwards and matched Jesse's eyes, although Jesse's were wide in panic, and Gus' were narrowed in a joyful laugh. Jesse again reached out to his right as far as he could manage, and Gus simply watched him whiz past. As time slowed for the moment that Jesse drifted by, Gus clapped his hands in encouragement. He threw his fist in the air as he watched Jesse tumble in space, groping for his friend that was too busy cheering his death.

Hurt by the rejection, Jesse tried to stay firm. It was apparent now that he had to save himself, so he righted and peered into his plummet. There was yet another figure coming into view. This person was going to pass by right in front of him, he got both hands ready to reach out, hoping that it doubled his chances for rescue. But this person was rather petite by comparison to Gus, and if physics made any sense at all here, his terminal velocity was beyond the rescue of their petty grasp. It was Junia, she stared straight at him. Even in the distance as Jesse approached, he could see the same struggle of a want to hold on but a knowing to let go wrestling in her eyes. At first he thought she was reaching towards him. This might be his chance of rescue! But as time slowed, this time each second seemed to last 10, it was clear that Junia was not reaching, but pointing. With one hand she pointed at him, with the other, she was pointing further down. Jesse was crying in desperation as he slid past her. Her eyes pleaded that he understood, but Jesse didn't understand why no one was catching him as he fell. He lazily followed her point, to further down into the black, and assumed that it meant he was destined to die. Ready to accept his lonely fate, he watched for what would come.

But instead of the end, a last object was coming. This one was big, and on fire! Flames shot out and around from behind the circle racing towards him. As it approached, it approached fast as if it was racing upwards as he fell downwards. He had mere seconds but he could make out details: Fins, thin and sharp. Rivets into metal paneling, smooth down the sides. A sharp tip to slice through friction on the front. It was a rocket! Blazing directly for him!

Jesse twisted himself to the side, so that perhaps if he made himself thin enough, it would miss him. He squeezed in his gut and did so just in the nick of time, the rocket narrowly missed piercing his side with the nose cone. He slid down its smooth cylinder, pushing himself away from the approaching fins by shoving off of the fuselage. But after he thrust himself away from the rocket, he noticed numbers etched into the side of the rocket. The numbers, 419, were everywhere. All over the rocket. On the nose cone, wrapped around the fuselage, cresting the tips of the fins. Quite literally, everywhere on the rocket. Jesse saw all of this, as time slowed, this time completely to a stop.

He was no longer falling, but floating. He could move, in all three dimensions, however he wished. Jesse felt weightless but could push himself along as if swimming. He circled the rocket, over and again, pondering the numbers. Then he gazed to see if he could determine where it was going. Following the angle of the nose cone, it was aimed precisely at the bright star that he had reached for from the grey Earth. Its rainbow of hues still danced in the blackness.

The rocket was still. Its engines still spewing fire in billows out into space, but making no sound, and making no movement forward. Jesse drifted towards the rocket. There was a detail he noticed that he had overlooked. A handle. Embedded into the side of the rocket. It was ergonomically designed, and when he reached out to grasp it, it had finger grooves that seemed to fit his hand perfectly. On the back side of the grip, Jesse could feel a trigger pull. With no reason to trust this other than his gut feeling that it was the right thing to do, Jesse pulled the trigger. The rocket exploded into life with the loud crackling of the engine's now deafening sound, and Jesse streaked right along with it towards the only bright light in the black nothing.

◆ . ✦ . ◆ . ✦ . ◆

Bleep, Bleep, Bleep, Bleep!

The alarm was buzzing on the view screen at the foot of his bed. He tried to sit up to turn it off, but his stomach muscles weren't strong or awake enough to get him there. So he slumped back into his pillow and stretched his right leg out to tap the OFF icon with his big toe. Luckily, that did the trick, and the bleeping quit. He huffed as he relaxed back on the bed. Last night was nightmarish in more ways than one, but he wanted to attend to the dream he had had before it slipped away from him.

It had felt just like the other two, deep in meaning and weighty. It was increasingly obvious to him that something deep and spiritual was beckoning him to space travel. There were still problems to solve with it though. If he is supposed to follow God to a colony, which one? Is he supposed to follow right away, or is he supposed to wait for a while? What did the numbers mean on the side of the rocket? He needed to talk to someone who he could trust with these matters. Someone who might have more insight than he had, and didn't have any ulterior motive based on which choice Jesse would make. It was only now 07:30, which meant Gus was probably in the middle of slinging breakfast to the less fortunate of Low Point. He would have to wait to reach him, so he figured he could do breakfast himself in the cafe.

He hopped off the bed and sorted his satchel. That's when he remembered he had no clean clothes of his own. Maybe they had a laundromat? Jesse started pulling all of his dirty clothes out of his satchel in one swoop, and threw the bag back onto the dresser. When he did, the old Bible that Gus had given him slumped onto the floor in a messy clump of pages. As he looked past the mess of clothes in his arms, he considered. *Is 419 something to do with the Bible?* It would stand to reason that if these dreams were a message from God, that His Word might have a connection as well. Jesse threw the clothes back down on top of the bed, picked up the Scriptures from the floor, and perched on the edge of the bed.

He paged them open and started considering which books in the Bible might have 41 chapters. *Genesis?* He thought. Jesse turned the old book towards its beginning and scanned for Genesis chapter 41. He found it after a moment, scanned down to the 9th verse and read: 'Then the chief cupbearer said to Pharaoh, "I remember my offenses today."'

Ummm, nope! That doesn't make any sense. Jesse thought he remembered that verse having something to do with Joseph but wasn't sure. He considered other books. *Maybe one of the prophets? Which one is a big one... Jeremiah?* He turned to Jeremiah 41:9: "Now the cistern into which Ishmael had thrown all the bodies of the men..."

No, no, no... Jesse didn't bother reading the rest of that one as it was definitely the wrong verse. He turned and checked Isaiah, the book just ahead of Jeremiah in the Bible. Isaiah 41:9 said:

"You whom I took from the ends of the earth,
   and called from its farthest corners,
  saying to you, "You are my servant,
   I have chosen you and not cast you off"

Well, now that's interesting... Jesse thought to himself. A slight chill ran down his spine as he read the words again. He felt special, as if the prophet was speaking directly about God and His actions towards him. He could feel the words resonate within his chest, and he was touched in the same comforting reassurance as if his very own mother had whispered her love to him. The hairs on his arm stood up in the realization that the Holy Spirit was alive and active, and that he was in communion with the Almighty.

Jesse basked in that moment for a long while. Tears of relief were welling behind his eyes. He closed them tight and prayed for the first time in a long time. He thanked Jesus for revealing himself to him and asked for forgiveness for his wandering. Jesse spent the most time thanking God for this confirmation but also pleaded for specific direction. He closed his prayer with not one, but three loving 'amens' and he stood, filled with joy for breakfast and ready to begin what the day might bring.

If he was going to leave the Solar System, maybe for good, Jesse needed to get his goodbyes in order. He wasn't for sure yet if the most recent Venture Colonies excursion to Toisee was where he was called, but the call was definitely confirmed. He hadn't known Gus for long, but he felt close to the man. His warmth and welcome was exactly what Jesse needed at the time, to say nothing of his words of wisdom as well. Jesse left the Venture barracks right after he finished a quick bite, and headed for the red gravimorphic transport tubes back to Lunar Side.

A few stomach-churning minutes later, the tube doors slid open for Lower Lunar Point. Jesse walked briskly through the patrons of the Dragway, lighter in step than he had previously trod. His mood seemed to mismatch with the aura of Low Point now, but he considered he felt probably a fraction of what made Gus such a necessary presence here. Those who are lost and broken, finding no comfort and respite within themselves, need someone on the outside of their predicament to retrieve them from their wallow. Jesse had jested that Gus' wisdom was wasted down here, slightly mocking him for claiming this was his purposed station. He knew now how foolish of a statement that was.

Jesse found the nook where Neu Retter Church was tucked into again, with not a little bit of difficulty. The sign was so obscured by steam today that the only way he could find his way back was through memory. He jaunted inside, squeezing through the restaurant patrons in line outside.

Gus wasn't in the kitchen. Jesse looked around, didn't see him behind the line, his normal spot was occupied by another under his *He who has ears, let them hear* Jesus quote. So Jesse backed out of the cafeteria and proceeded to check in his office in the back of the sanctuary. That wasn't necessary though, because as he walked through the sanctuary's double doors he spied Gus, standing at a podium in the middle of the room. Gus looked up when he saw movement of someone approaching.

"Well, hello young man! Good to see you again!" His voice boomed even from this distance as Jesse approached, striding down the aisle between the pews.

"Good morning, Gus!" Jesse slumped his bag down on the front pew and was wrapped up in Gus' big arms in no time. Gus was enthusiastically patting him firmly on the back. Maybe a bit too firmly. Jesse tried to return the favor, but it felt paltry by comparison, so he gave up and backed out of the embrace. "How's things this morning?"

"God is good all the time, Jesse. All the time!" Gus rested his left arm on the podium and leaned into it. "Where do you find yourself now? I half expected you to come back last evening, but figured something good must have happened to you when you didn't show."

"Ya, I'd say. If not good, it's definitely big, that's for sure." Jesse sat down on the pew behind him, next to his satchel. "I went to see a friend of mine that works for Venture. She's offering me the opportunity to join in an expedition for a new colony."

"Wow, that is a big opportunity!" Gus grinned from ear to ear. He pointed at Jesse. "Do you know when I prayed for you last night, I prayed that your calling would become clear?"

"Well, it seems to have been working." Jesse worked at opening his satchel.

"And it seems to match with that dream of yours, if I recall... Something to do with reaching for the stars?"

"Ya, well, sorta, ya. That's actually what I wanted to ask you about." Jesse started paging open the Bible Gus had given him. This naturally made Gus' heart skip a beat, seeing this prodigal thumbing through the Scriptures with purpose and excitement. Gus sniffled once.

"Whatcha got there?" Gus asked.

Jesse spoke as he was trying to find the right page and chapter. "Well last night I had another one of those dreams, about falling off the earth and the one star." He stopped when he found the verse he was looking for. He put his finger to it and looked up at Gus to finish explaining. "But in this one, I was falling past people. I kept reaching for them as I fell but none of them tried to help catch me. You were one of 'em." Jesse pointed playfully at Gus.

Gus put his hand to his chest. "Lil' ole me? I was in your dream? And I didn't try to help you?!" He folded his arms with a smart grin. "Well, that just can't be right!"

Jesse smiled and shrugged his shoulders. "I mean, ya didn't. Just kinda laughed at me like you're doing now."

Gus relented. "Fine, fine, what else happened?"

"Oh, ya. So, I was falling still, until this massive rocket shot past me. I was able to grab hold of it though, and saw it was flying straight at that star. The one from before, the one that was calling to me. And all over the side of the rocket were the numbers 419."

Gus was now stroking his beard, considering the interpretation of Jesse's dream. "Hmmm, 419." He looked down at the Bible in Jesse's lap. "And you think it's a Bible verse?"

"I know it is! Check this out!" Jesse looked down at where his finger was holding and read. "Isaiah 41:9:

"You whom I took from the ends of the earth,
   and called from its farthest corners,
saying to you, "You are my servant,
   I have chosen you and not cast you off."

"Gus, when I read that my heart stopped. It was as if Isaiah was talking straight to me!"

Gus stepped over to the podium and opened his own Bible to Isaiah as well. He started scanning the verses for himself. "That is pretty remarkable! That seems to match exactly what you have been experiencing in your dreams."

"That's what I thought! And, Gus, It's not like I knew that verse or anything. Jesus must have led me straight to it!"

"That's really invigorating for your faith, isn't it? Having the Word of God speak directly to you?" Gus now held his finger in his open Bible as he spoke back to Jesse. He had a bit of a knowing glint in his eye. "Do you know what you're supposed to do now?"

"Ya! Well, I mean... I think so." Jesse's excitement waned a bit. "I know I'm called, and God's made that obvious, but there's a lot of options still there. Am I supposed to leave right away? Am I supposed to wait? Am I supposed to … I dunno, talk to other colony companies?"

"How do you figure you're going to start finding out what to do with yourself? Where should you begin?"

Jesse had felt this kind of leading questioning before, especially in a church setting. "I should probably pray, huh?"

Gus nodded with a grin. "That's what I'd do."

Jesse sighed and settled in the pew. He bowed his head and closed his eyes. "Jesus. I want to thank you again for calling me. There's been a lot going on and… I mean, you know. Right now I know you're trying to get my attention on something big. And I want you to know I hear you. I want to follow, but Jesus, I need some more guidance on what to do. Please reveal to me what you want me to do. Amen." He opened his eyes and lifted his head fast enough to see Gus do the same.

"Amen." Gus looked down at this Bible and back up. "You ever study Scripture in context?" Jesse shook his head. He'd heard the phrase before but wasn't sure he knew what he meant. "It sounds like God is speaking to you through verse 9, most definitely, but it might help us to understand why, or what He's saying better to look at the verses around it. Look at the ones right before."

Jesse looked back into his Scriptures. He started at the beginning of Isaiah chapter 41. Scanning through the verses, he found understanding exactly what the prophet was talking about difficult to grasp. What he was able to decipher was that God is showing off his strength, then claiming that He is going to imbune that strength into the nation of Israel? Jesse struggled to see how that applied to him directly.

"It sounds like God is claiming to be the one who is in charge, and that He is going to use his might to strengthen Israel?"

"Sounds like a good synopsis to me." Gus said. This was a bright kid, he realized. "Anything jumping out at you there? Giving you some more light on your situation?"

Jesse considered. "I mean, if I'm the one he chose, like he chose Israel in the past… maybe He's saying that he will strengthen me?"

"I'd say that's right for anyone God calls His own, right? Does that help any more with your questions?" Jesse shook his head. "If it doesn't feel like it gives you clarity on your choice right now, what about the other side? Check the verses after 9."

Jesse looked back to his Bible and read through verse 13:

Fear not, for I am with you;
  be not dismayed, for I am your God;
I will strengthen you, I will help you,
  I will uphold you with my righteous right hand.

Behold, all who are incensed against you
  shall be put to shame and confounded;
those who strive against you
  shall be as nothing and shall perish.

You shall seek those who contend with you,
  but you shall not find them;
those who war against you
  shall be as nothing at all.

For I, the Lord your God,
  hold your right hand;
it is I who say to you, "Fear not,
  I am the one who helps you."

Jesse stopped. He was visibly shaken by the verses, Gus could see it, but he wanted to give him a moment to think through what he wanted to say. His mind was circling back to the warning that Junia had given him the night before about the Venture expedition to Toisee. About how C.D. Horizon was the sponsor for the trip, and how dangerous it was going to be if Jesse, as a Christian, were to go along. Was God telling him not only to go on a colony excursion, but to go on this particular colony excursion? Was He encouraging him to go on this *dangerous* of a trip?

"Gus," Jesse said. "Do you remember me telling you about my brother?"

"Ya, I do." Gus responded somberly.

"He said he was 'called' to follow Jesus into a dangerous situation. I didn't understand what he was trying to tell me, or why he felt so compelled to go. I didn't see what he was going to get out of it. And then he died doing what God called him to do." Jesse looked up at Gus, obviously worried. "What if He's calling me to do the same thing?"

"What if He is?" Gus returned. "Would that change anything about how you feel about being called by God?"

"No… I mean, well, if I'm honest, ya. I understand how my brother felt called now. I definitely feel that, too. But what Jesus is showing me through this verse… Why would God call me to follow into a situation so dangerous? I feel very… not ready to do that."

"Are you sure that He's asking you to follow Him?"

"Ya, very."

"Then Jesse, that's probably all you really need to know for sure. You asked for clarity in prayer before you read that, then the Holy Spirit showed you these verses. Verses about trusting God in danger because He's fighting with you and for you. He's just encouraging you to do what you already know you need to do. To simply follow Him."

Jesse sighed, resolved but now heavy. "I'm scared, Gus. I'm not my brother."

"No, you're not. He was called to Illinois. You're called to somewhere else. You don't have to be your brother, you can't be him. Jesus called you, he wants you."

"This all feels so quick, but also so sure. The verse that God gave me here is speaking directly to everything I've experienced in the last day or two."

"While Jonah was happily comfortable, being a prophet for the King of Israel in the palace, God suddenly demanded he sail across the sea to preach to people likely to kill him for his faith. God has this habit of grabbing folks when they don't feel ready, but I think he does it on purpose. I think it forces them to rely on their faith in Him instead of themselves." Gus strolled over and sat next to Jesse on the pew. "Jesse, you and you alone can answer this call. It's only for you. But God isn't forcing anything on you, this is an invitation."

"Ya, I know." Jesse leaned forward and rested his elbows on his knees, letting his head hang down. At this point, things that he thought he would never experience were coming alive in Jesse. He had always longed to feel a smidge of what Stephen did, because Stephen was always so alive with his faith. But now that he was given a call of his own, Jesse was terrified to follow it. Terrified and yet compelled all the same. How was Stephen so joyful, following Jesus into such dark and threatening circumstances?

Gus threw his arm across Jesse's back. "There isn't a right way to follow Jesus, Jesse. Jesus simply said to follow him. You can follow Him in confusion, in anger, in sadness, in doubt… That's because the following gets you closer to Him, living a life right alongside the Maker. And the closer you are to Him, the more you'll feel the joy of following. It makes more sense the more you do it."

Now that made more sense. Jesse had been expecting to feel joy at simply heeding the call, and to be fair it did make him feel special and singled out when he realized it. But now that the cost and responsibility was coming into view, he had been feeling less and less honored at the nomination. Jesse couldn't expect to suddenly gain back so much familiarity with Jesus when he had been running for so long. It still felt too foreign to yet be familiar. But Jesus was wanting him, and that was tempting enough for Jesse to try and follow where He was called to go. Surprisingly to Jesse himself, apparently even into danger.

Jesse sighed quickly, steeled his resolve, and stood. He looked over to his friend who stood with him. "Gus, thank you." Jesse wrapped his arms around the man as best he could and squeezed. "Thank you so much." He let go. "I don't know when I'll be able to see you again."

Gus grinned and clapped his hands in minor excitement. A move that oddly reflected the actions that Gus took while Jesse was dreaming, clapping and cheering him on. "My brother, my cup is filled every time we talk. I will miss you, but I am happy to send you forth." Gus grabbed Jesse's shoulders. "Godspeed to where He leads!"

Jesse took the gravimorphic tube back to Mid-Terra Plaza, which was a bad move. The speed and shifting gravity was a bit much to handle twice in under a couple hours, and Jesse embarrassingly had to use the vacuum vomit receptacle. Why did the transport have to be so full this time? He allowed everyone else to exit the tube before he did, as he sheepishly awaited to exit. He believed more people noticed or cared than actually did.

He weaved his way between the traffic back towards Colony Way. Junia had said that he needed to make his decision this morning, but she neglected to say by what time exactly. This put Jesse a little on edge, especially now that he had made up his mind. He was hurrying across the cobbled pathway, darting this way and that.

At the corner, when he was turning down Colony Way in front of the receiving office of Intrepido Explorar, his ears perked up and he looked around. Did he just hear someone call his name? Most of the conversations between the patrons here were in Spanish, and no one was immediately looking to him for attention. Jesse stopped for a moment and turned around, scanning the passersby but didn't notice anyone he knew, so he moved on.

He halfway considered stopping for a paleta at the next cart, but the line was a little long, so he thought better of it. He had to get to Venture before the opportunity expired anyways. Jesse considered that traveling along in the middle of the street would be quicker with fewer colonists to dodge, so he jumped the curb and quickly walked along the edge of the scooter lane in the middle.

He kept shoving the panic down in his mind. Not over if he was going to make it in time to talk to Junia, but the worried thoughts of what he was leaving behind. Earth was home, and it was familiar. All of the shops he was hurrying past wouldn't exist, all of the convenience of going to the nearest store for clothes or food or drink. None of them would be there. He and the other colonists would have to work to recreate everything that they took for granted here in the modern world. Sure, the HomeMaker's amenities would be rather plentiful. They wouldn't be primitive camping or anything. But could he even breathe the air on the planet he was going to? Was the last time he was on the Earth really be the last time he would ever breathe air freely without the stale taste of recirculation?

THWACK!

Suddenly, Jesse felt something hit his back. Just as he looked down to see a small apple roll past him, a rickshaw scooter blew past his right shoulder. He stopped and watched after it, alarmed at the close call but also trying to determine the passengers. Did he know them? Did they throw the apple or was it an accident? Jesse watched the scooter stream further away and neither of the passengers turned around to watch their apparent prank through to fruition.

Then a hand gripped Jesse's elbow and wiped him around. It was his father, Ben!

"Dad!? What - what are you doing here?!" Jesse was thrown into a sudden embrace with his father. Looking over his dad's shoulder, he could see his mother half jogging to catch up with them in the middle of the street.

"Once we knew you were here, we just had to come see you." His father's voice was full of warm contentment at finding his son among the crisscrossing chaos of Colony Way. His mother, Deb, had caught up with them and the second Ben let go of his son, his mom grappled on.

"Did you throw an apple at me?!" Jesse exclaimed.

His father nodded, proud of his aim. "It was all that I had! You were getting away from us so I had to get your attention somehow!"

"Mmmmm, it's so good to see you!" She squeezed him tight, leaned back and kissed him on the cheek.

"It's good to see you, too." The familiar smell of his mothers homemade shampoo filled his nostrils. The nostalgic memories of being a boy among his parents were all coming comfortably back. He had only been away from home for a couple weeks, but without an end to his fleeing in sight, it was a great relief to be with them again. He fell instantly back into the niche of being their son, and he relished their care for him. Especially enough for them to drop everything and hunt him down on a space station of thousands, and yet, he still had to ask so he could hear what he already knew in his heart.

"Why are you here?"

"We had to come, sweetheart." His mother was still hugging him. "We wanted to see you."

"Here, let's get out of the street." He removed his mother from his body, but grabbed her by the hand to lead her to the wide sidewalk. With Ben following, they found their way over to a nearby cafe on the corner across from

Venture's headquarters. There happened to be a free bistro table and chairs out front that Jesse brought them to. They sat down and his father dragged over a chair from another table.

"Jesse, we love you so much." His mother started. "We got dressed right away after our holo this morning, so we left for the shuttle station right away. Thank God there was a flight available to us!" When Jesse had called at just past midnight last night from Archway, it was nearly 6 AM for his parents on the earthen homestead in Asheboro.

"We've been traveling all day! Fortunately you used the scenic holobooth with a view of the Moon in the background, so we knew where to look!" His father stood up and started for the cafe doors. "I'm gonna grab us some coffees."

"OK, thanks, dad." Jesse said, forgetting his rush for time, or at least placing it purposefully on hold in his mind. He looked to his mother. "Mom, I'm sorry. I shouldn't have ended the transmission like that."

"It's ok, Jesse, we forgive you." She sighed and shook her head. "I know we don't fully understand each other lately…" It'd been most of Jesse's young adult life, actually. Ever since he was able to start questioning what, where, how and why.

"Mom, there's just always been things I need to figure out for myself. I wanted to believe like you and dad, and Stephen, but I just couldn't."

Deborah's eyes glistened a little, and she knocked her head curiously sideways. "Couldn't you say? That's past tense, Jesse. What's happened?"

As Jesse tried to frame his newly reborn, infant faith, his father returned, balancing three mugs of black coffee with him. He carefully set them on the table in front of each family member and then he sat down next to his wife. They both leaned in to listen to their son.

"Well, I told you about the dream and my calling, right?" They nodded enthusiastically. Jesse couldn't help but think them a tad daft for being blind to the danger he was going to be submitting to. But seeing them here, he felt it was endearing of them and not as insulting as last night. "I think I got confirmation in another dream last night on where I'm supposed to go."

"That's great, son!" His dad sipped then said. "How do you know?"

"I'm pretty sure God gave me a Scripture verse that spoke directly to my situation and what's been happening. It was too perfect… too spot on to be coincidence. That and I don't remember ever reading that verse before."

"What verse was it?" His mother asked. Deb jostled in her seat, knocking her knees together in anticipation. She was thrilled to have the privilege to watch and listen to her son disclose his very specific, God given calling on his life.

"The numbers I saw in my dream were on a rocket, it said 419 all over the place."

PSSHHTTT! His father spit out his coffee a bit across the table. His mother's eyes went wide but remained excited, so Jesse shot his dad a look of bemusement but continued. "And I felt like a number that specific must mean something, so I grabbed my Bible and started looking around until I found Isaiah 41:9. Let me dig out my Bible... but it said something like... Are y'all ok?" His parents were both obviously captivated by something he said. Jesse thought it was pretty miraculous, but they seemed comically overwhelmed.

"You said 419?" His father checked.

"Ya, why?"

"Jesse, sweetheart, did you know that your brother had a verse that he said Jesus gave him? He claimed God gave it to him when he was called to found the mission in Chicago. The verse was Matthew... 4:19!"

"Come, follow me and I will make you fishers of men!" His dad recited.

Jesse sat back and smiled, completely taken by the notion that not only did Jesus use the same method of a Scripture verse to get both of the sons of Heartshire, but He used the *exact same numbers!* What could the chances of that possibly be? Jesse's resolve to follow after this Messiah grew solid and bold in that moment. Had this been the only evidence he'd ever receive in his lifetime in the proof of God, it would be enough. His faith was sealed.

"What did your verse say? What was it... Isaiah 4:19?" His mother inquired.

"Isaiah 41:9!" Jesse corrected, "Here, I'll show you."

He drew out the love worn Scriptures that Gus had given him, and Jesse opened to the chapter and verse he was talking about. After the revelation, over the next hour, the small family poured memories and blessings and laughter upon each other. Time stood still for the Heartshire's as they rekindled. More than a couple passersby noticed the energy flowing from their table, which elicited feelings of awe or jealousy, depending on their own perspective. Another was looking down from her office window, her hand resting upon a golden spyglass. She watched the family relish these moments they had together, father, mother and son, and a few tears traced down her face. It gave Junia peace to remember that she had shared a similar moment with her own son the day he had left for Tau Ceti. It gave her peace as well to know that Jesse would be able to leave, chasing after his own purpose, with the blessings that she had given Leonard.

As she watched Jesse stand and hug his mother and father, so hard and so long, she wiped the tears from her eyes, and picked up her tablet. Junia adjusted a few notes and checks on Jesse's colonist profile, most importantly switching his status from inactive to confirmed.

CHAPTER 9
INTO THE WILD BLACK YONDER

The next two days were a whirlwind of activity. The instant that Jesse was added into the Toisee manifest of colonists, he had a lot of catching up to do. Most of which could be achieved on the back end of the journey, once the Toisee HomeMaker starship had arrived in the vicinity of the star.

Even with the amazing travel method that the slingshot gateways are, with their cutting away of lightyears of distance and centuries of generational travel, there still were a few months to account for on the tail end. The physics behind the gateways themselves accelerated the starships on the front end, nearly instantaneously catapulting them across the vast reaches of space. However, the deceleration process was more gradual. Ships would arrive in the outskirts of the star system and then launch massive reverse thrusters that would fire for weeks on end, gradually bringing the HomeMakers to manageable velocities once nearby the planetoids of their choice within the system. This also gives those on board time to analyze and assess which planets to focus on for colonization, utilizing more accurate scans and sensors that are limited in range. Expeditions have a very good idea of the planet they are aiming for at the onset of the initial launch from the gateway, but some systems have multiple options within the habitable zones of their systems and therefore most captains and crews will finalize their destinations upon arrival.

This also meant that for Jesse, he had time to catch up on some more specifics of his official duties with the time that the Toisee HomeMaker was in its final approach in the star system. What he did get caught up to speed on in the two days before launch was mostly intrapersonal and official.

Jesse had contracts to sign and agreements to shake on. First of all, he had to review and sign his allegiance to the Toisee's Colony Charter. Each new colony is effectively self-governing upon establishment as the impossibility of communication with Earth prevents any remote oversight. This one was fairly standard practice in terms of governmental structure:

1. The HomeMaker Captain, Tristan Yale, would be the Colony Director, overseeing all colonial aspects until the construction of the return slingshot gateway was complete.
2. Upon successful completion, the colonists would hold their first democratic election process and found their own particular bill of rights.

Ultimately, as long as the gateway was constructed and the sponsors saw a return on their investment, it was up to the colonists themselves how they wanted to conduct their own governance. The sponsors could not meddle in these affairs directly, so if they wanted to have any influence in this process, they would select captains and crew sympathetic to their own particular interests. This was the part of the charter that made Jesse a little nervous.

As Junia had warned him, while reading Jesse discovered that the Toisee Colony Charter explicitly forbade any "establishment of a church, convening a religious assembly, or participating in any recognized practice of faith" within its official outline. Most don't read the fine print, but Junia had insisted that Jesse pay attention to this clause, as she knew it affected him greatly. Charters cannot control what each individual believes and practices within themselves, but they can stifle the physical exercise thereof. Jesse signed the document with great hesitation, with his calling from the Lord actually driving him to obey. He knew he was in for rough seas.

Based upon his Venture assessments and the colony's needs, Jesse was assigned to the expedition officially as a Horticultural Specialist. This placed him within the Agricultural Wing of the HomeMaker starship, as well as assigned him the duties of assisting in creating a sustainable method of harvesting grown food where the Toisee Colony is planted. A tall order, but he was not without help.

His director, Shea Willow, carried a doctorate in Soil and Crop Sciences, as well as managed her own 3,000-acre farmland in Kentucky. She was recruited by Venture Colonies to act as a trainer for colonist agricultural recruits but was convinced to leave her established farm on Earth for a new one in the stars with the promise of enormous grants and endowments from the European Union. Shea was also guaranteed a prestigious consultant position within the Union's agricultural department, which would grant her certain privileges when it comes to purchasing and trading across the ocean. This gave her a great personal drive to see the colony succeed and return home as soon as possible. Shea, as the Toisee Ag Director for the colony, had Jesse and 77 other hands underneath her.

Jesse had shaken hands with most if not all of them, but not many of the names had stuck yet. Most of the crew he was assigned with were of similar rank as him. They were day laborers seeking a better outlook, folks looking for a fresh start or some looking to escape from Earth with either good or bad motives. Jesse assumed many were looking for a way out of criminal conviction based on their demeanor. Luckily they all were in good spirits. They were getting their chance to start again, and they all knew they had to rely on each other in order to survive.

Obviously he hadn't found anyone yet with a similar conviction as his own, being called by God and all. He wasn't expecting it, but it did make him sad and a bit lonely to consider he might be the only Christian on board.

Jesse now found himself in an odd moment of Deja vu, standing in a line with his other colonists approaching the double DEPARTURE doors in Venture's main office. It wasn't even a week since he first set foot in this lobby, hoping to simply land a job and now he found himself boarding the shuttles to the Toisee HomeMaker. Above the doors, the text had changed to *Toisee t-minus 00:21:44:56*, with the seconds counting down. They seemed to be diminishing rather quickly to Jesse, but maybe that was just his nerves.

He had never considered that he would never set foot on Earth again, but now the reality was beginning to sink in. His onboarding for the excursion was truncated and hustled, but by late last night he had found time to slink away. He didn't have the freedom to walk the Earth once more, but what he did have was Luna Side Gardens.

◆ . ⁺ . ◆ . ⁺ . ◆

Jesse could have simply stayed on Terra Side and visited the gardens there. He would have then been able to avoid the stomach-churning ride on the gravimorphic lift back to Luna Side, but he longed for the familiar feeling of being home. He hadn't yet been to Terra Side Garden, so he opted for the closest he could get to somewhere that felt at least a little homey and nostalgic.

The moment his toes hit the gravel walkway again, he breathed a little easier. He purposely slowed his naturally brisk walking pace for a slow meander instead. Jesse drew each breath deep and slow, obviously craving the taste of fresh oxygen from the local flora, but also sniffing for scents that he might never again smell. Who knew what types of plant life he would encounter at his new home? The mission was bringing some crops along with them to grow on the HomeMaker, and hopefully cultivate on the planet in Toisee, but perhaps the growing conditions would limit what was successful. He wandered, not with much direction.

In his heart he knew this moment was fleeting, time ticking on without his consent. He stood a number of times, savoring private plots of plants where the gardeners had paid special attention to detail and created interesting floral pairings. In his grazing of the gardens, Jesse didn't mean to end up at the keifer shack and yet he still ended up there anyways. Of course, due to the hour it was closed. Jesse didn't mind though, as the lack of people was a welcome quiet. He pulled up and took a seat at a bar top that looked out over half of the garden space. Stretching out before him was at least a ¼ mile of beautiful, patchwork arboretum.

Pulling up his satchel from off of his arm, he rested it on the stool next to him. Jesse opened it, shuffled some things around, and pulled out Gus' Bible. He held it in his hands for a second, rubbing the soft, faux leather cover with his thumbs. He had debated whether or not to send it home with his folks. It might be dangerous or at least troublesome for him to be seen with it while in the colony. He needed it though, to stay close with God. He knew the basics of his faith, but Jesus had used it to speak to him recently so he had to bring it to stay close to the light. He would just make sure it was well hidden and only out when he was alone. Jesse wasn't ashamed of his faith by any means, according to him anyways. But he didn't want anyone to know he was a Christian. Not yet.

It made him grin to admit it, but another major reason he decided to keep it was because of the smell! Jesse opened the Bible to the Psalms, and he bent over and shoved his nose in the Scriptures. This particular page had some scribbles and notes written in between a few verses with big looping letters. Drawing in a deep breath, he could picture his friend Gus, joyfully smiling through steaming trays of food. Jesse believed he could detect traces of fried oil and stale coffee when he closed his eyes.

He turned the pages to Isaiah 41, and he drew in a long inhale through his nose again. This time he smelled his mother. After they said their goodbyes and prayed, he pulled out the Bible again and had his parents 'imprint' on it, for lack of a better word. Deborah lightly misted the page with a naturally essenced perfume that his father had made her from the flowers in their backyard. Rose and lavender, with a touch of lemon balm and a hint of sage. Scents that reminded his dad of his mom. Ben, his father, had a nickname for his wife, so he named the vial *Sweetie Spray*. Every time Jesse heard his father describe it as that, he cringed and rolled his eyes, but now it made him smile. His attention was so drawn to the smell of his Bible, he hadn't noticed the approaching footsteps in the gravel pathway.

"Getting in a little light reading?"

The words were sharp to Jesse, as if he had just been grabbed from behind. He jumped, clutched the Scriptures to his chest and shot to a stand.

"Oh, my gosh, I'm sorry!" She giggled. "I didn't mean to scare you so!"

Jesse whipped his head around to see a young woman. She was wearing the same colonist outfit as he, even trimmed with the same green lining around the arms, neck and waist. This indicated that she was a member of the Ag Wing of a HomeMaker starship.

Jesse breathed a sigh of relief. "Geez…" He was slightly annoyed at the fright and felt a tad exposed. He didn't know if she had been watching him, but either way he decided to shove the Bible back in his bag and start to pack up.

"I didn't know anyone else would be here, let alone from a starship." She pointed at his matching uniform. "You're in Ag too, huh?"

"Ya." He was throwing his satchel up on his shoulder.

She read his actions. "You wanted to be alone. Me too. That's why I came here to Luna Side. I'll let ya be." She smiled in goodbye and started walking past Jesse's bar space towards the other side of the garden. As she passed him, he could see the Toisee expedition badge on the shoulder of her uniform. She also smelled as pretty as she looked, so he stopped her with a comment.

"You're on Toisee?"

She stopped and turned. "Yup!"

Jesse flung his left shoulder towards her, exposing the same badge she had. "Me too. My name's Jesse."

"Oh, would you look at that! I'm Elena." She approached him curiously. "But I don't remember seeing you at any of the meetings?"

"Ya, I joined late. I signed up only two days ago."

"Hmm, well are you excited to leave? Or are you here for the same reason I am?" She glanced out over the view that Jesse had been enjoying the gardens.

"I am, but ya… feeling a little homesick." He set his bag down. "I can't see home so this is the best I could do."

"I know the feeling. I wonder if we'll ever see Earth again."

"Ya."

They both traced the gardens into the distance, each of them focusing on this plot or that. Jesse was drawn to the grove of pine trees in the distance where some one had tried to recreate a small slice of Appalachia. Elena's eyes were fixed on a tropical looking oasis only a few plots away. She had been heading there before she noticed Jesse sitting at the bar and she grew curious.

"Why are you leaving?" She asked without turning to him.

Jesse had been practicing his excuse in his head, as he could no longer use his anger against his parents as a convenient excuse for his running, but he couldn't trust everyone with the complete truth of his calling. "I feel like my future is out there. Things here just don't fit anymore."

"Hmm." She pondered. When she didn't respond right away in return, Jesse looked at her and probed.

"What about you?"

"Oh, I don't even know anymore. I was excited to explore. But now I'm wondering if I'm going to be disappointed."

"Why would you be disappointed?"

She still spoke without looking at him. "Look at all this, Jesse. This is just a sample of the life we have here on Earth. What if the planet we end up on… what if the planet is ugly?" Jesse huffed and smiled at the notion, so Elena turned and leaned against the bar with her lower back, crossing her arms. "I'm serious! What are we even looking for out there? We have all of this here." She presented him the gardens with her arms. "What if the planet we find, we can't even breathe the air? We will be stuck with recirculated air for the rest of our lives!"

89

That exact thought had occurred to Jesse, which is one reason he came to the gardens. The HomeMaker has a rather large garden within the starship itself, but it's much more commercialized and still a great deal smaller. The gardens on Archway actually gave you the impression you were on Earth again. He thought for a moment before deciding to be encouraging to her.

"We're grasping at hope, right?" She looked at him. "I mean, ya, we have all of this and it's great. But there is something in us that longs to explore the universe. It's not to escape the good on the Earth, but to discover more of it. Almost as if we have an implanted drive within us to… to…"

"To know just how much good there is out there?" She finished for him.

"Ya, exactly!"

"How is that hope then? Doesn't hope mean we are wishing that it was good but it may not be?"

Jesse shrugged. "Maybe, but that's not how I see it. Hope isn't a wish that things work out, it's a knowing that it will. Hope is a sure thing."

Elena furrowed her brows at him. He was speaking to her soul, nourishing it while remembering why she felt compelled to the stars in the first place. It bothered her for some reason that he should be so insightful. Maybe because she desired to discover these things on her own and was threatened that others would know more than she about herself.

"Hmm." She looked back out towards the gardens for a moment. Then she righted herself off the bar and extended her hand to shake his. "Well, it was nice meeting you, but I'm going to continue my walk now."

Her smile was nice to see, but Jesse could also see it was dismissive. He took her hand and shook. "Ya, same here. Nice meeting you."

As she walked away down the gravel path, Jesse again gathered his satchel and threw it up on his shoulder. He had successfully had his first conversation with a member of his crew without exposing the nature of his decision to join Venture. He was happy that the conversation went smoothly, and it seemed his explanation worked well. But what drew his thoughts was the surprise that not everyone is looking forward to this expedition in the same way he was. Either way, he had had his moment with the transplanted remnants of Earth that he was looking for, so he turned and made his way back to the transport tubes.

✦ . ⁺ . ✦ . ⁺ . ✦

CHIK CHIK CHIK CHIK CHHHHHIK!

Jesse yanked down on his shoulder straps, clicking them into place. He was part of the final boarding group to arrive on the HomeMaker and it was standard procedure to enter the slingshot gateway with all non-flight crew strapped into the escape pods. There had yet to be an incident where the crew needed to jettison from the starship during launch, but there was no reason for them to be anywhere else.

Jesse was now experiencing the launch from the perspective of the escape pod porthole directly in front of him, whereas just the day before he had witnessed the Venture HomeMaker departing for Gilese from the vantage of the Venture transfer shuttle as he and others boarded their HomeMaker. He was both impressed and disappointed seeing the HomeMaker starships in person for the first time.

The HomeMakers resemble something similar to a 4-sided, multi-story building in space, complete with a white moon attached to the top of it via a long rod. This of course is the starship's singularity drive, which pulls and powers the entire ship through its journey in space. It's dwarfed by the Archway Station, but HomeMaker starships are designed to be as comfortable as possible while in transport, which makes them large and roomy. They are 18 habitable levels high, with each level consisting of ¼ mile wide decks. From the mid-section of the ship, bulbous mechanical love handles protrude. These are the massive reverse thrusters required to slow and stop the immense velocity that the gateways generate when "throwing" starships across the galaxy. Directly underneath these is the detachable section of the HomeMaker starship, the half that then separates and divides into 5 planet landing pods. These pods provide colonist housing, terraforming and the planetary tether required to transport materials back into space for construction of the returning slingshot gateway.

All of this is an impressive feat of engineering. Still what disappointed Jesse was the fact that the HomeMakers themselves were obviously completely designed with function and efficiency in mind, with nary a thought to the aesthetic. It was a floating, disgusting-looking refinery in space.

I wonder if Elena is even more depressed about the ugliness of where she has to live for the foreseeable future, Jesse considered. He watched as the Gilese HomeMaker starship entered the slingshot gateway.

The gateway resembles some kind of unraveled and stretched spring, held in place in orbit on the dark side of the Moon. A network of reinforced scaffolding, bolstered by energy storage batteries on all 4 sides frame the spiral as it winds from a large to small opening. The gateway is aligned and oriented to the system they are traveling to by maneuvering thrusters, and starships enter the wide side of the gateway, aiming down the middle of the spiral and then "park" in the middle. Massively complicated calculations are processed and adjustments to the intensity of the slingshot are filtered into the machine. Once the energy build has reached critical mass, it is released from individual nodes on the circling spiral arms that wrap around the starship, painting it in fiery blue light.

This was an incredible sight to behold, at least for as long as someone could behold it. The windows of the transfer shuttle, as well as all transparent surfaces on the Lunar surface, were coated to protect them from the massive discharge of blinding light. Actually, the gateway was built on the far side of the Moon because of this light, as it was unwanted pollution for Archway Station and Earth as well. It had been said ever since its first firing, this light was so intense that the initial flash from the launch of the slingshot was visible even through solid walls. This is of course ridiculous and untrue, but the rumors persisted, nonetheless.

Jesse closed his eyes and shielded them with his hand when the Gilese starship launched, and he could still see a bright pop. When he opened them, he was surprised to see the starship still in its launch position in the gateway! This is due to a phantom phenomenon in the slingshot gateways design. Because of the incredible amount of energy discharged, a ghost image of the launched starship remains for 2.56 seconds after it is physically gone. Jesse blinked to make sure his eyes were working, and the ghost ship was gone within the blink of his eye.

Now, he was inside the starship as the slingshot charged itself outside this port window. He glanced down his left and right, looking at the other 20-something faces strapped in with him in this pew shaped escape pod. No one took notice of his gaze as they all were mesmerized by the action outside. Rays of fiery blue lights spiraled in sequence outside, each one of them impacting the hull of the HomeMaker, painting it in energy. The shots coming from the spiral reminded Jesse of being behind glass while it was being sprayed with single sprays of water. Each impact thudded as if a snowball had struck the window. When the ray splashed against the porthole, it left behind what looked like electrified goo that his experience on Earth said should have dripped downwards. Instead, the goo stuck and spread with skips and jumps outward from the initial impact. Each time a tiny spark flashed, the goo would jump in the direction of the spark. With only a couple passes of the fiery blue rays, all of the portholes were covered, and assumedly so was the rest of the starship.

Then came a building glow from each node on the spiral arms of the slingshot gateway. This glow was discernible through the opaque goo, and the brighter the nodes grew, the more the goo on the outer window of the porthole was electrified. A deep low rumble began and quickly became a roar in their ears. All of the passengers in the escape pods closed their eyes tight to the light, gripping their restraints, unaware of what to expect. Jesse gritted his teeth and tried to pray through the gripping anxiety. Without warning, a loud POP exploded within the starship. The sound was that of a large balloon that was pin pricked inside of a cathedral. Jesse opened his eyes as the echo of the release progressed through its slow, reverberating retreat.

Outside the porthole was nothing but streaks of white against the black. As if every star in the sky was drawn from a singular point to an infinite line. Then one would suddenly end, and others would spontaneously begin. They were traveling beyond the speed of light but slowing. The streaks were getting shorter, but not by much.

Interestingly, the stars were streaking from the bottom to the top of the porthole. This was due to the direction of gravity within the starship itself. The singularity drive was at the front, which meant it was at the bottom in terms of gravitational pull. Jesse and the other crew members were flying sideways, feet first, through space. This gave the initial impression that they were constantly falling through space. Jesse thought about the dream he had, falling away from the Earth. Chills ran down his spine as the prophetic nature of that seemingly insignificant detail was realized.

Suddenly an announcement over the intercom:
Crew members, remain in your seats. We will be firing reverse rockets momentarily.
CHU-THUNK!

A bang resonated through the walls behind the heads of the passengers in the escape pod pew. Outside the HomeMaker starship, the four bulbed reverse thrusters detached from the main fuselage. They dropped away at the four corners of the starship, attached by long near unbreakable cables to the inner framework. There was a quick jerk towards the back of the starship felt by all of the passengers on board as the braking thrusters fired. Plumes of red rocket thrust streamed out against the passing streaks of stars outside the escape pod windows. The streaks of the stars began to slow more visibly now. Another announcement came over the intercom:

Crew members, we have stabilized our deceleration. Please, commence the application of your duties. Begin preparations for arrival, t-minus 43 days and counting. Welcome to Toisee!
The voice over the intercom was the starship captain, Tristan Yale. Jesse and the other passengers started to unbuckle and file out of the escape pod. As he waited for those crew members ahead of him, Jesse peered out the windows more closely. The stars were still streaks, impossible to recognize, but they still felt so foreign to him. He half-heartedly looked to see if he could find any constellations. Of course, they would look different from 100 light years away from Earth from a completely different perspective. In actuality the system of Toisee was found in the constellation of Dorado when viewed from Earth. He felt a poke in the back from behind, and Jesse shook himself from his study of the stars and filed in with the other exiting crew.

CHAPTER 10
SETTLING INTO THE INTERSTELLAR

Jesse looked for the internal directional signage and followed fellow crew members with matching green insignia to the Agricultural wing. He only had an image of the internal levels of the HomeMaker to review once, and it's a big ship. In a lot of ways, the HomeMaker starships were laid out similarly to Archway Station. The gravity pull from the singularity drive was at the technical "bottom" of the starship, and the Ag wing was placed at level 8. This meant the gravity at the level was nearly identical to that on Earth. The drive on the HomeMaker starships were much smaller and weaker than those on the station, so there isn't much difference in gravity in the levels, but the designers wanted to give the ships their best chance at growing sustainable crops successfully.

He paused at a T-junction on his current level and read the signage. There Ag wing was divided into 4 sections, and his first duty was to ensure the safe transport of the ships' crops, but he couldn't remember which section he was assigned to.

"Section B, Mr. Heartshire."

He turned to his left to see his superior, Shea Willow, approaching quickly. She blazed by him, followed by a couple of other specialists. Other than the direction she gave, she offered no other interaction.

"Yes ma'am, thank you." He half bowed in an awkward acknowledgement of her authority, that and he was embarrassed in front of his boss. Jesse followed the arrow to the right of the junction towards Section B. He entered into an immense greenhouse with stacked rows of vegetables. Section B was mostly vines of beans and of berries, at least the beginning of this row. Jesse considered whether that was coincidence or design, either way it felt goofy.

He slinked along the rows, scanning back and forth. He adjusted a vine here, removed a broken stem there. Most of the plants seemed to be intact as far as he could tell. They looked healthy as if they were growing at home. He leaned into a rather thick patch of blackberries, sorting them out as it looked as if they had become entangled. He had to be careful due to the thorns and —

"BOO!"

Shockingly a face appeared behind a wall of berry leaves. Jesse shot back and nearly lost his balance. It was Elena.

"Geez, Elena." Jesse hated being jump-scared. It was unsettling.

She giggled a little, causing the shrubbery to shake. "That was an intense ride, huh? Feels kinda surreal to imagine that an hour ago we were 100 light years away."

"Ya. It's hard to accept. I don't think it's sunk in yet." Jesse changed the subject. "You seem in a better mood."

"I mean, I still am excited about the possibility of what's out here." She backed out of the blackberries, and started down the row again on the other side of Jesse. They walked together, completing their checks.

She glanced up at one of the HomeMaker status monitors. These were placed throughout the starship to inform the crew of pertinent information. On the screens currently was a big banner stating "Welcome to your New Home" circling above the only habitable planet in the Toisee system. It was the same digital render as before due to the fact that they were just now in range of more detailed scans and telescope views of the planet. The render just hadn't been updated yet. There was also a countdown to the landing, 42 days and 23 hours.

"I wonder what it's going to look like."

Jesse followed her eyes to the monitor and then kept going. "*Hope*fully a lot like home." He smirked at her. She looked at him incredulously but smirked back.

"Ha ha."

They kept working their way down the row. Jesse had been considering what the new world would look like quite a bit actually.

So far, 20 colony missions had been sent to distant stars, and although only a handful had traveled back, none of them had yet mentioned discovering any kind of intelligent life. There were new plants and animals, sure, but to Jesse they seemed to be more of the same kind of life you would find on Earth. In their first return journey, Centauri had returned samples of corn-like vegetation that tasted like apples and had captured animals they called Tritzi's, which looked like squirrels the size of dogs. He had found it interesting to see, but was ultimately disappointed in the discoveries. It would stand to reason that other Earth-like worlds would feature Earth-like animals and plants. Jesse was hoping for a bit more diversity in the universe.

After checking on the HomeMaker's sustainable crops, Jesse was relieved of usual work details of the ship to finish his studies on his role as a Horticultural Specialist in the new colony. For easy travel within each deck, the starship had two central hallways that circled the middle and outer portion of the level. Jesse's quarters was on the inner circle of the residential level, with all of the other lower ranked crew members, which meant he was not entitled to a window, at least not yet. He decided to take the outer loop around, where there were lounge areas to overlook the stars outside. As everyone else was preoccupied with their various duties, the lounge was empty. Jesse settled in with his tablet to work through the reading and study his job required, but the view made it hard to concentrate initially.

The reverse thrusters were still firing at full burn, as they would be for the next few weeks to slow the HomeMaker into its approach to the planet. From his vantage point, Jesse couldn't see the thruster itself, but its elongated plume burned in an intense red against the white lines of the stars. The blurred lines that were the stars were simply dashes now and still getting shorter. Soon they would be the simple dots that all Earthbound folks were used to seeing, although with none of the usually recognizable constellations.

Will we rename our own stars? Jesse considered. Granted the colonists would be on their own, maybe forever, but surely some of the stars they could see from here are still the same stars that are visible from Earth. *What parts of Earth will we keep, and what will we remake? We could rewrite history and no one would know.*

The thought scared Jesse to consider. Not only could they name the planet and the plants and animals they find, but they had the power and potential to rework what it meant to be human. There was potential to completely erase or create anew anything they wished. It was an intimidating and terrifying and yet electrifying and invigorating notion. It also became a little clearer why Jesus would call Jesse to come along on this adventure.

Of the other 312 crewmembers on the Toisee HomeMaker starship, everyone brought key and critical skill sets and knowledge bases. Even though officially a Horticultural Specialist, Jesse felt his most important role might be to preserve Christianity. He knew that the charter of the new world was going to try and delete faith in God in this recreation of humanity, but that meant to Jesse he was going to have to work even harder at preventing that from happening. His heart burned with a passion of meaning and reason that he hadn't felt ever on Earth. It wasn't up to him to keep the faith alive there, but here, it was.

He tore his attention from the view outside and actually switched to another seat on a couch that did not look out to the stars. He started to read the next section of the text on Extra-Terran Soil Analysis and Management. Despite the riveting material, nearly instantly his mind was distracted again. This time he was considering what Scripture verses he was going to study tonight in his quarters. New stars, new world... The obvious choice seemed to be Genesis.

With his new beginning, Jesse wanted to be reminded of the old beginning. That even in this distant and foreign environment, he was still within God's creation. He always thought it was laughable that of all the infiniteness of the universe, the Bible barely spent all of two sentences describing it. *What did it say? Something about the stars...*

It felt dangerous to pull out his Bible right here and now, in the open of the lounge. Curiosity was knocking rather loudly and everyone else was "at work" in other parts of the ship, so he gave in. Jesse looked around, listened for approaching footsteps, and slowly pulled his Bible from his satchel. He kept the Scriptures below the top of his tablet, attempting to hide the open book behind it even though the tablet was only a bit bigger than half the Bible's size. He paged it open to the front, and found Genesis 1:14 & 15:

And God said, "Let there be lights in the vault of the sky to separate the day from the night, and let them serve as signs to mark sacred times, and days and years, and let them be lights in the vault of the sky to give light on the earth." And it was so.

From the start of everything, it would seem that Earth was the center of creation. Jesse pondered the verses. What caught his attention was that he was now out among the stars that God made so that the earth had light… And could tell time? *To mark times, days and years. So all of the entire universe was made so that we could know what season it was?* That seemed to be a dramatic overkill to Jesse. What does that mean about telling time here? The colonists would adjust to whatever the day/night cycle is on the planet for sure. But what bothered Jesse about the verse was that it implied that Earth is the epicenter. That the planet itself is where the most important aspects of his faith had happened. Does that mean that everything that he does out here still yields to what happens on Earth? When he would witness, when he attempts to keep the faith alive, would he have to keep pointing back to the planet they left behind? Would their new life and world be perpetually second to the Earth's ranking of first in God's eyes?

His thoughts were interrupted by the sound of fast approaching footsteps. Jesse panic packed the Bible into his satchel just as two crew members ran past the lounge towards the lifts to the other parts of the station. They didn't even pay him any attention. This could be because of their rank, as the insignia and color of their uniform indicated they were part of the command crew, maybe members of the piloting or leadership team. Jesse couldn't tell when they sprinted past so quickly. But they also might not have noticed him due to the worrying look on their faces. He couldn't tell for sure, but Jesse thought they looked scared.

No alarm was sounding, and after they passed and all was again quiet, Jesse decided he was not going to worry about it. He did take the moment to remind himself he needed to take his studies seriously, and so he settled into the couch again with the tablet and made a strong effort to know as much about dirt as he could.

Jesse grabbed his brush and started straightening out the mess that was his hair. He was a bit worn out from reading for the last few hours, and after the shower he wanted to stay in his room. But still, the gathering was mandatory, and he wanted to at least make an effort to look his best, even if he'd rather not attend what amounted to a giant mass dating shindig.

Tonight, as was a tradition started on the very first Venture Colony HomeMaker, is GEM Night, or the GEnetic Matching list release party. This is when the lists of approved genetic matches are first presented to each colonist. In an effort to get things off to a good start, the starship captains host an evening of feasting, dancing and libation fueled relationship encouragement. Alcohol wasn't forbidden on board, but it was highly monitored. And everyone needs a little diminished inhibitions when they are nervous to meet those whom they may one day wed, especially if they discover they are expected to wed multiple women. Jesse was one of only 97 males on board the starship. An intimidating pressure to be sure. Especially considering a colony on par for growth is expected to double in size by year 3 and again in year 5.

Jesse felt like he needed to throw up. He had hoped he could avoid it with his studies, but it appears Captain Yale was excited to see his prospects. He made it a ship wide, mandated attendance event. Even the Captain himself was part of the pool of potential candidates, and that meant Shea, Jesse's director, was too. He shuddered and forced unwelcome thoughts out of his mind as he threw on a fresh uniform. There were no available dress clothes as of yet, those were only produced once the textile facility was up and running on the planetary colony.

He checked his breath once more, and unlatched his quarters, stepping out into the bustling residential level. Everyone, like salmon up a river, was walking the same direction, down the hallway to the lifts, to the lyceum deck, level 16. Here was located the only large and open space on the starship, dual designed as a multipurpose ship wide meeting location, as well as the town hall and market center of the colony once founded on the planet's surface. As Jesse and a mixture of other colonists filed into the packed lifts, he and the others glanced around at each other. The glances were friendly on the surface, but everyone was hiding their true feelings beneath. Peaks of interest or disgust spiked in everyone's mind as they pictured futures with each other, unbeknownst to their comrades.

Soon as the lift doors opened, Jesse and the others took in the fantastic sky of stars falling in reverse, raining away from the sides of the HomeMaker starship. Level 16 was on the "top" of the ship, the furthest away from the singularity drive that pulled the ship along in space. That meant that above the colonists was a spectacular view of where they had been, as if one was watching out the back of a transport train. It provided a rather romantic setting, especially when coupled with the lyceum's diminished lighting and engaging music. Jesse scooted and excused himself through the crowd to the beverages. He wanted something to hold and sip in case the conversations got awkward, which he expected that it would. He scanned the crowd from the bar area.

The vast majority of the colonists were in their 20's and 30's, and Jesse surmised that he was on the younger end of the spectrum. It wasn't rare that a captain or other senior command member was well into their 40's, but they were the exception, and only due to their advanced skill sets. Those in leadership roles were still expected to "reproduce" in other ways, such as passing on inherited knowledge and wisdom to the next generation. But colony life was mainly for the young, those who have many childbearing years ahead of them.

Jesse was also not looking forward to GEM Night for other reasons. He had always been taught that marriage was between one man and one woman, and that the polygamous relationships of the Jewish patriarchs were not God's design. He did end up studying Genesis for a while after his soil readings were done. And there he confirmed what he had always assumed: that marriage was indeed God's design and that it was reserved for only two people. Jesse was pleasantly relieved that his own feelings of unease were justified. However, this was going to pose a problem with him fitting in with his crewmates. His withdrawal of "taking his fair share" of the duty to build the colony population isn't punishable, but command would demand to know why, and simply stating he didn't want to would probably have consequences.

After a few minutes the lyceum was full of milling colonists, anxiously awaiting the start of GEM Night. Jesse found a corner, and faced the windows of receding star streaks. He pretended to be overly fascinated with them until Captain Yale took to the stairs of a small stage that had been erected in the middle of the floor. Spotlights highlighted him from all 4 sides of the room as he raised his hands for their attention.

"Citizens of Toisee! Citizens, lend me your ears for a moment!"

The crowd hushed quickly, as they were eager to get underway.

"Welcome to your new home!" There was an excited applause, with a few sprinkled cheers. "Well, we aren't quite there yet, but every second we soar closer! I have asked our cartography crewmates to highlight something for you, if all of you would look right here." Yale extended his pointer finger towards a spot on the ceiling of glass. It was just over his right shoulder, nearly directly above him where a bright yellow circle appeared. If you squint hard you could see a slight speck of a star in the center. "That's Sol, where our journey began. Over 100 light years away. We are now the furthest away that humanity has ever traveled from our origin planet. I say this with great pride, but also great determination."

His voice was definitely commanding the colonists attention. Jesse could tell at least one reason he had been chosen as the HomeMaker's captain. He could demand ears to stay focused with his vocal tone alone.

"It is up to me, and you, and you," he pointed out into the gathered crowd of colonists. "It's up to all of us to see this colony be the most successful it can be. That is why tonight is a night of celebration! Each one of us has the skills needed to make this happen, but tonight it's all about the fun fueling it!" The crowd laughed, some like Jesse, uneasily. "So, let me cut myself off, and order each one of you to pull out your Venture issued tablets."

These tablets were small enough in size to fit in a back pants pocket. Roughly 3.5 inches wide, 7 inches long. They housed a number of features and specs, and each colonist was issued one to assist in the completion of their duties on board. Jesse pulled his out, and noticed a command bulletin announcement at the top, right as Yale continued:

"You will notice a personalized command announcement at the top. Opening this message will direct you to your approved genetic matches, listing the most compatible on the top of the list. Now, this is not the time to be shy! I encourage you, as your captain, to not enjoy your first night here in Toisee alone! We have over a month until we are to decide upon a landing site to establish our new home. Use this time to mingle with your fellow crewmates. Get to know each other, as I also look forward to getting to know you! To a happy GEM Night! May you all find a diamond!"

The colonists applauded and quickly started scanning their tablets, looking about the room for facial matches to those on their GEM profile. Those incharge at Venture decided not to put name badges or any other information on uniforms, which meant you had to ask and get to know someone by their name. Some said providing too many details "took the magic" out of forming a relationship. With the genetic matching, in order to find true fulfillment in choosing a mate, there needed to be some semblance of control or choice. The matches still happened anyways as the colonists mostly focused on those whom they were provided with. And all you were provided was a frontal photograph and a match percentage. That's it.

Jesse scanned the photos quickly. He searched for those whom he knew so far, Shea and Elena. The first he was hoping he did not match with, for who wants to marry your overly driven boss? The second, he wasn't too sure about yet, but they did seem to have some chemistry in common. That and she did have a cute smile. Before he got too far into his list, a sultry voice got his attention.

"Hey, you."

Jesse looked up, hoping he wasn't the voice's intended target, but he was. A young woman, Jesse guessed a few years older than him, approached with her tablet in hand, holding it to the side to compare with whom she was now face to face with.

"Jesse, right?"

Dang it. "Ya, that's me."

"Hey, I'm Charlotte."

Jesse nodded, "Nice to meet you." He didn't mean it yet though.

"You too!" She tucked her tablet into her back pocket and rested her hands on her hips. She nodded towards him. "So, where are you from?"

"Carolina. What about you?"

"Rio. Brazil. What do you think about our journey so far?"

"I dunno, I mean, it just started." He glanced at the view behind him. "I like the view though."

"Do you? I'm not so sure. The stars are too cold. I hope our new place has a beach! I'm used to it being warm."

"Ya I'd bet. I guess it's hot in Brazil?"

She laughed. "Ya. Ya, it can be."

Jesse had no idea what to talk about with her. Both of them knew why they were having this conversation, but only Jesse seemed to feel like it was a ridiculous way to start a family. She was attractive, but God's design in marriage and child rearing wasn't just about having children. There was something more to it, wasn't there? Jesse felt uneasy about all of this already, but he was becoming more sure that he had read something in the Bible about this.

"You want a drink?" She was trying to ease him up a bit, and even in Jesse's inexperience, he knew that much. He forced a yawn while he fought for an excuse to escape.

YAWN. "No, I'm sorry but I didn't sleep much last night, worried about all this. And I've got the early shift in the morning." A lie but God would probably forgive him given the circumstances.

"No, you don't! Didn't you hear? Captain Yale suspended all shifts until 10 AM tomorrow! We can sleep in!" *Shoot. Maybe He wants me to be honest.* Jesse thought, annoyed that he wasn't getting out of it that easily.

He looked around, sheepishly avoiding her gaze. "Look, I'm sorry but this is all a little fast for me."

She smiled, "Aww, aren't you a sweet one? That's ok, Jesse. How 'bout we just talk some other time?"

He sighed a little too visibly in relief. "Ok, thanks."

She side eyed him a little as she strolled away, pulling out her tablet to peruse for another target. "Good night."

"Good night!" He felt really embarrassed now, but he was relieved to have escaped from the uncomfortableness of that conversation. *Thank you, Jesus.* He thought to himself.

He glanced around the lyceum quickly, noticing that most everyone else was engaged in conversations with those around them. Most men had at least 2 or 3 women hovering around them, which a few seemed to be relishing. Jesse decided that this was his opportunity, and he found a way around the backside of the bar to avoid anyone else that could single him out. He kept his head down until he was to the lifts, and only when the doors slid shut, did he feel complete relief and breathe easy.

Once he made it back to his quarters, he slouched onto the small sofa. He picked up the Bible that was sitting next to him and pressed it to his forehead as he prayed. He knew that God had revealed Himself and that He had called him to this mission to Toisee, but Jesse wasn't trained. How exactly *is* he supposed to live out this calling? God hadn't given him any instructions, any vision on his purpose, any clear direction on what he was supposed to be doing. In his prayers, he expressed his frustration to Jesus that he barely had an idea as to why he was here, but now that he was, how is he supposed to do this?

Jesse cracked his Scriptures open to 'his' verse, Isaiah 41:9. *You are my servant*, it says. Jesse wished it said what a servant of God was supposed to do here. But then it hit him, the Holy Spirit gave him a nudge. *Doesn't how I serve Jesus look the same here as anywhere else?* He thought. He knew that to serve God meant to simply follow Jesus and live according to His commands. Those commands don't change depending on if he is on Earth, or in Toisee. Jesse breathed a bit easier upon that revelation, because he might not have a direct command, but he did know how to live a life following Christ. He was already, and is currently, living the purpose that God called him to here by being a Christian in Toisee.

He sat back against the sofa and closed his eyes and considered what to do in his predicament. Due to the fact that women outnumber the men 3 - 1, he knew he was going to have to approach this problem starting again tomorrow. How does he hold them at bay without sounding the alarm, so to speak? With the emphasis that Capt. Yale put on them tonight, it was almost as if his job depended on —

Wait! That's it! Jesse remembered something from Scripture, especially the passages on marriage, that reference *working* for Jesus. That marriage actually gets in the way of that. He started paging through Paul's letters to the churches, scanning the titles of each section, until he happened across 1 Corinthians 7:32: *I would like you to be free from concern. An unmarried man is concerned about the Lord's affairs - how he can please the Lord.*

He had found the answer! If he worked hard, harder than any other colonist, delving deep into his studies and preparations for Foundation Day (the beginning of the colony on the planet's surface) he could effectively 'hide' from the expectation to... procreate? *What a cold way to describe bringing new life to the world,* Jesse thought. But that would work. To his superiors, he would simply be a perfect, model citizen, but to Jesus, he would still be living his life in respect to God's expectations for family.

Jesse resolved within himself to dedicate his free time to working visibly outside of his quarters. He would need to be seen being studious and driven and not slink away to his room. He wanted others to see him changing, as he noticed deeper changes within himself. Here merely weeks ago he was running from his parents, running from his life, and running from God. Now he had nearly forced his way onto a starship to live out his Christian faith, and he was devoting himself to Christ in ways he never considered. Especially being alone out here, with only God to lean upon, he felt he could almost tangibly watch himself mature in thought and mind. The person he was before was slowly eroding away, and the rebirth within his soul was all he knew mattered anymore.

CHAPTER 11
IMPRESSIVE DODGING

 It had now been a little over two weeks into their journey to Toisee. The HomeMaker had continued to slow, visibly in the stars motion outside the ship that were now still points of light as if it was surrounded by a perpetual night sky.

 Their first detailed scans of the planet, its atmospheric composition as well as its visual appearance have been coming into view. Toisee is roughly earth-like, and rough is definitely the right word to use. It is definitely higher in cloud concentration, with only peeks of the surface showing through occasionally. This indicates a much more consistent temperature throughout the planet, which has its positives, except for the fact that due to Toi, the star it orbits being a red dwarf, the solar energy received to the planet's surface is much less. The average temperature on the planet will be considerably colder than what most are used to on Earth. Still habitable, but perpetually autumn or winter conditions will be likely. Some in the crew were excited for the potential of blustery conditions, but most were saddened by the idea.

 A calm was permeating the crew as well, where the initial excitement in the revealing of GEM Night was winding down and being replaced by monotonous preparations for Founding Day. Dates between the crew were still occurring, but those who had been chosen first had been chosen. Official marriages would not begin until the colony had been established on the surface, but declarations and simple proposals would happen occasionally. The betrothed colonists seemed happy with their hasty engagements, but all the rest of the crew were settling into the idea of being second or third, which had put a damp on overall morale. Those women were occasionally prickly to the men or the first chosen women, but this phase is expected in colony ships. Jesse, who had still not chosen anyone, was successfully avoiding the notice by navigating his way into the hearts of both the command staff and his peers.

"How did you figure that out?" Elena was looking over Jesse's research in the herbology lab. They had been working together quite a bit. Side by side anyways.

"There's a long history of plants like this being used for medical purposes. They've been using them for thousands of years." Jesse said smartly.

"Well, ya, I know that. But I mean how did you get them to cross AND adapt to the soil modifications?"

"I was playing around with the magnesium and potassium levels, due to the rich iron content on most of Toisee. That got the germination and viability rate way up. Then I just considered how similar blue lupine was to wild flax, dabbled with the genes a bit, and voila!"

He waived over towards the small plants growing in receptacles next to them. They were spindly, tall and thin while being less than a foot tall so far. Buds were beginning at the tops of the sage colored main stalks, and by the looks of the hue on the outside, the flowers were going to be numerous and violet. Elena brushed her hands over one of them, gently squeezing the buds.

"I can't believe you did this! What did Shea think?"

"She's been so busy with command meetings, I haven't seen her yet personally. But she did send me a message and sounded rather impressed." Jesse cracked a large smile.

"Don't get all proud on me, Heartshire." She chided. "But, wow, it is impressive. I bet they'll be beautiful."

Elena walked back over to her station and sat. Both of them were the only ones working the herbology lab today. There were many preparations to be done, especially in terms of readying infant crops for transport to the surface. In the horticultural wing, supplanting pre grown crops to the surface was much easier and yielded faster results than attempting to grow from seed on an alien surface. Sustainability was the key focus, especially considering the procuration of meat wasn't as guaranteed. There was a small livestock wing of the ship, where the horticultural specialists received regular transfers of manure, but those animals were in a state of preservation and depended on the success of grown crops as much as the human crew did. Other than the small pre-slaughtered supply brought from Earth, the crew was effectively vegetarian until founding of the colony.

"So, found anyone yet?" Elena called over to Jesse. This used to make him nervous when crewmates would ask, but he'd gotten good at his excuses.

"I honestly haven't had the time. I've been so busy with developing things like this," he pointed at his plant babies. "I haven't really considered it."

Elena looked around and nodded in agreement with him. "You certainly have been busy." She glanced at his other works. Exceptionally large varieties of lettuce and kale were his first attempts based on the new info he was getting from commands study of the planet. This was based on the scans of lower average temperatures from Earth, then when he considered the immense cloud cover and high humidity of the planet, he modified varieties of Taiwanese long beans to overproduce in colder environments. These vines could be seen through the glass case refrigerators at the end of the room, where spade shaped green leaves pressed against the glass, trickling down water.

"Have you even looked at your list?"

"Not much. I glanced at it night one but then fell asleep with it on my chest and woke up with these ideas. I haven't checked it again." This was God's honest truth. Jesse didn't want to know who he'd been paired with. He usually could tell based on the increased attention anyways.

"Hmmm." Elena thought he was telling the truth, but she still didn't buy it. Jesse seemed to her a thinker and a dreamer, not a studious scholar. "Can I ask you something? What did you mean that night on Archway that hope is a sure thing?"

She didn't even wait for him to respond. "Because I'm starting to wonder if you're right. Here nothing has happened yet for me, the scans we are getting of the planet are showing a cold, clammy and cloudy world… I'm just getting this sense that depression is knocking on my door and it's getting harder to ignore."

Jesse looked over at her from his work. He didn't know what to say, and apparently his face told her so.

"I'm asking you because you don't seem affected by all of this like everyone else is. Everyone else is trying to land a catch, and you're here happily ignorant. The planet we are going to be calling home is dreary, and you're finding creative new ways to make it better. How is hope so easy for you?"

Elena pleaded him with her eyes. This question felt more exposing than the folks asking him about his lack of a dating life, but Jesse did feel safe discussing these things with her. He had gotten to know Elena more over the past couple weeks working together. She hadn't been chosen by a man yet, and up until this point, she didn't seem bothered. It was nice that she hadn't been acting differently around him. *I guess we aren't a match.* Jesse had figured.

"Why did you join with Venture? Why did you wanna come out here in the first place?" Jesse asked, leading her to answer. He was feeling rather intuitive at the moment and brushed aside the notion that his faith could be discovered.

"I was excited about what I might find, but I was worried it would be ugly. It looks like it will be."

"Who says that it's ugly?"

Elena huffed, dumbfounded that anyone would call it anything else. "It IS ugly…"

"But the planet isn't ugly, or even beautiful for that matter. The planet is neutral." He could feel his Genesis reading coming back to him. "We make the planet what it is. The created world is simply there. How you approach it, what you do with it, how you see it. That's what determines if it's 'ugly' or 'pretty'. How you look at it."

He let a word slip in there that he was hoping she wouldn't notice. It didn't seem like she did. Luckily, some expressions in speech are seen as simply that. Expressions.

"So you want me to give into the power of positive thinking? Is that what you're saying? Just think differently?"

"No, that's not what -"

"Cause that's not easy." Elena didn't like hearing the idea that her mind was what was broken, not the world. She simply looked at things and felt. How she felt was based on external stimuli, not her perspective.

"No, what I mean is I used to feel a certain way about my life. I used to see things that happened or how the world was, and I would react. But then I finally understood, I… elevated my reasoning… no, I…" Jesse looked around as he grasped for the right words to say. His sight happened upon a pair of protective glasses, and he grabbed them and put them on. "I started to see things through a different lens!"

He pointed to his face. "Now, when I look around at the world, I'm hopeful because I see through these instead."

Elena was curious as to what Jesse was getting at. She was tracking him, but he wasn't telling her everything. "So then, What type of glasses are you using?"

"I trust that everything is going to work out."

He still didn't say anything, really. "Ya, I get that, but why? What do you trust in?"

Jesse opened his mouth to respond, but he had no idea what he was going to say, so it sat open for a moment.

SCHTUNK!

The laboratory door slid open and Director Shea strode in. She had a determined look, but then again, she always did.

"Mr. Heartshire. Come with me."

"Yes, ma'am." Jesse laid his glasses down on the table and scooted his stool back. He exchanged a glance with Elena. His said goodbye, hers said whatever. Jesse knew he was being dodgy, and he wanted to trust her, but he was scared. They weren't even on the planet yet, and things were going well. He didn't want to jeopardize the purpose that God had sent him for.

Shea was a fast walker and so Jesse, or anyone who walked with her, followed a step or two behind. Even at Jesse's normally brisk pace, he felt the need to half-jog occasionally. She talked over her shoulder as she led them on through the corridors.

"Where did you say you came from before here?" She grilled.

"Uh, I grew up on a farm."

"Just a simple homestead, right?"

"Ya, in Carolina. It was -"

"You're a veritable diamond in the rough, Mr. Heartshire! I really didn't think we would have someone so capable hidden in a Specialist position," She mentioned sarcastically.

Jesse took the compliment, as he chose to see it as one. "Thanks!"

"Because of your apparent ability, I'm going to be placing you on a special assignment once we reach the surface. I'd like you to start preparing for that.

I'm bringing you to a closed meeting with the others on your team. You'll be part of CAPA, Cultivated Asset Procurement and Analysis. Here's your tablet."

She handed back to him an upgraded Venture tablet. This one had attachments on it, such as an upgraded camera, an atmospheric dongle and a fold out analysis tray. Across the back were the letters CAPA, designating the authorization of the user.

"You'll find it already matches your bio-signature." She stopped and spun so fast that Jesse almost ran into her. "You must understand that this tablet never makes it into anyone else's or anything's hands."

Her eyes were so dead serious that it wasn't until after he responded, "Yes, ma'am, of course," that he fully heard her.

Anything's hands? What does that mean? Like an animal? Jesse's confusion was shaken off when she turned and he was attempting to keep up with her pace again.

"You will have to present yourself to security for clearance before you can access the tablet. You will then report directly to me in all CAPA related matters, and this assignment takes precedence over your current responsibilities." She turned the corner and grabbed an open lift. Jesse was about to follow but she held up her hand to stop him at the door. "I expect your first draft of suggestions to be ready by our initial meeting at 0800 on Command Level. Don't be late."

The lift door slid shut on him as Jesse responded with yet another "Yes, ma'am, I won't." He glanced down at the tablet, pressing on the dual thumbprint readers on the surface to unlock it, but as Shea had said, his access was denied. Jesse called the next lift, and proceeded to the security wing of the HomeMaker.

Obviously, there must always be need to know information in any official operation, Jesse knew that. But when he got to the security wing of the starship, there was much more action than he expected. Granted it wasn't much action to be fair, but Jesse and every other crewmember didn't have much reason for security other than tiffs between crew, or establishing policing after Foundation Day. Due to this fact, the security wing itself wasn't very large in terms of space on the HomeMaker. It was actually designed to land and expand once on the planet. Slits and creases in the walls and ceiling revealed this compressed fact, where extra material for expansion was hidden.

Personnel from command were leading a few various specialists from nearly every department to and fro, each of them with the meager members of security in tow, discussing whatever topics were pressing to their assignments. There was a central counter directly ahead, so Jesse waltzed up. The attendant wasn't frantic, but definitely frazzled at the increase of excitement on the level. "Excuse me, I was given this tablet that I need clearance for?" He held it up to the man on the other side of the desk.

He glanced at the tablet in Jesse's hand and pointed down the corridor to the left. "You need Ocular Identification, third door." He turned back to his

OF WHAT STARS SING

work behind the desk and Jesse started wandering down the way. As he started down the hallway, he noticed Captain Yale discussing with other members of the command staff, including Shea Willow. They were calm but direct in their body language.

Why was this so busy? Is there some danger of a mutiny or something? He turned the tablet over in his hands. *What does Cultivated Asset... whatever mean? Doesn't cultivated mean 'grown' or 'managed'... something like that? How could an empty planet be cultivated?*

He looked back up and realized he was in front of the door labeled Ocular Identification. As he pressed the access screen on the side of the door, which denied him entry.

BRRRRT! ACCESS DENIED.

Jesse looked blankly at the screen, about to turn back to the central desk, when Shea leaned past him, swiping her hand in front of the screen. To this, the lock chimed and the door slid open. Jesse was about to enter, when he heard a bassy voice from behind him.

"Is this him, Miss Willow?"

Jesse turned to see that not only did Shea sidle up behind him as he attempted the lock, but the rest of the present command staff did as well, including Captain Tristan Yale, whom he now was face to face with.

"Yes, Captain, this is Mr. Jesse Heartshire."

The captain extended his hand towards Jesse. Jesse took it, and Yale pulled him a little closer to him. His grip was stronger than it needed to be, and he smelled expensive and important. Yale gave instant authoritative energy, from a distance and especially so in close contact. His direct and piercing gaze, even coupled with is friendly political smile, made Jesse uncomfortable and he glanced away a lot.

"Mr. Heartshire, it's a pleasure, sir. Shea here has told me many great things about our surprise horticultural specialist!"

"Yes, sir, thank you. Just glad I can be a help."

"You're going to be quite the asset for our CAPA team. Looking forward to working with you, but remember," Yale pulled Jesse close to drive the point. "This will need to be handled delicately and with discretion. You understand?" His breath was minty and cold.

"Yes, sir, Captain, I do." Jesse still had no inkling of what he was being thrust into. He had been very studious lately to keep his head down, but apparently his hard work was so noticed he was even on the mind of Captain Yale. He was intimidated, and simply wanted to be let go of so he could discover just what this new assignment was that he had the privilege to be a part of. Blessedly, Yale released his hand.

"Good man!" Yale boomed and turned back to his command staff. Shea smiled politely but dismissively as she offered her hand towards the Ocular ID door, indicating to Jesse to leave. Jesse bowed, literally, out of the conversation and entered the Ocular ID chamber.

It wasn't much larger than a walk-in closet. A singular stool in front of a large machine on a desk. The machine looked both sinister and innocuous at the same time, having protruding lenses that looked invasive for the eyes, but everything colored in pastel green and orange hues.

HELLO! PLEASE TAKE A SEAT.

Jesse apprehensively sat, the two gun-barrel lenses aimed at his forehead. The apparatus gently shifted to life and lowered, centering itself delicately so that the lenses were on eye level with Jesse's height. The way it moved seemed as if the machine knew it looked intimidating but was trying to be soft and as disarming as possible.

LEAN FORWARD AND PEER INTO THE LENSES FOR OCULAR IDENTIFICATION.

Jesse followed the command prompts of the machine, and tentatively leaned into the lenses. At the back of the barrels appeared to be a floating, miniature replica of the HomeMaker starship. The detail was quite impressive.

REMAIN SEATED WHILE YOUR OCULAR IDENTIFICATION IS ASSESSED.

Jesse studied the miniature model. Soft, low-fi beats started to eliminate from the machine, which somewhat masked the sound of electronic fans kicking on and whirring in the background. He took in the shape of the vessel, traced the lines of the outer hull, imagining what the detached pieces would look like as they floated down to the surface.

I'll be on one of those. He thought to himself. Of course Jesse was going to be on the planet's surface, but based on this new assignment, he would most likely be one of the first. That was both a thrilling and terrifying consideration. Especially now with the secrecy of the CAPA team. What other teams were being created? Was this part of the normal procedure and Jesse was just ignorant? He didn't believe so. If this was normal or expected, there would be no need for secrecy and increased security. What was going on then?

OCULAR IDENTIFICATION COMPLETE. Jesse Hearshire, IS NOW AUTHORIZED, LEVEL 1 PERSONNEL. YOU MAY EXIT THE CHAMBER.

Gladly, Jesse leaned back away from the machine. No sooner had he backed away, the restful music stopped and the pastel scanner gently gilded back to its starting position. His curiosity was gnawing at him, so before he opened the door to exit, Jesse pulled out his tablet. It beeped in recognition of his new clearance, evidenced by the tablet unlocking and his name appearing as logged in at the top.

There was nothing much that was more special on this tablet so far than what his previous tablet had, aside from a new subdirectory, titled Mission Prerogatives. Jesse tapped it, and opened the menu, which was still annoyingly unrevealing. His first assignment that Shea had mentioned was there, listed as 'Onset Toisee'. It's description was as follows:

OF WHAT STARS SING

Upon arrival of an alien world, challenges await those who would seek to establish any permanent foundation of colonial living. Considering the hypothetical possibility of cultivated crops to preemptively exist, what would be your recommendation for utilization of such horticultural assets?

Jesse's mind was boggled, not only by the wording of the question which made his head spin, but also what he was being asked to answer. He took two wrong turns on the way back to his quarters as he pondered the answers.

Preemptively existing? Is command suggesting that prepared crops were discovered on the surface of the planet? No, they did mention that this was a hypothetical situation, and there was plenty of precedent for being prepared for things that aren't necessarily so. In fact, in his brief Venture training before departure, there was a chapter on encountering alien life on other worlds. It centered on non-intelligent animal life mainly, and that expectations needed to be broadened with how any such species might differ from life found on Earth. Bringing preconceived notions of how such animals respond to human interaction on Earth most likely will not help in similar situations on a new planet. Or maybe they might, they are all animals after all. It was a very confusing chapter of his training.

But, anyway, Venture was not saying that animal life was even present at all where he was going, but just to be prepared for it in case it was. Perhaps this was a similar assignment. Captain Yale and Director Willow were not saying that there WAS cultivated crops on Toisee, but if there was, they wanted to be prepared. This was an odd and specific consideration for an assignment to be sure, but Jesse clung to that explanation to not be carried away by imagination. He was also still fairly proud of himself for being selected to not only a special assignment, but a unique mission team as well. As he neared his quarters, he passed by the lounge area on this side of the starship residential level. A few crewmates mingled here, and one in particular was waiting for him.

"Jesse!"

Elena started quickly from her seat. Jesse stopped.

"Hey, Elena." His voice was a bit distant with thought.

"What'd she want? Where did Shea take you?" She eagerly prodded.

"Oh, I'm on some new assignment. Something command wanted done." Jesse discretely held the CAPA tablet behind his back.

"Hmmm, there's a few of those going on. Murphy and Griffith got called away too. With you gone, that's gonna make life harder over in Ag Wing." She crossed her arms disapprovingly.

"I dunno how long it's gonna be. Probably not more than a day or two. So, it shouldn't be too bad." He tried to paint it positively, but he had no idea what to expect himself, so he couldn't be too reassuring.

"Ya, let's hope so." She was standing, still and waiting, but Jesse said no more. It was awkward for a moment, but what Elena wanted to get out of him, he wasn't going to give here in the hallway. "Look I've gotta get back to the nursery and finish Murph's duties for the day, but I'd like to get together and, ya know, just talk and stuff. Would you want to meet up at the 1303 tomorrow?"

The 1303 was a restaurant and bar on level 13, encompassing the 3rd wing of the starship. It was where the crew could spend some of their earnings back on extra meals, snacks, drinks and entertainment not included in their daily rations. There was no money earned or used to buy things, but on starships crewmembers were awarded points for jobs well done that they could turn in for various perks. Each crew member of a HomeMaker starship is expected to perform their duties to adequate levels, and then directors would add additional incentive to motivate progress beyond the mediocre.

"Sounds great, I'll see you there, then!" *Did she just ask me out?* Jesse thought.

"Fun! I'll be there by 2030, probably." She said while she checked her watch. "Bye!" When Elena rushed by Jesse, she squeezed his arm. Was this a goodbye squeeze? A move outta my way squeeze? A looking forward to our rendezvous squeeze? He couldn't tell. Jesse did know that she was not matched with a man yet, as she expressed frustration at that earlier. He wanted to watch her go, to see if she turned back, but he didn't. He just continued his progress to his quarters.

Once there, he settled into what comfort the desk chair provided. Every crewmate, regardless of position or rank, is afforded private quarters on board the HomeMaker. Upon arrival at their planet, the residential levels separate to form the floors of an apartment style housing arrangement. From there, they can be built upon and expanded for family accommodation. Here, it was modest but complete. A work desk with swivel chair, full size bedding, personal toilet and shower combo in suite. All of this sleek and streamlined. A definite upgrade from the meager stay Jesse had on the Dragway in Low Point.

Jesse laid the CAPA tablet out on the desk, opened the Mission Prerogative and rested back against his chair. This was going to take some effort. Fortunately, he'd been studying a lot over the past weeks, and so he felt confident as he began dissecting the possibilities of the 'what if'. He found his mind was a bit distracted by the thought of seeing Elena tomorrow. Her face kept popping back up in his mind, especially the moment she asked him to meet her at 1303. They've hung out numerous times, had dozens and dozens of conversations, but all of it was always in the context of the Ag Wing, or the lounge area of the residential wing. But the way she asked this was different. She wanted something, and Jesse had a hunch that Elena might be after him. The thought was flattering enough to keep him daydreaming for the first hour he intended to solve the riddle command had provided.

CHAPTER 12
THE PREEXISTENCE OF CULTIVATION

Jesse was early when he arrived at the 0800 CAPA meeting, but apparently, he was still the latest arrival. He crested the doorway to Command Meeting Room 2 at precisely 7 minutes to the hour, and yet everyone seated looked as if they had already been settled in their places for quite a while. It didn't help that Shea reinforced the notion with her welcome.

"Ah, Jesse, you're here! Good we can begin." She motioned towards an empty seat at the corner of the large and open-middle square table. "Please, have a seat."

Other than Shea, there were 4 other crewmates present who had all stared at Jesse upon his arrival. He moved around the back of the one in front of him as he shuffled his feet to the right. This was a gruff looking security officer by his uniform. He scuttled with his head lowered to his corner seat, avoiding eye contact with anyone who was annoyed at his early yet late timing. All confidence that Jesse had had when he had awoken this morning had faded in an instant.

"As you are already aware, you 5 are the members of our Cultivated Asset Procurement and Analysis, or CAPA, team. You have been chosen for this role, and that is because you have shown exemplary performance in your duties on board this starship." As Shea began her opening monologue, Jesse quickly scanned the room.

To his left was the security officer, a rough-looking individual who'd seen a couple bar fights by his appearance. Shea stood in the front of the square meeting table. In between her and the security bouncer was another Ag Specialist, Rin Sato. Jesse knew her, she was considered the go-to specialist for horticultural chemistry and botany genetics. He had asked her for help a couple times when creating his hybrids. To her right was an unassuming woman with medical attire, and further between himself and Shea was a junior command officer. She sat so stiffly Jesse considered her a mannequin at first.

"But what I am here to discuss with you this morning has to do with when we arrive at Toisee. You've no doubt wondered about the nature of the assignment you were given. I believe this may help you to understand:" Shea reached into her pocket and withdrew her own CAPA tablet, where she worked a couple controls. Suddenly, over the intercom speakers in the room, music began playing. Or at least what sounded like music.

The rhythm was slightly irregular, almost as if the timing was conducted well but then sped up every 4th beat, only to slow back down afterwards. What sounded like muted trumpets or some other horned instruments followed the same pattern. It reminded Jesse of an old-fashioned analog music player, made of pressed wax or magnetic tape, where if the playback surged the audio would speed up momentarily. The quality of the playback itself was grainy and distorted sounding, as if it was low quality or cheap. Then a voice began over top of the instruments.

THEIAAAAAAA LOU TI AN THEIAAAA! SICK AI LOU, SICK AI LOU! THEIAAAAA!!

The language was definitely unrecognizable to Jesse, and looking around the room, the blank faces of the other crewmates with him said they didn't know it either. Still, it was vaguely familiar, as if he had overheard the dialect before, but it sounded almost as if someone was speaking (or rather singing) in organized gibberish. It did seem like it was matching rhythm with the horns, or at least attempting to, so he figured it was a performance of some type.

Shea abruptly turned the audio off. "What you have just heard, was what we perceived not long after we arrived here in the Toi system. As is standard procedure, our communication team began to activate their equipment and send our arrival notification back to Venture on Earth, when we noticed we were receiving radio transmission." The command and security crewmates shuffled forward in their seats, as they seemed to pick up on what Shea was saying a bit quicker than the others. "This transmission was coming from Toisee. Toisee, as it would seem, may not be uninhabited."

The stunned silence was thick with shock and awe. This was not the new and undiscovered animal life that Venture had prepared them for. Definitely not. Jesse noticed his mouth was literally hanging open, and he realized when someone finally spoke.

"What the hell are you saying!? We've got little green men on Toisee!?" The security crewman blurted out what everyone else was thinking.

"Well, Mr. Kincade, I can't tell you what they look like, but, yes, it would appear there is intelligent life on our planet."

"Why didn't we see this before we left?" Astutely asked Mr. Kincade, looking to lay blame by the sound of his voice.

"This star system is just over 100 lightyears from Earth, Mr. Kincade. And all radio scans of this star, and all others around it, were negative. As it was explained to me, this signal did not exist before we got to this system."

"That means that the signal must be new, having originated only in the last 100 years. We didn't hear it on earth because it hadn't reached us yet." The junior commander finished for her, with a condescending tone.

There was another long pause after she spoke. Shea had come to terms with this a couple weeks ago. She was now going to try her best to bring her team to this point as fast as possible. Direct download of the information was the route she chose to take. She was about to speak again when another teammate at the table spoke.

"I suppose that was bound to happen at some point. After all, it is a very big universe. Lots of opportunities for life to begin." Finally, said Zuri, the medical specialist. In actuality, this was the general mood of most of those who wondered about what lived among the stars. It was a discussion that was popularized after the invention of the slingshot gateway and the first colony missions, speculation on not what if there was life out there but about when they would find it.

"What does that mean for our mission? How are we going to found a colony? What if they are hostile?" Rin was ripe with questions, none of which seemed to stem from any sort of surprise at the existence of intelligent alien life.

"Miss Sato, as of this moment our mission remains the same. We are a HomeMaker starship and we are equipped to run indefinitely on our own here in space. However, we have some reasons to believe that may not be necessary. This is why you are here. We plan on moving forward with Founding Day 17 days from now."

"We cannot stop or alter the course of the HomeMaker until we are nearly in orbit, Rin. She's carrying so much inertia, we have no choice but to approach Toisee." The junior commander seemed to accept it rather quickly, already towing the mission line. "So, we might as well see who we are dealing with, right?" She looked up at Shea for approval, as if a puppy looked to their master for consent.

"Yes, Miss Mueller, that is correct."

The members of the team kept bringing up this or that question, but Jesse's mind was distracted by this point. *Aliens?! What does that mean?!* Jesse was perplexed, and very much of it surrounded his faith and what this would do to Christianity. *Is this why God called me out here?*

The existence of intelligent life on other worlds had always been a possibility, especially if one prescribed the theories of evolutionary origins of life. And as was just stated, it was considered by most to be a foregone conclusion, even among Christians. But not many of those, including Jesse, had considered what that would mean if they had found them. If God created humanity on Earth, it would stand to reason that He would have also created the life found on other planets as well. What confounded Jesse and made him nervous, however, was that in his reading of Genesis lately, it implies that humanity was the pinnacle of creation. "In the image of God he created them; male and female, he created them."

If God created us in his image, does that mean he created aliens, but not in his image? ... or does this disprove that God exists at all? Jesse's panic was growing. He knew he was called, he knew he had had dreams he couldn't explain. But did he? Doubt was swimming within his thoughts. His ears perked back into the conversation when he heard his name.

"Jesse, what suggestions do you bring?" Shea looked at him expectantly, as did the others at the table. He fidgeted and clumsily laid out his tablet on the table, enabling presentation mode. He welcomed the shift away from his inner conundrum and vocalized what appeared holographically in front of them.

"Umm, if cultivated crops exist, we can probably assume most are safe to eat." His holograph displayed the math and figures behind his conclusions. These were displayed as if projected onto a sphere in the middle of the table, so that each person could view the material, convexed to their particular seat. "Based on what we know of the surface composition of Toisee so far, there is little reason to expect any unknown contamination. But we actually don't know a lot, yet. Plus, a lot of crops are grown on Earth for non-edible reasons..." He displayed various pictures of commercial farming on Earth, which he could see now felt out of touch with the subject matter at hand. In his defense, he had no idea what he was walking into.

"So, ultimately, yes or no?" Shea pressed.

Jesse immediately felt embarrassingly inadequate for this position on CAPA based on what little he could contribute. "I can't say for sure. We have to be there, and analyze the crops to know."

Shea turned to the more qualified member of the Ag Wing, "Rin?"

"Unfortunately, Jesse is correct. We can make an educated guess and definitely assume that if crops are cultivated, they are safe for consumption. But we don't know anything about the bio-makeup of the alien race, or the plants themselves. We would need to be present on the planet to determine these things."

Shea acknowledged her response with a single nod. "Very well, we will move forward and reassess on the surface. Mr. Kincade, you were tasked with analysis of any security risks to our mission efforts we could encounter. What can we expect in terms of hostility? Can you speak to that?"

"Who the hell knows?" He threw his hands up in frustration. "With the information command provided, I don't know what to expect."

Shea opened her mouth to reply, but Mueller responded first.

"Surely, you were given all the information we have. You really can't make an estimate?" Mueller was direct and instigating. Rather forward considering her superior was running the meeting.

Roger Kincade shot her a look that accepted her challenge. The security specialist tossed his tablet onto the table, and swiped forward, thrusting the holographics from his presentation over top of Jesse's. "Here are the visuals I was provided by command."

A holographic visual of Toisee digitally sputtered into view. The planet glowed from the projectors and was actually encouraging to see 'in person' finally. Jesse watched the cloud patterns swirl, some lightly greyed, some thickly charcoal. Mini flashes of lightning sparked here and there across the more tumultuous sweeps of cloud clover. When they appeared, his eyes shot to peeks of land here and there, revealing that there were broad patches of blues, greens and browns beneath the grey, but the glimpses were brief.

"Do you see anything there? How am I supposed to analyse potential threats when I can't see squat?" His comments were directed towards Mueller, due to her overstep. Shea brought the focus back under control.

"Mr. Kincade, what about broadband frequency communication? Radiation signatures? Energy registers?"

"Ya, zilch. There's a fair bit of radio chatter across the spectrum, but nothing I can decipher. Sounds like some of the same stuff you just showed. Loads of light pollution at night too in various spots, so best I can do is tell you where the majority of the population centers are. It would have helped if you would have told me this was for real and not some hypothetical assignment. I would have taken it more seriously." He glared at Mueller sarcastically. "Das ist alles!"

Shea ignored Roger's comment towards Anneliese Mueller. She instead turned to the last member of the team who had yet to speak to their area. "Miss Masando here is our xeno-biological specialist on board. Zuri, what can you tell us about what to expect from the lifeforms themselves?"

"Well, I'm sorry to disappoint you, but as with everyone else, I can not say anything for certain." She was soft spoken and careful with her words. "What I can tell you is that the atmosphere of Toisee is thicker than what we would be used to on Earth. It will feel like breathing in a sauna, and that the effect that could have on the life we find will be altered but most likely undramatic. It will be cool, humid and dim." *Would be like a northern rainforest,* Jesse thought.

Shea was visibly disturbed by the lack of solid facts and figures to go off of. She sighed and hung her head, leaning forward on the table. Even with their training, and some level of experience in each of these areas, those onboard this starship were selected as colonists with areas of influence. None of them were anywhere near the top of their class in terms of expertise. First contact with an alien race was an unexpected surprise, as the deep space scans from Earth revealed nothing to indicate this was a populated system. Captain Yale had said this when all of the command staff met to discuss the discovery of the radio signals. Still, Shea was aspirational. She expected more from her CAPA crew. Without lifting her head, she directed her next question to Annaliese.

"Miss Mueller, do you have anything to add from the command perspective?"

The young junior commander perked up, "Yes, ma'am." She swiped and took charge of the holographic projectors. The swirling display of Toisee dimmed and was replaced by a tactical graphic of the planet, severely digitized and rough. The planet was black, with outlines of blue for oceans and green for landmasses, presumably. A red outline of the HomeMaker sat in orbit above.

"We will not be on the first contact landing party, but we will be with the second, before the third with the rest of the Founding Day team. Command will be sending a delegation to an area on the outskirts of a major city, and then broadcast a welcome signal to invite conversation with the indigenous population." Accompanying her words, red dotted lines descended from the HomeMaker to Toisee, planting an X on the location where the party would land. "After this first contact, a flyover of the planet beneath the cloud cover will have to commence first to determine a suitable landing area for the colony's foundation."

"We're still going to establish a colony? On an inhabited planet?" Rin questioned.

"That is still the plan, as Director Willow has stated."

"Are we sure that's a smart move? Will they let us?" Rin's worry had no quit, but they were still common-sense questions. Jesse had them as well.

"We don't see any evidence of air travel within the atmosphere. No planes, no rockets, nothing. Probably means their level of tech isn't on par with ours. That's another thing we can tell, I guess." Roger consented, throwing his hands up briefly.

"So whether they consent or not…" Medical Specialist Zuri Masando started.

"We are a colonizing starship. We have no other alternative but to attempt a colony on this world, especially if we want any hope of constructing a returning slingshot gateway. We need the materials on the planet, plain and simple."

"Alright, thank you Miss Mueller." Shea worked on her tablet. "I am assigning each of you your next Mission Prerogatives. Work with each other to accomplish the parameters of the landing on Toisee 16 days from now. You are dismissed."

There were many loud squealing noises from the chairs being pushed back. Everyone stood and started for the door, except for Jesse. He was trying to let the notion sink in that they were not alone in the galaxy anymore, but the 'wow' factor wasn't coming. Only worry and doubt in who he was anymore. Shea Willow noticed her horticultural specialist was lingering in his seat.

"Heartshire? Are you alright with this?"

"Ya, I mean. Yes, ma'am why wouldn't I be?" He asked dodgingly.

She collected her tablet from the table, and deactivated the holographic projector. He hadn't looked at her when he responded, so she could tell he was struggling. "Mr. Hearshire, I chose you for this mission based on your demonstrated ability over the last two weeks. Also, your profile indicated, how did Director Fresco put it… 'a unique and unquenchable desire to see your purpose fulfilled'? What would you say your purpose is in being here right now?"

A sharp-edged question that stabbed at the heart of his internal wrestling, for sure. He couldn't answer too honestly. "This is where I am supposed to be." He stopped but then provided more detail. "To be the best specialist I can. To ensure the success of the colony." Jesse didn't lie, as it still was his convenient guise after all.

"Exactly!" She pointed at him. "This is why I chose you. You understand your role in all of this better than most, and your determination in your performance has shown it."

He nodded and took the compliment. Shea believed that she was encouraging him in what he needed to hear, so she began for the door. He had heard her, and she was a good mission director. "We had Venture training in the inevitability of encountering alien life. I suggest you continue your vigorous efforts and review it."

She exited the meeting room with Jesse still seated, watching her walk away. The training she referenced was shallow at best. Jesse's hiding space in doing the best job he could had just exposed him to a fact that was now wrecking his faith. The situation was thick with irony, as he had been working hard to hold onto his purpose and following his calling from God, only now to have that work ethic land him into a situation where he doubted his calling at all. Not that he doubted that he'd had the dream, no. He was wondering if he misunderstood. Was it actually God? Was it all coincidence? Was it some innate human Deja-vu that tricked his mind? Was he really still just running away?

The lifts back to the residential level seemed slower after the meeting. Probably also because he shared them with a couple other crewmates. A young and scared looking security woman and an engineer with very hungry eyes. Neither of them spoke when Jesse entered. He could feel the air in the lift was ripe with a heavy topic, most likely they had just come from a similar meeting with another director. Jesse then realized that he wasn't told to keep it a secret, that alien life had been discovered on Toisee. Just the mention from Captain Yale to be discreet. Due to the nature of the discovery it for sure felt this news needed to be quietly hoarded until an appropriate time. Not something you just casually discuss like the weather, this realization that humanity wasn't alone in the stars.

When the lift hit the residential level, the engineer quickly passed Jesse out the lift doors, striding with determination. Whereas the security woman stayed behind as the doors slid shut, with no destination selected. Jesse thought he heard a sniffle as he made his way down the corridor. He understood both reactions, as most of the crew is going to have to come with the same realization as he would. Although, most of the crew probably isn't struggling with it in the way that Jesse was.

Once to his quarters, he locked the door and took out his Scriptures from underneath his mattress. It was overkill to hide it so much, but he wanted to be cautious. Now all that caution felt a little silly to him, especially considering he was wavering so much, wondering if his faith even mattered any more. *Does this presence of intelligent alien life disprove God?*

Theologically, Jesse couldn't remember any sermon he'd ever heard, nor any

Christian ever saying that their existence would threaten Christendom. Why did he feel this way then? Jesse had this sense that he'd just discovered Santa Claus wasn't real, that he'd caught his parents red-handed with the presents in the living room in the middle of the night. Then it hit him.

Because if intelligent life existed elsewhere in the universe, if it was sentient, the foundation of faith that Jesus died on a cross on earth for the sins of humans would seem very egocentric. The discovery of other life would challenge the notion that humans were created special, as God's image bearers, as the Bible says from the very beginning. The words Jesse had read in Genesis popped into his head again: "They were made in His image."

On earth, in his image. Not across the galaxy. If mankind alone was the pinnacle of God's creation, that put humanity front and center for the entire redemption story. Jesse paged open to Genesis 1 again and read. Yep, the words were as he remembered; the reason the stars were made was to aid in telling time and serving as light, to humanity exclusively, as if they were the only life in the universe. Jesse's faith was fleeting.

He looked inside the front cover again, to Gus's play on words: *If lost, please return to JESUS*. Jesse was definitely lost at the moment. And maybe the gospels wouldn't be a bad place to read when you're looking for some reassurance. He thumbed to the tail end of the Bible, guesstimating about where the Gospels show, and opened the words. He landed on the tail end of the Gospel of John, towards the end of chapter 17. Desperate for some reassurance, Jesse read.

"My prayer is not for them alone. I pray also for those who will believe in me through their message, that all of them may be one, Father, just as you are in me and I am in you. May they also be in us so that the world may believe that you have sent me."

Gus had written above the first lines, circling 'those who will believe'. He wrote, *THAT'S ME!!!*, large and all in capital letters. The three exclamation points at the end got slightly bigger than the one before it. Jesse hadn't noticed that before, but this prayer of Jesus was directed at him too. Indirectly, as a believer who believed in Jesus by the words of others, Jesus would have been praying for him too. He kept reading.

"I have given them the glory that you gave me, that they may be one as we are one— I in them and you in me—so that they may be brought to complete unity. Then the world will know that you sent me and have loved them even as you have loved me."

Jesse didn't feel very glorious right now, nor did he feel very connected to the Godhead, or even any other believers. He was alone. Way out here in the throws of outer space, 100 lightyears from the Earth Jesus walked on. He could feel his eyes glistening with tears and his breathing was heavy. This passage wasn't very comforting, and now he didn't feel like looking for another one. Jesse shut the Bible, and scooted it away from himself across the desk. Then he leaned forward, resting his elbows on the desk and cradled his head in his hands. With his eyes closed, Jesse began to pray, hoping that God was still there, and still listening.

The day continued to drag on. Jesse made it through his work, but he had to leave his quarters, and the Bible, behind to do so. He didn't bother hiding it this time, but left it directly on his desk. What was the point? At this point in time it was simply a memento to remember friends and family in the Solar System. But the day felt like an eternity for another reason too.

It's standard practice for HomeMakers to begin to acclimate the colonists to life on their new world before they actually land on it as a way of easing them into the differences. The first stage is adjusting to the new day/night cycle of the planet they are founding. Yesterday on board the starship, the lights dimmed at 2100 hours for the evening. Tonight however, the lights did not simulate night until midnight, 2400 hours. A complete day on Toisee is nearly exactly 30 earth hours as the planet spins slightly slower than Earth. Shipwide duty detail still let out at the same time for the day, affording each crewmember extra down time for the night.

This meant by the time Jesse reached the bar at 1303, the place was jam packed with crewmates. The HomeMaker might not have been in 'night mode' yet, but it was perpetually dusk here. Every HomeMaker starship is built relatively to the same specs as the one before it, but there are opportunities for customization along the way. Each starship has a 1303, but each starship's 1303 has a different flavor. Captains are allowed a voice in the design and theme of the recreational space for their crew, and many use this privilege as a way of earning increased support within the ranks.

Captain Yale's rendition was a socializer's dream, with classic games and many comfortable and gently lit tables and armchairs. The entire space was themed as if an old English pub atmosphere was thrust a few hundred years into the future. Deep, dark wood accents and faux support beams lined the walls and ceiling, but instead of being rough cut and hundreds of years old, they were polished and slick. The walls held flamelike sconces, but the flames themselves flickered from nearly invisible bowls which were held by sweeping and sharp iron works. These also held the old-world charm and color but with new world polish, precision and perfection. Along nearly every wall there were modern dartboards, but with gently digitized scoreboards. Billiard tables a plenty, with red and orange carpeting, metallic cues and crystal glazed balls. A dance floor, 3 different bar fronts, 7 mini bowling lanes, and even a legitimate antique record playing jukebox. Yale's 1303 even had misting systems that could influence the olfactory experience with fragrance depending on the mood. Tonight, there were hints of orange, peppermint and jasmine in the air, which encouraged energy after the extra-long day.

Jesse wasn't in the mood for a crowd, but he did find it comforting to be around others who were not as bothered as he was. Checking the time, it wasn't quite 2030 yet, so he decided to wait out front for Elena. Turns out, it wasn't necessary.

There was a grip on his arm. "Hey, Jesse!"

Turning he was face to face with Elena. She was holding a red-orange iced drink of some kind and seemed fairly happy to see him.

Jesse forced a smile. "Hey Elena. You're already here, huh?"

"Ya, come on! I've got us a table." She tugged at his arm, letting go but pulling his shirt a little as well. He followed her in, passing by various groups and tables of crewmates. It felt as if nearly everyone was here. With the extra time off, Jesse probably shouldn't have been surprised. He couldn't help but wonder if they were all talking about the discovery of life on Toisee. He watched the faces as they passed. Laughing, smiling, annoyed, flirtatious, listening, agreeing. They all seemed normal considering a night out at the pub. Of course, not everyone was a part of some special assigned group like he was, but they all were going to the same destination. Everyone is going to find out eventually. Wouldn't they be telling each other? Was he going to tell Elena? He realized then he wasn't planning on it. Arguably the biggest news in the history of mankind, and he didn't want to discuss it.

Elena brought him to a 4 top table snuck into a corner. It was still in the middle of the room, as there was a step and then railing behind them, with another set of chatting tables. Jesse discovered here that maybe this wasn't the date he thought it could be, as another man was awaiting their arrival.

"Jesse, this is Hector. Do you know him?"

Hector half stood and extended his hand. "Hey brother! Don't believe we've met!"

Jesse shook it, nodding his head in hello. Hector squeezed hard. He was assertive.

"Hector is a Structural Engineer." Elena said as she sat in the armchair between the men, crossing her legs and sipping her beverage.

"LEAD Structural Engineer. I've gotta oversee the landing site on Founding Day, make sure all 5 of the big HomeMaker sections get a great start." He smirked cockily at Jesse, then turned to Elena and winked. "You could call me the 'founder' of Founding Day."

"I can't believe it's only a couple weeks away! We're literally going to be standing on an alien planet two weeks from now!" She raised her glass.

"I'll cheers to that!" They clinked glasses and sipped. Elena realized that Jesse was still standing there. She quickly swallowed and stood.

"Oh, my gosh, Jesse, I'm sorry! Let me go get you something!"

"Oh, no it's ok!" He put his hands up in protest, but it wasn't strong enough.

"No, hold on! I'll get you what I've got!" She stepped around the table again and pulled his chair out. "Here, sit down! I'll be right back."

She nearly skipped away with all her youthful excitement for the night. Jesse watched Hector watch her until she was obscured by other crewmates. Hector then turned back to Jesse and tipped his chin towards him.

"You ain't claiming that one, are you?"

The thought had occurred to Jesse, but he said out loud. "No, why?."

"Alright!" Hector smiled. "I've been looking for a second." He rested back into the chair, looking Jesse up and down judgingly. "So, plants and stuff, huh?"

"What?"

"You're in Ag Wing with Elena."

"Oh, ya."

"I bet that's pretty easy. Watering seeds, pulling weeds... Not a lot to think about there I'd guess." Hector's smugness was already grating.

"It can be." *So that's how he's gonna be, huh?* " But then there's all the soil dynamics, gene splicing and botanical chemistry. That's where it really gets you." Jesse defended himself.

"Ya, I'd imagine trying to decide what flowers grow where is fairly difficult. Dunno how you gardeners do that."

"It helps when you know how to read." Jesse grinned. "Hey, when you decide what building blocks to play with, is it really hard, or do you always put the big ones on the bottom and just stack from there?" The tension was rising a bit, as did the corners of Hector's mouth in his response.

"Oh, son." He laid heavy emphasis on Jesse's role as his inferior. "There's quite a fair bit of advanced math involved. I wouldn't expect you to understand, but you want to make sure the surface has enough subsistence and subterranean mass to withstand the tonnage we are landing." Hector wasn't backing down. Jesse knew this was a stupid pissing contest, but the thought of watching him trying to win over Elena the whole night coupled with his poor attitude made him venomous at the moment.

"All the math, ya. I'm glad you know all of that because we wouldn't be able to decide whether to land on rock or sand without you."

With that Elena had reappeared behind Hector with a drink matching hers, which was now refilled. She extended it to Jesse and returned to stand over Hector's seat to his right.

"Thanks!" Jesse sipped it.

"You like it? They call it the Toisee Sunrise. They say a red dwarf looks a bit like our sun at dusk, more red and orange than white."

"Ya, it's sweet."

"I dunno if it'll be like this or not, but the idea of the sun on the surface looking like this... It seems more romantic than I was thinking before. Definitely not ugly!" She giggled a bit. She was obviously referencing back to their quick conversation last night, and she was always so unsettled about what to expect on Toisee. Right now she was leaning towards the lighter side of things. Jesse held the same sentiment, but now he was the one that considered the future ugly.

"Are you both getting to know each other?" The fellas nodded and exchanged glances of animosity, unbeknownst to Elena. "Oh, hey, Jesse, what was that special assignment you got yanked out of Ag Wing for?" Hector's interest was slightly piqued, as his competition might be stiffer than he realized. "The CAPA meeting? Had that this morning! Stands for Cultivated Asset

Procurement and Analysis." Jesse wanted to make it sound important, and to ignore his feelings of inadequacy. They wouldn't know if he didn't show it.

"Shea said she pulled me specifically because of the worth I've shown in the last two weeks. Captain Yale even expressed his gratitude towards me, saying he had heard great things from Director Willow."

Elena's eyes went wide. "Wow! That's great! Good for you!"

Hector was annoyed, clearly. "Psh. But I do like Tristan, he's a good man. I'll make sure to mention we met next time we talk. We're gonna meet about Founding Day on Monday." He sounded casual, as if they chatted often.

"So, what's the new job?" Elena pried.

"Well, we're gonna go down early, before Founding Day, to study the cult – to study the plants on the planet. Ya know, see what naturally growing flora we can cultivate." He almost let slip the fact that they had reason to believe there are pre-grown crops already there. This reminder pushed his competition with Hector to the background. Jesse found himself feeling his forlorn for the discovery of intelligent life again.

"Oh, you're going early?" Hector inquired. "Won't there be plenty of time for that after we've established the colony? Is there something wrong with the supply we are bringing with us? Maybe you should have stayed in the Ag Wing to help."

Elena was on her own train of thought. "I'm excited to see what life we discover down there. I wonder what it will look like!"

Jesse wasn't so enthused. "Ya, who knows."

Elena crossed behind Hector and sat back in her chair. She turned her knees towards Jesse and sat forward.

"By the way, I wanted to bring back up. You were mentioning seeing the world through a different lens earlier. I think I know what you mean now."

"Do you?" Jesse wondered.

"I mean, I was so worried about it being an ugly place to live, all these unknowns. But, and this is gonna sound so dumb, but I kinda had this realization." She opened her arms and swung them around elegantly. "Life is beautiful."

"What do you mean?" He wasn't so sure right now.

"Life, Jesse! Just the fact that it is life, is beautiful!" He wasn't tracking, obviously, so she backed up to her epiphany. "So after we talked, and you mentioned your lens, I had to run to cover Murph's shift, right? I was moving along, working the legumes, and I wondered what life there would be on Toisee, and it hit me. Life was right in front of me already!"

"The bean plants?" Hector scoffed. She turned more towards the middle, to address both of the men.

"Ya! I mean, not them specifically, but before we left Archway I went to the gardens to see the life of Earth one last time. I was so sad I would never see it again. I felt like I was leaving not just my life, but all life behind. But working in the Ag wing today, it finally sunk in that we are bringing this beautiful, amazing life with us! It doesn't matter what life we find out there, we have this life here already!"

Jesse considered her words silently. He knew what life they were about to find out there, and whatever it was, it was probably nothing like what they were bringing with them from Earth. But Elena's perspective was true, and it even applied to Jesse's secret Christianity. He was still tasked with bringing life, the life of Jesus, to the stars. Maybe he still had a purpose. He still carried the life of the Holy Spirit within him.

"I love your outlook, Elena." Hector commented, pawing at her knee with his hand. "It's refreshing to imagine what it will be like after Founding Day. Creating and exploring our own personal planet!"

She smiled back at him, beaming with joy at her thoughts. Jesse's mood was lightening on the subject as well. He wanted to feel the hope he felt before, and he considered the words of Jesus he had read before in the Gospel of John. *I have given them the glory which you have given me.* That's the true life, the hope that Jesse was bringing with them.

Regardless of how enthusiastic Elena was feeling at this moment, he had been around her long enough to know that her moods were fickle. Her outlook on life was surface level, based on how she *felt* about what was going on, not based on what is. Jesse was envious of her joy at the moment, but he did know enough to know it wouldn't last. The second things were hard again, or doubt crept into her worldview, she would swing back to hopelessness. He had just experienced it himself. Both in his runaway state on Archway and now in his realization that the Bible says nothing about extraterrestrial life.

Oh my gosh, she is me! His internal realization of this fact was externally expressed. Elena saw Jesse's face change from neutral to bemused without her saying anything more. She narrowed her eyes at him.

"What's that look?"

He chuckled. "Nothing. Just you reminded me of how I was feeling earlier." Jesse sat up. "But you're right. We're all so concerned with what life we are finding, that we aren't even thinking about the life we are bringing to the stars!"

"Exactly!"

Hector wanted to contribute, so he wasn't forgotten in their moment. "I can think of a few aspects of Earth I'd wanna leave behind though."

"But what we bring that is good far outweighs the bad that could linger." Jesse trumped.

"So you've accounted for our viruses, diseases and human born malice? We've literally destroyed parts of the Earth just from our being there. Our 'life'." Hector wanted to sound smart here but ultimately sounded like a nagging naysay to the growing energy between Jesse and Elena.

"The good life I'm talking about bringing is beyond that. It elevates us above what bad things our lives have done, or the physical harm we've caused."

"Ya!" Elena was swimming with the flow, even if she didn't follow Jesse's deeper meaning.

Hector wasn't allowing him to be vague. "What takes us beyond the physical?"

"Faith." Jesse said, smiling. But the second the word left his lips, he felt his smile fall, but he grabbed it back. He caught it fast enough as to not give away his slip, and only if the lighting was bright enough would his table mates have noticed.

Hector laughed. "What kind of fairy tale are you living in? Faith? What does that mean?"

"Faith in us." Jesse recovered. "Faith in what life lives within humanity. The Spirit that gives glory to life." How in the world Jesse was able to say the precise truth without completely revealing his true purpose was beyond him. Something, perhaps the Holy Spirit himself, seemed to give him the right delicate words.

"Hmph." Hector shot back the remainder of his drink. "I don't think I share your optimism. I'd rather leave all the old world behind us, and focus on what we can do here. Bring something new."

"I think you'll still have your chance, Hector. After all, I'd bet there's still plenty of new life to discover on Toisee." Jesse was feeling good again.

He didn't have the answer for what life on Toisee meant for Christendom. He had no idea what to do for the next Mission Prerogative for CAPA. He especially had no idea how to witness to alien life forms about the love of Jesus. But he did feel re-invigorated in his own purpose for being on the HomeMaker. He wasn't the brightest or the most capable, but he was entrusted with the glory of life from the Creator of Life, Himself. He was called from his home to bring Christ to the stars, and that hadn't yet changed.

CHAPTER 13
A TOISEEAN ENCOUNTER

There were a number of incredible happenings over the next couple weeks. The first was that Hector did not get his second wife from Elena. It wasn't too surprising to hear that after that night, she didn't see him again. At least not in a personal way. Elena was feeling the indirect rejection from the shortage of males on board, however she had made peace with it. She had noticed that there were a handful of men, Jesse included, who had not yet invested in this pursuit which bolstered her resolve as well.

The second incredible happening was that there was no widespread panic, excitement nor really any discernible reaction that any outsider would notice among the crew when Captain Yale made his ship-wide announcement about the discovery of intelligent alien life on Toisee. There were many questions and speculations floating about, but because no one could provide answers, everyone on the HomeMaker seemed to be in a state of suspension. Yet the air was ripe with the mildest of tensions, mild but tension nonetheless, as the inhabited planet inched closer in every viewscreen.

This was probably due to the fact that by now, every crewmate was assigned specific teams with their own special mission prerogatives. All of them answered to directors and command staff that were attempting to piece together a first contact plan with zero help available from Earth sponsors or governments. There was a pretense of know-how from those ordering about the specialists, but everyone knew this was breaking ground into an area where no one knew what to expect. There was still a hierarchy, but many of the groups banded together as peers and partners rather than lords and peasants, each of them trying to figure the best way to approach this unprecedented problem.

After all, when the Toisee HomeMaker set off, the star system of Toi was quiet. No radio noise or any other indication of intelligent life was present. This meant that the expedition was not expecting to find anything but a ripe world for their own colony.

Jesse's CAPA group was still expected to land after the primary landing party of the Captain and a select few, but now they were descending at the same time, landing in a much more remote location. The cloud cover of Toisee was constantly generated by the solar energy from their red dwarf star which worked in partnership with the increased amount of water in the air. But there were occasional breaks where more and more land masses were being further revealed in detail. There was now a decided landing location for first contact, into the hills only a mile away from the edge of a town, nearby to the largest city they could locate.

What was also revealed was the sheer amount of water on this planet. Toisee was approximately 1.5 times larger than Earth in size, but also seemed to have about the same available land mass. The oceans were impressive in size on Toisee, which would account for the increase in atmospheric humidity and cloud cover.

Elena had been assigned to a special work detail that was busy fabricating fertilizers to supplement what work Rin and Jesse had done on the Earth grown plants. They had started to show signs of non-viability with the Toisee soil estimates, and their harvest production had slowed to worrisome levels. This meant that Elena and Jesse had spent even more time together, comparing notes. Jesse or Rin still had their own mission to address, so they would provide ideas and follow up with Elena on their success or failure.

Jesse's intuitiveness and inventiveness continued to impress Rin, and more importantly, Director Shea. This was stressful as Jesse didn't feel he had a firm handle on what was going on, but he was also grateful for the opportunity to lose himself in the work. He felt that the more he tried to overthink the problems, the more he would lose his edge, so he found a specific flow of his assignments that seemed to work. Letting go and letting his mind work at its pace. He was still reading and researching, readying himself as much as he knew how for what Founding Day would bring, but it wasn't consuming him. He floated on the surface of his duties and of the unknown. He trusted his instincts, and this was bringing dividends.

Now, the day was here for the descent. For the first time, Jesse and the other members of CAPA exchanged their casual, color coded Venture HomeMaker uniforms for what amounted to intense hazmat suits. They were sealed and sterile full body suits, complete with filtering breathing units and polarized helmets. Once donned, the suits hid the identity of those wearing them completely. Only with the personalized name tags, or the digitized voice emitted when speaking could you determine who was who.

"Isn't the air breathable, you know, because we can see that creatures live down there?" Roger asked as he struggled putting the boots on after he had already secured his gloves.

"Do you assume you can breathe water just because there is fish in it?" Zuri,

OF WHAT STARS SING

the xeno-biologist quipped. "Besides, we have never been exposed to the viruses and bacteria on Toisee. Do you want to risk that your immune system can handle it?"

"Nah, but maybe Mueller wouldn't mind testing it for us?" He said under his breath.

"I heard that, Kincade." Annaliese Mueller was performing her pre-flight checks. She didn't look up or sound amused.

Roger wasn't embarrassed, but laughed heartily. Then he turned to Jesse who was dressing next to him, slapping him hard on the back. "What do you think gardener? Have you got your shovel packed?"

Jesse chuckled politely with him, "Ya, got my pail and bucket in the back already."

"See! The gardener gets it! Everyone here is so tense."

Jesse, 'the gardener', was actually about to puke before Roger slapped him on the back. His mind was churning as much as his gut. This was it. This was the day he would step foot onto an alien world, further away from Earth than any human had gone before. And what phenomenal opportunity had given him this chance? The fact that God made him good with dirt.

It was an absurd notion when considering what would be going on about 25 miles away, where the so-designated First Contact team would set up a welcoming camp outside of the large city. Jesse and the others doing vegetation recon had the stink of less importance to it. However, that fiction was far from the truth, as the HomeMaker needed to be able to thrive on this surface. It was very important work that CAPA was doing behind the scenes, just not as iconic or memorable.

They would set down as quietly as possible, hopefully on the edge of a forest or even better a cultivated field. Their chances of locationing one once beneath the cloud cover was good, but the more they flew around that low to the surface, the better their chances of being seen by the alien population as well. Mueller, as CAPA's team lead, had mentioned in their briefing that zero contact with anyone was the goal. Simply get in, get the data they needed and rocket back to the HomeMaker. It was a very covert-op assignment that 10 year old Jesse would have adored in his childhood, relishing the spy-craft and sneakiness involved. Now, the espionage of it all gave him a sense of hesitation. If they wanted to earn the trust of this alien race by seeming unassuming and welcoming with their First Contact team, it would mean this assignment, if discovered, would destroy that whole premise. Besides, a lot of what they needed to know could be determined by simply analyzing the soil beneath the First Contact landing site.

Still Jesse wavered between the fracturing of his nerves; caught in the middle of crippling anxiety and pure, unfiltered bewonderment. Sure it made him nervous to consider what dangers lie ahead with all that could go wrong. But he also was so ready to be on the planet, so eager to explore this unknown corner of God's creation. He was the first to strap himself into the jumpseat of the landing shuttle, kicking his legs like a little tike on an amusement ride.

The landing crafts that Venture had equipped the HomeMaker with were actually the exact same vessels used to ferry passengers from Earth to Archway Station, but heavily modified. Looking around, the refinements or niceties had been stripped away, exposing a lot of blandly painted grey metal and bulkhead. Instead of dozens of rows of seating, there were only the very front 12, close to the flight cabin. Behind these the rest of the length of the shuttle's interior was used for cargo hauling and storage. The equipment that CAPA was bringing with them on this journey was minimal and there were a number of large storage bins for collecting samples to be analyzed on board the starship. As Jesse peered behind him, it looked like the back of the shuttle had been modified to open wide as well, where all the cargo must have been loaded, and where they would off load themselves at landing.

T-minus 5 minutes before launch!

The announcement echoed through the mostly empty shuttle interior. Jesse had selected a seat next to a window, as he wanted the glimpse of Toisee as they descended. Rin, his horticultural cohort strapped in next to him, with her helmet already latched on. He gave her a thumbs up and a smirk. She tapped her face mask and said, digitally, *"You don't want to breathe?"*

Jesse realized he had yet to don his, so he grabbed it off the floor and slipped it over his head, spinning the latches at the front till they clicked. When they did, his oxygen flow began with a gentle hiss. He could hear his breathing within his head, similar to the sound of sticking your fingers in your ears and then drawing breath in and out. His tactical, heads-up display flickered to life in his field of vision as well.

Inside each helmet, the wearer's vision is flanked by pertinent information. There were atmospheric condition readouts, such as temperature, pressure, and chemistry makeup. As well as a compass, radio communication logs, HomeMaker command announcements, and the most fun toy, the visual analyitor. This handy bit of technology would constantly scan the wearer's field of vision and provide ID tags and act as an audibly cued database for everything the team would encounter. Its information bank was fairly empty at the moment, but the more time they spent on the surface, the more information the database could relay to the wearer.

PREPARE FOR TAKE OFF! Mr. KINCADE, SECURE YOUR STRAPS!

Jesse then realized that the voice he had thought was a computerized announcement was actually the pilot, who apparently was Annaliese. He couldn't see but her shoulder from inside the flight cabin, flicking switches, reaching this way and that. Roger, who was seated in the row in front and diagonal from Jesse, threw up his right hand in a gun pose, aimed at the flight cabin.

"You got it, Annie!" He yelled to her as he pulled his straps tight, and then twisted on his helmet. Not a moment too soon either, as before he had it secured, the shuttle lurched with upward thrust and Jesse watched out the porthole as the interior of the HomeMaker shuttle bay was gone. Gravity was left behind with his stomach the second the stars replaced the starship's shuttle bay interior as the shuttle left the dock.

They rolled and cruised to the... right? Based on the movement of the distant stars, Jesse could make an educated guess. With the movement of the stars outside, came Toi, the red dwarf sun of the system, panning into view outside the port window. It wasn't near as red as its name implied, but it certainly wasn't the tinged yellow white that Sol, the sun of Earth was. She glowed with a deep orange white. Toi was also much smaller than Sol, only about 40% of Earth's star, but you'd never guess from this perspective. Toi loomed large, very large outside the window, multiple times larger than the Sun would have been from this distance. This was due to Toisee's much closer orbit to its star. Toisee was only .16 Astronomical Units from the star Toi, compared to Earth's full 1.0 AU from Sol.

And there she was. The shuttle rolled back to the left, and Jesse watched the planet Toisee rise slowly and gracefully from the bottom of the shuttle window. It was a sight to be sure! Every nerve in his body melted away, all the anxiety ceased, as he watched the waft of clouds encircling the planet. The beauty and grace that this simple orb in the universe conveyed was too magnificent for words. It didn't matter that Toisee's clouds were so thick that they couldn't see much of where they were headed. In fact, now that Jesse could see it with his own physical eyes, the swirling blankets of grey magnified its glory. The waves reminded him of the way an elegant dress sways when a woman dances. Highlights of the sun's rays crisped the tops and edges of each pattern in a brilliantly orange caress.

He wasn't the only one on board taken away by its beauty. Zuri, in the seat ahead of him, sniffled and attempted to wipe tears from her eyes. Her hands hit the front of her helmet as she had forgotten she had it on. She dropped her hands quickly and let out a slightly frustrated sigh.

"I can't believe it. It's gorgeous." She whispered to herself, but Jesse could hear her as her coms were on. *She's got that right*, he considered to himself.

Atmospheric entry in 10 seconds! Hold on!

The nose of the shuttle pitched downwards, directly towards the planet, and instead of Toisee rising from the bottom of the window, now it approached from the right side. Minor vibrations started to shake various bits of the shuttle cabin. Glowing orange and red streaks started to appear outside the window, trailing away as the friction of their descent ignited the gases. A rattle in the cargo hold behind them began and grew so loud Jesse could hear it through his helmet. He tried to turn to see that the equipment was secure, when suddenly a large screw bounced up into his face. It startled him something awful, but amazingly the visor seemed intact and unscratched. He reached to feel for an impact crease, but the jostling, dipping and tossing of the shuttle made him drop his hands back to the grips on the side of the jumpseat.

All view outside the window was gone now, only flickering red, amber streaks with dark grey beyond. He could now feel under the seat the torquing of the metal of the shuttle, struggling to hold together under the duress of their descent. It was an odd and unsettling sensation, and although the movements in reality were too small to perceive, he swore he could see the front two legs of his jumpseat twist and turn. Then, after what seemed like forever, the stress dissipated. With a final BUMP, the shuttle now coasted like an airborne plane. The gentle rolls to the left and right were smooth, and the rattles had ceased.

Outside the window, the dark grey had turned to wisps of white. Then, for the briefest of moments, the clouds broke to reveal what had been so well hidden below. Patchwork is what Jesse saw, the same sort of mostly organized patchwork of farmland one would see if they flew a commercial shuttle across the rural parts of Earth. It was so familiar that for half a second, Jesse believed that he was about to land back in Carolina. The shuttle was swallowed again into the clouds as Annaliese pulled back on their descent.

They wanted to use the cloud cover to conceal their arrival as much as possible. Fortunately, the shuttle's contrail was hidden by this as well. But even with the cloud cover, they had no idea what kind of technology the aliens possessed to track their landing. Obviously, it would be noisy, so in the flight cabin, Commander Mueller switched on ground scanning radar to determine the most remote but also the most immediate landing space.

As his CAPA team neared the surface, Jesse closed his eyes. He remained facing towards the port window so no one would guess that he was praying. The mission was about to touch down and his purpose was screaming in his head. He wanted to calm his inner spirit, so he sought the presence of Christ. While Jesse prayed in moments like this of intense stress, he resorted back to a focal method he practiced when he was a young boy.

"All of the disciples were scared and hiding. They had a lot of friends with them, but they still felt scared because bad men wanted them to stop believing in Jesus." Mrs. Brown was his Sunday School teacher, back at his family's Neu Retter church in Asheboro. She was the sweetest woman, and most knowledgeable, that he had ever known. "And as they prayed, they were filled with the Spirit of God for the first time. Jesse? Would you mind reading verses 1 through 4?"

Little Jesse pulled himself off the floor. He didn't really want to read in front of his classmates, but his knees were hurting from sitting criss crossed anyways. He wrestled with his floppy Bible for a moment, finding the verse beginning with his finger. Then he read as best he could.

"When the day of Pen... Penta..."

"Pentecost." His teacher read for him.

"Pentecost came, they were all together in one place. Sudden... Suddenly a sound like the blowing of a violet -"

"Violent."

"Violent wind came from heaven and filled the whole house where they were sitting. They saw what seemed to be tonguesses -"

"Tongues. You're doing great! Keep going."

Jesse kept going. "Tongues of fire that separated and came to rest on each of them. All of them were filled with the Holy Spirit and began to speak in other tonguesses... tongues as the Spirit enabled them." He stopped here and sat back down among his young peers.

"Perfect! Thank you, Jesse." His teacher, Mrs. Brown, placed her hands on her knees and leaned over the students. "Now, remember, all the disciples were scared. They were scared because they followed Jesus and bad men didn't like that. What do you do when you're scared?"

A few students around him raised their hands and responded. Jesse was still trying to imagine what the tongues of fire would have looked like, so he didn't remember what they said.

"Yes! And just like you, they hid because they were scared!" Mrs. Brown continued. She always got more excited to share and teach when the little tikes were listening so well. "But Jesus had told them to stay and wait in Jerusalem. They knew God's purpose was for them to stay in the city, even when it was dangerous. We just read that something helped them by giving them a strong power. What was that?"

Jesse definitely knew the answer to that, as he was in awe of the flames. He raised his hand. "The fire! The Holy Spirit!"

Mrs. Brown pointed at him. "That's right, Jesse! The Holy Spirit gave them amazing power, and a boldness to speak the truth no matter the danger!" Jesse beamed with pride. He got it right and everyone else heard. "What was the first super power the disciples got after the Spirit landed on them?"

"To fly!" "To go invisible!" "To be saved!" Many of the students threw up answers.

"No, no." Mrs. Brown gently corrected them, her voice was so soothing, Jesse recalled. "Look at your Bibles, what happened after the Spirit fell on them?"

The students looked down to read again. Josephine raised her hand.

"Yes, Josephine?"

"They spoke in tongues?"

"That's right! Does anyone know what that means?" Mrs Brown scanned her students faces before moving on. "The Holy Spirit gave the disciples the super power to speak languages they didn't know! Isn't that amazing!"

"What does that mean?" Yuri asked from the back.

"Do you know how to speak Spanish, Yuri?"

She giggled, "No!"

"Well, if you were given this power from the Spirit of God, you could! Or German, or French, or Zwahili... anything!"

Josephine stood up, "Look, I'm full of the Spirit! Bleh, bea boo! Wree wree, thess la toot!"

Jesse and the other students giggled at the ridiculousness of her gibberish, but the image of the flames is what stuck with Jesse the most from that memory. It's what drew and connected the disciples to Jesus, even when he wasn't there. He had used the imagery many times since as a way of concentrating on prayer when things were hard or distracting.

The moments before the shuttle touched down were exactly the kind of hard and distracting times to pray in. So, when Jesse closed his eyes to pray, he focused on imaginary flames dancing on the top of his head. As he started to speak to God, the flames danced in slow motion. For some reason he only ever imagined them in sepia, tones of yellowish brown and tan, ethereal and misty. But they also stretched high, higher and higher still as he continued to reach out to Jesus. The flames ignored the bounds of the shuttle ceiling and danced and stretched towards the heavens from whence they came.

The shuttle tossed and jostled a bit, then with a definite THUD came in contact with the ground. They had landed on Toisee. When he opened his eyes, the other members of the CAPA team were unstrapping and scuffling around the cabin. He quickly stood and started gathering his equipment for extracting crop samples. The backloading door of the shuttle had not yet opened, and the other members of the team gathered for a quick meeting.

"Alright everyone, listen up. Luckily, we've managed to find and land in the midst of a thick fog bank. This will hide our visit while we conduct our collection of samples and then back to the HomeMaker." Annaliese stood with the other teammates around her. This is when Jesse learned of the smart features of their polarized helmets. When in close proximity to others in Venture suits, the helmet auto-detects and clears the polarization temporarily from the front of the glass. This way, others can see the faces of whom they are talking to. Her voice was still digital, piped directly to Jesse's helmet speakers.

"Let me reiterate again, we are NOT a first contact team. This was made very clear by command. We are to have no contact with any intelligent life form out there. Are we understood?"

The team shook their heads yes in their helmets. "You don't have to tell me twice. Who knows what those freaks look like." Roger stated.

"Fan out, keep watch on your positions. No one drifts more than 50 meters from the shuttle. Mr. Kincade, you will stand guard at the shuttle door. Miss Sato, Masando and Mr. Heartshire, you have 30 minutes to gather what samples and specimens you can. Communicate to me and I will act as liaison and help you transport everything back to the shuttle. Are we clear?"

Again, they all shook their heads yes. "I'm so ready! Let's open the door!" Rin was uncharacteristically excited.

Commander Mueller reached over and threw the hatch release. Slowly, steadily the ramp lowered. Hydraulics hissed and eased the ramp downwards. Too slowly for Jesse's liking, but once the ground was visible, he realized he wasn't missing much. The fog was indeed thick. Roger, pulling up his automatic rifle, walked to the edge of the lowering ramp and descended down with his guard up.

Everyone was still. The mood was quiet and palpable, and most noticed they were holding their breath. They edged to the top of the ramp, watching Roger aim left, then aim right, scanning the area carefully. Once the ramp touched down, he sent out an etch-ping and watched for movement. Jesse couldn't see the results from his vantage point, so he waited anxiously with the others. Slowly Roger raised his hand, and then waved it forward, the signal that the immediate area was clear, and all 4 of the remaining team members shot down the ramp.

Jesse hesitated for the briefest of moments before his feet hit the grass. Grass? Well, it looked like grass at his feet, but the color was off. It seemed a tinge blue. But as he was looking down at his first step onto Toisee, the first step onto an alien world, it felt kind of like stepping into his own backyard. At the thought, Jesse's helmet and hazmat suit felt silly. Almost as if he was playing pretend.

He looked up and watched the others tentatively walk into the dense, orange hued fog. It seemed as if they were walking through an earthen dust storm by the color, but Jesse remembered that Toi was a red dwarf, and the colors cast from it would cause the rays to be a bit reddish orange. He looked up to the brightest part of the fog bank, but even the large star was unable to break through this mist. He could just make out the massive disk, as from this distance, the star Toi was much larger in appearance than Earth's sun. A loud click was heard from the back of the shuttle and ahead of him, his team was then outlined by the next etch-ping.

An etch-ping is a fog penetrating laser blast. Other than its emitter, it silently strobes out in all directions, slicing through the vapor and illuminates any hard surface. Once the laser hits an object, the object's raised edges reflect the lime green glow back. The outlines of his comrades glowed briefly, but then also did the tree line about 15 meters or so to his left and right. Straight ahead nothing pinged back, which meant that for however far the ping shoots, there was not much ahead but a field.

"We're situated on the corner of a cultivated field. The edges seem to be lined with trees and thick hedges. Sato, Heartshire. This is your area, begin collecting your samples and taking measurements." Mueller pointed as she spoke.

"Yes, ma'am." Rin Sato replied back. Jesse pulled out his CAPA tablet and unfolded the small sample analysis tray as he took another few steps forward. Now his boots were kicking the soil, soil with rows of small crops embedded between the plowed dirt. He was breathing fast. This was exhilarating. There wasn't much to see yet, but wow. An alien plowed field!

"Kincade, keep an eye on them. I'm going to escort Masando to the tree line on our left."

"I've got 'em." Roger stood a few steps behind Jesse, Rin a few steps beyond. Jesse knelt down and pinched a bit of the topsoil, drizzling it into the sample tray. He worked the tablet, and waited for it to cycle. While the numbers crunched, Jesse turned his attention to what they were growing here.

He reached down and gently stroked across the baby leaves, then rested his hand under them, lifting them up. He wished he didn't have his gloves on as he couldn't feel the texture or weight of it at all. But the plant was muted violet, flat leafed and lettuce looking. Given the spacing in between each plant, the crop was going to be rather large. Maybe a type of spinach? He pulled a few up, roots and all, and placed them in a compartment in his sample tote. With a ding the soil reading was complete, so he dumped out the dirt and folded back the tray.

Jesse stood to resurvey his surroundings. The fog was so thick he could watch patches of it slowly rolling across the field, almost like tumbleweeds of mist. Sato was still scratching at the ground a bit ahead of him. Another etch-ping traced her back as she hunched over a small piece of coring equipment. Jesse scanned the treeline to his left and right. His anxious excitement was calming, now he just wanted to explore.

"Rin, you good over there?" He hollered.

"Damn, Jesse! It's an intercom, you don't have to yell!"

"Oops, ya, sorry." Talking to someone in a normal voice while watching them from a distance was throwing him off.

"But, yes, I'm just about to start burrowing. I'm going to collect some shallow core samples."

"Great. I'm gonna head for the tree line. I'll gather as many samples as I can."

She didn't respond. She was busy activating the coring machine. Jesse decided to make for the trees on the right of the ship. Mostly because Mueller and Masando went to the left, and he could potentially find samples that they would miss. That and Jesse wanted to experience this world a little on his own at the moment. He started to feel comfortable here, probably against his better judgement. But being cooped up on Archway and then the HomeMaker, he hadn't felt dirt beneath his feet for months. It was really very strange to him that this alien world, an impossible distance from Earth, would feel so much like his home. There was most likely massive unknown danger here, but the blanket of fog and his own hazmat suit gave him a confident sense of protection.

"Don't wander far, and keep your line open. You've got 24 minutes left." Roger chirped at him as Jesse crossed the soil towards the trees. He couldn't see them yet, but the etch-ping had shown him they were only a few meters ahead. Jesse determinedly stepped forward, carefully watching his steps so as to not trample the diminishing rows of purple crops. He knew he had to be close, as the edges of the fields the sown plants grew the smallest.

Shapes began to appear ahead of him. Large, looming and intimidating. The dank and dim shade of the trees was cast even deeper into the fog, darkening the already dark corners of the edge of this... forest? He had no idea how deep it went, but he could tell it wasn't just a treeline dividing fields. As he got face to face with the specimens, he again had to remind himself he wasn't home. At least at first.

The tall growing weeds, the bushes, the trees... it was all so eerily similar to Earth. But the more he gazed upon the forest, the more alien it seemed. In the fog he first couldn't tell clearly, but the forest seemed a bit darker than it should be. As he closed in, he realized why. The plants were deep in color, mostly shades of light to dark blue!

So much for feeling like home! Jesse thought to himself.

There were bunches of deep royal blue ferns, but their branches held much fewer individual leaves. The plant had the same overall shape, fanned out all its branches from a central point, low to the ground, and red lines ran through it. The stem was red, nearly ruby in tone and a stark contrast to the blue leaves, and as Jesse turned it over so was each vascular bundle, the veins that transport water through the plant.

As he scanned the flora, his helmet ID tagged each new vegetation species he happened across. It would briefly flash, highlighting the outline of a specimen that he hadn't collected. Once these plants were named and their composition known, the information would also populate on the side of the screen in his field of vision. For now, rows of question marks and blank dashes is all that the helmet could report to him.

Removing a few of the fern branches for collection, the space revealed turquoise mosses with giant, bright yellow spore pods. The moss was thick and deep. Jesse pressed his gloved hand into the moss and watched it disappear! It was so fluffy, and reminded him of shag carpeting. And when he took a few steps forward, he could see it literally acted as carpet in the forest. It covered nearly every empty space on the ground, except for a few barren spots and a couple fallen tree trunks.

But how some of these trees could have fallen was beyond him. They were probably the most alien thing he had seen so far, aside from the dramatic colors of the plants themselves. It was their trunks, they were thick, massively thick. Jesse estimated he couldn't have wrapped his arms around it if he had tried. They reminded him of baobab trees of Madagascar, but what made them so alien looking wasn't their enormous girth, but their staggeringly short height. Maybe 8 or 10 feet high at the most? They were topped with branches that reached out in 5 directions, equally spaced, like a drawn star. Each branch was thick with multiple, broad leaves, whose thickness and shape reminded Jesse of a magnolia, however the leaves were easily 2 to 3 times the size.

As he progressed ever so carefully, he discovered the source of the dark shadows overhead, as there were also taller trees deeper into the forest. Jesse's tote was rapidly filling with cuttings and pulled leaves, but every step he took, there was something else new. The fog seemed to clear a little further he went from the field, mostly due to the ground rising a bit as he explored. He trudged up a hill towards the towering trees on the ridge. Jesse was so enraptured by his surroundings he didn't realize he was now nearly 40 meters from his shuttle. It appeared he had left the penetration of the etch-ping, and he hadn't even noticed.

    As he crested the ridge, Jesse was coming to somewhat of a magical looking clearing. The ferns were more sporadic and smaller here, and a gentle brook bubbled through the middle of the clearing past Jesse. The brook trickled its way to the other side of the glade to his right of the ridge that Jesse had just climbed. The orange fog caught incredible rays of reddish light, flickering and dancing through the gentle sway of the branches above. They had landed sometime in the early morning, and the light of the sunrise was getting stronger.

    The tall trees here created a beautiful canopy of deep but spotty shade, and what looked like white flower petals dropped and drifted down from above as the tree tops swayed gently in the breeze aloft. As he approached the taller trees that he was originally aiming for, he could see these trees were surprisingly smooth on their trunks. As if all their bark had been peeled away, but as Jesse studied the trunks he could tell this was as the trees were created. He stood at the base and scanned upwards, not seeing a single rough spot. It was like looking down an impossibly long arm, and as the tree swayed slightly from the breeze at its top, the curves of its trunk looked like muscles flexing. It was a thin, but sturdy-looking tree. The branches were few, until near the top, where similarly to the squatty trees, the branches reached out far and long. These resembled the shape of mimosa tree leaves, fernlike and many, and they seemed to be the tree that was dropping the flowers.

    Jesse reached out to try and catch the white pods as they fell. They spun as they dropped, similar to the helicopter seeds of maple trees, except these were on 4 sides of the flower pod. They weren't much bigger than a couple inches across, so catching one was difficult. Jesse was having fun with the challenge though. He could have chosen a few off the thick mossed ground, but he decided that he had to prove he could catch one in mid-flight. Reaching to his left, he was just too short. He took a couple steps into the clearing. He tried again, grasping at another drifting to his right, but it spun faster and fell further away than he could get. Gravity on Toisee seemed to feel very relative to earth, as Jesse couldn't discern a difference in his body, as well as the drifting of the pods. Then one more dropped nearly on his helmet, so he stepped back and stumbled slightly. He caught his balance on the carpet beneath him, reached out his hands to infront of his face and clasped them both around the pod. He brought it close to his helmet to examine. His helmet readout gave him the same question mark response to its visual analysis of the pod.

    Then, the second he dropped his hands from his face, he froze. His helmet ID system had flashed to outline a new species of flora across the clearing, however based on its shape, this was no bush or tree. He was being watched, and the realization terrified him. He was exposed, unarmed and had nowhere to hide.

There were two pale figures on the other side of the short clearing that had caught him with their attention. They were standing directly in front of him, and staring directly at him. They hadn't entered the clearing fully, and so they were still partially obscured by the fog bank. They were maybe 15-20 meters away? Jesse couldn't see details, but what he could make out was sending his perception through a loop of confusion.

They appeared to be human. Jesse knew this couldn't be, but here he was looking at them. They looked to him like two, pale white, dark haired humans. They were about average height, one about a foot taller than the other. They seemed to be holding hands, and the little one had a basket. Their attire was loose fitting, flowy and brightly colored. And they just watched him. They didn't move.

Neither did Jesse, for a good long while. Sweat rolled down his temple on the inside of his helmet. He was speechless. Does he radio this in? Does he turn and run? He realized he was still holding the white helicopter flower pod in both his hands, so he slowly reached over to his sample collection and he carefully deposited it inside.

When he did this, the human things started walking towards him. Actually, it was the littler one first, apparently dragging the other taller one by the hand. As the small pale person trod over the thick moss, coming towards Jesse determinedly, he panicked. He took a step back, gripped his shoulder strap of his sample tote, ready to turn and run. But he didn't. He lingered as he still struggled to believe his vision. This little person seemed to be a little girl, a pale, long black-haired little girl. Her hair was straight and fell down on either side of her face, past her shoulders. He could now make out that their clothes seemed tattered at the edges, as if from long wear without repair. She was watching her step, especially across the brook, and for good reason because she wore no shoes. Jesse was fascinated to see 5 toes on each foot, just like a human. An odd thing to notice, granted, but each new detail revealed another aspect of what he had in common with this alien. Was it even an alien?

He watched her approach, her eyes shooting up to him then back at the ground, eyes that looked strikingly green. They flashed as emeralds every time she looked at him, a brilliant contrast to her ghastly pale complexion. She stopped only a few feet from Jesse's standing shock. Surprisingly, her gaze did not match the awe and unbelief of his own. She looked up and down at Jesse and his suit, her face curious and bemused.

Her companion was a different story. He was male in appearance, shorter hair, not falling past his ears. He had the same striking green eyes, ghastly skin and had a look of fear and unease on his face. His grip was tight on both the girl's hand and what Jesse thought was a knife at his waist. Jesse would have done the same if he had remembered his suit was equipped with a utility knife.

The girl's eyes looked at Jesse's sample tote, then she tried to let go of her companion's hand. He didn't let go, nor turn his eyes from Jesse's helmet. Jesse then realized they couldn't see his face, but he could see theirs. He gained a little confidence from the notion, similar to how someone feels they can hide behind sunglasses. The little girl shook her hand free from her companion's grip and she reached over to open the top of her basket. Inside, she selected one of the same white flower pods that Jesse had grabbed. Apparently, she was collecting them as well. She let the top of the basket fall when she retrieved one, and she took the final few steps towards Jesse.

"Thy'alla!" The boy protested. Jesse didn't understand if this was the girl's name, or if he was telling her to halt her approach. Either way she ignored him. Was this her brother?

She stopped just in front of him and offered the flower up towards his chest. Jesse was instantly charmed by this foreign but cute little girl, offering him a flower. Now that she was this close to him, he swore her eyes were larger than normal humans. Ever so slightly though, and they were glistening white pearls, with embedded emerald gemstones. Jesse looked down from her eyes to the flower she offered.

"Stu di." She said gently, offering the flower within her open palm.
Jesse hesitated, but then slowly reached out and took the flower from her. As he grabbed it from her, she recoiled her hand a bit quickly from the touch of his rough gloved hand, but she did not retreat. She watched him open his tote, and drop the flower in with the others. She watched him curiously, standing on her tippy toes to see deeper into the vessel.

He was touched to see her childlike curiosity. With that, Jesse was reminded in the Spirit of the reason he was there. He was called, by God, 100 light years away from his home, to find his purpose among the stars. It came suddenly, as if a notion was dropped into his mind, more than a thought, a feeling. An impulse, an intuition that came from beyond his own mind. He felt compelled, disregarding reason and caution, to remove his helmet. He wanted to reveal himself to her in the same brave way that she revealed herself to him. So he slowly reached up for the clasps and twisted them to disengage the airlock. It popped and made a sharp, short hiss that frightened the little girl, so she jumped back and stood slightly behind her companion. Instantly, crisp air stabbed at his lips and cheeks. He breathed in its freshness for a moment, tasting the alien air for the first time. He was given no indication from his helmet readout that the air was toxic to him but trusting that did give Jesse pause. He lifted the helmet over his head and held it with both hands in front of him.

When Jesse revealed his face and the alien humans took sight of him for the first time, they gasped together. They now held the same face of confusion as Jesse looked very much the same to them in every way, except for all of the details. His hair, skin complexion, eyes. All the differences that Jesse had perceived, they now saw and understood. Maybe they didn't fully understand in the way that Jesse did, as they have not seen where he had come from, but they did know that there was more to this person than just a funny looking full body suit. He looked strikingly different from them, and yet familiar enough to feel safe.

He tried to make his face friendly, so he smiled. It was forced and awkward, and their confused looks did not change. In fact, they both started to look worried and take a step backwards in retreat.

How am I supposed to do this?! Jesse's mind was a rush. Here he was in a true first contact situation, alone, probably in loads of trouble. Most assuredly in trouble now with this situation, but when command finds out what are they gonna do with him? *What was I thinking?! I have no idea how to communicate with someone I can't speak to! How do I show them —*

His mind stopped on that notion. He just had to show them. He didn't have to tell them anything. And she already showed him how to love a stranger. Jesse smiled again, but this time it was genuine. That kind of smile you make when you're going to give a gift to someone that they are sure to enjoy. And at least she recognized it and smiled back. Jesse set down his helmet and pulled his tote bag around to the front of his body and opened it. He started moving this box and that, looking for something specific. She could somehow anticipate that whatever this strange man was doing, it was for her, so she stepped around her brother again, who still had his guard up. He put his hand on her shoulder to keep her from getting too close, which she allowed because it made her feel safe.

Jesse stopped when he found what he was looking for. He looked up at her, met her eyes with his, and grinned playfully. She was excited to see what he would reveal, she bopped on her knees, up and down, waiting playfully. Jesse popped the top of the sample tray, reached in and produced his favorite sample so far: a pink flower, with petals in the shape of the Star of David, and a yellow stamen in the middle.

Her eyes grew even bigger. She clapped her hands together and then extended them, hoping that Jesse would deposit the flower in her palms. She took it, holding it up to the light so that the color of the petals glowed slightly. She then brought the flower to her nose and smelled, holding it there as she smiled back at Jesse, sheepishly hiding behind her new treasure. Jesse felt proud that he could return the love that she had shown him. At the conclusion of their moment, her brother tugged on her arm and started to turn.

"Thy'alla, gor roe." He commanded her. She understood that he was serious and she turned, holding his hand back across the small brook. Her brother kept turning back, watching Jesse as his little sister struggled across some rocks of the brook. He wasn't letting his guard down for a moment. Jesse simply watched them leave, smiling after them, still trying to soak up as much of this moment as possible. He wished he could take a picture.

As they were reaching the edge of the trees, the little girl turned and yelled back towards him, waving her hand up and down. Jesse couldn't make it out.

Her companion tugged at her again. He seemed annoyed that she would stop and yell something back to him. But she wouldn't budge right away. She kept waving at Jesse, obviously hoping he would reciprocate, so Jesse waved back in the same way she did. He waved his hand up and down, and realized he could yell anything back at them, and they wouldn't know what he said. He used the opportunity to witness for his faith, and love them with his words, even if they couldn't understand.

"God love you!" He yelled back at her. When he did, the boy's head shot quickly towards Jesse. It was hard for Jesse to tell from this distance, but the boy's face appeared to be extremely surprised. The girl didn't seem to think anything of it, but Jesse had the feeling he had said something to disturb the boy. He hurried her along, more forcefully this time. She gave in and trotted off with him, into the fog and out of sight.

CHAPTER 14
INTRODUCTIONS ALL AROUND

Jesse had returned to the shuttle with less than a minute to spare. Rin and Roger were waiting, and were interested to hear what he had discovered, but before Jesse could consider how to lie about his encounter, Annaliese and Zuri appeared out of the fog. They carried a number of small traps and containers, one that they struggled to hold between them.

"Grab some of these, will you?!" Mueller ordered. Jesse and Rin stepped forward to meet the other two as they approached the bottom of the ramp. Their sample cases were full of various "biological samples" as Zuri would call them. Various insects or worms and a rodent-like thing made up most of the smaller sample containers, but the big one between them was the real surprise. It had a collar, so whatever it was, that meant it was domesticated.

"Did you steal someone's cat!?" Roger exclaimed.

To be fair, it did resemble a long haired cat at first glance. Something similar in size and fluff as a maine coon. Until you noticed that it possessed a pig-like snout and three sets of legs, or to be more clear, 4 legs and a pair of curved mandibles coming from its front shoulders. The mandibles were in line with its head, and seemed to work like an ant's; designed to grab and shove things towards its mouth. It was cute to an extent and seemed to be more confused at being captured than aggressive. Now with free hands, Mueller and Masando grabbed either side of the cage and hoisted it up the ramp into the cargo hold of the shuttle. The others followed with their samples and totes.

"Did you see anything like that out there?" Roger turned to Jesse as he was the last up the ramp, elbowing him with enthusiasm.

"Ha! No - nothing like that." Jesse was quick to respond. It was true, as he still had no idea exactly what he saw.

Were they really human? The brother and his sister (he still assumed that's what they were) looked and seemed human enough. But how was that possible? What does that mean? He wondered how the first contact situation with

Captain Yale and the others was playing out. He doubted that they were exchanging flowers with each other, but he did hope that it was as friendly. Maybe they would get more answers than Jesse was able to figure.

As he and Kincade crested the top of the ramp, Annaliese pressed the button to fold up the ramp.

"Secure your samples for transport and strap yourself into your seats. We're dusting off in 1 minute." She demanded. The engines were igniting and whirring to life. The high-pitched squeal of high velocity turbines was sure to grab the attention of the boy and girl, or anyone else who happened to be out there. As Jesse sat down, he peered out the porthole window facing the woods he was in. He pleaded with them in his mind not to appear on the edge of the forest. The fog was clearing much more now, and the tree line was easily visible, but thankfully he did not see any pale figures emerging from its borders.

"I can't believe we just did that." Rin was strapped in next to him. She was relaxed back in her chair, and she turned her head to face Jesse when he turned around. "We were on an alien planet. Our alien planet."

"It was incredible wasn't it?" Jesse agreed. "But it's not our planet anymore is it?"

Rin smiled at him. "You mean because it's inhabited?" Jesse nodded his head. "Do you think that's going to stop us from creating a colony here?" Jesse stared blankly at her.

"But we can't just drop our HomeMaker here..."

"Where else is it going to go, Jesse? The other planets in this system are unlivable. And besides, are the natives really going to stand in our way? Whatever they are, it's apparent that they are technologically inferior to us." Jesse had a look that said he was offended at her statements, so she continued.

"Oh Jesse, come on. I'm not saying we're going to invade and slaughter and enslave. But we have to land somewhere, and I'm sure this planet is big enough for the both of us. Heck, they might even want us here! That means that it's as much ours as it is theirs now."

Rin wasn't wrong, at least in the sense of the necessity to create a colony. At the very least, materials were needed to reconstruct the slingshot gateway to return to Earth or advance on to another star system. That meant that some kind of deal was needed with the Toisee HomeMaker and the Toiseeans themselves.

Jesse turned back to the porthole window as the shuttle ascended back into the clouds. He did not end up seeing any of the pale humans, nor even a building or piece of equipment in the distance. The secret of their encounter seemed to be safely contained between himself and two he happened upon in the woods.

Once back in the HomeMaker docks, Mueller got word that first contact was made between Captain Yale's party and the Toiseeans. There was an immediate command meeting to be held upon the captain's return, so she gave quick orders to her team before she departed. Everyone knew the next steps already, but Annaliese felt the need to maintain control of what she could control. Jesse could relate.

The initial shock and excitement of meeting fellow alien humans had worn on in his mind on the shuttle ride to the starship, and now Jesse's thoughts were filled with what this meant for his faith. As he had considered previously, new intelligent life does not necessarily negate the Bible's witness, nor does his mandated witness and purpose change. But the presence of other human life? He wanted to return to his quarters, crack open the Scriptures and dig, but his duties kept him busy for the next few hours. Analyzing the soil and flora samples was pressing as command was expecting them right away. The countdown clock for Founding Day was still ticking with only 22 hours to go.

Elena was waiting for him at the horticultural lab. She was leaning against the doorway when Jesse rounded the corner, totes of samples draped over his shoulder. She popped up eagerly and approached him, offering to take the tote from his shoulder with her hands.

"You harvested quite a bit, huh? Find anything interesting down there? What's it like?" Her questions berated him.

He laughed, "Jeez Elena." He let her take the tote off his shoulder, holding his helmet in his other hand. "Can I get out of this hazmat suit first?"

"Pft, fine." Her voice was pressed with the effort of carrying the surprisingly heavy tote.

"Ya, that's a bit heavy."

"Thanks for tellin' me! Such a gentleman." She strode into the lab, making a b-line for the nearest analysis table. She thought about tossing it on top, but considered again and slumped it down by the base. She started unzipping the cover and removing the sample boxes, looking into the different colored trays as she placed them on the table.

Jesse slouched into a nearby lab chair and began work peeling off the hazmat suit, starting with the ankle and wrist connectors.

"Wow." Elena said slowly, studying the turquoise moss. "I had no idea that it would look so different. They look nothing like anything on Earth!"

"That's what it felt like down there too. The ground, the trees and plants... the shapes all seemed so familiar and yet so exotic. As if someone swapped my eyes with... I dunno. Someone colorblind or something."

Elena set the yellow moss flower sample down and looked over at Jesse, a look of a bit of hopefulness and dread at the same time. "Did you see anything else?"

Jesse conveniently tugged at the zipper on the front of his suit, as it was a bit stuck. He used the distraction to hide his fib. He knew what she was asking. "No, I didn't see any little green men." Actually, it wasn't a fib. He hadn't. Then why does it still feel like I'm lying?

She sighed. "I guess we will know when Yale gets back. This communication silence thing is crazy." Elena was referring to the command order to cease all external communication from the shuttles to the HomeMaker. Their explanation was that they didn't want anything to tarnish their first impression with the native life on the planet. It was doubtful that the tech level of the inhabitants were even capable of hearing their communication, much less understanding it.

"When is Captain Yale supposed to be returning?" Jesse asked.

"They didn't tell you? I guessed with you on this secret mission that you'd be in the know. I'm the lowly outsider here." She crossed the room with a couple samples to study under the microscopes.

"No," Jesse stood and laid out his hazmat suit on the chair. "I'm the gardener. Mueller hasn't said anything about that. Actually I'm pretty sure the other members are in the dark as well."

He reached into the tote and pulled out the violet crop sample. It was wilting in the box, but still held its purple hue well. Actually, under the color temperature of the pure white recessed lighting, the crop was even more purple looking. Like a light purple cabbage. Jesse laid the sample on a dissecting tray and began slicing into the stem, leaves and roots.

"What do you think about all this?" Jesse asked her. He crossed over to a nutrient grading machine and laid the samples inside. Pushing the button to begin the cycle, he looked over to Elena because she hadn't answered him.

Elena was staring down into the microscope. She must have felt him looking at her because she answered without looking up. "What do you mean?"

"How do you feel about finding out that we aren't alone in the universe?"

"I'm not surprised if that's what you mean." She still didn't look up and she changed the subject. "Cellularly these are remarkably similar to plants on earth, aside from the color. It looks like the chloroplasts have evolved to absorb this planet's light spectrum. So that's why they are blue in color."

Jesse glanced back at the nutrient analysis of the violet crop. Remarkably, the machine was able to recognize every component of the plant. Loads of iron, but also Vitamin K, A and C, also folate and magnesium. This plant was definitely edible and nutritious for mankind. Jesse then realized he himself wasn't shocked to discover this, especially after seeing the humans on Toisee. He still didn't know for sure they were human exactly, but the evidence was mounting.

"Elena, why aren't you surprised about finding intelligent life on Toisee?" Jesse was pressing now because she was dodging the question. She finally leaned back and shrugged her shoulders.

"I don't know!" Elena huffed and spun in her chair to face Jesse, her arms across her chest. "I mean, it makes sense right? We find the right planet with the right components and chemical makeup, the right distance from its star for water to form, and it happens right? Life? When you find that, it seems that out of all of the millions of planets out there, there's bound to be one with intelligent life like us."

"So you wouldn't say there is anything special about us?"

"Who, you and me?"

"Ya, us humans."

"No. I mean, not in the sense that we should be proud of ourselves or anything. If life happens on Earth, why shouldn't it happen on Toisee? Remember that life I was talking about the other day in 1303?"

"Ya."

She stood up and held out the sample tray. "This is it, this is what is amazing. That life happens. And if it happened on Earth, it's gonna happen elsewhere. Life itself is amazing and remarkable, not the fact that it's here." She held up her finger to him to emphasize her point. "The fact that intelligent life is here is great and all, especially that we get to discover it, but it's routine for the universe."

Finishing her point, she looked depressed. The thought hadn't occurred to her, but if finding life was a guarantee, the excitement was gone about the discovery. She was back to being disappointed in the life she wanted to be in awe of. Vocalizing it just now finally brought that realization to the forefront of her mind. "Life is routine." She said slowly.

Jesse wanted to tell her so badly about his own discovery. From their analysis of the plants having the same components to horticulture on Earth, to the apparent fact that humankind is not limited to that same planet, the life that she was seemingly disappointed in was much more of an exciting discovery than she might realize. Finding life when life is expected is one thing, but finding you have brothers and sisters across the galaxy? That's beyond incredible. If anything, the notion of the evolution of life from nothingness is drawn into question, if not utterly destroyed. But unfortunately for Jesse, so is the truth of the Bible.

Why would God create human life here too? Did Jesus die for these people too? Are the Toiseeans made in the Image of God? Both Jesse and Elena were now lost in their own thoughts, and the room sat quiet. She wrestled with the lack of awe she felt at the new life discovered that was also expected. He attempted to fathom what humankind on Toisee meant for Christendom. New discoveries all around them, and yet frustration at what they already knew. She shook herself of it first.

"Well, we might as well finish. I am still curious as to what type of creatures we are going to be sharing this planet with."

"Ya, I wonder if they're blue too." Jesse smirked and Elena chuckled a little.

Captain Yale's crew shuttled back to the HomeMaker a few hours later than expected. This put the launch time to Founding Day at less than 13 hours on the countdown clock. After a quick meeting with his command personnel, Yale called a ship wide gathering in the Lyceum.

The gathering of the crew was ripe with questions and anticipation. Jesse and his CAPA team's reconnaissance mission was not widely known about, and after they presented their findings to command, they were dismissed and told to join the ranks of the rest of the crew at the gathering. Jesse was glad for this as he did not want the constant barrage of questions about the planet's surface that was sure to come. The badgering of others in the Ag Wing was enough already. He was looking forward to the gathering as a way of placating their curiosity once and for all.

Yale had ordered the flight crew to maneuver the HomeMaker so that the planet Toisee was directly above the glass of the lyceum ceiling. Its clouded splendor filled most of the visible space, slowly swirling as if tossed by the breeze of the cosmos. Captain Yale erected his platform again in the middle of the floor, and the second he ascended the stairs, the crew grew quiet.

"My fellow citizens of Toisee, what a splendid and invigorating announcement I have! Most assuredly, you all are curious as to our next steps, watching the countdown of Founding Day inch closer with each second. I want to guarantee to you today that we will indeed continue right on schedule with the founding of our home away from home."

With that reassurance, a number of crewmates clapped and hollered their approval. About half of the crew remained silent though, as their biggest questions were not whether or not a colony would be created, but what creatures they may have met on the planet surface.

"But before that day, I would like to introduce you to our new neighbors. And despite all of your fantasies and imaginations, you will discover just as we did, that we have much more in common with these new friends than you might believe. Sherii, come forth!"

At this invitation, Captain Yale raised his hand and beckoned someone to the stage with him. The individual was cloaked and slowly ascended the few steps. Many of the crewmates jostled, leaning on each other, climbing to their tiptoes to catch a better glimpse of exactly who this being was. A murmur was building in the lyceum, and all eyes were fixated on the stage. Jesse turned to watch Elena's face, as he already had a good idea of what to expect.

Sherii stepped forward on the stage in line with Captain Yale, reaching pale white hands out from behind their sleeves. This drew some small gasps of those watching with strict attention. Sherii's hands gripped the top of the cloak's hood and threw it back, revealing sleek black hair, trimmed long in the front and short in the back. His face held a beard as well, but it was shaven short around the chin and ears. As with the girl and boy, his eyes were bright and slightly larger than the average Earth born human.

The crewmates began a restless agitation. Some threw questions of "How?" or "Who are they?" Others dismissed it as some kind of joke made in bad taste. They cursed towards the stage in disbelief. The uproar of the crowd was growing, despite Yale's hands raised to quiet them. Jesse watched Elena's face turn from curiosity to deep thought to realization, when she turned to look at him. His eyes must have given something away, as she seemed surprised that she caught Jesse watching her instead of the reveal. She pointed at the stage, and cocked her head sideways, insinuating a question that Jesse might have known something already. He felt discovered and so he quickly turned back to the stage and tried to look bewildered. She watched him fake it.

"Fellow citizens, please! Let us speak!" Yale tried to calm the crowd, but it was to no avail. Whatever the crew was expecting out of alien life, it was not that they would look nearly identical to themselves. Who would?

Sherii, who showed no sign of worry or concern that the crowd seemed to be in disbelief of his authenticity, stepped forward and raised his hands over the crewmates.

"Took te dah, took te dah jest de alles!" His voice instantly silenced the crew. If this was a ruse, it was an elaborate one. Sherii's voice was bold, calming and assurant even if they had no idea what he had said. The crew was engulfed by his presence nonetheless. He spoke with an accent that seemed so comfortable and yet foreign, a perfect mix of the familiar and different that kept them quietly waiting for the next syllables.

"De ti Sherii Angil, sun my gretta boost te fungallend jet te dah toy. Oost quin sun my gretta. Jekabah de angil soot jet te hunandara vest tiya myst toy."

Sherii stood still, his arms still raised towards the ceiling. The crew watched and waited for him to continue, but he did not. Moments passed before Captain Yale stepped forward to address his citizens, and only when he did did Sherii lower his hands to his side. He also began to remove his robe while Yale spoke.

"As you see before you, our new neighbors are much like us. Very much like us. And, in all incredibleness, exactly like us." Sherii laid the robe aside to reveal his trimmed and prestigious looking attire. It was a dress suit, complete with slacks and jacket, although its design was definitely not of Earthen origin. The cut was relaxed and casual looking, while maintaining an air of sophistication. Similar to Sherii's hair style, kept neat except long and easy. Yale continued.

"What I mean is that Sherii here, one of their leaders, has allowed us to take him on board and conduct a DNA test upon him. And to our happy surprise, he and the rest of his kind are human. We are the same humankind!"

"How? How is that possible!?" a voice erupted from the crew, with not a few cries of agreement and confusion.

Not how, but why. Was the question in Jesse's mind. Why would God create more humans on another planet?

"I've been conversing with our command staff and the answer that explains all of this the best is Universal Seeding. The Toiseeans, or as they call themselves, Jolethitee, are relatively un-surprised to discover there are more of us in the universe. Why? Because they, like us, know that a universe that creates life within itself and has existed for billions of years, must have had ancestors. Our common ancestors in the stars explain how even light-years apart, we can find our brothers and sisters in the far corners of the cosmos! It was only a matter of time!"

To this declaration, the crewmates acknowledged and began to clap in agreement with their captain. The concept of Universal Seeding was a theory that developed long ago to explain how life spontaneously developed on Earth.

That instead of life evolving from non-organic components, that Earth and potentially other habitable planets had been "cultivated with life". Human life was planted, its DNA somehow embedded into the Earth in the planet's early stages of development. This then eventually brought forth the humankind we see today, and if it was what happened on Earth, it certainly could happen elsewhere.

This proposed solution triggered a new response within Jesse. In the past, his faith would waiver and the resolve in his understanding of Biblical truth would hesitate. But instead, this time he felt offended. The indignation of humankind to assume that the only solution for the existence of fellow humans on another planet is that some unknown entity put them there aggravated him. If God had put humans on Earth, God also put humans on Toisee. Or Joleth? Jolethite? Whatever they called their planet. He furrowed his brow at the excitement of the crew and their willingness to accept what command told them was true. He didn't realize that Elena's eyes were still on him.

"You may have noticed that the countdown clock to Founding Day has not ceased counting. That is because Founding Day is still on!" Applause and cheers from the crowd. "Our new neighbors have graciously given us space to form our own colony upon their world. A beautiful location along the mountains, which are rich with the materials we need to build our gateway back to Earth. Citizens, we could not have hoped for a better new home than our beloved Toisee! A new world, and new friends to share it with!"

With this statement, Yale gripped the hand of Sherii and lifted it high with his own. Sherii was caught off guard for a moment but then followed suit and raised his own hands with Yale. They exchanged smiles between each other and peered out on the crowd as a united front of new humanity.

After the meeting concluded, the crew was nearly falling over itself to prepare for the Founding Day landing. Half of the crew lingered in the lyceum in an attempt to get a closer look at Sherii the pale human. The other half was rushing off to finish their last-minute duties before the ship broke apart.

Founding Day was the largest effort in the life of a HomeMaker starship. If the gateway jump was the appetizer, and the massive retro rockets slowing the ship was the salad, then the Founding Day starship division was the main course. HomeMaker's are designed to be everything that the colonists would need to survive on a virgin world, including the very colony structures itself. The starship will divide into 5 different main components that will then penetrate the atmosphere and land permanently upon the planet's surface, establishing the Meeting & Market Hall, Residences, Engineering, Agricultural and Excavation wing. Once launched from the main body of the HomeMaker starship, there is no going back as there is no way to reattach each wing. The last remaining piece in space, called the Gate Base, serves as the beginning structure for the slingshot gateway. There were many preparations needed to ensure this vast endeavor went off as smoothly as possible.

Jesse, Elena and the other Ag members were hard at work either securing the crops for delivery or planning and preparing for the installment of their first Toiseean garden. Jesse and Elena, along with Director Shea, were studying the maps provided by command of the landing sites. In all of the chaos they, nor anyone else for that matter, had a spare moment to themselves to weigh all of what just happened. There was simply too much to do.

"How many acres did you say we needed for adequate wheat production?" Shea asked out loud as she studied the layout of the farmland.

Elena considered a moment, then answered, "4 or 5 would be plenty, ma'am."

"Alright, we can use this last bit here -" Shea pointed towards the far corner of a plowed field on the map. "After the rest of the grains. That will keep all of them together in the same category. Nice and neat."

She stood up and checked her watch. "I will need you two to finalize these plans and get them submitted to command for approval. Once you have the go ahead, begin outlining to the reapers and seeders their first fields to cultivate."

"Yes, ma'am." Chimed both Jesse and Elena at the same time. Director Willow turned and walked briskly from the room, her mind already set on the next task to be accomplished. When Elena turned to Jesse to finally get some answers, Jesse had turned to the digitizer and was already inputting the cartographic data.

"So, Sherii is a pretty crazy sight, huh?" Elena leaned on the remaining maps of the farmland.

Jesse felt the inquisition coming and he couldn't stop it. "Ya, it's weird to see them for the first time." He never was a very good liar.

"Jesse, look at me."

He sighed and turned reluctantly. He looked at her as a child who is about to be chided.

"In the lyceum, instead of fixating on this big reveal of the first intelligent alien life form, you watched me as if you were sharing your favorite movie. As if you knew what was going to happen next. Why?"

"Look, you can't tell anyone. I didn't report this."

"I won't." Elena sat at the cartography desk, her attention all on him.

"It was supposed to be a covert mission. No one was supposed to see us."

"Ya, I know, Jesse. What happened?"

He looked around the obviously empty room. Mainly he was checking for security cameras, as some of the advanced labs had them. Noticing no surveillance equipment, he confided in her.

"I was wandering in the woods by the field we landed on. Collecting samples and just exploring a little. I came to a clearing in the forest, with a brook and everything. It was very pretty. And once I was in the middle of the clearing, I noticed two people watching me."

Elena's eyes shot wider. "What did they do?"

"I was about to run, but they came up to me. At least the little girl did."

"They were kids?!"

"I think so. I mean, the girl was probably 6 or 7? Her brother looked close to being a teenager."

"Did you talk to them? How did you know all that?" Her surprise was mounting. She figured he had seen someone from a distance or something like that. She didn't realize that Jesse could have experienced such an intimate connection with the Jolethitee.

"No... Well, ya. Yes, I did say bye when they were leaving." The memory came back to his mind of when he yelled God love you as his witness-goodbye, and he recalled the face that the boy had made. The shock and... fear? Was that what was on his face? It was hard to see, but Jesse did have the impression that he had said something wrong or offensive. He continued recounting the story.

"But, no, I just guessed that they were brother and sister. They held hands, he was protective of her... it seemed to fit. But anyways, she approached me and gave me a flower, so I took off my helmet and gave –"

"You took off your helmet?!" Elena held her hand to her mouth. "What were you thinking!? Jesse, you could have anything from that planet!"

"Ok, ok, calm down." He raised his hands towards her, attempting to placate her exclamation while looking at the door and windows to make sure no one was in earshot of her yell. "I did because when I got a good close look at how human they were, I felt like I was hiding behind a mask. They took the first step towards showing me a loving gesture, so I responded. I took off my helmet and gave her a flower from my sample tote."

"Ok, cute, but have you seriously not checked yourself for contamination?"

"That's what you're worried about? We're literally landing on this planet in a few hours."

"Just make sure you're one of the first to get inoculated, ok?" She lowered her hand back down slowly, deciding to trust that he is ok, regardless of her intuitive caution. She thought for a moment, breathed, and then spoke again.

"Wow, Jesse. I mean, that is a beautiful first encounter." She smiled at the imagery of him and her exchanging flowers in the woods.

"It scared the mess out of me. I had no idea what to do. But it was much easier when I could see just how like us they are. Honestly, I think the discovery of humankind elsewhere in the galaxy is more incredible than finding anything else weird or different."

"Why is that? You don't consider it just more of the same?"

"Well, think about it this way." Jesse was going to be careful with his words, but with this confession, he felt he could start to trust Elena more. "Captain Yale said that Universal Seeding is what explains finding humanity living on another planet other than Earth, right? What that would mean is that we are all created. Created by the same beings, or whatever, in the past. That unites us in ways that we never considered. Or at least never gave much thought to."

"Us and the Jolethitee? Ya. It's pretty neat to accept the gravity that we have others in the universe that are just like us." She was agreeing with him, but the tone of her voice said she wasn't getting the full picture yet.

"Ya, but what I mean is how it will unite us on Earth. Do you remember learning about how impossible it was to build the Archway Station? All of the nations and peoples of Earth bickering about this or that. Earth nations have so many different ideas and perspectives, it's as if we are living among aliens on our own planet sometimes. When we reveal to them that humanity exists on more than just one planet, all of us will realize that we truly do have a Creator that made all of us. That may break down every wall of difference we ever had!"

Elena nodded slowly, hearing what Jesse was saying. "A common Creator, huh?"

Jesse's eyes flashed in exposure for a quick second before he recovered. "Ya. Whoever did the Universal Seeding."

She nodded again. "I understand you. You're not wrong, that would be a big reveal to Earth. I'm not sure if it will solve all our problems, but you're right. It should get our attention on the bigger picture."

Inside Jesse's mind, a Scripture verse came to memory. Every tribe, tongue and nation will bow at the foot of the throne of Jesus. Was the reason he was called to this system so that he could preach to the Toiseeans? Or the Jolethites? What were they going to be called?

Jesse wanted to get back to his quarters and dive into the Bible verses that he could partially remember. His mind was beginning to fathom that the Scriptures about Jesus dying for the sins of the world... could that be Him dying for the sins of all the worlds where humans existed? At first consideration, believers of every tribe, tongue and nation could easily encompass these other humans on Toisee, right?

BRRRRRRRNNTT!!

His train of thought was interrupted by the ship intercom on the far wall.

HEARTSHIRE, AQUINO - WE NEED THOSE HORTICULTURAL PLANS TO COMMAND, ASAP!

"Yes, sir!" Elena responded. She gathered the other gaudy paper maps and set them down next to Jesse's digitizing terminal. "We'd better get on these before they throw a fit."

WHAT WAS THAT, AQUINO? DIDN'T COPY THE LAST STATEMENT.

Her and Jesse's eyes met and shot open wide. Jesse stifled a laugh as Elena slightly panicked.

"I said yes, sir! We are on our way shortly!"

GOOD, COMMAND OUT.

As Jesse erupted into laughter, she threw a pen at him. He wouldn't let her forget it for the next few minutes as they modified and prepared the crop plans for the colony garden.

CHAPTER 15
FOUNDING DAY

 These long days really felt long when they were full of so much duty to perform. Jesse had been up late the night before, obviously not able to sleep due to the upcoming covert mission to the planet surface. Even with the excitement of the landing and his chance encounter with the Jolethite siblings, the stress of keeping most of that to himself was exhausting. It felt better to release it to Elena, and with the rest of the crew being quickly exposed to Sherii after first contact, the danger of someone discovering his benign chance meeting seemed low in terms of consequences. However, he didn't want to let his guard down.

 Expressing to Elena his understanding of the origin of the humans on Toisee, as well as on Earth, felt like a guise. It wasn't a lie, but he still felt guilty about not coming full circle with his beliefs on the matter. He didn't know what she would think about his explanation that the Universal Seeder in all of this was not an ancient alien race, but the Lord Almighty. After all, the official charter of the colony itself was still an abolishment of any religious practice, and even if she was understanding of his position, he doubted others would be.

 This is another reason Jesse very much wanted to return to his quarters. He was fatigued, but also the answers for some of his questions lay in the Scriptures he was hiding. With the witness of the Bible, maybe he could convince her how God could have created the humans on Toisee just as easily as an ancient alien race could. In fact, he hoped that the principles of Occam's razor would apply: that the simplest explanation tends to be the true one. And what would be more simple… ancient aliens or an all-powerful God? He knew he would say that YHWH was much more likely, but would she?

 Unfortunately for him, however, immediately after transferring the digitized copies of the horticultural charts to command, he and Elena were ordered to report to their "landing seats". As with the launch of the HomeMaker from the Lunar Slingshot Gateway, this meant they got to watch everything from the cramped escape pods as a precaution. At least the perk was since they were together, they sat side by side.

Many of the crew as they made their way to their seats were high-fiving and shouting for joy at the excitement of landing on the planet. The mood that had been tense before first contact was now the exact opposite, where tension and nervousness was replaced with elation and ease. Now, the general expectation by most was that things were going to be easier when establishing the colony as previously expected. With the planet populated already, they apparently had friends nearby to help with the move in. There was no need to create an elaborate or overly secure perimeter against unknown aggressive animals or another danger. The engineers didn't have to clear and raze the land in order for the agricultural personnel to even consider how to start planting crops. Everything was going to come easier as the colonists themselves didn't have to start from scratch. Actually, a few of the crew started to refer to themselves as immigrants and not colonists at all.

In consideration of the local population, mandates were coming down from command already on how the colonists should conduct themselves among the Jolethite. This started as a way of combating rumors that were being spread about how an entire planet of other potential spouses existed meant there was no need to collect GEM matches anymore. Captain Yale and the HomeMaker leadership wanted to make it clear that although we will be sharing space with the Jolethite, this was still going to be a Venture colony and it needed to conduct itself as one. Strict guidelines were distributed to every crewmate's tablet, including prohibitions on excursions beyond the territory allotted to the colony by the Jolethite, as well as rigid requirements for any Earther to Jolethite interaction. According to the new mandates, Jesse's encounter with the siblings in the forest was punishable by imprisonment in the brig and forfeiture of all shipwide rank, rations and privileges. A steep punishment he would like to avoid.

As he strapped himself into the seat, and Elena alongside his right, he began to pray. Eyes open, staring blankly into the stars beyond. He looked for familiar constellations but could of course find none. There was no comfort to be found in them in terms of any homey dearness to him. They weren't his stars, but he did know that they were God's. This is what his prayer centered around, that although he will be settling into a place so very foreign to him, that he would remember that YHWH is God of the Universe. All of this is still God's domain. He prayed that he would come to accept it, and see God's loving touch in it just as much as he saw it on the family farm in Carolina.

There was a jolt. A deep shudder whose waves vibrated so low in frequency that Jesse could barely perceive them, except for the enormous power behind it. Elena's hand reached over to his and latched upon his knuckles as he gripped the handlebars. He looked over at her.

"You don't mind do you?" She asked with a bit of a shake in her throat.

He shook his head at her. "No." He tried to lean over but the straps were so tight he barely managed an inch. "It's going to be alright. We're taken care of." He let go of the handlebar and held her hand on top of his thigh.

She nodded and returned her eyes to the stars that Jesse had used for prayer inspiration. The intercom spoke to life.

HOMEMAKER LANDING SEQUENCE HAS BEEN INITIATED. ALL CREW AND WINGS SECURED. DIVISION OF WINGS WILL COMMENCE IN T-MINUS 10 SECONDS.

The landing pod applauded and cheered. Jesse watched Elena close her eyes. She held them tight as the numbers dwindled.

10… 9… 8… 7… 6… 5… 4… 3… 2… 1… DIVISION COMMENCE.

The low-level rumble that had continued suddenly slowed. BANG! Only to release in mild violence as the bottom 11 levels detached from the remaining top 5. They stayed static and still in close proximity to each other. The decks were separate but not separating further, two large buildings floating in orbit.

PREPARE FOR LOSS OF GRAVITY. DEACTIVATING SINGULARITY DRIVE. BING BING!!

The lights inside the escape pod, as with the entirety of the starship, gave an audible and visual warning for the loss of gravity created by the singularity drive. This was needed because when the drive is cut on or off, gravity or the lack thereof instantly follows. There is no cool down period. As the lights of the pod resumed their normal glow, a number of small items began to float around. A few specks of dirt, a pencil… and a half drunk bottle of soda? The crewmate that had brought the bottle reached out for it but was unable to secure the bottle before it drifted out of his grasp. In his effort, he knocked the lid off, and globules of brown cola began flowing from the open container. This brought chuckles from Jesse and moans of annoyance from someone else down the line of seats. There was another loud bang, but this one felt distant. Far from where this escape pod was situated on the side of the Ag wing.

COMMAND SECTION GRAPPLE COMPLETE. ELEVATOR MOTOR ENGAGED. LANDING THRUSTERS FIRING.

There might not be gravity at the moment but the thrust of the landing jets pushed the occupants of the escape pod upward against their shoulder restraints. The landing thrusters were giving the landable sections of the HomeMaker a push down towards the planet, away from the singularity drive and command section that will remain in space. This portion is tethered to the center of the colony buildings down below, and acts as a miles long materials elevator to transport components to space to build the gateway. The drive acts as an anchor for it from orbit in space.

RE-ACTIVATING SINGULARITY DRIVE. GRAVITY ANCHOR ESTABLISHED.

The detached buildings of the HomeMaker were steadily making its way towards the planet with the tether attached to the command section. The pull of the singularity drive was now going to lower the attached buildings in a controlled fall towards the planet by way of the elevator tether. Landing thrusters were gently radiating from the bottoms of the buildings already, as the atmosphere was beginning to burn red around its foundational edges. Due to the immense size of the multi story buildings that were landing on Toi, the occupants didn't experience much more than some minor jolts and jostles. Elena's hand remained gripped firmly to Jesse's palm, and despite the pain of her grasp, he didn't really mind.

The entry of the landing sections of the HomeMaker was slower than that of a shuttle's atmospheric entry to Toi, but it was still fast enough to be dangerous. From the ground, the sight would have been extremely unsettling, seeing a giant fireball descend from space onto your home land. And with the thickness of the atmosphere of Toi, the light show was increasingly spectacular. The landing thrusters shifted the trajectory of the falling buildings left and right, ensuring as best they could that the precise location decided upon was where they would end up. Once landed, these structures were unmovable again.

Out the porthole window Jesse and the others saw nothing but grey clouds for what seemed an eternity. But just as the ride smoothed out, the clouds broke instantly. The canopy of the grey sky continued to recede and revealed a remarkable view of what would be their new home. As they cruised steadily lower from 2 miles up, the expanse was breathtaking.

Rocky mountains, cragged and jagged stretched from the left side of the window out towards the horizon. There, a few miles away, they seemed to turn and run right, completing a snowy peaked backdrop for the lowland valleys before them. These valleys were the customary shapes of plowed farmland, but without all of the usual color. There were not many green nor brown shades to be seen, but varying shades of blues, turquoise and purple. Fields that appeared to be filled with royal to navy tulips or another equally bright variety checkerboarded the landscape, alongside forested areas puffy with trees sporting azure, violet and even occasional ruby foliage. Jesse and Elena knew that these fields were most likely not flowers but crops to feed the Jolethites. It was going to take some getting used to, eating a salad of blue vegetation. They hadn't discovered any livestock yet, but Jesse had considered within himself that he could stomach blue lettuce, but he didn't know about green or yellow meat.

FINAL DIVISION OF HOMEMAKER WINGS IN 3... 2... 1... NOW!

The occupants of the escape pod shot forward against their restraints. Elena's hand nearly broke Jesse's but he still refused to let go. Each of the wings completed their final separation from the descending center of the colony starship. With that came a brief but nightmarish full second of freefall, until the Ag Wing's own retro thrusters fired and caught the building's descent. A few crewmates, including Elena, let out a startled yelp when they felt the rockets catch the wing's fall. Now each of the wings drifted away from the meeting hall in the center, which the elevator tether remained attached to.

Seen from above, the separation looked very symmetrically pleasing. Each of the 4 wing buildings drifted simultaneously apart from the center, and large, ground penetrating studs began to emerge from their bases, sharp and looking like athletic shoe spikes. There were many of these leveling supports that dotted the soles of the buildings. Retro rockets fired loudly and with enough force to toss grown trees aside, clearing the ground for touchdown. Dust and debris from all 5 buildings grew so high that nearly half of their height was lost in the swirly tempest. Then, while feeling the twist and tip of the Ag Wing tossed about by the rocket's thrust, suddenly came a solidly immovable THUD to Jesse and his fellow passengers. Hydraulic whines emitted from the walls behind them that grew louder with effort as the foundational studs were forced into the ground beneath them. The building was steady but contortions and creaks could be heard as the studs leveled out the wing. These eased the view out the porthole window ever so slightly more to the right, evening the foundation. And with a final hiss of the release of the hydraulic pressure, the Ag Wing was settled into its final rest upon the surface of Toisee. Founding Day could now begin.

    Most of the preparations and events for Founding Day were celebratory and not necessarily progressive for the colony itself. However, It was progressive for the mood of the colonists themselves, and even if the original idea was to commemorate the breaking of virgin ground, the Toiseean Colony was still the beginning of a new era for humanity. Even with the language barrier, Jolethite Leader Sherii had understood enough to provide some local food and drink to participate in the Founding Day party. This was incorporated into a feast that was planned and prepared by the 4 wing directors. Agriculture Wing was bringing the rest of the food essentials, Excavation was to prepare the space, Engineering the facilities and Residential to provide entertainment. A normal Founding Day celebration was designed to only last a single day, as establishing the colony itself was a looming task in the back of everyone's mind, but with the welcome of Sherii and his people this was not nearly as pressing of a concern. There might even be leftovers for another day or two.

    The cool, crisp air of Toisee was welcomed by all. All except for that Brazilian lady that made a play at Jesse on GEM Night a month ago. It was an overcast day, of course, but the large red sun was still radiating light through despite the coverage of clouds. The blazing color of the clouds made it feel odd that the ambient temperature was close to 40 degrees. It was a pleasant sensation on the cheeks and exposed arms to feel the warmth of the star against the cold breeze.

    As Jesse and the other Ag specialists brought out the food carts from the main entrance of the Ag Wing building, he could finally witness exactly how prepared the colony site already was. A pressed gravel roadway met them as they descended the Ag Wing ramp, and by the look of it, it had been there and used for quite some time. This was the exception, as the other colony wings did not have an already prepared space to disembark, but it did reveal that this area was already lived in before they planted the colony. Light poles were also present along the gravel road, and could be traced going into the distance, following the road into the nearby blue forest. Each pole had a cable attached, which meant they must have run by some type of electricity, and as Jesse followed them back towards the Ag Wing with his eyes he noticed that the last pole nearby the Ag wing had a cable attached to it that disappeared under the wing itself.

Did we land on something? Jesse pondered curiously. He tried to remember any kind of crunching or squishing during the landing, but then instantly abandoned the hope of the memory due to the enormous girth of the Ag Wing building. If they had landed on anything other than solid rock, it would have been crushed as if it were made of paper or dust.

He continued to follow the train of specialists and party supplies to what will now be the hub of all colony activity, the City Lyceum. This was of course the gathering place used by Captain Yale to introduce GEM Night and Leader Sherii aboard the starship version of the HomeMaker, but now it was the central building in the middle of the colony complex. It stood the shortest of all the landed wings at only 3 stories high compared to the wing's 10. Although, because it was connected to the gateway elevator tether, it appeared to reach past the heavens. The elevator was attached to the rear of the building, climbing out of its roof as if an impossible chimney with no end. The glass top of the lyceum was still the same as from the starship and it was apparent this is where the party was to take place as the building glowed and lights danced from this crest. 1303 was the City Lyceum's right cornerstone and the colony command offices were on the left. Jesse and the party train were heading straight into the middle of the building, where the entrance was widest and led straight to the glass toped gathering place.

As Jesse scanned the horizon line around the colony, he could trace the gravel road emerging from the forest a mile or two away. It seemed to lead into a small village, where simple homes or huts were erected along the roadway. It would appear they had neighbors that were not too far off. Parked around these homes were what Jesse had first thought were vehicles, but looking closer he noticed that at the front of one of them was some kind of large animal similar to a horse. It honestly could have been a horse, from this distance he couldn't see detail, but based on that cat thing they found yesterday he very much doubted it. Living further out from the city must have meant these Jelothite were not as technologically privileged. Jesse remembered the look of the siblings he ran across, their tattered clothes and lack of shoes.

"Heartshire, your supply and Smiths are going to 1303." Junior Ag Director Ralph Kitting was standing with his tablet by the entrance to the City Lyceum. Apparently, he was in charge of this end of the organization.

"Yes, sir." Jesse acknowledged and redirected his cart, Jolean Smith turned hers as well a few specialists behind him. There was no path here, and in actuality it seemed they were trudging through a formerly farmed field. The wheels of the cart were occasionally stuck on the ruts and valleys of the previously tilled soil. Jesse's brow creased as he realized this field had the appearance of being tilled recently. A loud machine whirred to life somewhere behind him, and as he turned to look, he could see excavation specialists manning some kind of paver.

The machine started to smooth a pathway from the entrance of the command offices on the left of the City Lyceum. It moved easy enough due to it being the same tilled ground that Jesse pushed across. The excavation team then turned it back towards the command offices again. Instead of a pathway, the team seemed to be building out some kind of large patio area in front of the lyceum, but across the way in front of the residential wing, Jesse could spy another paving team doing the exact same thing there. Perhaps the goal was to smooth out an entire courtyard between all of the colony buildings? That would make sense.

Jesse turned back to pushing his cart, wishing they had done his current section already due to all the small rocks and ground divots he was hitting. Looking up and forward towards his destination of the ground entrance to 1303, his eyes then scanned the far wing and the forest edge past the City Lyceum's right side. Past the corner of 1303, the wing in the distance was the Engineering wing, where exiting its large, rolled doors was what looked like drilling and electrical equipment. He knew that the ag wing had automatic watering systems that would be installed within any fields they cultivated, so the water wells would need to be dug, plumbed and powered. Also, he had not seen any lakes or rivers nearby, so they must be setting up the entire colony's water supply.

Beyond all of this commotion was the forest tree line, where Jesse also caught glimpses of pale figures standing against the blue hued foliage. Local Jolethite's seemed to be watching all of the colonist action unfold. Jesse started to wonder what might be on their mind, watching all of this organized chaos and commotion. He thought about if these alien humans even understood much of what they were doing or if –

They're sad.

Jesse stopped his cart momentarily, only a few steps from the entrance of 1303. He'd had a thought enter his consciousness that was not his own. His own ponderings were taking his mind along a path of consideration wrapped up in what these Jolethite humans thought of what these Earthlings were doing, not what they were feeling. But Jesse suddenly had a strong external intuition that those who watched from the forest were saddened and hurt by the colonists' arrival. He felt like the Holy Spirit was trying to tell him something, and that something was that he needed to teach others to be gentle around the Jolethites. Why?

Because they just lost part of their home to us. Jesse glanced again at the site of where the Ag Wing had landed. The gravel pathway the colonists had trod, which was flanked by the electric light poles... Is their home under our building?! Jesse's heart now hurt at the realization that they surely have crushed something dear to the locals. Oh Jesus, please don't let there be anyone buried under our colony!

He looked out and around at the plowed field that was being made level and walkable by the excavating team, who was now also beginning to pave the courtyard with another machine. Jesse's empathy was again drenched by the idea that not only did they crush a home, but they are demolishing their livelihood by paving and then partying upon their food supply. He shot his eyes again towards the tree line, looking for the locals, trying to devise a way to help heal the hurt his colony had caused.

"Jesse, move your damn cart, will ya? What are you doing?!" Jolean had caught up with him and was nearly running over his heels with her supply wagon. Jesse reacted quickly and hoisted his cart over the dirt humps and into the entrance of 1303.

"Ya, sorry!" He hollered over his shoulder at her. Once he was in the clear, he parked it to the side and trotted to help her with her load.

"Thanks. Daydreaming about the new world already?" She asked him, as it was apparent his mind was elsewhere.

"Ya, a bit, sorry." He apologized again. They both guided their carts into the storage area of 1303 and emerged again at its entrance. Jesse scanned the tree line for the locals, but they had disappeared. Jolean glanced out towards the right where the rest of the Ag Team was milling about in front of the City Lyceum, having finished their loads too. "Are we done?"

"I dunno, they aren't too busy it looks like." She pointed to the other Ag Specialists, but then pulled out her tablet. "I don't see any more command announcements yet."

Jesse retrieved his CAPA tablet as well. He also had no more general announcements, but he did see a communication notification from Shea to all CAPA members. Apparently, there was a new mission prerogative that Jesse and Rin had just been assigned. Looking through the first few lines, it seemed like it had something to do with follow up on their covert spy run yesterday.

"Oh, I've got something for CAPA though." He mentioned.

"Alright, well, have fun with that!" She said dismissively and started off for the rest of the Ag group. Jesse did feel special not to have to deal with all of the party preparations, but when he noticed Elena chit-chatting with another couple men in the crowd, he did feel a twinge of jealousy that he couldn't head over himself.

Before reporting to the CAPA meeting room, Jesse finally had a few minutes to retreat to his own quarters. After unlocking and opening the door, he slumped into his desk chair and let out a tremendous sigh. The dimmed light of the evening was casting an ominous red hue upon everything on his desk in front of him thanks to his new window. Jesse had no view of the stars at all from space, but due to his quarters sharing a wall with another wing of the HomeMaker, now that they were detached, he had a tremendous view. Outside the clouds hid what must be a spectacular sunset over the mountains, where ruby red rays of setting sun stabbed through weak points in the grey blanket shrouding the valley. From his vantage point, he could see the far village more clearly. Even with the darkening of the valley, the village had not yet illuminated its streets or homes. Jesse could still make out their outlines in the fading sunlight, and perhaps a small flashlight or torch here and there, slowly drifting down the main stretch of road. And a torch must have been what it was, as when the light happened upon a streetlamp, the single glow multiplied into two. The locals appeared to be lighting the streetlamps manually.

Jesse, being short on time, tore himself from the view and fetched his Bible from its hiding place. It had been pressing on his heart from the moment he exchanged flowers with the little girl, and he now wanted to validate his feelings on the matter. How and why is it possible that God had created humankind on multiple planets?

How, well, that seemed explained easily enough. If God had molded Adam and Eve from the dirt, then breathed life into them on Earth, obviously He did the same thing for the Jolethites. Jesse thought that God creating 2, 200, or 2 million humans by hand, or by word of mouth, did not seem hard to wrap his head around. You could even use the vernacular that Jesse had borrowed from Captain Yale, that God himself was the Universal Seeder that planted humanity among not just one star, but all the stars where they would appear.

Jesse looked again in the beginning of Genesis for his peace of mind, where Genesis 1:27 said "God created mankind in his image." By his own logical understanding, it would mean that as long as Earthlings and Jolethites carried the same DNA, they would both be considered created as the Image Bearers of God. With his special CAPA clearance, he was given privileged access to some command files that the general population was not allowed. He trusted Captain Yale and his own eyes enough to see that they were as human as he was, but to be completely sure, he would need to see the DNA readings themselves.

So, he typed out a message to Director Willow, claiming he needed access to Sherii's DNA files to compare nutritional requirements and absorption rates to test our own digestibility of Toiseean vegetation. He wasn't lying, as this was also a part of his normal responsibilities, to ensure that the colonists could ingest local food without incident. But his ulterior motives might have been a bit more discrete.

While he waited for a response from Shea, he turned his attention back to the other side of God's purpose in creating multiple humans on multiple planets. Jesse was frustrated that he could only use the Bible he had in front of him for this research and wished he had been in more practice before leaving on this mission. At home, he could use his tablet to find commentaries, theological discussions and sermon notes to find his answers quickly, but any such search within the database of the HomeMaker would be discovered and traced back to him. In order to stay under the radar, his research had to remain cognitive, prayerful and analog.

God does like diversity, right? Jesse thought. *The different races of humans that exist prove that God must enjoy similar things to be slightly different. Same way that an apple doesn't taste like an orange, or a banana, or a kiwi. God didn't have to create diversity in flavor or color. He could have made a bland world, but He didn't. Is that why they were here? Just another different flavor of human?* Jesse didn't love that explanation. His insight made him feel it had to be another reason.

What is the main reason that you're here? There was the Holy Spirit again, dropping ideas into his mind. Jesse considered then answered in his thoughts.

To love God, to love Jesus in return.

Deeper, Jesse.

To live life with God? ... I don't know what you're getting at.

Jesse, You, specifically, why are you here?

You called me to follow you to the stars.

"By this the world will know you are my disciples..."

Jesse's head was starting to get confused with the internal dialogue between himself and the Spirit. Maybe next time he would try replying out loud instead of speaking and listening internally. But the Spirit was quoting a passage to Jesse. He needed to find it.

He opened to the gospels, and the first one he hit was the Gospel of John. By the quote it sounded as if Jesus was speaking to his disciples, so Jesse instinctively started reading just the red text lines. He had always been annoyed at red-letter Bibles. If the whole Bible is the Word of God, and all of it was 'God-breathed', then why draw special attention to the words of Jesus as if they are more important? It was as if the printers were claiming these particular verses are double blessed. A silly notion, but one he was grateful for at the time as it made his skim-reading faster and easier.

Soon Jesse found himself scanning the correct passage in John 13, where he found the beginning of the verse that the Spirit had reminded him of.

John 13:34, "By this all people will know that you are my disciples, if you have love for one another."

"So, love? That's the reason?" Jesse thought aloud, but there was no answer in the Spirit. If it was simply about love, he supposed God in his infinite love could have made more humans just to love them more.

But wait, the Spirit quoted this wrong... Jesse noticed that when the Holy Spirit had mentioned in his head to look for this verse, the Spirit had said "so that the world would know", not that "all people would know". As he started looking at the other verses for context, his eyes happened across Gus's notes in the margin of the page. Written off to the side was: "Our love for our fellow Christ-made souls is our witness to the world."

I called you here to love my church.

Jesse heard that. He heard it loud and clear. Gus's words provided the understanding that he needed so he could hear what the Spirit wanted him to know. Jesse was brought 100 lightyears from Earth, not to do anything new and special, but to continue to do the same thing that the 12 apostles were told to do by Jesus, himself. He was called here to follow Jesus by loving others. To love Christ's people, as a witness to the world.

Wait... the world? Is that just Earth, or could that mean the 'entire universe'? Jesse glanced to see if this Bible had any footnotes at the bottom that could give him any idea. Unfortunately, there was nothing. He dove into his memory, to see if there was any other verse that would come to mind. For God so loved the world... John 3:16?

He thumbed his way over to the beginning of the gospel. Without much effort this time, Jesse found one of the most famous verses in the Scriptures and he read.

"For God so loved the world, that he gave his only Son, that whoever believes in him should not perish but have eternal life." Jesse read it out loud to himself, trying to get used to speaking the words of Scriptures out loud. It felt weird reading them to himself in his room, but he thought that he was going to need the practice. And there were more of Gus's scribblings in the margins, with an arrow coming off of 'the world'. It read, "The world = Kosmos, all of creation".

Jesse's heart skipped a beat.

Did the Bible just say what he thought it said? He read 3:16, then Gus's notes again. *Kosmos? As in the whole of the universe?* Jesse threw caution aside and jumped onto his tablet. He felt he could at least explain away one curiosity if he was questioned about his usage.

He typed into the research screen, 'meaning - kosmos', and allowed the tablet to compile the information for him. Is 'kosmos' the same as 'cosmos'? The entirety of the universe? Sure enough, the definition that came back confirmed his speculation.

KOSMOS - GREEK ORIGIN, MEANING ORDER, ARRANGEMENT. ALSO UNIVERSE, THE WORLD.

Jesse looked back into the Scriptures and wrote above the word 'world', the word KOSMOS, and then he re-read the verse out loud.

"For God so loved the KOSMOS, that he gave his only Son, that whoever believes in him should not perish but have eternal life."

Jesse was in awe. His mind was bouncing with joy and elation, astoundment and wonder. According to his new understanding of this verse, Jesus died not only for the Earth and for humans, but he died for Toisee and the Jolethites. With every breath in this moment, his purpose and reason for being on this mission was becoming more and more clear. His determination was solidifying into a faith that he didn't think was ever possible for himself. Seeing this verse and understanding it in its vast meaning for the first time ignited something within Jesse. A fire so intense now that he couldn't put it out even if he wanted to.

Jesse was eager to get to the Founding Day celebrations, which had started without the members of CAPA nearly an hour ago. Supposedly this meeting was brief, and although everyone was seated and ready, Director Shea had yet to arrive. Glancing around the room, the other members of the team were equally as annoyed. Kincade let it be known.

"Mueller, it's nearly 20 past now. Can't we assume that Shea ain't gonna be here and we can get to the party?" He had his feet up, but dropped them and readied himself for his departure from his chair and the room.

"Mr. Kincade, the festivities will still be there no matter how tardy Director Willow is."

"Ya, but everyone else will be at least 2 or 3 drinks ahead of me! I don't want to be the late and sober one!"

"Well, I am the bearer of bad news, I'm afraid. Captain Yale had made it clear to command that this was to be an alcohol limited event."

Kincade thrust his hands out upon the table, open palmed in disgust. "What!?"

"He set the limit at only 3. There will be Jolethites present tonight, and we don't want to set a poor first impression."

"Isn't that his problem? Why are they gonna care about some drunk guard?"

"Because we met this planet's population only hours ago, and I'd rather we maintain our established reputation, Mr. Kincade." Captain Yale had entered behind Roger's seat, with Director Willow in tow. He circled around the meeting table, where each one of the members of CAPA straightened themselves and looked with attention at the captain.

"Surely, even a grunt like yourself understands that you don't present all of your faults on the first date?" Captain Yale stopped and stood behind Mueller, his hands clasped behind his back. He stared down Roger Kincade and ensured he understood the seriousness in his tone.

"Yes, sir." Roger sighed, but it was a sigh of submission. "I understand."

Yale stood up straight and looked about the room. "Members of CAPA, I have relayed your mission prerogatives to Director Willow, but I wanted to stand before you to ensure I have impressed upon each of you the weight of your next mission. The lifeblood of our successful colony here on Toisee is embedded in the Ag Wing's ability to sustain us independently from the Jolethites. They have provided us this territory in order to do that, and they will be providing support along the way. However, in order to maintain the hierarchy of our arrangement, I want this colony to be self-regulated by the colony's first crop cycle." The hierarchy of our arrangement? What did that mean? Jesse's mind captured that mention from Captain Yale and mulled it over.

"Once our crops have yielded fruit and our livestock follows suit, I want us to be experts in Toiseean agriculture. This will ensure that our continued colonial growth minimizes outside influence from the local population, and only ever remains dominant in our negotiations. Am I understood?"

Nods and 'yes, sirs' murmured throughout the room. Apparently, Captain

Yale had the upper hand when arriving on this planet and he wanted to keep it that way. Jesse could imagine Leader Sherii and the others being generally in awe of the arrival of a space vessel when they had no such technology. Then to realize that the alien race was identical to themselves, the impressiveness of the advanced knowledge would ebb away to a realization that it could be theirs one day given enough time, or trade, or theft. Yale seemed to understand that his relationship with Sherii and the Jolethites was most beneficial to the colony when they compromised due to needing or wanting things from him, and not the other way around.

"Of course, we have established a colony within the borders of their country, and so interaction with the Jolethites is a foregone conclusion. However, due to the nature of your assignments, you members of CAPA will be in direct, close contact relationships with the local population. Each one of you, even you Kincade, are acting ambassadors for this colony, and that means I am expecting each one of you to act with the consideration of what is best for us in mind. At all times, and in every interaction, you will guard what you have and know as privileged members of Toisee Colony as if it were your very life. Because it is."

At this point Mueller interjected, eager to sound authoritative in front of her boss. "You all have read and reviewed the Local Jolethite Command Mandate?" She looked around the room for assurant nods, but moved on without confirming. "That is the baseline expectation for all colonists. As members of CAPA, we are entrusting you to follow that exactly. Do not relax among the Jolethites. They are our neighbors, not our friends."

"Thank you, Mueller." Captain Yale watched the faces of the CAPA team. Each one, including Jesse, was listening intently and absorbing the seriousness of the situation. He seemed content with what he saw in their eyes. Without looking down at his subordinate below him, he spoke.

"You have each performed very well so far in your assignments. I am aware this is not what we were expecting, strangers upon our planet. But with time and care, this will still become the Toisee that we had planned for all along. Members of CAPA, go enjoy yourselves for the night, and report in for the beginning of your special duties at 0900 tomorrow."

Yale glanced down at Roger Kincade, who was sitting and listening as a model citizen. Those who knew Roger well knew he was simply turning on the charm a bit, and there was little to no doubt that Yale knew it as well, but that didn't stop the captain from dropping one more bit of influence over the CAPA team as a treat for good behavior. He looked right at Roger but spoke to his junior command officer.

"Mueller?"

"Yes, sir?" She responded.

"Allow the CAPA team 2 extra alcohol rations tonight."

Roger grinned and clapped his hands. "Thank you, sir!" He yelled enthusiastically. The other members of the CAPA team clapped briefly as well.

Jesse, who was already feeling free to enjoy himself tonight through the revelation of the Scriptures earlier, clapped as well. He had heard the restrictions on sharing tech and knowledge with the Jolethite people, but he remained undeterred. He wasn't interested in sharing anything with them but himself and his faith, one way or another. This new assignment was exactly the excuse he needed to interact face to face with the people that God had called him lightyears away from home to. And he couldn't wait to get started.

CHAPTER 16
PREACHING TO THE CHOIR

The Founding Day celebration was quite the festival. It felt like another GEM Night, except bigger. The Ag and Residential Wing were told to spare no expense in their preparation of food, and the buffet lines showed it. Although, the most popular line of the night wasn't those nor even the drinks table (surprisingly, but most likely due to the limit), but the Jolethite offerings of welcome. Most of the colonists seemed to take to their first introduction to Jolethite food rather well.

The tables included various raw fruit and vegetable offerings, paired with sweet, spicy, and savory dips. The fruits resembled Earth fruits, but with a twist such as purple peach-like things or miniature granny smith-like apples. On the vegetable side, the surprise hit was the 'wheat bananas', so called due to their shape, color and even texture, which was similar to a ripe banana, but that tasted bready and was served with a garlic butter like sauce. There were also salad offerings of the purple spinach plants that Jesse had analyzed on their covert mission, mixed in with other 'greens' that were not green at all but blue and hazel.

After the sun had descended behind the far mountains, the temperature had dropped a little. Due to the near constant thick cloud cover of Toisee, the ambient temperature didn't actually fluctuate too much. It only felt cooler due to the lack of bright red sunshine. The colonists' breath could be seen, and everyone was wearing their matching Venture Colony jumpers and jackets. These were coveralls and matching coats that had been issued to each member of the colony. Due to the sea of green and gold, it wasn't hard to find the strangers among them.

Jolethite men and women were there, alongside Leader Sherii, who were watching and bowing to all who would acknowledge them. The language barrier meant they mostly smiled and nodded and waved their hands towards the food offerings they had brought, welcoming the colonists to sample again and again.

They even had some speakers set up, playing Jolethite music that sounded very similar to the broadcast that got the HomeMaker's attention initially. Apparently, that radio signal they received once they arrived was the first nationwide broadcast that United Joleth had ever attempted. It was part of a national holiday celebration, where songs, food and mirth were lavished upon the citizens of the country in extra portions.

A number of the crewmates were approaching the Jolethites with their tablets, having cleared the screen and using their fingers, they attempted to communicate with them using rudimentary pen and paper like drawings. This was mildly successful at best and at least elicited a few laughs and easy connections between the races. A few of the colonists offered Earthen food to them as well, in an effort to see if they would enjoy things or not, but the Jolethites smiled and refused. Either they knew they didn't like it already or they were instructed to be polite and distant from the festivities.

There were also many games the colonists could participate in. Amazingly, in the span of the long afternoon after landing, the Excavation wing was able to clear and level the entire courtyard area of the colony and erect a soccer field as well as a baseball diamond. While obviously not to scale in terms of its officiality, the colonists rotated in and out casually while making their rounds back to the buffet tables, or to the dance floor inside the City Lyceum.

The glass top of the lyceum sparkled and flashed with the brilliance of the northern lights, throwing rays into the night sky that were reflected back by the low hanging clouds. Inside the mood was jovial and light, and the music chosen for the evening reflected that. Most of it was poppy and uptempo, with a slow number tossed in occasionally. This is where Jesse had found Elena, slowly shuffling with her arm around a big excavation professional.

He watched them for a while from a distance. Jealousy played with his emotions, especially considering how close and firmly he had pulled her, but mainly he was trying to decide what he truly felt about this situation. Elena and he had a great relationship, they were good friends, and he felt he could confide in her, to an extent. And that was what he was considering. If he was going to have any kind of romantic relationship with anyone, he needed to be completely honest and transparent about why he was here. And, ideally, she would have to reciprocate that purpose. At the very least, Elena or whoever would have to be supportive, but realistically she would need to convert.

Is that right though? Should I be 'converting' my future wife? If she changed her views for me, would that mean she did it because she loves me, and not Jesus?

Jesse continued to fight his feelings, and because he could feel his envy rising beyond rationality, he decided it would be best to participate in the games outside. And so he was distracted and eventually lost himself to running among his fellow crewmates. The crisp air burned his throat and lungs, but he didn't care. It made him feel vigorously alive. He thanked God in his mind for the gift that this journey had been so far. For all the things he had discovered about His creation and Jesse's own life. The Founding Day celebration was a great time, running about on the soccer field, and in the morning, he would be running again, this time onto his mission field.

The Cultivated Asset Procurement and Analysis team assembled in front of the City Lyceum at 0900 the following morning. Looking at the sky, the sun may actually have a chance of appearing directly as the clouds were high and thin. Glimpses of blue could possibly be seen in the distance. But looking around at the faces of those ready for their adventure into town, the disposition was less than sunny.

Each member of the team, aside from Jesse, wore long faces that had a want for longer rest. Even Junior Command Mueller seemed a bit off her game this morning, her hair a bit disheveled and out of place. Jesse tried to curtail his excitement, especially around Roger who seemed as if he would hit the first person that wished him a 'good morning'.

"Alright, everyone gather close." Mueller pulled out her tablet and flicked forward on the screen. Each member of CAPA pulled out their own tablets and selected the map that Annaliese had shared with the group. It was an aerial photo of the nearby village and surrounding countryside, assumedly taken from a recon drone.

"We are tasked with entering the local village and securing relationships with the local populace. Our goal is to establish means of communication, then eventually curry favor in effort to elicit support of the local cultivators to support our own independence."

"Good gosh, woman. English please!" Roger rubbed his head.

"You've read the mission prerogatives, haven't you?" She retorted. Roger stared at her blankly. Rin piped up.

"We're going to make friends with the village, and get them to help us start our farms, Roger." She stated simply.

"Why didn't you just say that?" Kincade pointed at Mueller and waved in dismissal. "I'll just watch your backs. You do the talking."

"That's exactly what we are hoping for, thank you." Mueller responded sarcastically. "The same pairings as before, Rin, you and Jesse. I'll stick with Zuri. Kincade, stay with the Scouts. Let's get going." Her use of Roger's last name and the others first name insinuated her disdain for him. Although, they had supposedly shared a dance last night, which led Jesse and the others to believe that they were GEM matches, and they both hated every bit of it.

The Scouts that Annaliese had referred to were beefy, all terrain, electric scooters that each member of the CAPA team had been issued for this morning's mission. They had multiple saddlebags and containers to hold whatever the members needed, and enough ground clearance to make it over most landscapes with relative ease. Jesse and the others mounted up, and following Mueller's lead, they set off down the beaten gravel pathway towards the local forest and the village beyond.

As they scooted past the excavation wing, they had to dodge the unloading of the massive and complex looking mining equipment. Apparently, the excavation team was starting right away this morning as well. No doubt they had their sights set upon the mountains nestled behind the colony to its west, rocky crags that grew in size and viciousness rather quickly as their height ascended. All preliminary scans said these mountains were exactly what they were after in terms of raw materials to build the slingshot gateway in orbit. They only had to get at them.

Just around the corner of the Excavation wing was the edge of the forest. Nearly instantly upon entering the azure overhang of the trees, the members of CAPA were enveloped in more than just shadow. Dramatic scents invaded their nostrils, the most overpowering of these was a damp mustiness. By the look of it, it was similar in shape and feel to a cold weather rainforest. Jesse could identify a number of varieties as they cruised past that he had seen in his first endeavor into the woods. The blue, red veined ferns were the same. As well as the wide alien looking trees. Some of the tall, thin and muscular ones stood proudly by the edge of the pathway, and they squished a few of the dropped white helicopter petals as they drove. There were a few new varieties here as well, short flowering shrubs and some kind of vibrantly purple vine that snaked its way within the highest branches.

Jesse and the others could not but look quickly as they followed the curves of the path, also flexing their legs when anticipating the dips and rises in the way among the trees. In their ears as they neared the exit of the forest, they could make out a few songbirds, chirping back and forth. At least all of them expected it to be songbirds. Mueller pulled her scout to the left side of the pathway, waving her hand to slow and to be cautious. As the rest of the team fell in-line behind her, Jesse could see why. A couple small, long tailed mammals were bickering and chasing at each other on the path ahead. Their fur was slick with dew or water, but also a dull turquoise in hue, a slightly dimmer color than the shaggy moss that covered the forest floor. They hardly seemed to notice when Jesse and the CAPA team cruised by. Zuri, the last in line, tarried to snap a photo with her recording equipment.

Incredibly, the scene exiting the forest was bathed in red-twinged morning sunlight. The clouds over the valley had broken, but by the look of the sky probably not for long. The CAPA team had found themselves a patch of glowing Toiseean sun which lit up the fields they found themselves between in brilliant vibrancy. On their left was the violet spinach, however it was looking fully grown here, 2 feet tall and spread just as wide. On their right were rows of growing 'wheat bananas', the stalks of which were sturdy looking and azure blue, standing proudly at least half as tall as Jesse was. Jesse smiled and shook his head again as they scooted on towards the village that sat now only a few hills away. It was certainly going to take some time to get used to walking out into this world, expecting to see green and only finding blue.

Ahead along the pathway were the first few buildings of the village, and they could finally get a good look at them. They looked simple, squared and blocky in shape, with a plain door in the front and a porch and windows. This particular building might have been a utility shed of sorts, as the porch was littered with baskets and gardening tools leaning against the walls. Its color resembled rusted metal, with what also looked like metal sheeting on the roof. As the CAPA team started to slow, cresting the last hill into the village, Jesse could get a better look at the siding material of the building and realized it was in fact wood, but with deep orange and red swirls. It didn't look as if it was stained that color due to the weathering patterns and dry cracks on its surface, which revealed brighter variations of the same outer color.

Mueller brought her scout to a stop about a ¼ mile from what looked to be the center of the village. Jesse could see why, as a number of Jolethites were stopped and standing still, watching the approaching CAPA party. It didn't appear that these folks were as smiley and welcoming as those at the Founding Party last night, as there was a definite tension in the air that Jesse could perceive even from this distance.

"Let's pull our scouts to the side of the pathway just before we get to that first building on the left." Mueller nodded towards it with her head.

"They seem scared." Zuri commented.

"It's hard to tell from here isn't it? We need to get closer and show our intentions." Rin insisted. She hadn't let up her grip from the scout's handlebars.

Mueller started off slowly again, and the rest in line behind her. As they approached, a few of the Jolethites started to clear the pathway. The women hid their children behind them or scooted them along out of the open street and into nearby buildings. A few of the men began to gather closer together in the middle of the pathway. Their reactions seemed to be careful and slow, and Jesse noticed that they had not set aside their various tools. If anything, they held them tighter.

The CAPA team pulled to the side and stopped right behind a larger, a bit more up-kept building to the left, just as Annaliese had said they should. They threw their kickstands down and dismounted their scouts, Roger actually leaning his up against the back of the building. He rested his hands on his pistol on his belt and puffed out his chest, initiating his guard duty over the scouts and his team.

Junior Command Mueller strode confidently towards the group of men, so much so that a few of them took a cautious step back. She was choosing who she should speak to first. They all looked like they worked hard for a living, based on the dirt on their clothing and boots. Their dress was a stark contrast to the sleek look of Sherii and the other Jolethites, as these were similar to the siblings that Jesse had encountered in the woods. Dark stains were visible on their knees and up to their elbows on their sleeves, indicating they labored on with their hands quite a bit. Their shirts and pants looked to be made of a thicker material, maybe wool or something similar.

There was an older-looking fellow in the middle of the group. He held no tools, but his clothing suggested he had seen work in his day. His demeanor was that of a leader due to his stance, inquisitive and bold, with his chin extended towards Mueller's approach instead of shying away from it. So that's who she chose.

She stopped a few feet short of his stand. "Hello. I am Junior Commander Annaliese Mueller."

There was an awkward pause, as Mueller did not offer any pleasantries with her introduction. She simply stated who she was and stopped. No handshake offers, no smile.

The man she addressed looked beyond her at the rest of the CAPA team, making eye contact with each one, then looked back to Annaliese and spoke.

"Yessip tor di." He gave a slight nod of his head towards her, perhaps as a hello. Then he touched his chest with his open palm. "Formanglan Sillias chu."

Mueller, seemingly content with how this exchange is going so far, continued. "We are here to learn about your village and viable crop cultivation. We will not be in your way, but we may have some questions. Thank you for your cooperation."

As she spoke, she drew a crude picture on her tablet. When she finished speaking, she flashed it towards the man. The drawing was that of a stick figure person, who then was being led in a circle by a large arrow that wrapped around the screen all the way back to the back of the stick figure. The man narrowed his eyes as he studied the image, and then softly nodded as if he understood.

"Di su yessip todare." He then gently opened his arms and offered his palms to her, as if he was giving her permission to do exactly what she had asked.

Annaliese turned her back to the man, concluding their business. The man cocked his head back and chuckled slightly under his breath. Jesse could read his face, surprised at the incredulousness of Mueller but also amused at her cold seriousness given this was the first time they had met. He turned and addressed his own people, while Mueller relayed instructions to the team.

"Alright team, you know your assignments. Let's get as much as we can here today." She turned and looked down the stretch of roadway, craning to see past the group of Jolethites. "Zuri, there looks to be some kind of horse and buggy on the far side of the village. That's where we will head."

. "As well as animal pens. The drone photos revealed they are on that side as well." Zuri added. She stepped forward and joined Mueller as they set off down the pathway. As they passed the group of discussing men, they paid them no attention, but the Jolethite men watched them pass with curious unease.

Rin sidled up to Jesse's left. "Would you say that looks like some kind of grocery store?" She pointed across the street to a building with baskets and boxes of produce on its front porch. A woman and 2 children were watching from there as well.

"Could be, I guess."

"Probably a good place to start to find information on how they cultivate this stuff." Rin started directly for the building, with Jesse in tow. As they passed by the discussing men in the street, Rin also ignored their looks. But Jesse met a few of their eyes, and didn't know what else to do but smile in greeting. Of the two or three that he smiled at, only the older man who seemed to be the leader of the group smiled in return. His eyes seemed kind and confident, and Jesse only broke his gaze when it was a twist on his neck to maintain it.

They approached the store, and the woman with her two children. The kids seemed to be just at school age, maybe 6 or 7. She looked to be in her late 20's, with long black hair that was mostly braided in the front and then hung down her back. Her eyes were a bit shocking, as Jesse had never seen naturally orange/yellow eyes before. Rin did not seem to notice, or at very least care, and started speaking to her right away.

"Hello! My name is Rin, can you tell me about how you grow these plants?" Rin's approach to the woman was at least welcoming and gentle in tone, but still straight to the point. The woman looked to the men, and then back at Rin.

"Torey torey. Loe sore klimate." She gently shook her head, obviously not understanding what Rin was after. One of the men walked past Rin and Jesse and took his place by her side, most likely her husband.

Rin, using her tablet, drew one of the violet spinaches to the best of her ability, and then a question mark next to it. She flashed the screen towards the couple, and repeated herself.

"Can you tell me how you grow these plants?"

"I don't think they will know what a question mark is, Rin." Jesse commented.

"Oh." She turned the tablet to herself for a second, then back towards the couple. "It's fine, I'll try something else in a second."

The couple squinted at the images she had produced, then at each other. The man gestured with his hand towards one of the boxes on the porch, which was full of the spinach plants. His wife, the woman, bent over and picked up one of them out of the box and offered it to Rin.

"Yes, those, how do you grow them?" Rin spun the tablet back around and tried to draw something resembling a watering can, or an ugly cloud raining. Jesse turned and started looking around at the other boxes. They were halfway full of produce, and most of it looked freshly picked, maybe this morning or yesterday. Glancing into the windows, the rooms inside did not look like a store but more like a living room. Chairs and tables, what looked like a pantry or kitchen space in the back. Lamps were lit and flickering inside, which gave it a homey glow. There appeared to be electric lamp sconces on the walls but they were turned off.

Jesse then turned around to survey the rest of the downtown area of the village. The village seemed to comprise of about 7 to 8 homes, situated in a rough circle, with what was most likely a well in the middle. Each hut or home was relatively the same. They had either produce boxes out front, chairs and tables, or various tools hanging on their front walls. Most also had hanging plants, with purple vines growing down that wrapped around the supports for the front porch roofs. This sported yellow fruit that grew in small bunches of less than ten, golden looking fruit in the vein of grapes.

Rather absentmindedly, Jesse meandered back into the street and towards the well in the middle. His excuse was that the purple vines grew thicker there and he casually wanted a closer look. Glancing back towards the group of men, some of which watched him, he took in the largest building where they had parked their scouts. This appeared to be the only two-story structure in the village, but now looking at it from the front, he didn't believe it truly had a second floor. The front windows were broad here, and large and tall. The structure itself seemed stretched and pulled up, and on its roof was the most peculiar adornment. A pillar of stone, similar to a church steeple, was the roof's pinnacle. As Jesse walked, he got more of a glimpse of the inside which revealed that the rock was not only the pinnacle of the building, but was what the entire structure seemed built around. A large, tall and thin stone stood in the middle of the building, its peak poked through the ceiling. It had to be at least 12 ft tall. From what Jesse could discern, chairs were situated around the rock, each one pointed towards the middle. And the same oil burning lamps as was in the home sat on tables around the stone, casting beautiful shadows and highlighting its chiseled surface.

Jesse was so intrigued by the rock building that he nearly ran into the well he was on his way to see. He turned his attention back just in time to not catch a purple vine to the face. This was in fact a well, as Jesse confirmed by peering down into its depths. A red wooden bucket hung by a winched rope over the hole, and there was a small table nearby with metal utensils such as a ladle and spoons with slots in them. Jesse, just now remembering that he was supposed to be collecting information that would lead to successfully cultivating Toiseean crops, looked back over towards Rin. Her conversation was continuing, with perhaps mild success as the couple looked a bit more relaxed. He then turned his attention to the golden grape berries of the vine.

He plucked a few, daring even to taste one before he had analyzed it. It was sweet, near honey level, also with a similar honey viscosity to its juice. After he had bitten into it, the rest he squeezed gently and watched the thick juice drip from the fruit onto the stone well's sides. Then out of the corner of his eye, he perceived movement.

As Jesse turned, his eyes met that of a father and daughter who had come up from the other side of the well. He assumed it was a father and daughter, as the man was easily a couple decades older than this pre-teenage girl. They were holding hands and approached with caution. The man also pulled behind him a large metal container on 2 wooden wheels. Jesse, recognising that he is what is causing tension here and maybe preventing this family from their water supply, stepped back away from the well. The girl looked to her father, who spoke.

"Julie aya."

She nodded at him, let go of his hand and started to grip the winch, spinning it to lower the bucket down the well. Her eyes shifted back and forth from what she was doing, to watching Jesse cautiously.

"It's ok, I'm just looking around." Jesse reassured her. He knew they couldn't understand him, so he focused most of his speech effort on his tone and cadence. He held up one of the golden berries that he had eaten.

"These are delicious, by the way." Then he thought of the little girl in the woods. "Do you want one?" He offered the berry to the girl as she wound the bucket down. She smirked shyly and shook her head, which he took as a no. Jesse turned towards the man, and offered the same. He smiled at the offer, but put up his hand in a stop gesture, and shook his head as well. Jesse nodded in understanding.

As he watched, the girl had reached the bottom of the well, and was now winding the rope back the other way. It seemed it took a little effort, but not so bad that she needed assistance. She was using both hands on the pulley system, and although the method was crude, its operation seemed smooth and well designed.

A Biblical passage now came to mind as Jesse watched her lift the bucket of water out of the well and towards the metal container they had brought. He was of course not considering this young girl to be some kind of outcast sinner, but he was reminded of the story of Jesus and the woman at the well. Jesse's farm in Carolina had a well, but it was obviously much more technologically advanced than this one. It was amusing to him, seeing a part of this Scriptural scene play out before his eyes, especially considering he was impossibly far from where that scene had taken place on Earth. Lost in the moment, Jesse spoke his remembrance of the verse outloud, knowing full well that they wouldn't understand him anyways.

"I will give you living water that will spring up to a well of eternal life."

The girl startled and sloshed the bucket of water down the side of the metal container. The man that was helping her stared at Jesse with an open jaw. Then the impossible happened.

"Yes, eternal life." She looked up at him. "Wait, what did you say about this well?" The girl asked Jesse, perfectly understandable.

Jesse's face matched that of her father's.

"The water... "

"Yes, what did you just say?"

Jesse swallowed. What was happening? His mind was stopped, fixated on the incredibleness of this moment, but his mouth kept moving anyway. "The water - living water, will be a spring inside you, welling up to eternal life."

She looked over at her father. He himself was too stunned to speak. She turned back to Jesse.   "You know how to speak Joelle? How?"

"I... don't... know..." Jesse stammered, now visibly shaking. She repeated herself.

"Di tick seya see Joelle? Seya see?"

Her words were indiscernible now. Jesse blinked and tried to listen again, wondering if what had just happened had happened at all.

"Seya see di vermongus. Di Joelle fune tapa!" She looked frustratingly at her father, who was trying to piece this puzzle back together as well. The other men had taken notice of the excitement around the well and were moving over towards them, with the older gentlemen in front.

Jesse, now feeling exposed and intimidated by the attention, started back for Rin. Roger Kincade had noticed the increase in commotion as well, and stood at attention, his hand on his sidearm. Jesse waved over to him, indicating that all was well. He could hear behind him the girl speaking over the men in the group. She was probably trying to convince them as to what just happened in the same way that Jesse was trying to convince himself.

How did she understand me?! How did I understand her? She wasn't speaking English, and neither was I! Without explanation, Jesse was able to communicate to her. He hadn't meant to but suddenly had the impulse and ability to say what he had said. It was very confusing and disturbing to his mind, to be in complete control of himself, but to utter sayings and expressions that his mouth seemed to do on their own. It was almost as if a translator had stepped in between his thoughts and his mouth and relayed exactly what he wanted to say into understandable speech.

… and all of them began to speak in other tongues, as the Spirit enabled them.

Did I just speak in tongues? Like, real tongues?!

Jesse paused and turned back. He wanted to go back into that moment and relive it. He wanted to try again and see what would happen if he spoke again of Jesus to them. But the father was ushering away his daughter with their cart of water. The men were now gathered around the well, with their elder out front. He was smiling large at Jesse, as if he had just been laughing.

No, not now. The moment's passed. Jesse thought to himself. He returned and joined Rin just as she seemed to be finishing up her discussion with the couple about the violet spinach plants. She met him, stepping off the porch.

"Geez, finally. I think I understand their methods now, but they pointed to that shed we passed on the way up here. Maybe some kind of special fertilizer or something." Rin stopped and looked past Jesse to all the men at the well, watching them. Jesse tried to ignore their eyes on his back.

"What'd you do? The whole village seems interested."

"I helped a girl get some water. I think they're just happy I helped." Jesse shrugged, covering for himself.

"Ah.." Rin seemed to be alright with that. "Alright, let's go see what we can find in that shed then." Jesse and Rin walked side by side out of the village center and headed towards their next objective. Jesse's mind was definitely not on what interesting fertilizers they could find, but when he could come back alone. There were some definite God things happening, and he needed to discover what all of that meant. Remarkable things that he had to try again to believe.

The rest of the CAPA team's jaunt into the Jolethite village was less than eventful. Rin and Jesse did indeed discover some unique chemical mixtures within the shed that enlightened them on the secrets to growing successful Toiseean crops. When they had returned, so had Mueller and Masando. They had quite a tale to share involving being chased by a bull of the cattle that the village was raising. Unfortunately for the villagers, the story ended with the Mueller escaping through the open gate, and the bull along with it. They had skedaddled in the ensuing chaos, and at least Masando was feeling guilty about it. Mueller had her mind too dedicated to extracting the information they needed from this primitive group to care about their personal wellbeing. Jesse was embarrassed to have his intimate and God-touched exchange be tainted by the actions of his fellow colonists.

On the return journey, he was wringing out imaginative ways to return to the village. His current position seemed to be the most explainable reason to do so, however by the sound of the discussion between the teammates, they themselves had little reason to return. Rin was fully convinced that they could fabricate the fertilizer compounds, and Mueller had already indicated that her report would list the village as inconsequential and only mildly resourceful. Jesse was going to need a specific reason for command to allow him to return.

On their return to the colony compound, Jesse returned to his quarters to shower and change clothes, upon recommendation by Zuri for the entire CAPA team. A precautionary measure against the spread of any unknown disease or contamination. Jesse used the opportunity to investigate within Scripture why, how and what just happened to him at the village well.

Settling into his desk chair, he tried to recall the moments where folks had spoken in tongues in the Bible narrative. His childhood memory of the tongues of fire came quickly back to him, so he opened the old Bible to the book of Acts, chapter 2. He did not need to read far into the chapter before he came across verse 4:

And they were all filled with the Holy Spirit and began to speak in other tongues as the Spirit gave them utterance.

He was well aware already that this was a sign of the movement of the Spirit of God. He knew that in the rest of the chapter, the disciples here were filled with the Holy Spirit, and what proved that to the unbelieving crowd outside was the fact they spoke in languages they shouldn't or couldn't have known. A chill ran down Jesse's spine as he recognized that the very same thing had just happened to him. His heart was pounding with a humble pride that God would have used him in the exact same way as the original disciples of Christ.

Looking into the margins, Jesse prayed and thanked God for Gus and his scribbled notes in these Scriptures, because written into the margins was this reminder: "Unknown languages made known. 1 Corinthians 14:6." Jesse paged over to the letter to the Corinthians from Paul, found chapter 14, verse 6 and read:

"Now, brothers, if I come to you speaking in tongues, how will I benefit you unless I bring you some revelation or knowledge or prophecy or teaching?"

Now this was interesting. This was what he was hoping to find. While Jesse was speaking to the Jolethites but having nothing but normal chit-chat to say, he spoke in English. First of all, it was all he knew, just like they only knew their language. Joelle, was it? Is that what she had said? Anyways, what Paul seemed to be saying here is that when Jesse started to speak to them of Godly things, the Spirit intervened and interpreted what he was saying because his speech was of prophetic or revelatory value.

Jesse didn't consider his comparison to this girl at the well to Jesus at the well outside of Samaria, but obviously it was a more important conversational transaction than he could perceive. Maybe the girl and her father needed to hear the knowledge or teaching that Jesse was saying? He thought back on the moment. Didn't she respond at first as if she had heard those words 'eternal life' before? Was Jesse correcting a misunderstanding that she had heard at that church of the rock, or whatever that building was surrounding the stone pillar. It definitely had an air of worship to it, and maybe what Jesse was bringing to the village was a correct knowledge and understanding of who and what they should be worshiping.

He continued to read the passage in 1 Corinthians. Jesse came across statements such as "if with your tongue you utter speech that is not intelligible, how will anyone know what is said?" and "strive to excel in building up the church". Based on these, he was now fully convinced he needed to return to the village. God was apparently using him to make known, or intelligible, the things of God to these people. Jesse's purpose here was to build up the church, as he deciphered from verse 12, as he had been gifted this ability by the Holy Spirit to do so.

With this renewed determination, he now had to devise a way he could get back, hopefully alone, but that was doubtful. Either way, he would have to convince Director Willow of the need.

The pressing need turned into an abject lesson in patience for Jesse, as days passed without the reason nor even opportunity to revisit the village. Director Willow had given the entire Ag Wing as much as they could handle, plowing, planting and fertilizing the fields that the colony had been gifted by the Jolethites.

By this point, their continued interaction with Leader Sherii had yielded more and more understanding between the colonists and their hosts, whom they had discovered were actually citizens of the primary country upon the planet. Nearly the only country. Sherii was the leader of the United Joleth, a position he had inherited by popular vote after the former leader had passed away. The United Joleth came into being a few hundred years ago, where the victors of a global conflict decided to restore peace to the planet by using massive governmental oversight of every aspect of society. All business and agriculture, military, all the way down to individual professions and education, it all was done under the umbrella of a benevolent government, which was headed by the Sherii as the Prime Leader.

The real incredible aspect of this system was that its citizens seemed very content to live under such strict oversight and management. As the Toiseean colonists discovered, this was due to their government backed comfort and care. Great lengths were taken by the government, which was also the largest employer in the United Joleth, to ensure that every need was met and usually exceeded for all of their citizens. Poverty and crime was virtually non-existent, everyone had enough to eat, everyone had a comfortable lifestyle.

All of this knowledge and learning was made possible by a number of exchange programs that the Toiseean colonists and Jolethites had begun, including excavation and mining laborers, mineral shipments and trade, as well as linguistic cooperatives. The Toiseean's submitted a team of education specialists, the Linguistic Exchange and Commonality Team, or the 'Language Brigade' as called by the colonists at large, to the closest Jolethite city where their task was to know and learn as much of Jolethite culture as possible, including learning the language of Joelle.

Another interesting aspect that was becoming apparent is why the Jolethite's had only recently discovered certain technological advances, such as the radio broadcast that tipped off the colonists on their arrival. Without the external drive of conflict among any other nations, innovation and scientific discovery was slowed and even halted in some regards. When the United Joleth came into being, their main focus was of course rebuilding and restoring the broken planet, but most of all they subdued the wants and needs of the people. The closer that they came to a nearly 100% satisfaction and contentment level among their people, there was no drive to make things better. To the masses, life was as good as it could get already, so what need was there to improve and innovate?

But there was resistance. Namely a 'small religious sect' as Sherii had called them, referring to the village outside of the colonies allotted territory. Apparently, they, among other small patches of Jolethites, had resisted the control of the government and retreated to far corners of the planet, as far away from their influence as possible. The small patches of dissentients were benign by their nature, resisting vocally but not violently, and so they remained largely ignored by the government. Even when Sherii allowed space-faring foreigners to land and confiscate over half of their crop producing land. According to Leader Sherii, it was Joleth land and as Prime Leader he had every right to grant it to whom he willed.

Jesse did see them occasionally, but from a distance. Working their own fields or watching the colonists from the edge of the forest between them. The agreement between United Joleth and what Captain Yale had ordained as the Toiseean Charter Colony was clear in the strict prohibition of contact with the local village of 'religious extremists'. Every colonist that Jesse knew wanted nothing to do with the locals anyways, as they were most concerned with the very real possibility that the construction of a slingshot gateway was only a month or two away from completion.

With the help of the nation of Joleth, and their supply of day laborers to mine and excavate materials, the construction timeline was halved, then halved again, then halved again. Every HomeMaker is designed with the ability to excavate and construct their own gateway, a process that takes up to 5 years even in the best of conditions. But with the presence of a host nation that has prepared materials for construction, and a force to excavate even more as needed, the construction crews in orbit have been able to work at a non-stop rate. As fast as the colony could supply the orbiting command section of the HomeMaker with materials, they were molded, manufactured and assembled into place. Every colonist, who previously had said goodbye to Earth expecting to never see it again, was elated at the idea that they could traverse back before many of them even had another birthday.

Even so, the Toiseean colonists were still expected to behave as if they were under contract and were colonizing a brand-new world all to themselves. Marriages were happening nearly daily, with 27 together in a joint ceremony at once in one instance. Some of the social pressure to find a GEM match was dissipating due to the progress on the gateway meaning they could bring more folks from home to join them. But, as that hasn't been assured, command was still holding the crew to the previous expectation. Director Willow had pulled Jesse aside to inquire about why he isn't seen fraternizing and dating among the crew like everyone else.

"I don't believe I need to remind you that nearly half of all the males have selected their first mate by now." She sat behind her desk, her hands folded, her tone accusing Jesse not holding up his end of the bargain.

"I've considered it. I've just been so busy that by leisure time, I just don't have the energy." His facade was easy to hide behind, especially when it was so mingled with truth he didn't have to lie. CAPA had been reassigned to take oversight on a number of horticultural projects, most of which were long days outside.

"Hmm. And yet the rest of the crew has made time for this. You do realize the importance of it?"

"The long-term success of the colony? Of course, but with the gateway coming–"

"Which is not yet finished."

"Yes, but -"

"And we can't assume that it will be. Any number of faults or construction setbacks could waylay its completion indefinitely."

Jesse sighed. "Look, Director Willow. I understand, and I will make it a priority as soon as I have the fields in a good rhythm."

She narrowed her eyes and leaned back in her office chair. She really didn't try to hide how important her position made her feel. "Mr. Heartshire, I admire how dedicated you are to your duty here in Toisee Charter. But I need you to understand your complete purpose here."

"Yes ma'am, I do."

"Hmmm." She considered. "I have a new assignment for you. You are to engage in a prospective social activity with one of your GEM matches. You will have 3 days to complete this assignment."

Jesse couldn't help but smirk at the ridiculous order. "You're ordering me to have a date?"

"Yes, Mr. Heartshire." She wasn't laughing. "I want to see you make a concerted effort in fulfilling your entire purpose within this colony. That is the expectation of all colonists."

"I am on a special assignment from command." Jesse protested.

"CAPA? I'll see that Junior Command Mueller is informed. In fact, I'll see that your duties are suspended for the rest of the day." She scooted her chair back and stood. "Is your assignment understood?"

Jesse threw up his hands in a shrug and giggled a little nervously. She stared at him, her eyes expecting an answer.

"Yes. Yes, ma'am." Jesse sighed defeatedly.

"Then I wish you happy hunting. Good day, Mr. Heartshire." She waved her hand towards the door, welcoming him to leave.

Jesse exited her office and shook his head. He had played his part well, being lost in his work to avoid any suspicion, but it was bound to catch up with him. The pressure to discover his wife was now fully on. It was still an incredibly odd assignment ahead of him, being ordered to find a 'genetically compatible mate'.

He exited the command offices and made for one of the outdoor tables that had been set up in the courtyard of the colony outside of 1303. Everything still had this new freshness to it, the same feeling that a well-manicured lawn or garden embellished after it had been gone over with a mower and trimmers. There was grass growing now, in the field areas between the wings of the colony where the crops of the local village had been. And the freshly poured concrete was a bright, dusty white around the entire City Lyceum. The tables that Jesse sat at were simple, picnic style and bench seated, with a Venture colored green and gold umbrella shooting through the middle.

He sat down and laid his tablet out in front of him. The irony of the fact that he had just finished reading the Biblical passages of Ephesians chapter 5 was not lost on him, the passage in particular about husbands and wives in the church. And now, here he was, having to pick out one. He at least knew where he wanted to start, and it didn't have much to do with genetic compatibility.

This was still the first time that he'd honestly reviewed his matches, something he had been trying very hard not to do in his resistance to the mandate for marriage, and so it felt just as awkward as he thought it might. Seeing the faces of those whom he was expected to seek out felt like selecting from a mail-order catalogue. It just wasn't what he would call natural. Scrolling past the 90th percentile, the 80th, the 70th, he was relieved not to see Director Shea Willow, but he also was confused at not seeing Elena Aquino either.

They had been still working together occasionally but Jesse had decided to put some distance in between their relationship ever since seeing her with the grunt at Founding Day. If he wasn't going to pursue her, which that night he had decided against it, then he needed to let his feelings dissipate as well. Now however, he wasn't so sure. On the one hand, they seemed to have a great connection and the convenient yet ever-so-romantic assignment from command was a good excuse to try to date her. But on the other hand, he didn't know if she was one to compliment his mission on Toisee. Scripture taught that it was better not to marry because you are more free to do what God has asked of you. If he is wedded to her, or any other non-Christian, that would severely hinder his purpose.

Even while Jesse debated this in his head, he was actually starting to wonder if Elena was an option at all. In Jesse's GEM matches, he had scrolled past the 50th percentiles now. Venture does not recommend, realistically even allow, colonists to marry anyone less than a 40% GEM match. A nervous butterfly was loose in Jesse's stomach. If he and Elena tried to marry at a less than 40% match, command would consider there to be far better options available and insist that they both try their luck again with a higher percentage match.

48... 45... 44...

THERE SHE IS!

Elena's picture finally graced upon Jesse's tablet screen, her smiling face highlighted in red next to her percentile of 43%. In small lettering underneath, the words Not Recommended were underlined. Not recommended means still allowed. Jesse reassured himself. Well, that was that. She is in fact one of his matches, albeit a low one, but a match nonetheless.

He checked the time on his watch. 15:37. Elena had been assigned under Rin's oversight, and he knew they were fertilizing the western grains, past the forest between the colony and the village. Lunch break began at 16:00, so Jesse left the picnic table behind and made for his Scout parked in front of the the City Lyceum.

CHAPTER 17
HEARTS LAID BARE

It'd been almost a full 3 weeks since Jesse and CAPA had landed in the fog on their recon mission to the planet, and yet he was still not used to the crispness of the air as it stung his ears. He had heard from the colonists that had come from the parts of Earth with typically colder climates that one does get used to the temperature. He wasn't getting used to it fast enough and he often forgot about a beanie. Unfortunately, he had all the time in the world to adjust.

Toisee's climate did not change. It was perpetually fall or early winter feeling, dense humidity with a relative temperature between 30 - 50 F. Altitude affected that of course, but due to the planet's rotation, atmospheric makeup and minor axis tilt on only a 37 day year, the climate never had a chance to change. It explained a lot, from the plants broad leaves attempting to catch every ounce of sunlight they could, to the pale complexion of every Jolethite they had met so far. Some of the miners on loan from United Joleth were so white the Toiseean colonists claimed they glowed in the dark.

Jesse cruised along the side path of the grain field just as the Ag Specialists were walking to their transport for lunch. The field was a bit over a mile from the Residential wing and so they would bring their lunches with them for the day instead of journeying back and forth. He pulled the scout up behind the truck and waited, scanning the incoming specialists for Elena.

In the vast field itself was the beginning of sprigs of green. Jesse surveyed the landscape. Here the colony was attempting to cultivate its first crop of Earthen winter wheat, and the view was a very welcome reminder of home, seeing green plants popping up in rows instead of blue or purple.

"Do we meet with your approval?"

Elena's voice came from behind him. She had a sandwich in hand and held her water tote in the other. Apparently, she had already started lunch and he had missed her in the transport.

"It's a nice view. More homey than all of the blue." Jesse replied. "The fertilizing going alright?"

"Yes, sir." She was kurt with her words and distant with her tone.

Jesse got off of his scout and kicked its stand. "How about you?"

She nodded sideways with a mouthful of sandwich, adding a little shrug, indicating 'meh' to Jesse.

"Ya, I was going to see if you wanted to ride back and get some lunch with me. We could catch up, but–" He motioned towards her sandwich and drink. She held it up and showed it to him.

"Already eating it." She said a little annoyed. She was being prickly. Jesse had known they had drifted apart a little, but maybe it was more than he had realized. He was saddened and embarrassed to have let their friendship dwindle.

"What about after your shift then? Would you want to get together at the 1303?"

"Oh, like a date?"

"Ya!" Ooo, that was too fast and eager. "I mean, we just haven't had a chance to see each other in a while."

"It'll have to be early, because Miller is taking me out tonight." She took another bite of her sandwich and with her words.

Utility Foreman Rhett Miller was the large grunt of a man that he had seen her dancing with at Founding Day. Jesse's sadness began to increase. Hopefully he hadn't missed his chance with her.

"Ah, ok that's fine." He lied. "I'll see you there, at what, 2130? Is that early enough?"

She lifted her sandwich in acknowledgement and started to walk away. "Sounds good, Heartshire. See ya then."

"Bye!" Jesse stood next to his scout and watched her walk away.

He felt foolish and hated being in this stupid position. Jesse mounted the scout scooter and started back for the colony.

He had been doing so well, keeping his feelings and emotions in check, especially in terms of curtailing any distracting level of attraction for Elena. But now, with the pressure from command, he had to open his heart to the possibilities, and it hurt because now he might be too late. The more he considered it, Jesse had decided that he did love her to an extent, and he could tell that she loved being around him too. At least she did.

He started to pray on the ride back, asking God for guidance and direction, but not before Jesse let Him have it for the timing of it all. If this was His plan from the beginning, why didn't God make it obvious on the HomeMaker? Maybe he could have played this differently and instead of withdrawing from the GEM pool, he could have been swimming in it with Elena already. Maybe she would even be open to having faith?

No, it was the right thing to do at the time, and the Holy Spirit had shown him that in Scripture. And even still, his studies had shown him in Romans that it was better not to marry to begin with. Or was it Corinthians? Ephesians?

Whatever, it didn't matter. It was there, he knew it. If it was better for his Godly mission to remain single, maybe he needed to just lock up these emotional distractions and stay single. He could date around for a long while, simply going down the list of his GEM matches, and claim that he was trying all while he bided his time. Yes, that was it. His 'date' with Elena will simply become a reunion of friendship and nothing more. That was what made the most sense.

Reaching this conclusion, Jesse noticed his ride was getting darker than he remembered it being on the way over, so he finally glanced around himself and noticed where he was. He had passed the turn back for the City Lyceum and was riding north up a small pathway that ran alongside the forest towards the village. He could see it in the distance over the hills, a mile or two ahead. He could also see the rain band coming, which had darkened the sky so much that his scout's lights had auto-switched on. Within a minute or two, he was going to be in a downpour, and that did not mix well with his scooter's traction on these loose gravel pathways.

Quickly, Jesse swerved his scout off the path and to the woods. He found a small niche in the thickened ferns and parked under a couple of the fat umbrella trees, just as the downpour came. He dismounted and stood, maybe too surprised that the broad leaves prevented so much of the heavy rain from drenching him and his scooter. The temperature had dipped a bit with the incoming weather, and Jesse shivered as he shoved his hands in his pockets. Looking up, he couldn't see any of the charcoal grey sky through the canopy. Simply a few streams and drops of rainwater falling down in small waterfalls through the leaves.

While gazing at the canopy, he did also notice an orange glow illuminating the tops of the trees from further into the forest. It flickered like flame, although he smelled no campfire. Curious, Jesse tried to see beyond the thick forest between him and the light's source but couldn't see anything from his vantage point. He listened for any speech or sound, but all that came, rushing to his ears, was the roar of the rain pounding the trees and plowed ground behind him. He decided to investigate and so he began to push his way through the ferns and branches.

He was shivering from the cold, and maybe now also the excitement of what he might discover. The wetness of the plants, although preventing him from being soaked by the direct rain, was still pressing in on him from all sides and so beginning to seep into his coat and pants. But still he pushed through. He was marching fairly directly now, uncaring about the sound he made due to the rain above. The glow was getting brighter as he closed in.

Then, as if in a cinematic reveal, the next giant fern branch he pushed aside laid plain the source of the glowing light. It was a man-made clearing, where stumps of smaller trees were still visible as 3 or 4 inch pokes coming out of the turquoise mossy ground. Tall lit torches were the source of the light, but their flames produced no smoke or odor. However, their orange light did reveal 3

Jolethite villagers huddling around a small collection of large trees that Jesse had not yet seen.

The trees were barked deep red, with a garnet like sheen to them. They were maybe a couple feet in diameter, but impossibly tall compared to the rest of the forest around them. The trunks disappeared as they rose past the lower trees' blue topped bunches. These tall garnet trees were most likely the source of the hints of red that Jesse had seen in the forest when they had landed, as he remembered the leaves looked bright as fall ruby reds on Earth.

Jesse craned his neck to the left and right and shuffled as gently as possible around the outside of the clearing while remaining hidden by the foliage. He was trying to see why all three Jolethites were huddled close to one of the trees. One of them quickly turned and set a bucket down on the ground behind them, full of a thickly viscous liquid. He grabbed another one and as he turned back, Jesse could see that there was some kind of a tap or nozzle attached to the tree trunk. He glanced at the other few large red trees in this clearing, and sure enough there were taps attached to them too. It looked like they were harvesting the sap from the trees in a similar way that Earthers would harvest maple syrup.

Suddenly there was a bright flash and an immense thunder clap. The sound startled everyone, the Jolethites nearly dropped their buckets and Jesse tripped and fell out of the tree line. He caught himself before landing on any of the stumps on the ground and pushed himself to his feet. But glancing back up at the harvest scene in front of him, he was met by 3 pairs of crystal blue eyes. Fortunately for Jesse, they all looked just as scared to see him as he was scared to be seen.

Jesse slowly straightened up, and lifted his hands, palms towards the Jolethites.

"Hello." He said gently. "I'm sorry, I saw the light and was curious." He knew they couldn't understand him but he hoped that his soft tone was relatable. They looked at him, then looked at each other. The man in the middle looked familiar to Jesse. He felt he had seen him in the group of men at the village, chatting and watching with the old man as Jesse was at the well. The man on the right and the man in the middle said something and motioned towards the man on the left. He shrugged at them and shook his head 'no'. But the other two seemed insistent and the man in the middle even pushed him forward a step. A bit nervously, the man on the right turned to Jesse, and took a deep breath before speaking.

"Heelo."

Jesse cocked his head sideways and smirked. "Hi."

"Heelo." He said again and slightly bowed his head down and back up.

"How… How do you know english?" Jesse was instantly relieved and puzzled by hearing his language being spoken by a Jolethite. It warmed his heart and his shivering stopped.

"I go… c-city. I am learn." He was struggling quite a bit with the words, closing his eyes tight while he spoke, trying to remember the vocabulary. Jesse was still beyond impressed as this man could only have been learning English for 2 weeks at most.

"Good!" Jesse tried to limit his own speech to be more easily understood but not come across as condescending. "You sound good!"

"I thanking you." The man smiled back at Jesse.

Jesse pointed at the tree behind them and the buckets. "Why? What are those?"

The man followed Jesse's point. He motioned towards one of the full buckets and his companion handed it to him. "Drink." He held it towards Jesse.

Jesse, being completely curious and not at all cautious, took the bucket and started to tip it towards his lips.

"Henya! Henya!" The companions said and threw up their hands towards him. The man on the right did the same.

"Henya, uh… NO. NO!" He said and Jesse stopped. The man speaking English held up one finger and then made a motion, dropping his finger as if dipping it, then bringing it to his mouth. He said again, "Drink, small."

"Oh, I understand." Jesse said. He gave the bucket back to the Jolethite and dipped his finger in the liquid and pulled it out. It drizzled slowly back into the bucket, as Jesse looked at him for approval. The man nodded and so Jesse brought his finger to his mouth and tasted. At first the bitterness made him pucker up something awful, and the companions began to snicker. Jesse started to feel like he was the butt of their joke, but then the sweetness came. A warm sweetness that swept over his entire mouth that tasted of strong coffee and caramel.

"Wow, that's good!" Jesse exclaimed.

"Medi-sign." The man informed Jesse and then set the bucket down. Jesse understood him to have meant medicine. When the man set the bucket down on the forest floor, a necklace dangled out from behind his collar. It was a long singular pointed stone, wrapped at the top in leather or string. Jesse glanced at the others, and sure enough, they wore one too. He was reminded of the worship building built around the tall stone in the village. Jesse pointed to the man's neck.

"What is that?"

The man stood straight and looked down at his shirt, feeling on the right and left side of his chest. He looked back at Jesse, pinching his shirt.

"Gistad?"

"No, that. Your necklace." Jesse pointed more emphatically and directly. The man felt his neck and pulled on the pointed stone.

"Gistad?"

"Yes, that." Jesse nodded.

The man looked back at his compatriots who gestured for him to tell Jesse. So the man thought for a moment, seeming to consider if he knew the correct words or not. Finally, he spoke.

"Gistad ti Drodd." He considered again, working on the English. "This…

the - the Rock?"

Jesse pointed out towards the village. "Is it the same as the rock in the building?" He made a ball with his two hands and stretched them vertically apart from each other. "The big rock in the building, through the roof?" He finished his hand motions by bringing his fingers together, making a point like a pitched roof with his flattened hands.

The man seemed to quickly understand Jesse's hand charades. "Yes, the Rock." He said again. "My forgiving."

Now, that was an interesting statement for him to make. Here was an opportunity for Jesse to witness to them again. Similarities in their faith were beginning to share connections with Jesse's Christianity. The stone was their symbol as the cross was his, so he decided to show them as best he could. Jesse stooped and drew in the dirt, making a large cross with his finger. He looked back up at the men.

"This is my forgiving." He said.

Jesse turned his attention back to the ground, where he outlined the best he could with his finger and dirt, a stick figure of Jesus, with arms stretched upon the cross. He pointed to the drawing, looked at the men again, and let a Scripture verse flow from his mouth, this time in perfect Joelle.

"For God so loved the world, that he gave his only Son, that whoever believes in him should not perish—"

"--but gain new life eternal." The man finished the Scripture verse for Jesse. Jesse could feel that he had spoken in the Spirit again, in the tongues of the Jolethites, and that now the man was speaking back to him in Joelle, but Jesse could understand it. Just like the girl at the well. But what startled him this time was not that he was speaking in tongues, but that the man had finished John 3:16 for him.

Jesse's wide eyes mimicked the man's. They apparently were both not lost on the impossibility of this moment. The man quickly stooped down to Jesse's level and drew a long straight line on the ground. Then he spoke, while drawing a stick figure of a man whose arms were wrapped around the top of the stone.

"For God did send his Son to save the world through him, and not for its condemnation." He said, finishing the sketch in the dirt. They both studied the drawings they had made. Jesse and he saw the definite and stark echoed comparisons. Not just in the symmetry of the words they spoke, but in the image of a man lifted up. The only difference was upon a cross or a stone.

The rain continued to fall. A thunderclap rumbled from across the valley floor. The hairs on Jesse's head dripped with water. This moment stayed still, all of its members struggling to believe what seemed to be true, but was not possible.

"Can- Can you take me to your place of worship?" Jesse managed to get the words out, even though they were just above a forced whisper.

"Thekya?" The man questioned, speaking in unknown Joelle again. The Spirit enabled speech seemed to be gone. Jesse tried his question again.

"Can I go to your village?" He pointed at himself, at the men, then towards the village. He knew the mandate forbade him to have contact with the local village, and he definitely knew that this exchange would not qualify as a valid reason for contact by command. But what he just experienced had to be seen through. He had to discover if his hunch was true. If indeed the connection that they shared was more than religious coincidence.

The man stood and looked at his companions. They were just as flabbergasted as he, but seemed to agree that Jesse could go along with them. He turned back to Jesse.

"Follow... me. Us." With that, the men picked up their buckets and began down a narrow path with Jesse in tow, through the waterfalls among the branches.

They trekked silently through the forest and over the hills to the village. However, the noise in Jesse's mind was loud as he had been praying constantly the entire time. *God, what is this? Give me your wisdom. Please, reveal and help me to understand what this is! I do not want to be deceived. I will only trust what You show me as truth. Continue to reveal the truth to me, O Lord!*

Over and over his mind circled around and around, attempting to make sense of what had just happened. *The speaking in tongues is heavy enough, but now the remarkable similarity between their verses? How did he know how to finish it? What is the Spirit trying to disclose to them?*

They made their way up the last hill, where the other two men ran ahead towards other Jolethite villagers who were sitting on the porch where Rin had talked to the couple. The man who Jesse spoke Scripture to turned back as they approached.

"They get Sillias."

"Sillias?" Jesse questioned.

"Yes, Sillias. Umm... Village... led?"

"The village leader?"

"Yes, Sillias is village leader."

With that clarified, they stopped and stood under the awning of the large, stone worship building. Jesse peered into the large windows. Inside he could now see better the layout of the worship space. The massive, tall stone in the middle had a number of words carved into it in various places. It was still illuminated with tall candles on either side, they were asymmetrical in height and girth, but all still tall enough to cast light up half of the stone, some even reflected off of the ceiling. There was a podium directly in front of it which faced a number of short looking backless benches that maybe sat 3 or 4 each. The benches were arranged in a semicircle, all facing towards the stone in the middle.

"Heelo, Toiseean."

Jesse withdrew his gaze into the worship building to face Sillias. This was the same man that had smiled at him, with the same kindness in his eyes. His eyes now also held a knowing intrigue, assumedly because he had been brought up to speed on the miracle that happened in the woods. He held his hands behind his back, standing as if expecting for Jesse to perform his feat of tongues again. Instead, Jesse extended his hand in an offering of a handshake.

"Hello, Sillias."

Sillias looked down and put his hand in Jesse's, unknowing what to do with it. Jesse gripped it with mild firmness, which Sillias reciprocated again. He then used his other hand to gesture to his chest.

"My name is Jesse."

"Jesse. Heelo, Jesse." Sillias repeated, probably ensuring he remembered it. Jesse looked past the shoulder of Sillias at the man he had spoken to in the woods. He nodded towards him, implying he wanted his name. Apparently, he understood.

"My is name Thorold." He said, tapping his chest.

"Can I...?" Jesse let go of Sillias' hand and pointed to the worship space behind him.

Sillias nodded. "Yes."

He stepped past Jesse and gripped the door handles, pulling them outwardly open. He then stepped aside and smiled at Jesse, indicating that it was alright that he entered the building. Jesse eagerly strode past the old man and into the worship building.

The scent of a piney cedar struck his nostrils first. He had not yet been in any other Jolethite building to know if this scent was common, but he had a feeling this one had a special air to it. He walked past the benches and approached the stone at the center. The flickering candlelight, now disturbed by the breeze accompanying Jesse and the others' entry, was dancing across the smoothed reddish and grey surface. It bore the marks of chisels, so it was definitely hewn by hand, most likely from the mountains just past the village itself. Jesse traced his fingers upon the stone. His fingertips felt the grooves and divots of the imprinted words, feeling the cool of the stone upon his palm. He then stepped back and pointed to the chiseled text.

"What does this say?" Jesse asked towards Thorold, who was the next behind him.

Thorold opened his mouth to speak but then hesitated and glanced over to Sillias. Sillias cleared his throat.

"Words of Isstar."

"Isstar." Jesse repeated. He thought for a moment. Jesse turned to face them and pressed his back up against the stone, lifting his hands above his head in an attempt to mimic what Thorold had drawn in the forest. "Isstar? Isstar on Drodd?"

Sillias nodded in affirmation. "Yes, Jesse. Isstar died on Drodd."

Jesse felt a chill run down his spine. This was getting very, very strange and even more exhilarating. He quickly pulled out his tablet and switched to the external camera, twisting back to face the surface and take pictures of the words etched into the stone.

Behind him, Thorold opened his mouth in protest, and was about to approach Jesse to stop him, but Sillias held up his hand. He shook his head gently and said a few quiet words that Jesse could not hear.

Jesse crossed around the other sides of the stone, looking for each imprinted text and took picture after picture. It would appear that the Jolethite here worship a person who died on a rock in a similar way that Jesus died on a cross. And based on what Sillias had said, these were some of the words or sayings of what Isstar had spoken. The evidence was mounting that maybe his reason for witnessing to the Jolethites had less to do with him bringing the truth of Jesus to them, but maybe connecting the truth of Jesus between them? He had to compare their verses to the Bible in his room.

When Jesse had captured the verses he could see clearly, he turned back to Sillias, Thorold and the others who had now filtered in. The word of the miracle of tongues had been circulating the small town. Jesse saw that the father and daughter from the well were there too. He scanned the gathering crowd from behind the podium, suddenly recognizing the gravity of the situation to them.

He'd been so wrapped up in the enormity of his own purpose and mission from God, getting closer and closer to some divine cosmic connection shared between them, that he wasn't considering the perspective of the Jolethites themselves. What did this look like to them? Only weeks ago did they discover that they themselves weren't alone in the universe either, that mankind existed beyond their own planet. Then these technologically advanced humans landed, destroyed and made themselves right at home on top of their land. A group of them then rudely pranced around their village, where they demanded answers to difficult questions in a foreign language, only to shun them and pretend they weren't neighbors.

This village and its people had been open and kind to him, regardless of his obtuse comrades. All of that emotion flooded upon Jesse. These villagers, who share such a similar faith as his own, felt the most like home in Carolina than anything he had experienced with Venture or the Toiseean colonists yet. He teared up as he looked out upon their expectant faces, where he found himself standing behind the podium.

"I'm sorry." He started and wiped a tear from his eye. "I'm sorry that you probably won't understand much of what I say, but I feel that my God wants me to say it." Their faces were fixed on him with such focus. An intense focus. Not even a breath was heard among them. "I am here because of Jesus, the Christ. I came with all of the other colonists, not because I wanted to create another world in the name of Earthen humanity, but because my God revealed to me in my dreams that I have been called here. He called me from Earth to the stars. To your stars, to tell you about Him, and to bring you the gift of eternal life in Jesus Christ our Lord."

"Jesus, the Messiah." A voice from the back spoke.

"Isstar, our Savior." Another said aloud.

What is happening?

"Isstar, the King of Kings!" A woman shouted.

"Jesus, my Lord and my God!" Thorold exclaimed.

Numerous voices among the crowd, maybe all of them, were shouting in Joelle and also English. Jesse had yet again spoken in tongues, the Joelle tongue, to the villagers without realizing it, and they had understood and responded in kind. The same Holy Spirit, moving among him and them, declaring the same truth about both Jesus and Isstar. Ascribing to them both the names that the Bible used to describe the Messiah from the line of Judah. Such a fervor filled the room, each participant prophesying aloud with hands raised to the ceiling. Jesse blinked and couldn't believe his eyes at this moment. Was he really perceiving small, sepia toned flames dancing on top of their heads, or was it his imagination?

"Praise be to Isstar, Christ Our Lord! All glory and honor and worship be His, in all worlds lift His name above all other names! Amen!" Jesse declared, palms open to the ceiling. His heart, pounding more vigorously than it had ever in his life. The voices stopped as solemnity rested lightly on the bowed heads of the Jolethite congregants.

Oh my God, what have you just shown me here? What have you just shown us here? Jesse thought as he attempted to save every aspect of what just happened to memory. He stored it away, locked where fear nor doubt nor anything else could ever retrieve it. He knew now why God had sent him to Toisee, and it had nothing to do with bringing Jesus to the Jolethites, and everything to do with bridging connections in the Body of Christ.

Jesse spent the rest of the afternoon with the villagers, whom he discovered called themselves Isstarleans, or "Followers of Isstar" in Joelle. Neither he nor they could make direct sense of it yet, how they both could come to worship the same Messiah, but the more they discussed in the limited vocabulary that they had between them, the more they confirmed the movement of the Holy Spirit. Jesse and the Isstarleans had this Pentecostal moment as an anchor point to build on, and they both trusted that as they communed more, the Spirit would reveal more understanding.

He would have stayed with them all through the night, as getting any sleep after this revelation was going to be difficult. But he had a date that he was looking forward to, and the rain was breaking so that he could get back to his quarters in time to change clothes before meeting Elena. So with handshakes to Sillias, Thorold and many others in the village, Jesse said his goodbyes for the evening. Forbidden mandates or not, he was going to come back as often as he could.

When Jesse had arrived back into his quarters, he showered and changed as quickly as possible. He had debated within himself the entire way back from the village what he was going to tell Elena. It was firmly decided that he needed to come clean to her to an extent, but he couldn't go into dramatic detail with what he called the Spiritfall of Rue, the name of the village. He needed something to show her, something to prove to her that there was a connection between Christianity and Isstarleanism. Fortunately, Jesse believed he had just the thing.

It was a very difficult endeavor, but Jesse was able to use what little that Sillias, Thorold and another woman from the village named Esth knew of their English lessons to roughly translate the Scripture verses on the Drodd, the cross-stone. They brought out their instructional pamphlets from the city with some pens and paper. There were 7 inscriptions in all, and 5 were beyond their ability at this time. But two of them were able to get fairly close.

According to their translation, the stone etching read: "I, Isstar, tell you, come my way and live true and live alive forever, because no one will be presented to the Father except by me." They had scribbled it out for him with a number of cross-outs and mistakes. It didn't matter though, as Jesse had a strong suspicion he knew exactly where to find a verse that reminded him of that phrase. It sounded a lot like one of Jesus' 'I Am' statements found in the Gospel of John. When he had turned to it, he paged past "I am the bread of life" found in John 6, and the "Good Shepherd" of John 10. Skimming through the chapters, he came to John 14, where in verse 6 the Bible says: "Jesus said to him, "I am the way, and the truth, and the life. No one comes to the Father except through me." That was it. That was the one he was thinking of. Jesse wrote these passages, one on top of the other, on a piece of paper and compared.

Jesus and Isstar were speaking, they both mentioned following them on the way, to truth and to life. Then they both insisted without doubt the only way to get to the Father was by themselves. John 14:6 matched right up with what Esth had written as Tren 327.

Jesse smiled as he held the paper, then carefully folded it and tucked it into his coat pocket. He checked the time, and he had only 6 minutes to get down to the 1303. Based on how Elena had responded to him earlier in the day, he felt the need to hurry as she might not wait for him, so Jesse rushed out of his room, boldly leaving his Bible splayed open on the desktop for anyone to see.

Crossing the courtyard from the Residential wing to 1303 meant approaching the City Lyceum from the back. This was where gateway building components or the raw ore that was extracted from the mine was delivered, where the materials elevator was, and things were always really busy back there. Because of the influx of additional miners, plus shipments arriving every other day from United Joleth, refined material and completed gateway components were lifted to orbit multiple times a day and night. Even now there was a line of refined structural components being loaded into the elevator, passing the Engineering wing.

Some raw material would be transported via ground vehicles to the

Excavation wing, which housed refineries, melting pots and smithing machines designed to fabricate every component needed to build the slingshot in space. This created quite a loud banging, clanging and hissing from that side of the colony, industrial echoes that would bounce back from the mountain range. The Toiseean Charter Colony was very excited to set an unprecedented record in returning to Earth so quickly, and so the efforts ran nearly round the clock. Only each evening dusk, from 2200 hours to 3000 hours, or roughly from dinner to midnight on Toisee, did the machine shop take a break and the courtyard was much more still. Shipments still ran on the elevator all night, but the din of noise was curtailed quite a bit.

Jesse came around the corner of the City Lyceum on the right side where 1303 was, on the dot at 2130. Scanning the occupied tables on the patio, he didn't find Elena right away, so he ducked inside for a peek.

The mood was jovial as usual inside the bar, where Jesse found it about a third full. Crewmates and junior commanders were mixed and mingled, at tables, at pool or at the bar. Still no sign of Elena, though. It was hard to see towards the back, so Jesse started passing the entryway to see— wait, there she was. Elena was at the bar, facing the bartender and chatting it up. She held what looked to be another Toiseean Sunrise, the drink that she introduced him to weeks ago on the HomeMaker. Jesse took a breath and readied himself to be honest, weaved through a couple tables and slid onto the stool next to her.

"Hey Elena!" He patted her on the shoulder.

She was still facing the bartender in front of her and just finished laughing off something he had said. "Alright Trent, how about I let you know how tonight goes, alright?"

"Fair enough, beautiful." He winked at her. Trent took a quick glance Jesse's way, but must have decided he was much of a threat and he walked away down the bar. Jesse turned to Elena curiously.

"What was that about?" He asked.

"He wants to marry me." She smiled, but Jesse couldn't tell if she was being sarcastic or if she was actually flattered.

"Wow. Miller, now Trent, huh?" Jesse was playful with his tone.

"It IS nice to know you're wanted." She halfheartedly toasted Jesse with her drink. "I mean, isn't that why you're here too? I'm being chased on all sides." She sipped.

"Ya this is our little date I guess, huh?" Jesse said. "But, you're part of this too, right? Aren't you here for me?"

"Jesse, I've been here for you for a while now." She turned to look Jesse directly in the eyes. "You're the one who's comin' a bit late to the party. Now, you have to get in line."

Jesse nodded to himself. "I have been pretty busy up until now —"

Elena huffed and turned away from him to face the back of the bar. "Oh, come off it, Jesse! You haven't been so busy that we couldn't have gone out. We'd been working together so much, you could've asked at any time."

Jesse was taken aback. She seemed really upset at his lack of pursuit, but he didn't know that she had been interested in him at all. Was he that daft? He thought back in his memories of their time together for clues as he responded.

"Elena, I didn't know you wanted me to."

"Ya, Jesse, I'm just that flirtatious with everyone." That one he knew was sarcastic.

"Ok, I'm sorry for waiting for so long. I was nervous about it all and –"

"And now all the good ones are taken, right?"

Jesse was sweating now. This was definitely not how he saw this evening going. Maybe she would have rejected his faith, but he wasn't anticipating her being so upset over his persistent cold shoulder. Plus, he thought she was being unfair with her accusations, as she had never made any kind of pass at him… had she? But what was this now about the good ones being gone?

"All the good ones? What are you talking about?" Jesse then tried a little charm, with a small smile to break the mood. "I've got the best one right here!"

She shot him an angry look that told him now was not the time for jest and flattery. Not the time at all.

"Jesse, do you really not realize that I see the same GEM match scores that you do?"

"Ya, I do." No, he hadn't. Of course she would see their match percentage, she's the other half of the match! Jesse hadn't considered that.

"We match at only 43%. We're literally NOT RECOMMENDED to pair according to Venture." She spun and faced him directly again, her eyes hot and brows furrowed. "I wondered why we had such good chemistry but you never pursued me. You never even hinted towards it. Then you even started to distance yourself from me. You kept holding back when we would work together. It wasn't the same anymore, and it hurt but then I figured out why. You saw the same number I did and ran. I knew then what I meant to you."

She gulped the last of her drink and slammed it on the bartop. Trent and the others a few stools down shot startled glances. Trent then stifled a giggle at Jesse's dumbfounded face. Elena then scooted her stool back and started for the entrance. Jesse hesitated for a moment, still reeling from her confession. He felt incredibly foolish now for the way he handled things, so he chased after her.

"Elena, wait!"

She kept on, speeding her steps to the front of 1303. When she got to the double doors she pushed them both open with one thrust. They flew open and she stormed through. Jesse, though a few steps behind, was able to still scoot through the opening while the doors were still gently closing.

"Eleana, hold on!" He was almost able to grab her arm, but she stopped suddenly and spun around, causing Jesse to throw on the brakes or run into her. She had a tear running down her cheek.

"Why, Jesse? What's the point? We know what the purpose is in all of this, and even if you want me now, it doesn't change the numbers."

They were standing in the middle of the entrance way to 1303 and Jesse needed more privacy than the multiple eyes that were on this scene right now to say what he had to say. He reached out and rested his hand on her upper arm, where he turned and tried to encourage her to an open table.

"Can we sit? I want to tell you something."

She shrugged and walked out of his hand to the table. She sat, leaning her forehead into her palms. Jesse sat next to her instead of across from her. He wanted to be discreet and also intimate with his words.

"What did you mean the purpose of all this?" He asked, but asked in a way of setting up his own counterpoint. He was asking her to clarify so he could rebut.

"GEM matches, Jesse. We're given them to marry, and produce children for the colony. That's their purpose, not to find love but to find a 'mate'."

"And you think that's why I didn't ask you out until now?"

She shook her head yes.

"Elena, I'm gonna be honest and say that I haven't looked at my GEM matches at all until this afternoon, right before I came to see you."

She looked up at him, confused and trying to discern if he was lying. "Why?"

"Because I've been busy –"

She huffed again and started to stand up. "I told you, I don't believe you- "

Jesse reached out and grabbed her wrist. "Please, listen to me!" She glared at him but plopped back down on the bench. "I've purposefully not looked at that list. I didn't want it to distract me from the reason I joined this colony. Actually, I was thrilled to see you on my list at all. I didn't care about the number."

"The reason you came? We joined Venture to bring humanity to the stars. To establish a new world for us to live on. That's not why you're here?"

"And we found it already was here! It's probably already in other places too!"

"Either way, why did you come? If it wasn't for that, what was it for? Are you a criminal?"

Jesse shook his head.

"In debt? Are you running?"

Jesse shook his head again.

"Then what?"

Here it goes. Jesse thought to himself. He hesitated, she stared impatiently, and then he said, "I'm here because Jesus called me to this mission."

She stared at him and blinked. She wanted to disbelieve that he was telling the truth, but she knew Jesse well enough to know when he was lying. He wasn't.

"Jesus?"

"Yes."

"As in the founder of Christianity?"

"Well, the center of Christianity, not the founder… but yes. Him."

She waved him off. "Whatever, but, you know, they don't allow religion in these colonies. What do you think you're doing? It's illegal." She was actually starting to fear for his wellbeing, which annoyed her and her want to be angry.

"Well, I wasn't sure at first. I didn't know what to expect, but Jesus gave me these dreams, and I talked with my parents and a friend back on Archway... but then we got here, and Elena, we found other humans here on Toisee! I figured that Jesus had sent me as a witness or messenger, an evangelist to tell them about Him!"

"Uh huh." She couldn't believe her ears. This seemed like a strange fiction story she was a part of. "So, you're a Christian?"

Jesse nodded his head. "Yes."

Now Elena nodded her head. Jesse tried to read her face as it could have been interpreted as concern or annoyance. "So, what, were you just afraid I would find out and snitch on you? Is that why you shut me out?"

"No, not at all." Jesse looked around to make sure no one was listening in, and he continued. "You were talking about the purpose of the colony was to marry and make babies, right? Well, that's not the reason I want to marry anyone. That wouldn't be my purpose in wanting to marry you. I want to love who I marry for them. Not because some number says we would make good kids."

She nodded again, seemingly willing to accept this as his excuse. "Ok. I get the romance of it." It was what she had wanted in her heart as well, but didn't believe was going to happen. Especially after Jesse had rejected her.

"But most of all, my purpose was to bring Jesus and Christianity here. Or that's what I thought until we went to Rue."

"Where?"

"Oh, that's the name of the village over there." He pointed, forgetting that Elena, along with all of the other colonists, would not have visited it like he had. "We went there for CAPA after we landed, and since then I've met a couple of them."

"Shhh!" Now Elena was looking around as if they were going to be caught. She leaned in a little closer and whispered. "Jesse, we're not supposed to talk to them!" She looked him up and down, honestly surprised and slightly impressed that he was this conniving.

"I know, but once I discovered what... I mean, who they worship, I couldn't stay away. Look at this." He pulled the folded piece of paper out of his pocket and opened it flat on the table in front of Elena. She looked down at it, and followed where he pointed.

"This verse here, John 14:6, is from our Bible on Earth. The thousands of years old witness to the things Jesus said and did, ok?"

"Ok, 'the way, the truth and the life'?" She glanced at him to make sure she was understanding.

"Yes, exactly. Now in the village they have these verses written down of what their Messiah Isstar said long ago, here, on Toisee. Look what it says!" He pointed up to the verse above it, where Esth had written in her pretty handwriting.

She read it out loud. "Come my way and live true and live alive forever?"

"Yes! And they both mention God the Father at the end!"

Elena thought for a moment, trying to see what Jesse was so excited to show her. "Are you saying that Jesus and this other guy —"

"Isstar."

"Ya, Isstar. Are you saying that Jesus and Isstar are... What, the same person?"

"YES!" Jesse whispered emphatically, some much so that Elena had to lean back away from his breath in her face. "Sorry, yes, yes exactly!"

"Just because these kinda match?" Her voice was skeptical, but she did consider it off-putting how similar they were.

"Not just that, but remember when we discovered the Jolethites were here, and Captain Yale explained it by saying that there must be a Universal Seeder? That some kind of ancient aliens spread humanity, or at least planted the seeds for humanity throughout the cosmos?" She nodded. "Who's to say that wasn't God?! The Bible says in the beginning that God created the HEAVENS and the EARTH! What if God was the universal seeder, and He created humanity here and on Earth? That's why the same Jesus, or Isstar appears on both!"

She was guarded. The pieces that Jesse was describing fit together well enough, but it seemed too ridiculous yet. A divine being really did exist, and that's what created people? This Jesus person too?

"But, how did Jesus.. Or Isstar, or whatever. How did he appear on both planets? Was it at the same time?"

"I don't know. I'm not too sure of stuff like that yet. But, Elena, you're the only one I've told this to." He made sure that his eyes met hers. He was going to plead for her understanding with his gaze. "I'm sorry for what happened before, but I want you to know, you're the first person I've trusted to tell this to."

She swallowed and took some breaths. "Wow, I don't know what to think about this. You really believe it?"

"With all of my heart. This is the truth." His confidence was reassuring to her, but also troubling. She didn't know what to believe yet.

There was suddenly a dark shadow over Jesse's shoulder.

"Hey babe, what's going on?" The gruff voice of Rhett Miller loomed. Elena and Jesse looked up, but Rhett was only looking at Jesse though he spoke to Elena.

"Oh! Hey Rhett!" She smiled up at him, and he didn't seem to notice that it was forced.

"This gardener bothering you?" She looked over at Jesse, not sure what to say.

Jesse spoke up. "Well, thanks for looking at that for me, Elena." He took the paper off of the table and stood, folding it into his pocket. "I was a little stuck, but I think you helped me out a lot." When Jesse stood, he pushed into Rhett's chest to do so. The way Rhett didn't move seemed like the man wanted to make sure Jesse noticed that he was at least 6 inches taller and solidly built. Jesse noticed but didn't really care. He looked at Rhett, then back at Elena.

"I'll see you out there in the fields, Elena. Have a good night guys." Jesse smiled at them both, Elena the only one smiling back, squeezed tightly by Rhett's arm around her waist. Jesse felt good about his confession to her, so Rhett's attempt at intimidation didn't even phase him. He could walk away from this conversation knowing that he expressed what he needed to, and it felt good to have let someone know what's been going on. It was a good trial run at what he would be doing a whole lot more starting tomorrow.

CHAPTER 18
A PROPHET IN HIS HOMETOWN

He wasn't cold. Jesse was on top of an epic peak, scanning the Toiseean horizon for miles and miles. The vast distance was mesmerizing. He could perceive rivers and oceans, hills and valleys, mountains and forests. In every direction it stretched on for what looked like infinity, until his eyes were no more use against the fog of distance.

The snow was still around him. It hadn't fallen since he had arrived, and yet his footsteps had disappeared, covered by a lush blanket of glistening white. But yet, instead of feeling the chill at the top of the world, he felt warm. Comforted, as if wrapped in a weighted quilt. This was where he was supposed to be. This was home.

Wait, home… Where is home? Where is Earth? Jesse fought the feeling of comfort and turned his attention to the sky above him. It turned quickly from sky blue at the horizon to navy as he scanned towards directly above him, where it was pitch black. Soupy, thick, and swirling black. He had seen this black before, back when he was lost among the stars. From the capital peak of the Toiseean mountains, Jesse searched the black above him for the familiar stars of old. Which one was Sol? Which one brought light to his Earth?

Come, Jesse, come!

A voice, distant and faint, called from somewhere below him. He ignored it. Looking for his original star. That was his mission. He knew it already was ordained by God, so he gazed on.

Jesse, come!

This time it was louder, as if the wind was carrying the voice a bit better this time around. Still Jesse searched the deep space above him. He wanted to see home. He wanted to bring them the news of Isstar and Jesus. They needed to know. The news had such a potential to unite the planet, and Jesse had to bring it to them.

Suddenly, a bright golden beam shot forward into the black sky above him.

The beam radiated from the surface of Toisee, as if the planet itself was reaching out towards the heavens. Jesse watched as it beamed forever into the impossible distance of space. The black swirls encircled and spun around the penetrating golden beam, shooting further and further away. Jesse felt he was looking down through the top of a cyclone of black.

Until it landed upon a star, a sister star far on the other side of the cosmos. The star sparkled with yellow and golden rays that shone brighter when it was touched by the beam from Toisee, and the connection was made complete between them. Toi had found Sol, and the swirling void sat still, but it did not stop there.

While Sol, the star of Earth, spun and shot its tiny rays of light against the black, the golden beam split and split again. Jesse watched and tried to follow with his eyes the golden thread touching this star, multiplying and touching that star. A web of carefully interconnected strands filled the night sky, as if new constellations were being written and drawn in the heavens above.

Come, come and help us, Jesse!

That voice again from the valley! Jesse closed his eyes against it. Why are you calling to me?! I need to go back to Earth! He thought.

Please, Jesse! Come help us!

Reluctantly, Jesse tore his face from the sky above to the valley below. At the foot of the mountains was a village like Rue. Red buildings, a well in the center, and a taller Church of the Rock, complete with the tip of the stone poking through the roof. Jesse had impossible vision at this point, because he could see the man who had been yelling up to him. It wasn't Sillias, but he looked similar. Worn clothes and skin from working the fields his whole life. He was waving to Jesse, beckoning him to come down from the mountain.

Jesse pondered the tone of the voice he had heard. It was spoken in Joelle, yet he understood every word. And it was not spoken as a plea or beg, as he had originally perceived it. The man had been yelling to Jesse in a way that encouraged Jesse to join them, as if Jesse had a special gift or component to bring which would enhance what they were doing. Another, strong hand to pull the hard rope against the rulers and principalities of this world. And as Jesse was about to take a step down, he awoke.

Jesse sat up on his bunk. He hadn't had a dream like that one since before he left on the HomeMaker. It was special, and definitely the same timbre as those previously from YHWH. He wrestled with the meaning as he absentmindedly got up, dressed and ready for the day.

Do they want me to stay? Jesse's thoughts circled upon the warm reception and kinship he experienced in the village of Rue. They recognized as much as he did their deep spiritual connection, so it would make sense that they wanted him to remain with them.

But I need to tell Earth. They need to know that these Jolethite humans are here because of God Almighty. The potential that he had discussed with Elena, how it could bring the planet together in recognition of our shared humanity. It could elevate us beyond our differences to realize that not only are there others out there, but that Jesus and Isstar are what defines us as His creations.

So, was it my own want to be with the Isstarleans of Rue that compelled me to stay, or was that God telling me that's where he wants me to be? Well, that's the big question of the dream, isn't it? Jesse let this soak in, attempting to see which side was stronger in his heart. But nothing was coming, nothing that he would consider solid evidence to choose either direction. To stay here on Toisee, or to return to Earth as soon as possible. He prayed for direction from Jesus and the Holy Spirit, and for doors to be open or closed to him to make his decision easier.

In the meantime, it's time that others knew. "How then will they call on him in whom they have not believed? And how are they to believe in him of whom they have never heard? And how are they to hear without someone preaching?" His reading from Romans the other night came back to the forefront of his mind. He had duties to perform, CAPA assignments to oversee, but he would make sure to find the time this afternoon to stand up and make the announcement to the colony. He didn't know what to say, but he had some time to work it out.

The Toiseean day was uncharacteristically bathed in gorgeously orange sunlight. It was still mostly cloudy, but there were more peeks of blue in the grey cloud cover than usual. This enhanced the mood of all the colonists to a point where everyone was nearly jovial to be about their assignments. Because of the extra sunrays, the day felt warm as well. Warm enough that a few of the off duty Earthers laid out and basked or sunbathed across the courtyard in Toi's occasionally direct rays.

Jesse's rounds took him all throughout the Ag Wing. He was in charge of monitoring the nursery growth of about half of the Jolethite crops that the colonists were cultivating. He and Rin had worked to genetically modify a few of them to produce quicker and use less water, and the tested results looked good in the nursery. They were hardy, cold growing plants already due to the climate of Toisee, and so only a few slight modifications were necessary. Compared to the control group, the GMO Toisee crops were already twice their height and girth after only one week of germination. From here the infant plants would be carefully transported from the nursery and then transplanted into the southern fields that have been prepared for them.

This is where Jesse found himself spending the late morning before breaking for lunch. It was about 14:30 and Jesse, like the other colonists, was still having a hard time adjusting to the longer days on Toisee. He was tired and hungry, ready for a break to sit and eat, but the last of the transports were coming out and he had to lead them to the field for prep. He drove the front tractor, pulling the long trailer carefully along the newly graveled pathway to the section of the south field allotted for this crop of what they had dubbed Toiseean Lettuce. The baby teal leaves jostled and tossed behind him as he carefully navigated along, a train of 4 more behind him, making a grand total of just over 3000 plants to be planted.

All to be done by hand, to much bemoaning of the colonists. Transplanting was considered delicate work that could not be achieved by the colonists' machinery without a high chance of crop loss. Jesse had been assigned 32 specialists and a couple professionals from the Ag Wing to complete the job, but also 12 Jolethite locals had been hired as well. They were technically assigned to and being watched over by Junior Ag Director Kitting, as all Jolethite locals were carefully observed by members of the command staff. When Jesse and his train of infant lettuce pulled into place for transplant along the side of the section of field, he found Kitting and the locals already waiting.

Jesse parked and dismounted, as did his train of professionals behind him. Due to the lateness of the hour, they implored him to allow an early lunch.

"Hey kid, let's go ahead and break for lunch, alright?"

"Ya, we can start on these transplants in a few. They ain't goin' anywhere."

Jesse checked his watch and glanced at JD Kitting. Ralph nodded in approval from his perch on top of the Jolethite transport, so Jesse turned to his specialists and raised his voice for them to hear.

"Alright everyone, go ahead and take your hour lunch break. We'll start transplants at 15:45."

Each of the specialists reached among the horticultural transport jumper seats to find wherever they had stashed their to-go lunch pails. Jesse retrieved his from under the driver's seat of the tractor he drove and dismounted. Nearby was a small outcropping of trees and ferns, which is where most of the colonists took their breaks. Not necessarily to get out of the sun, but because the thick turquoise moss grew well there and it was a soft space to rest.

While Jesse and the others made their way to the small forest oasis, they passed by the Kitting and the Jolethite day laborers. Standing over them, he was scribbling on his tablet, and attempting to tell them it was break time, but they seemed to disagree with him. Jesse didn't understand their speech, but the one Jolethite that spoke back to Ralph seemed to protest. Jesse could see a necklace of Drodd hanging from the Jolethites neck, and as he looked for it on the others, he saw most of them did too.

Ralph Kitting threw up his hands in frustration and tossed the tablet to his seat. "Fine, y'all wanna work, go head!"

Ralph walked alongside Jesse as the Jolethites went to the lettuce transports and started carefully off-loading the crops. Others picked up shovels and started for the field. Ralph spoke to Jesse but was looking ahead to the forest oasis.

"If they don't want to eat, I suppose that's on them. But, I'm going to sit down for a while."

"They don't want a break?" Jesse asked curiously.

"We've been out here all day as they insisted that the field needed to be prepared. I told them that our plows had already cleared the weeds and opened the soil. All we needed to do was wait for y'all to arrive, but nooooo. They wanted to turn the field by hand, and then started using that horse thing over there to plow again what we had already done!" Ralph pointed to the side of where the colonists were resting. The horse thing, actually called a 'trace' by the locals, was grazing next to a three-tined wooden plow. The trace resembles a horse for the most part, similar in body shape except the coat was much thicker due to the cold, and the head was broad and bulky like that of a bull.

"Those Joel's don't know how to listen." Ralph used the slang term that colonists had begun to use when referring to the Jolethites.

"They have a determined work ethic, huh?" Jesse said. They had reached the mossy place of the tree line and Ralph slumped down among some of the other specialists. He tossed his lunch aside for the moment and laid his head down on the ground. Jesse remained standing above them as they sat.

"An insatiable one. I'm just here to do what command asks, and nothing more. I wouldn't even be out here if they didn't say so."

"Hey Kitting, couldn't we just let them do it all if they want to?" A specialist, Samier, threw out.

"Ya, if they want to keep going, we can just watch 'em right?" Another specialist, Jolean, asked.

"It's tempting, isn't it?" Ralph agreed. "Honestly, there's no one else out here to tattle if we did! They certainly couldn't tell anyone!" They chuckled together as they halfway considered letting the Jolethites finish their assignments for them while they rested in the moss.

Jesse turned to watch Joel's steadily work the field. From this distance he heard them chatting among themselves. But the more he watched and listened, he could tell they weren't talking but singing to each other as they worked. Observing the scene brought a Scripture verse to mind:

Whatever you do, work heartily, as for the Lord and not for men, knowing that from the Lord you will receive the inheritance as your reward. You are serving the Lord Christ.

Jesse said aloud over the chatter behind him. "They're working for someone bigger than themselves."

"Who? Leader Sherii?" Specialist Jolean, whom Jesse was helping on Founding Day was next to him, sitting on the moss. He hadn't noticed she was in ear-shot. Jesse looked down at her and corrected her assumption.

"They're working for God." He said plainly.

She scoffed and looked away, then back at him. "Oh, you're for real? Are they even religious? How do you know?"

"Who's religious?" JD Kitting said, leaning up on his elbows. Of course a Junior Director would be sensitive to hearing about someone else's declaration of faith. Command personnel were supposed to be the gatekeepers of Venture company policy.

Jesse pointed out towards the Jolethites. "They're out there working hard because they serve a God that they love."

"Oh." Ralph looked out at them, then laid back down. "Good for them."

Jolean repeated her question to Jesse. "How do you even know that?"

"I can see it. Look, listen." Jesse tilted his chin towards the laborers, and Jolean turned her head to the side, cupping her hand to her ear. She listened for a few seconds.

"I can hear them singing."

"It's worship. They're singing to God as they work."

"Hmm." She stayed listening for a moment, as the melody was soothing. A couple other sitting specialists had started paying attention as well, unbeknownst to Jesse. He started to feel compelled to explain more about the reason they work so hard while the colonists rest. The Spirit was nudging him to witness.

"You see," Jesse started. "Work for them isn't work, it's an opportunity. They get to work. It's a privilege for them because they work whole-heartedly as an act of service to their God."

"It helps that they're getting paid, too, I bet." Said a specialist behind Jolean.

Jesse addressed him. "Oh, no doubt it's an added perk. But then why are they working now while we rest? They would get paid the same regardless of if they took a break with us now or not, wouldn't they?"

The man was quiet. Ralph chimed in again.

"The way I see it, they're foolish for going at it so hard. They aren't gaining anything more but grinding on an empty stomach to finish, what, a few minutes earlier?" He argued.

"Have you ever done anything simply because you loved to do it?" Jesse pried.

"What, like a hobby?"

"A hobby, job, duty... whatever. Something you do not because you are told or you are expected to do it, but that you do it for the love of someone else."

Kitting thought for a moment. "I always got up early on my mother's birthday to cook her breakfast when I was a kid." A specialist resting near him said 'Aww', to which a few snickers responded among the others.

"And you did that, why?" Jesse was leading with his questions.

"Because I loved my mother."

"But you weren't getting paid, right? No other benefits?"

"No, but who wouldn't do that for their mom?" Ralph fought back.

"I'm just saying, that's why they serve God that way. They love Him so much, they work with no break, with a smile and a song, till the job is done. They do it out of love."

Ralph narrowed his eyes at Jesse. "How is it that you know so much about this religion of theirs?"

"I've spent some time with them in line with my CAPA duties. I understand their motivation." He hesitated, but it was time to start his witness. It felt like the moment was ripe to give an example from himself as well. "It's my motivation too."

Kitting sat up, as did a couple others in earshot. This conversation was getting personal, controversially personal.

"What are you saying, Heartshire? You agree with these religious Joel's?" Kitting accused.

"Think about that Universal Seeder stuff that Captain Yale told us about and consider something for a moment. We've travelled over 100 light-years from Earth, and we find other humans on an alien planet. Same exact DNA as us. And the best way we can explain how this could be is that an ancient alien race 'planted' them here, like they did to us, like they did to this field?" Jesse pointed out towards the working Joel's and the cultivated field.

"Or maybe an Almighty God created us and them, and then He put us here. After all, we knew there was life here based on a created radio signal. What the Jolethites had created. Isn't it safe to assume that God exists and created us both, Jolethites and Humans, because we are here? Because of what we've discovered?"

A few groans could be heard from those who listened. They didn't want to hear this while they were having lunch. This kind of bogus chatter was supposed to be left behind on Earth. But Jesse kept going.

"What they are planting is what we designed in a laboratory. It didn't exist before, we made it. And now we are taking it and very specifically planting it somewhere where it was designed to grow and flourish. How is that different from what God could have done with us?"

Ralph was now getting more annoyed. "You could argue the same thing about the ancient Universal Seeders, Jesse. That doesn't prove anything."

"Ok, do you want to know what does then?" Jesse didn't like the way his first witnessing opportunity was going. He didn't seem to have an ally in the crowd, so he was going to pull out all the stops. "What if I said that their history matches ours identically? If we grew and developed independently, what would be the chances that could happen?"

"They don't even have the technology that we do. Our histories don't match!" Ralph pointed out.

"No, but their teachings of Isstar match so closely with our teachings of Jesus... It's a miracle."

"Jesus?!" JD Kitting stood up. "What do you know about Jesus? Jesse, I thought you had more sense than that. You need to watch what you say."

"If I showed you, would you believe it?" Jesse challenged. Ralph was approaching him. "If I could show you that verses of our Bible match verses of their Isstar, two documents' thousands of years old. There's no way that they could have ever influenced each other, and there's so many matches it's beyond coincidence."

"Do you have a Bible, Jesse?" Ralph's voice was challenging him, he wasn't listening anymore. Venture colonies chose their command level personnel well, as Junior Director Kitting was fully ready to turn Jesse in simply for discussing matters of religion when it was prohibited.

Jesse wasn't backing down though. Actually, he felt a little desperate to turn Kitting and the other's hearts towards the simple possibility that he spoke the truth. The fact that he wasn't willing to hear him out, drove Jesse's desire to proclaim it all the more.

"Would you at least listen if I showed you?" Jesse's voice was a small plea against the junior director's threat. Ralph was directly in front of him, but silent. "One, small example. And then I'll stop." Ralph was still silent. Jesse took his quietness as an allowance to proceed, and so he did.

"Thank you." Jesse reached into his jacket pocket and pulled out another small piece of handmade paper from the village of Rue. He carefully unfolded it and then held it up next to his face.

"This was written down in the village, by the village elder, as he translated one of their sacred writings." Jesse pointed to the verse that Sillias had written down for him.

"Bear with your mouth that Isstar is Lord and believe in your soul that God raised him from death, and salvation is yours."

Jesse then pointed to the translation of Romans 10:9 that Jesse had copied from his Bible in his quarters.

"If you confess with your mouth that Jesus is Lord and believe in your heart that God raised him from the dead, you will be saved."

He held the verses in front of Ralph as still as he could, but due to all the excitement and accusation, Jesse's hands were shaking. Ralph tried to read it, but then frustratingly grabbed the paper with both hands to hold it steady for Jesse. There was a heavy stillness all around while JD Kitting read the paper. Ralph finished reading and looked back at Jesse.

"You believe in our scientific method, right Ralph? All I am doing is testing this hypothesis and it keeps matching with the data." Jesse lowered his arm and was about to put the paper back in his pocket, but Jolean snatched it from him. He was about to protest, except Jesse saw that she was reading and comparing too, so he let go of the piece.

"Where did you get that?" Junior Director Kitting was now asking less intensely.

"From the village."

"And the Bible?"

Jesse breathed, and then confessed. "It's mine."

"Hmm." Ralph said. Then he turned and looked around at everyone. Nearly all of the Toiseean Ag colonists that were with them had begun huddling around, listening to what was being said. JD Kitting swung his head to address them.

"Alright everyone. It's time we finish this job. Let's get to work!"

The specialists all slowly rose, putting away their lunch totes and pails and started back towards the transports to unload and plant the Toiseean Lettuce with the Joel's. Jesse remained with Ralph, who seemed to be waiting until all of the specialists were out of hearing range. He looked Jesse in the eyes.

"Jesse, you've done some great work for this colony. You have a bright head on those shoulders. But as Junior Director, I am going to have to report this to command." He sounded reluctant. Jesse sighed but was unphased emotionally.

"I know. I know what the charter says."

"I suggest you find a way to recant your position before you see Captain Yale. You're a member of CAPA, and been given special oversight privilege because of your demonstrated worth. He will want to keep you if he can. Make it easy for him to, do you understand?"

Ralph was being sincere, Jesse could tell. Maybe he was touched by Jesse's witness more than he wanted to admit? Jesse couldn't see it in his eyes. But he could see that he was acting out of duty and not want.

"Yes, sir."

"You're dismissed for the day. I would expect a visit from Captain Yale before too long." With that Ralph Kitting walked past Jesse and into the field. Jesse stood still and looked up towards the broken clouds in the sky.

It was still a beautiful day. The sun of Toi was bright orange overhead, large and looming, about the size of Jesse's palm if he held it up. It felt as if it was a giant eye, its focus fixated upon Jesse and his exposing confession of faith. Had he failed? Had he succeeded? He couldn't tell. It felt like failure, based on the argument and lack of any acknowledgement of the points he had made. All he knew is that he tried when he felt like he was supposed to. And so he would try to take comfort in that. After all, Jesus wants a heartful witness, and not necessarily a competent one, right?

Junior Director Kitting was correct, as it did not take long for Captain Yale to send for Jesse once he had returned to his quarters. Jesse was in the middle of prayer, trying to restore his confidence in his witness and confession, when a buzz came to his door. He closed his Scriptures and tucked them under his mattress. He then stood but paused, considering for a moment, and then withdrew the Bible from under the bed and looked around his room. He felt he needed a better hiding place and was quickly trying to consider where the safest place to hide something was.

BUZZ!! THUD THUD THUD!!

"Heartshire, you in there?!" A voice from beyond the door declared.

"Ya! One second!" Jesse hollered back. His eyes scanned the room, bed, desk, shower, hamper... Hamper! Jesse pulled all of his dirty clothes out from the laundry hamper, set the Bible on top of a pair of pants at the bottom, then piled them all back on top. He finished and then opened the door to two security personnel.

"Jesse Heartshire, Captain Yale requests a meeting with you."

"Yea, I've been expecting it." Jesse walked out from his quarters and followed behind the first security officer while the other walked behind Jesse. They lead him through the Residential Wing, then out across the courtyard towards the City Lyceum.

Jesse figured that they would be going towards the command offices, and so he started to turn towards them as they approached, but the officer from behind grabbed his shoulder. He forcibly redirected him back in line with the officer in the front.

"No, this way."

"Not to the command office?"

"Captain Yale is inspecting the progress of the gateway from orbit."

Jesse trotted back inline with the officers. He felt watched by all of the colonists that happened to be milling about in the courtyard, carrying out their assignments. In reality, only a few seemed to notice this security escort crossing around behind the City Lyceum to the materials elevator. One of those did care a great deal about what was happening. That was Elena.

The orbital materials elevator was an incredible feat of engineering. Again, another piece of technology that was only made possible by the invention of the singularity drives as it requires a massive amount of energy to perform its function. A dozen gigawatts of energy is piped down from the drive in orbit to the 1000 square foot mag-lift elevator. The deck of which has multiple tie down locations to secure materials and machinery as it is rocketed back to the waiting command section of the HomeMaker. And rocketed it is, albeit with electron magnets and not conventional thrusters. At lift off from the ground the elevator is relatively slow to accelerate, but once it reaches a few hundred feet in height acceleration reaches 3.5 G's all the way through the stratosphere. This part of the journey takes nearly 10 minutes, so for only the most pressing needs will the colonists make the trip as none of them enjoy the discomfort.

Jesse and the security officers entered the main lift bay, passing by a few engineering workers as they performed their final checks on the payload to be delivered to the gateways construction efforts. It appeared they were going to share the ride up with a number of structural components for the outer ring of the slingshot. Jesse recognized a few of the beacon lights that were attached to the outside of the Lunar Gateway from when he watched their launch from the Moon. He, like most, was surprised at their massive size when viewed up close. These parts of the gateway were a few feet taller than himself, and yet they only looked like small blinking lights from his perspective in the escape pod of the HomeMaker.

The security pair escorted Jesse to a line of simplistic looking, military grade jump seats along the back wall of the lift elevator. They resembled backyard folding sling chairs, but were definitely not near as flimsy. Jesse had to exert some effort just to fold his down from the wall. Once unfurled, Jesse sat in between the two guards and they all three started to strap themselves in.

Not a moment too soon, for as Jesse was finishing pulling his shoulder straps tight, a flashing yellow light strobed and an alarm sounded.

ASCENSION IMMINENT! ASCENSION IMMINENT!

Hisses and unbuckling lock sounds rotated around the inside of the elevator. The floor rumbled and creaked under the weight of the lift and its packed machinery. Jesse felt his stomach start to drop, and so craned his neck to see out the porthole window behind him. Sure enough the lift was starting to gently rise. The landscape behind the City Lyceum was the north side of the colony, which was the direction that Jesse's porthole faced. As the lift rose, he was able to see more and more of the blue forest, and then the hills beyond where redwalled Rue village homes started to appear. He longed to return there, but with this upcoming meeting with Yale, Jesse doubted it might be any time soon.

MAGLIFT ACCELERATION! MAGLIFT ACCELERATION!

5... 4... 3... 2... 1...

At one, a swelling and dramatic downforce pushed Jesse and his security companions into their seats. He quickly swung his head back and leaned it against his hard metal headrest. Jesse could feel weight pressing down on his chest and legs, as if he had just been covered with sandbags, and they were still steadily piling them on. Breathing was a chore, labored and forced. As the maglift powered to full force, he could feel his face being stretched by the acceleration, pulled down and aging his appearance by at least a few decades. Jesse knew that the worst phase of the elevator would last only about 10 minutes, but the seconds dragged on slower with each of his heavy breaths.

Then, blissfully, the crushing pressure lessened. The sandbags were starting to be lifted off his chest, face and thighs until only a few remained. They were still accelerating, actually much faster now, but due to the reduction of atmosphere at higher and higher altitude the ride was easier. Jesse craned his neck again to view what he could outside the porthole.

Toisee was drifting down and away from his sight. It's swirling greys now a familiar sight from orbit. Jesse remembered seeing it for the first time as they descended. How intimidated he was then at what lay ahead. He could never have imagined what they had discovered, what God had created and shown him. Jesse reminisced in his thoughts over the past few weeks, first with the first interaction with the siblings on the planet.

He remembered how touched he was at the bravery and compassion of the little girl, her loving offer of the flower that made for a perfect introduction to this new world. And his first attempt at witnessing his faith to them as they left. He recalled the face the boy had made, shocked and surprised. Did I speak to him in Joelle and I hadn't even noticed?! Jesse considered for the first time, as he recounted the event in his head. Every other time he had spoken of God to the Jolethites, the Holy Spirit had intervened and given him the tongue to witness to them. Jesse smiled at the realization that, yes, in fact he believed he did. He hadn't considered that was why the boy was so surprised at his words, but it made perfect sense now.

Then the encounter with the father and daughter at the well in Rue. Where his Scripture reading had inspired him to see the similarities in the scene he found himself a part of. It warmed his heart to place himself there again in his mind, and he closed his eyes to envision again the feeling of surprise and awe to be filled with the Spirit of God in that moment. To feel the words coming from his mouth, touched, organized and sent forth with the direct blessing of YHWH. He loved the connection he shared with the people of Rue, but most of all it was the connection they shared through Jesus. Or Isstar.

Jesse now remembered the feeling of the stone, the Drodd in their worship space. It's cool and smooth surface he could still feel as if it lingered on his fingertips. He could imagine tracing the words etched upon it, feeling the groves and divots, letting the rough places scrape gently on his nails. He envisioned the drawing that Thorold had made in the dirt, and he felt his eyes watering as Jesse pictured what Isstar would have looked like, tied to that stone. His blood running down his beaten and bruised back, making his footholds slippery against the rock. His arms tied above his head, exposing him bare to his accusers. The Christ, dying in place of Jesse and all of the other Christians on Toisee.

And now, what? Jesse had exposed himself to his accusers as well. The carefully guarded secret that could be a secret no more. How could he keep this to himself? Especially in light of this miracle news, that God created humanity and extended them across the cosmos, apparently giving Jesus to each one of them. How could he claim to love Jesus and reach out to the lost without telling them the truth about God? A truth that had revealed itself to Jesse with his first few breaths upon Toisee. Jesse knew the rules of the colony, and he correctly foresaw this punishment coming, but as the apostles in the book of Acts exclaimed to the Pharisees, he must obey God rather than men.

Their approach to the command section of the HomeMaker, the Gate Base, the acting hub for the construction of the Toiseean slingshot gateway, was subtle compared to the launch from the surface. Jesse's porthole did not provide a view of anything except the stars beyond and the white glow of Toisee below them. If he tried very hard he could look down towards the planet, but their orbit was so high it wasn't visible without effort. All he could do was wait, listening to the sounds of the retro thrusters firing intermittently. Even with him listening, Jesse was still surprised when the elevator itself fired its thrusters not to slow them, but to spin them. The entire lift twisted and rotated 180 degrees, flipping the occupants and cargo upside down. Then it struck him, they were on approach to the command section and the singularity drive's gravity was now pulling him 'up', away from the planet's surface. There wasn't much of a period of weightlessness in the elevator because the handoff between Toisee's gravity and the command section was so quick due to their speed. Jesse wouldn't have noticed aside from the noise and the stars spinning outside. Then there was the sound he anticipated, the retro thrusters slowing the elevator lift to its destination. Jesse and the security pair felt themselves lift off of their seats for a few seconds before the thrust quit and the gravity of the drive pulled them down again.

Lift docking procedure starting. Arrival to Gate Base in 30 seconds.

Jesse took a deep breath. He hadn't prepared anything to say. No doubt Captain Yale would have questions and strong concerns, but all Jesse could think to do was be as truthful as possible. The worst that Yale could do was disbelieve him, but Jesse's want and need for deception was over. He was ready to come clean, and even eager to do so.

The Gate Base, was the top 5 levels of the HomeMaker starship converted into the construction and assembly space for the orbital gateway. This meant that most of the colonist engineers and professionals worked in a rotation on board, and also that the place was in chaotic disarray on the usual. Pallets of heavy machinery, batteries and fuel canisters, electrical and mechanical components were stashed along every corridor. In the driven haste of Captain Yale, organization and cleanliness were secondary to assembly and completion. The eyes and faces of most crewmembers that Jesse's security detail passed were ripe with focus and determination. They didn't even look at each other, apparently existing only to move on to their next task or assignment as if busy bodied ants riled by their queen. Their king, in this situation.

The security pair walked Jesse to a makeshift office at the end of a packed hallway. The door slid open, and inside was Captain Tristan Yale and Ag Director Shea Willow. Both were seated across from each other at a basic cafeteria table, with papers and construction blueprints all over. A large window behind them overlooked the construction of the slingshot gateway, attached by multiple tethers to the command section. Numerous bots and manned assembly pods were flying here or there. Bright lights of the welding of pieces together shown where a bot was attached to joints in various places. The entire circle of the gateway was well over halfway complete, maybe 60-65% around? It was smaller in size than the Lunar Gateway, which made its construction even faster.

There was a chair unattended next to Shea, that Tristan directed him to.

"Heartshire. Have a seat." His voice was cold, not near the political joy he had heard from him previously when commended on his CAPA position. Jesse sat down, glancing over at Shea. She gave him a look of disappointment.

"Undoubtedly you know why you are here." Yale started, his hand touching on an open tablet. Jesse could see the top of the report that Junior Director Kitting had filed. "What you might be wondering is why I would prioritize this meeting and bring you here, now."

"I understand that faith is forbidden in the Toiseean Charter, if that's what you mean." Jesse said, directly to the point.

"Faith? No. No, Jesse, faith is most certainly not forbidden on Toisee." Yale looked down at the tablet. "In actuality, I want you and every other colonist to have plenty of faith." He pushed back his chair and stood. He leaned over the table, pulling an agricultural plan towards Jesse for his attention. "I want you to have faith that your duty to the colony means something." Then he turned his attention to the scene outside the window. "I want you to have faith that you're part of something bigger than yourself. Bigger than this colony. As big as the future of humanity." He turned back to Jesse with his arms folded behind his back. "I want you to have faith, but the correct one."

Jesse responded. "I do have faith in something bigger than myself. That's what I have discovered here."

"The God of Toisee?" Director Shea scoffed. "Jesse, we've already explained how these Jolethites came to be on this planet. Same as we came to be on ours."

"God being the Universal Seeder makes just as much sense as some ancient alien ancestor does. More in fact." Jesse retorted.

"Where is this God?" Shea counted her fingers as she spoke. "We can measure our DNA and compare it with theirs. We can see how life grew, evolved and matured on this planet the same as ours. We cannot see this apparent creator being you claim."

"I've experienced him, here and back on Earth." Jesse leaned forward in his chair. "Director, have you ever had a dream that you knew was more than just a dream?" He wanted to try to get her to understand.

She laughed out loud and looked over at Captain Yale, whose face was still stern. Shea turned back to Jesse. "A dream, Jesse? That's your proof?"

"A prophetic one, yes. I may not be able to show you what God showed me, but it's what caused me to sign up with Venture to begin with."

"Yes! Let's talk about you and your signature!" She raised a hand to stop him from speaking further and picked up her tablet from the table. She swiped it a couple times and then read it out loud to Jesse. "Paragraph 13, Section 4: Those persons who willingly participate as colonists within the scope of Venture Colonies, under this Horizon/Toisee Charter, are forbidden the establishment of a church, convening a religious assembly, or participating in any recognized practice of faith."

Shea offered the tablet to Jesse, pointing at the bottom of the screen. "This is your signature, is it not?"

Jesse had to admit, "Yes, it is."

"Your 'preaching' is an admission to faith that is clearly in violation of the terms of the Toiseean Charter." She seemed to relish catching Jesse in this trap. "Jesse, I have had such a high opinion of you and your work ethic. I am disappointed." She said these words, but Jesse didn't believe it based on her tone.

"The charter banning faith is ridiculous. Especially in light of –"

"A charter that you signed." She persisted.

"Yes, but when –"

"A contract you willingly entered."

Jesse sighed frustratingly. She wasn't going to let him finish.

"Director Willow, let him speak." Tristan Yale was still standing over the table, watching and listening to her handle the situation, but here he interjected.

"Yes, I signed it, you're right. But I have to break this contract. Director Willow, Captain Yale, I've experienced miracles on Toisee. Physical, spiritual and historical… all measurable and witnessed miracles within the village of Rue. What I've seen and done among the people there, I… I… I can't explain other than to say that God is real. That Jesus has done incredible things. That the Holy Spirit is powerfully moving here. It's beyond doubt, and I am sorry for how complicated this makes things, but I have to say so." Jesse found that exasperating to say and relaxed his posture. "I am compelled to."

Shea Willow shook her head, she still looked at him as if he was to be pitied. As if he was digging his own grave and she couldn't stop him. She glanced over at Yale as he spoke.

"Let me tell you what makes your faith dangerous, Jesse. We are leading humanity into this new frontier, and you are trying to pull it backwards. We have a partnership with Leader Sherii, whose nation has done away with these superstitious notions of deity a long time ago. The sect that you have interacted with in Rue are outsiders of major society. They are cessationists and decry everything that Sherii and the government is progressing for the Jolethites. But what United Joleth falls short of in terms of technology, they have superseded us in communal culture and governmental oversight. They don't need a God to provide for them the comforts, protection, guidance and discipline that Joleth provides. And neither do we."

Captain Yale sat back down in his large office chair. He folded his hands on the table.

"Your faith will lead others away from seeing the Toiseean Colony President as the one whom they should trust for their livelihood. And like how Sherii deals with the villagers," He made a fist and pounded his pointer finger into the table with his next syllables. "I will not let that happen."

Yale paused for dramatic effect, watching Jesse listen to his words, their eyes locked.

"So let me tell you what is going to happen." He pointed at his subordinate." You, Jesse, will cease and desist all expressions of your Christianity. If you wish to retain that delusion, it must be contained within your head. Any and all materials related to this faith of yours will be confiscated and destroyed. Based upon your actions and your refusal to recant, your privileges related to CAPA are hereby rescinded, including access to the village of Rue, or any other Jolethite personnel. And you will spend 3 days within the confines of the colony brig."

He turned to Director Shea. "You can provide him with a work detail that he can complete from his temporary home, yes?"

"Yes, captain." She nodded in agreement.

Yale looked back at Jesse, his eyes strong with warning. "You understand that any other infractions will have more dire consequences?"

Jesse's face was calm, but dejected. He had expected a harsh reprimand, and so he wasn't saddened by the punishment. It even surprised himself, but he was mostly disappointed in their callousness towards his story. He wouldn't even be allowed to show them.

"Yes, sir. I understand."

Captain Yale did not look pleased with his answer. Maybe he could read in Jesse's face that he wasn't defeated, only cast down. Either way, Jesse would be on his sensitive radar from now on. "Mr. Heartshire, you still have valuable contributions to be made here to the Toiseean Colony. I have faith that you are redeemable, but you must be willing. Either way, we will be watching and waiting for your rehabilitation." Jesse sat still, politely waiting for Yale to finish.

"Dismissed."

The security guards came back into the room and escorted Jesse back to the lift elevator. It was being loaded with engineering personnel who were rotating back to the colony for their time off. They chit-chatted about what they would be doing, what games they would play, how long they would sleep, or what they would eat in 1303. Jesse let it sink in that he no longer had those freedoms, and would be cold and uncomfortable for the next 3 days in the brig.

But still, he could feel his soul attempt to feel self pity over his predicament, and yet he could not. A fire was burning still inside his chest, a feeling of pride or self-esteem that simply denied him the ability to feel defeated after this encounter. The thought of the Scripture in Acts again came to him, where the disciples felt compelled to obey God in the face of persecution from the authority. Now, he very much understood how they felt, and why they had leaped for joy after being persecuted for the name of Jesus.

CHAPTER 19
HILLS AND VALLEYS

The first day in the brig was the most difficult. The worst of it was the difficulty in guesstimating the time. His cell was small, approximately an arms-breadth wide and maybe 8 feet long. Enough for a cot, and a chair that doubled as a sink and toilet. It was uncomfortably close together, and Jesse wasn't given to claustrophobia. But there was no window, and the lighting remained the same regardless of the hour of the day. Jesse didn't know if that was part of the punishment, or if the security personnel simply forgot to turn the lights down at night. Either way, his chances of being an escape risk must be low as the presence of the guards were nil until it was mealtime. This was his only measure of the passage of time, that he would be brought breakfast, lunch and dinner. He would have welcomed a bit of menial work from Director Willow, but the tasks never came.

When he awoke on the second day, or at least what he assumed was the second day, the full measure of the weight of his punishment was felt. Now he understood that the second day was actually the most difficult to endure. His personal pride in standing up for his faith was waning. He did not regret his decision in the slightest, but as time crawled away, he had more opportunity for it to feel less significant. The high of the moment was fading away as peaks of life often do.

His prayers kept him focused on Jesus' will for him at this moment. Jesse longed to hold his Scriptures in his hands, to feel the tangible love of God in his arms. The next time he was able to hold his Bible, that's probably what he would do. Simply hold it, hugging the Word close. It was a comfort he even wondered if he would have again as Captain Yale had mentioned they were going to confiscate anything religious he'd had. That means they most certainly will have searched his quarters while he was in the brig. He hoped that his last second hiding place would not be discovered, as who wants to go through someone else's dirty laundry?

By breakfast on the third day in the prison, Jesse began to feel surprisingly and satisfyingly renewed. With still no work from Shea, he had only his prayers, thoughts and an occasional hymn to bide his time here. He never was much of a singer, but the poetry of the words had always captivated him. They also seemed more poignant here. In a way, he was thankful now for the opportunity to excuse himself from his daily duties and be trapped here. He had no other temptation to distract himself from intimacy with the Holy Spirit. This caused him to talk to God a lot. He now knew exactly what he had to do once he was released from this cell, and it would most certainly land him right back in it.

Paul, Peter, James, John. All of these apostles of Christ and the believers that followed, they never prayed against persecution in the Scriptures. They prayed for strength to endure. Obviously, they didn't want to be persecuted, but something happened to them and the church when they were chased, beaten, imprisoned or attacked for their proclamation of Jesus. They were emboldened. They bravely went out and continued the work with fervor. Why, Jesse now understood completely, was due to the clarity of purpose and mission that persecution defines.

For sure, encouragement and acceptance makes the heart want to continue in its mission as well, but persecution for the church has always been the most effective driving force. Nothing else but suffering for the truth of the Cross, just as Jesus did, brings the believer into such perfect unity with the will of God. When the only reason that someone hates a Follower of Jesus is for simply being a follower of Jesus, faith is made crystal clear. Everything makes perfect sense when the world hates someone in the same way it hated Christ. A believer's heart is made assured of its election by God, of its oneness within the Body of Christ. And now Jesse shared that same tenacity of the abused early church. All he could think about was getting back to the work that he had been called to do.

The main door from the security hallway slid open to the holding cells. Jesse absentmindedly checked his wrist as it 'felt' early for lunch. He chuckled to himself when he noticed that he had forgotten they had taken his wristwatch, a fact he already knew but had looked out of habit.

But rounding the corner, coming into view at the end of the corridor was not the usual security personnel but Elena. Jesse sat up from his cot and stood at the clear polycarbonate cell door.

"Elena? What are you doing here?"

"I needed to see you. Are you doing alright?" Her face was set on something, but there was also genuineness in her voice. She did actually seem relieved to see him, regardless of how testy their last interaction was. Jesse wasn't so sure how she would receive him now.

"I'm great, all things considered. There's something to be said of how peaceful it is in here." He offered up his cell with his stretched and upright hands. "Are you alright?"

"Ya, I mean, it's different out there without you. They've given your job to someone else." Her voice was apologetic.

"Captain Yale told me as much. Who's over it now?"

"Silvia."

"The horticultural sciences professor?"

"Yes." Silvia Spritz was her name. Jesse didn't know her well personally, but she had worked as an assistant professor at some university he couldn't remember. "She had experience in farm management as well, so they set her over your specialists."

Jesse shrugged. "Good for her! I don't need that position anymore anyways." Jesse's demeanor was genuinely content, which seemed to strike Elena as odd as she cocked her head sideways at him.

"You don't mind what's happening to you?"

"I mind, but I'm at peace with it." He further clarified. "I accepted it when I joined Venture. I knew this would probably happen eventually." Jesse hadn't fully expected all of this to be fair, but he did know the danger of possessing and professing his faith in the colony. Actually, looking at the care on Elena's face, Jesse could tell she felt bothered for him.

"It's ok, Elena. I'm really ok."

"Ya, I see that." Her eyes looked down toward the floor. "I don't know if I am." She was also shuffling for something in her pockets.

"What? Why?" Jesse took a small step towards the glass. He couldn't get much closer, but he wanted to show in some way that he was concerned.

She withdrew her hand from her pocket and in it was a folded piece of paper. She glanced over her shoulder at the door, then to the camera directly behind her. It could see the entirety of Jesse's cell, which is probably why the guards came so infrequently, as they could see everything that was happening remotely. Elena unfolded the piece of paper close to her chest, so that the camera behind her could not see what she had in her hands. She was trying to move as inconspicuously as possible.

As she opened it, she held it slightly towards Jesse so he could see the writing. He noticed that the paper was much more worn than when he had held it a couple days ago, the edges were dirty from hands and the page itself was wilted from being folded and unfolded many times. It was the Scripture verses that Jesse had shown Junior Director Kitting out on the field.

"Jesse, this paper has made its way around to a number of different people in the last few days. When Cho showed it to me last night at 1303, and told me the story of how you stood up to Kitting, I was shocked." Jesse was shocked upon hearing this from Elena.

How did she even get that paper – OH! Jolean had taken it from my hand! Jesse was remembering now how Jolean Smith had taken the paper from his hand while he was witnessing to JD Kitting. He hadn't thought much more of it, as the pressing matter after that was what he was going to say to Captain Yale.

And Jolean showed other people? How many people? Then Cho gave it to

Elena? How many people have seen this now?! Jesse's mind was flooding with the possibilities. He had felt like that evangelistic effort on the side of the field was a failure, but were people curious? Elena definitely seemed to be. Curious… and worried?

"I didn't tell anyone else about what you showed me, but when Cho gave me this and said what you told Kitting, I got scared."

"Why? You didn't do anything wrong. I'm the one that showed you."

"Jesse, I'm scared of what this means." She quickly put it back in her pocket as discreetly as possible. "I don't understand, but it scares me that what you've shown me at the table and now this… It's terrifying to me."

Jesse fought within his head a moment, trying to see why she was so intimidated by the Scriptures aligning from Earth and Toisee. Then he realized the obvious. *She doesn't know Jesus.* Seeing this miracle connection, strong evidence that God has worked among humans and Jolethites. It scared her because she didn't know the power behind it all was benevolent and loving. Having a relationship with Jesus, Jesse's faith was strengthened by the connection, but without it, Elena's was shattered.

"I could show you." Jesse said, reassuringly. "I can show you why you don't need to be scared." Her eyes looked at his, heavy with tears.

"But how, they're going to be watching you."

"I'm going to think and pray about it. I'll find a way to show you why you don't need to fear God. He loves you."

She wiped the tears from her eyes and composed herself with a deep sigh. The moment hung heavy. All Jesse wanted to do now was hug her close and firmly. His heart went out to her as he felt a touch of what the Holy Spirit was doing in her soul. He was knocking at the door, and Jesse was anxious to introduce Elena to her Saviour. The glass between them seemed –

ONE MINUTE, MISS AQUINO!

There was a sharp voice over the loudspeaker in the brig. Apparently, Elena's time was near its end. She waived towards the door in recognition of the reminder.

"Alright!" When she turned back to Jesse she was forcing a smile. "I almost forgot! I had to come up with an excuse to come see you."

"Oh? What was that?"

"Well… I told them we were engaged."

Jesse's heart skipped a beat, and he stifled a laugh of bemused elation. She smiled at him, grinning with pride at her ruse. *Or was it joy at his reaction?* Either way, Jesse enjoyed the playful thought and he went along with it.

"Have we set a date yet?" He grinned back after he recomposed himself.

"Director Willow wanted to know that too, but I told her I needed to see you first, hence why I am here."

Wow, this is perfect! We can easily meet together now without arousing suspicion! Jesse thought first, then responded, "Wait, what happened with Miller?"

OF WHAT STARS SING

"I was giving into the idea of having to be someone else's number 2 or 3. I didn't want that but," she lowered her eyes and looked directly into his. "No one else was asking me."

Jesse's happy smile turned sheepish, "I told you why." He shrugged.

The door to the brig opened and a security guard stuck his head inside.

"Now, Miss Aquino."

She straightened and her tone became serious and business-like. "Alright, next Monday it is! I'll see you on the outside tomorrow, honey!" She started for the door and waved cutely goodbye.

"I can't wait!" Jesse said, waving back. "Sweetie!"

Did she blush a little on the way out? Jesse thought he caught a glimpse of it as she left the brig. When the door shut, and he remained standing at the cell door, the room instantly felt plain and sterile again. As if life had left the room. Jesse's thoughts and prayers turned to what tomorrow was going to bring. It was hard to concentrate, considering all of what had just been revealed, where Elena's heart was leaning. Was it towards both Jesus and Jesse? Either way, an old hymn had found its way into his mouth and Jesse started singing to himself as he paced his cell.

"I've got joy, joy, joy, down in my heart, down in my heart…"

◆ . ✢ . ◆ . ✢ . ◆

Once the morning had come, Jesse was released from his cell by Director Willow herself. She had given him a stern warning and reminder of the discussion that they and Captain Yale had had in orbit. He was officially relieved of his CAPA duties, which he already knew as Elena had told him about Spritz's promotion to his position. His new duty was that of a simple specialist again, performing various tasks assigned to him by the director herself. She had neglected to give him any tasks while in the brig but now that he was out, he had a mountain of mind-numbing paperwork. She was going to be using him as her own personal secretary which would make it difficult for Jesse to sneak or escape away for most of any reason.

Here was the genius of his engagement to Elena, as that afforded them the privilege of an excuse to get together, alone and away from the prying eyes of Shea Willow. Their marriage was officially scheduled in 3 days, on Monday by the Toiseean calendar.

With Toisee orbiting its star every 37.5 days, the years were only a bit more than an earthen month long. The colonists, having already adjusted themselves to the 30 hour days, wanted to attempt to keep some earth-like normalcy to their calendar if possible. This meant they officially called every 18 orbits of Toi a Toiseean Year. At 37.5 days an orbit, that gave the colony 342 days per Toiseean Year. Broken down into months, weeks and days, they had 9 months in the year, 75 days in a month, 15 weeks in a month and, finally, 5 days in a week. The colonists then kept the 5 days of the week as Monday through Friday.

Anyone would obviously moan and grown over the loss of the weekends, but the colonists' work rotations were only 4 days long, so each had a built-in day off.

Today was Wednesday, which meant that Monday, the day of Jesse and Elena's marriage, was then 3 days away. There was not much to plan, but there was a lot to discuss between him and Elena before then. Jesse was released from his cell by Director Willow at mid-morning and Elena was going to be busy with her duties until that afternoon. Willow had instructed Jesse to report to her for duty in one hour, so Jesse returned to his quarters to freshen up from his stay in the colony brig.

To no great surprise, when Jesse opened the door to his quarters he found it in disarray. His mattress was hanging half off its base, the sheets and blankets disheveled on the floor. His closet had been rummaged through, as was his chest of drawers. Even his toiletries and bathroom had been searched by its rough appearance. And yet, incredibly, Jesse's intuition to hide his Bible at the bottom of his dirty laundry hamper proved to be solid. As Jesse removed a few now rank smelling items, he discovered the Scriptures right where he had left it, on top of his soil-ridden pants. He picked it up and held it to his chest.

Jesse envisioned holding Jesus close at this moment. When he was in the cell, this is the moment he wished for, to be able to hug his Heavenly Father. So he clung to the only physical item he had for a few moments, even catching himself swaying ever so slightly. He breathed deep, pleasantly surprised that he could catch whiffs of lavender and sage from the Sweetie Spray that his parents had scented Isaiah 41 with. Still, he was sad now. Embracing a book, no matter how holy, is still just a book. Jesse sighed and let go, dropping the Scriptures to his desktop.

It's still not safe here. Jesse thought. If he was going to keep his treasured tome of God's Word, he was going to need to find somewhere else other than his own quarters. The forest? A forgotten corner of the Ag Wing? A ventilation duct? Wherever he thought of, the problem was not hiding the Bible but accessing it after it was hidden. He would need it to be somewhere he frequented in order to hide its discovery.

Come, Jesse, help us.

The memory of his dream on the mountain floated back to him. What about with the Isstarleans?

At first Jesse wanted to dismiss the notion of keeping the Bible safe in the village, as how would he ever get back there. But if he was being beckoned to help them, what better way than to allow them to study his Scriptures the way Jesse was studying theirs? Up until now, their relationship, while definitely being edifying for both, was mostly a one-way benefit to Jesse's faith alone. Jesse had been exposed to Isstar's verses, and it solidified his own relationship with God in monumental ways, but other than the words he had spoken to them in Joelle, they had not gained the benefit of seeing the words of Jesus in an earthen Bible. Suddenly Jesse felt convicted of being selfish and he made the firm decision that his Scriptures needed to be delivered to them.

For now, Jesse scanned around the catastrophe that was his quarters for another place to stash his Bible. The air vent was too small, the laundry not permanent and his bed not secure. What about IN the bed? Jesse pulled the mattress and set it on its side. He squeezed the springs, which came close together but felt far enough apart for the Bible to have space without being felt. He studied the stitching of the mattress, following the seam with his fingers for a weak point.

BANG BANG BANG!

"Hold on just a second!" There was a knock on the door and Jesse panicked. He clutched the Bible towards his chest.

"Jesse! It's me!" The voice of Elena sounded clear but hushed, as if she was pressing her face against the door.

"Elena! Hold up." Jesse tossed the Bible back on the base of the bed and let the mattress fall on top of it. He wasn't scared of her seeing it but he didn't want it left out in the open either. He had to be very careful now.

Jesse stepped over a few items on the floor and opened his quarters. As soon as the door slid open, Elena slipped inside and shut it behind her.

"Hey, I was just thinking about you but –"

Elena spun quickly around and grabbed Jesse, throwing her arms around to his back in a firm embrace. Her head rested briefly on his shoulders, where Jesse could smell flowers in her hair. He was taken off guard by her hug, so much so that he quickly realized he wasn't hugging her back. The second he wrapped his arms around her, his heart felt warm. Not just due to the embrace of a woman, but the hug he had longed for from his Savior could be felt in the wrap of her arms, the gentle clutch of her fingers on his back. She let go entirely too soon for him, and Jesse was pulled slightly off balance as he didn't let go as fast as she. He straightened up quickly.

"I was thinking about seeing you but I thought you had your duties to attend to?"

"I was. I am. I had to run back to the Ag Wing for another load from the nursery, so I had a moment to come see if you were here." She glanced around the room. "Oh, upset are we?"

"No," Jesse scanned the mess with her. "I guess Yale had them come and search my quarters while I was in the brig."

"Geez, they wrecked it. What for?"

Jesse lifted the side of the mattress and stole the Scriptures from under it. "For something like this." He handed her the Bible. She flipped it in her hands, opening the pages and turning a few. She looked at it and studied it as if she had never seen nor held one before. It both fascinated and worried her.

"Wow..." She said.

"What?"

"It's just... a book."

Jesse laughed. "Well, ya, it's a book.

"But I mean, I don't know. I thought it would be more... impressive?" She paged through the back. Startled, she pointed at the pages. "You even wrote in it?!"

"Not me. Gus, the friend that gave it to me back on Archway. I wrote some too, I guess."

"Why? Isn't this special? Didn't you say this was thousands of years old?"

"The words are, yea. Not mine." He looked bemused at her. "Wait, did you think I had some ancient document up here? Like wood and leather bound scrolls or something?"

"I didn't know!" She thrust it back to him. "Based on how you described it..."

Jesse took it from her. He held it in both hands in front of him.

"Elena, this isn't God. What makes the Bible special is that it's God's message to us." He thumbed the pages as he spoke. "This is just paper and typed letters, it's not the physical book and binding that make it His Word. It's the authority and gospel, the good news, behind the words that do."

"His Word? I don't follow you." She crossed her arms in front of her chest and pouted a little. She wanted to understand, and didn't like when she didn't. Especially something like this. She felt like she was missing the point to something very important. Important enough to make Captain Yale and the colony feel that Jesse was endangering their future. She didn't believe that, but she didn't want to trust what her heart was telling her yet either. So she remained cautiously curious.

"It's as if... if... " Jesse thought for a moment, then he smiled with his idea. "It's as if I told you, 'I love you'. Would you believe it?"

She half-smirked and tilted her chin. "I suppose it depends."

"Depends on what?"

"Depends on you. Your actions, what you do afterwards."

"Exactly! When I simply say, 'I love you', those are just words. I have to do something behind the words to give them meaning, right?" Jesse held up the Bible. "That's what I mean about this. These are just printed words, but what makes it true is the God behind it."

"Then why does command want it so bad?"

"They can't get to God, but they can try to destroy other things. Captain Yale said so himself. He told me I could keep my 'delusions in my head' but everything else he was going to restrict."

She nodded her head, her eyes darting a little back and forth. Elena seemed to be putting it together. Jesse said a quick prayer for her in his head, then he looked down at his non-existent wristwatch again. That reminded him to check and see if they had delivered it to his quarters as they said they would. He started sorting through the things on his floor before his desk and chair.

Elena watched him pick things up, so she started to as well, tossing his clothes in the hamper again. "When we're married, our place is NOT going to look like this."

Jesse stood back up. "So, that's really happening, huh?"

She stopped and stared at him, holding a handful of his clothes. "Are you saying no?"

"No! No, it was just a surprise is all. After our last conversation, you know, before I was arrested, I wasn't sure what you thought." He kept picking and sorting his things, rearranging the lamp on his desk. She threw his clothes in the hamper, making a disgusted face at the smell.

"You weren't picking anyone else." She started pulling up his sheets and fluffing them out to lay across his bed.

"No."

"Like I said before, I was waiting but you never made a move." She started to tuck the sides of the sheet under the mattress. Jesse reached over and grabbed her hand to make her stop. She straightened and looked at him.

"I told you, I wasn't going to marry anyone for the reasons that the colony wanted us to. But I do want to get married for the reasons I want to."

"And what is the reason you want to?" She asked him, leading him on.

"I would want to marry you because I loved you."

"And do you? Do you love me?"

"I guess it depends on what I do after I tell you, huh?" With that Jesse grinned shyly at her. His gaze into her eyes gave her butterflies, the direct genuineness of his pupils made her blush. He was worried about their relationship polluting his calling from God, and he was nervous about becoming 'her Savior' instead of Jesus. But at this moment he didn't care. What seemed to be the most pressing issue right now was assuring her that he did in fact have strong feelings for her.

They might have been genetically approved to be paired together. Director Willow might have pushed him to chase after someone, anyone. And they might be simply settling for each other so they don't get stuck with someone else. But God also might have been using all of these outside pressures to unite their souls in this moment. Jesse decided to trust the latter as the reason for their engagement, which also gave him the confidence to stick out his neck and kiss her.

His day working for Director Willow was monotonous to say the least. He had the high of his first kiss with Elena to keep his spirits up, but Shea was obviously doing everything she could to ensure he knew this duty was still a punishment. He sorted her agricultural plans alphabetically because she thought it would be easier to find things that way. Then after she tested it, she decided that they should be sorted directionally depending on which side of the colony the fields lay on. Even after that she didn't seem satisfied, but they moved on. Jesse also fielded her messages, responding to them as she dictated. He prepared her lunch and dinner. And reworked her schedule for the next day over and over until things finally fit just the way she approved.

He did all this to the best of his ability. Not only because he had smooched

Elena, but because he humorously decided he was going to 'love his enemies so that heaps of burning coals' would dump on her head. In the meeting with Yale, Shea Willow seemed to personally detest Jesse for his faith, and Jesse was actually enjoying 'turning the other cheek' each time she slapped him with another pained or menial assignment. She was trying to break him, but he and the Holy Spirit wouldn't allow it.

By late evening, Shea had tired herself out of finding ways to make Jesse work overly hard, so she released him. She was going to keep close tabs on his tardiness in the morning however, prepared to make him suffer for any minute he was in later than 0530.

One small and joyful assignment that Shea had given him was to choose a new double quarters for him and Elena. There were a number of different arrangements available, each one Jesse daydreamed over.

It goes without saying that their courtship was less than ideal, but given the circumstances, he was very happy. When the slingshot gateway was completed, he would be able to tell his parents not only the Godly news about Rue and the Isstarleans, but he will be introducing to them his wife. That felt just as strange in his head as he imagined it would be for his parents to hear the fact that he was a married man! Well, not yet, but in two days he would be.

Working within Director Shea's messages, he was privy to information even without his dissolved CAPA privileges. Incredibly, the orbital slingshot gateway was only a week away from completion. Captain Yale had tripled the amount of engineers assigned to the task and the gateway was already physically intact in orbit. What remained to be completed was all of the sciency stuff that Jesse barely had a notion on. Formatting the interstellar targeting system, calibrating each and every energy diode to the right frequency, connecting this to that, that to this and doing all of the maths. He didn't need to understand how it all worked, only that it was almost ready.

However, the first trip back to Earth was going to be a difficult one to procure a spot on, especially given Jesse's current reputation. Captain Yale would be onboard himself, as would be most upper members of the command staff. When a Venture colony ship returns from establishing a successful colony, a major celebration is launched at home called the Golden Spike Ceremony. This refers to the final connection made permanent between earth and its newest extension in the galaxy, borrowing its name from the union of transcontinental railroads of ancient times.

Each member of the command staff is then rewarded for their heroic efforts, claiming the prizes they had been promised when signing on with Venture in the beginning. Director Willow will be gaining her consultant position within the European Union, and most likely then remaining on earth to continue her farmwork. Captain Yale will be promoted to Colony Director, and then most likely voted in as Colony President. He would return with absolute power, reinforced now directly with Chao Daivi Horizon's linked-might behind him. It would be rather doubtful they would allow Jesse, or any

Isstarlean, the ability to reach the humans of earth with the Good News of God's united creation across the universe.

And this is where Jesse found himself stuck. He knew the need to get back to earth, to spread the news, but the only way he could think to do that was to stow-away. That was a problem in of itself, as he would need to somehow sneak around on a very small and publicly fanfared mission. The chances of him getting any kind of audience to hear this message was slim. What's more, his heart wasn't in it. Jesse knew the need, and yet this is not where the majority of his thoughts drifted back to. It was Rue. It was his dream. He knew they needed the Word of God that was hidden in his quarters.

Once he had gotten back, it was very late, and yet Elena was there in the residential commons waiting for him. And it wasn't just her, but a few other Ag Wing members were waiting for him. There was Jolean Smith, the crewmate that had taken his verse paper, and also Manuel, Kwame and Florence. These 3 were actually part of the livestock side of the Agricultural department, who managed the cattle, sheep and goats of the colony. Jesse had been rather tired before the lift doors opened. When he saw them all waving him over, and Elena's smile, his fatigue seemed to be left behind in the elevator.

"Hey Elena, guys... what're you doing here?"

"We were talking about our trip to the village tomorrow." Elena said, as Jesse slouched into the couch beside her. The others were in a semi-circle, facing the window that overlooked the mountains to the east. Ochre clouds hid most of the setting sun's rays, however spots of red-gold highlighted where the gloom was thinnest. They beamed out, over and past the mountain tops, highlighting the snowy tips in occasional bursts of ruby red. It was a breathtaking sight no matter how many times you viewed it.

"You all are going to the village?" Jesse asked curiously.

"We need some samples from their herd of... I dunno, whatever they are!" Manuel waved his hand towards the far wall in the direction of Rue. "Command wants us to look into the viability of cross-breeding their livestock with ours."

Jesse did recall seeing a procurement mission on the docket for the morning, but its location was not disclosed. "Is this that procurement mission I saw?" He asked and Manuel nodded. "Is this some kind of covert motive? You aren't stealing from them are you?"

Manuel chuckled and looked at his colleagues. "No, of course not. We aren't there to hurt your friends."

Jesse felt a little caught and looked down to downplay his response. "I don't know if I would say they're my friends."

Jolean leaned in. "How did you discover so much about them?"

"What do you mean? I don't know much."

"Jesse, you showed us their translated words. You knew they were singing worship songs." She protested.

"I talked to a few of them."

"But you're not in the language brigade, are you?"

"No, they knew a little bit of English, so that helped and…" He trailed off. The thought of entering the brig again crossed his mind so he shut his mouth.

"Oh, I'd bet they're part of the exchange program." Kwame said.

"Ya! That trade off in the city, right? Where they learn about us and we learn about them?" Florence commented back. They didn't seem to notice that Jesse had stopped short, but unfortunately for him, Jolean did.

"And, what?" She pushed.

Jesse looked at her, mock confused.

"Jesse, you said they knew a little bit of English and then stopped, but you were about to say something else."

"Look, Jolean, I'm not really supposed to talk about that stuff anymore." Jesse wanted to though, but Elena's hand was on his thigh and he really liked feeling her touch. He didn't want to lose this opportunity to grow this new relationship with her. Suddenly, he felt ashamed. He realized he was stifling this opportunity to witness.

Manuel picked up on his hesitation. "Ya careful, Jesse! I heard about last time."

"What last time?" Florence asked.

"When Jesse faced down Kitting!"

Her eyes got big. "Junior Director Kitting?! What happened?"

"Sis, you didn't hear?!" Manuel got excited and sat up straight, eager to tell the story. "Jesse here is a preacher! Apparently, Ralph was getting all mean with the Joels, callin' them fools or something, and Jesse gets all in a tissy and tells Kitting off! He calls on God and whips out a Bible right there! Right in front of everyone!"

Florence and Kwame stare with disbelief at Jesse. He held up his hands in protest. "Hold on, that's not exactly what happened."

"Ya, Manuel, you weren't even there. Jesse was mad that Kitting said God wasn't real, not about the Joel's." Jolean corrected, incorrectly.

"Does it matter? He's not!" Manuel insisted.

Jesse was burning inside. He looked over to Elena. Her eyes were curious as to where this was going. She looked at him, and insisted that he say something with her gaze.

"But then how do you explain what Jesse showed us? The words from the village matching with the Bible?" Jolean pushed back.

Manuel laughed. "You mean the stuff that Jesse made up? He could have written anything down on that piece of paper! Are you that gullible?"

"I didn't lie." Jesse said quietly. Manuel, Jolean and the others turned to him. "The Spirit led me to them." Manuel started giggling but as Jesse continued, he began to listen. "I came to this colony because I believed one thing. I thought my purpose in life was understood, and it was simple and straightforward. But then, things just happened."

He looked around at the eyes that were on him. "These last few weeks on Toisee, I have been experiencing things I can't explain, hearing things that are impossible, and seeing with my own two eyes results that could only mean one thing. God is God. He was at home. He is here. My purpose for coming to this colony has changed based on all of that. And now that I know, I can't go back to who I was. All I want to do now is keep experiencing what I've lived, and try to put it into words to tell everyone else about it."

The group was silent for a moment. It's hard to argue about someone's own personal experience, except for the fact that it is their own experience and no one else's. This is what Manuel keyed in on when he responded.

"That's great for you, Jesse." His tone was sarcastic. "Really great. You must love being in the brig on Yale's bad side." He pointed at him. "That's where you're going to end up again."

"So you don't believe him?" Jolean asked.

"I don't believe anything based on what one person says. Especially the crazy things Jesse is on about."

"What if I could show you?" Jesse retorted. "Would you believe your own eyes and ears?"

"Absolutely. I trust myself completely." Manuel said proudly. He meant it but it did make a couple of the others snicker at the egotistical statement.

"Alright, I'll meet you all in the village tomorrow." Jesse said assuredly. Manuel was being annoying, but he was also right. It would be a lot easier to convince them of the truth if he could show them.

Elena spoke up, concerned. "Aren't you banned from there? What about Director Willow?"

"She has meetings throughout the morning in various spots across the colony. She probably won't even be in till past lunch. Also, I have access to her interface. I'll add myself to the mission manifest."

"That sounds a bit shady there, pastor." Manuel said. "Will God approve of your espionage?"

"Who's to say that He didn't put me in her office just for this opportunity?" Jesse smirked back at him. The others changed the subject and continued talking about their actual mission in the village tomorrow morning.

Manuel was right, though. This was a very risky abuse of position on Jesse's part. Not only was he continuing to preach and spread his Christian beliefs to the colonists, but he would be circumventing his boss and then forging Shea's approval. Most assuredly, if he was discovered and caught, that would be the end of his colonial career.

Jesse hadn't considered exactly what that would entail. Obviously the colony would not keep him in the prison on Toisee for long periods of time. They were not designed for that, nor did they have any kind of court system yet established. Most likely Jesse would be transferred via shuttle back to Earth for trial or punishment. This aspect intrigued him, as it might be the answer to how he would return to tell everyone about the connection of Isstar and Jesus.

A squeeze on his thigh brought his attention back to his fiancee on the couch beside him. She leaned in and whispered in his ear.

"So much for our honeymoon." When she leaned back, Jesse looked into her eyes, reading that she was only slightly jesting and mostly saddened.

After an hour of chat, the conversation dwindled, and the others had left to retire until morning. Jesse and Elena retreated to Jesse's quarters for a few moments of privacy. Fortunately, because of their registered engagement with the colony, Elena had yet to be harassed because of Jesse's confrontation with Captain Yale. Maybe he was waiting to see if Jesse was going to recant? Maybe he was betting on Elena as a distraction to turn Jesse's faith back towards the colony's future? Either way, they were both grateful as they laid on their backs, side by side on Jesse's bed.

"How do you think this would have happened if we weren't here?" Elena asked.

"You mean us?"

"Ya. How would we have met? Would we have ended up together if the colony didn't exist to force you to date?"

Jesse chuckled. "The colony didn't force me to date. I still would have dated."

"But you know what I mean, right?"

"Yes."

"If we weren't in the colony together, would we still have gotten together?" It was a cute and bemusing topic, but her thoughts seemed sad. The way she asked the question came across depressively, as if the only reason this was happening was because it was encouraged by gunpoint.

"I don't know." Jesse confessed.

She expressed her disappointment. "You don't know because you wouldn't have dated me?"

"No, I mean, this is how it happened, because this is how it was supposed to happen." He leaned up onto his elbow to look over at her. She stayed focused on the ceiling as opposed to his face. "What God wants to happen, happens."

"So whether we were on Earth, or on Archway, or here on Toisee... we were fated to end up together?" She looked into his face for confirmation.

"I wouldn't call it fate, no." He focused his eyes on hers so she would hear his heart. "I still had a choice whether or not to love you, Elena. We still have a choice in it. Fate means we don't."

She looked at him confused. "Then what do you mean when you say what God wants, God gets?"

"What He wills to happen, will happen. He's not demanding like some super-powerful, divine child wanting only His way. He guides us to make choices, the right choices that lead us to His way, the right way." Jesse used his thumb to point back over his shoulder. "But we can choose against it. We can run away in the other direction and fight against God."

"So, then how do you know that our marriage is what God wants... Or wills? Could we just be making a choice, not knowing if it's good or bad?"

"Here, let me show you something." Jesse rolled off the bed. He grabbed the Bible from off his desk and started paging for a passage in the New Testament. He spoke as he searched. "You're right. It is hard to know if you're making the right choice sometimes. But I always found comfort in the fact that Jesus made it easy for us to know. Here, look at this:"

Jesse held the Scriptures open to her as she sat up on her side to see best. Jesse pointed to verses that Gus had underlined and Jesse had circled in the Bible, where apparently both of them had found inspiration.

"Then Jesus told his disciples, 'If anyone would come after me, let him deny himself and take up his cross and follow me. For whoever would save his life will lose it, but whoever loses his life for my sake will find it." Jesse read the verse to Elena, and she looked up to him as he explained it. "The way we know if we are following God's plan for our lives is if we let go of our own ideas, focus on what He has put in front of us, and move forward with our focus set on Jesus."

"You did this?" She asked him earnestly. "And it led you to me?"

"I did this and it led me everywhere. When I understood that God was calling me, I mean, asking me to look for Him, I let go. I trusted that He was guiding me, and I dealt with what was in front of me. It led me to Junia at Venture, Venture led me to Toisee, Toisee led me to Willow, Willow led me to you." She blinked at him, listening carefully and trusting his words. "I made the choice to follow after God in each of those situations, and after all of these connections, He led me to this point, where we are now engaged to be married in 2 days."

She blinked more, her lids attempting to wick away the growing moisture. "Jesse, I want to trust in God like you do." A tear escaped and slid down her face. "You make it seem so easy, it gives you so much. I'm trying but I don't know how."

He held her face with his hand and wiped her cheek. "It's hard to let go, I know. It was hard for me too. But when God showed me who He is, in ways that I couldn't explain, He made it easy for me to trust Him." He leaned over and embraced her. Jesse began to pray out loud over her. That Jesus would reveal himself to her, that the visit to the village tomorrow would be a new beginning for Elena's faith.

Jesse had no idea what he was asking for, and what God was going to do with their relationship. He simply was asking for guidance, clarity, wisdom and strength. These were the same things he asked of his Lord all of the time. The day was going to bring with it the same choices as before, following after Jesus or not. Denying themselves, or living selflessly. The same decisions as any other day. However, as often happens in life, normal, everyday, mundane choices tend to be the beginning of something much, much greater.

CHAPTER 20
CATALYSTS

Despite Jesse and Elena's conversation lasting past midnight, Jesse was not late for his 0530 punch in at Director Willow's office. He logged into his interface at 0528 to be precise. He was tired and yawning, but still proud to shame Shea's attempt at breaking his will. She had no concept of just how strong that will now was, based on his night with Elena and the mission to Rue this morning. Jesse had been in prayer the entire walk over in the bitter cold of the Toiseean morning, asking God to reveal Himself in the village to his comrades. He didn't want to start a revolution in the colony, but if others were asking questions, Jesse wanted Jesus to provide answers.

He had slipped his Bible into his satchel after wrapping it in another Venture colony shirt. On the off chance it had slipped out or become visible, Jesse wanted to provide another layer of protection from its detection. Other than demonstrating the amazing connections between Jesus and Isstar, he still planned on leaving the Scriptures safely in the hands of Sillias. Captain Yale would tear his own colony apart looking for it, but surely he wouldn't touch Rue. That wasn't his area of authority.

Jesse logged onto Director Willows interface to perform his assigned morning tasks as quickly as possible. He had a hunch that Shea set up some kind of verification process to monitor Jesse's work while she was out and about, so he wanted to cross each item off his list. This would throw her off and ensure that she was not going to come looking for him while he was snuck out to Rue with the others.

He reviewed the Ag Wing procurement mission's prerogatives. The mission head was Junior Director Yolanda Sterling. She was one of two Colonial Management JD's, and Jesse also knew she was still fairly green around the edges. If Yolanda was given this mission, then this was considered fairly run-of-the-mill. That gave him another added boost of confidence that he could pass the Bible and witness to the colonials and villagers without much guff from command. She might still file a report like Kitting, but he doubted as stern of a stance against his attempts from her as Ralph gave.

The mission departed from the City Lyceum at 0810, so Jesse headed down a few minutes early. He thought he would be able to have the Scout scooters ready for the trip, but as he approached the Ag wing bays from the back, he saw that JD Sterling, and all of the Ag specialists were only waiting for Manuel to arrive. As Jesse approached, Yolanda Sterling yelled out to him.

"Heartshire, can we help you?"

"Just reporting for my assignment."

"You're not on the manifest for this mission." Yolanda stated, but then pulled out her tablet to ensure she was correct. She reversed course soon after scrolling. "Oh, apparently you are."

"I have experience in the village. That's why I was added." Jesse, always careful with his words when being deceptive, made every effort not to lie.

"So… you have." She watched him approach and then start to ready his Scout. Clearly she was trying to discern if she should simply allow this last minute change, or if she should call in to Director Willow. Jesse read her hesitation and asserted himself.

"Want me to ride point, ma'am?" He suggested and then pushed his scooter out front.

"Oh, yes, that would be good. Thank you." JD Sterling had made up her mind to trust his word. He did have higher clearance than she did, didn't he? He was just in the brig, but is it back to normal now? She was lacking the confidence to feel good about him, but also unsure of herself to do anything about it. Jesse smiled and winked at Elena as he walked past her to the front of their group.

Shortly thereafter Manuel arrived with a tractor and trailer, ready to depart for their procurement mission. Jesse looked back towards JD Sterling for the go-ahead, she nodded her assent and off they went.

The Toiseean morning was chilly and grey, as per the usual. Although Jesse did see off in the east, before the team turned north into the forest on their way to Rue, that a storm looked to be brewing. The colony had experienced rain a number of times since their establishment upon the planet, but never yet a thunderstorm. The dark of the sky was menacing in that direction, and indeed the wind was blowing in from the east as it usually did. Toisee's orbital spin around its star was backwards compared to the earth, with its sun rising in the west and setting in the east. That meant that if the storm was in the east, it was most likely coming their direction. He didn't think much of it at the time, as from this distance it looked hours away.

Cruising through the forest was slower this time due to the tractor and trailer in tow. Jesse and the others were able to look around more at their surroundings. A few birds flew quietly over the pathway as they scooted along, their screeches and squawks very reminiscent of the species on earth. As the colonists observed more and more of the life around them, they would send pictures and questions to the members of the Language Brigade that frequented the closest city, a place named Juento. A Toiseean Encyclopedia was being compiled by a few of the Ag Specialists in their off time, which was shared to the whole colony publicly. Jesse was able to identify a number of species. He watched a Siren Hawk chase after a smaller bird called a Yellow Trimmed Snippet. White Ravens called from somewhere deeper into the woods, their loud and angry sounding mating call heard over the crunching of gravel beneath the scooters tires.

Being in the front of the pack, lost in the blue forest surrounding him, Jesse had nearly forgotten that a team of others were behind him. As the scooters emerged from the forest, he almost waved to the Rue villagers as the scooters approached the village center. He slowed, aiming to park along the same place he did with the CAPA team weeks ago, behind the Church of the Rock, but JD Sterling yelled behind him.

"Heartshire, not here! Keep going!"

Jesse turned and looked at her. She pointed ahead, her finger aiming over the village itself. "The animal pens are that way."

Jesse waved in acknowledgement and proceeded slowly through the village center. He looked around longingly as they cruised. The village itself seemed fairly empty, only a couple women and some children were scattered about. It was early morning and so Jesse assumed that they were already out in the fields, or performing whatever jobs needed to be done. That was until he turned to look at the church, where he noticed a number of them exiting, with Sillias holding open the door. The villagers looked agitated by the rumbling of the tractor and trailer as it passed by the church building on its way to the north side of town. Were they in worship? He thought to himself as he banked back to the left.

Jesse looped back, waving the group onward. This was his hoped-for opportunity, to see Sillias again and hand off the Bible. The Ag group would be distracted at the animal pens, wrangling or sampling whatever Toiseean livestock they needed to retrieve, and Jesse could safely secure the Scriptures in Rue.

But JD Sterling slowed the progression of the team, watching Jesse circle to the other side of the well at village center and dismount. Her mission was simple, and to her knowledge, everything had been already arranged. She looked forward to the cattle area, seeing in the distance that a few Jolethites had already assembled there around a couple colonists in Venture uniforms. She was given this mission's colonist manifest a week ago, and she wasn't informed of Jesse's addition. Now there were more out here as well? She couldn't make out who they were though, but the evidence was mounting that her straight-forward procurement mission was taking some curves, and she didn't like it. She slowed the progression of the team to a halt with the raising of her hand. The tractor and trailer banged to a standstill behind her.

"Jesse, what are you doing?" She yelled over at him, as he had dismounted and was walking towards some building with a rock coming out the top. The villagers were smiling at his approach. He hadn't heard her, or he was ignoring her.

"YOU ARE NOT AUTHORIZED TO SPEAK FOR THIS MISSION!" She yelled at Jesse, who now stopped and turned to face her, his hand on his satchel.

Jesse quickly considered his excuse. "Oh, uh.. This is Sillias!" He yelled back to her, pointing to the man. "He's the leader of this village. I'm confirming with him —"

"No, you are not!" She kicked her scooter's stand down and dismounted, striding towards them before her scout had settled.

"I'm just making sure that our mission —"

"I am the only person authorized to speak for this mission!" She cut him off again. By this point, she had outpaced him and was in between Sillias and himself. She turned to address the village elder.

"Hello, I am Junior Director Sterling. We are here for our agreed upon retrieval of livestock." She was a little rude in her tone to Sillias, but smiled and at least made an effort to be cordial. Sillias, learning from Jesse in their previous encounter, met Yolanda's eyes and extended his hand for a handshake.

"Heelo, Joonier Direct Sterling. I am Sillias." She took his hand and they shook, with her letting go fairly quickly. Sillias looked over to Jesse, grinning in hello, then back to Yolanda. "Why you heer?" His question sounded confused. The other Isstarleans who had exited the church with Sillias were huddled around the entrance of the building. There were probably about 30 of them in total. Men, women and children, all watched from a few yards behind him. Jesse could recognize Esth and Thorold in the crowd. He smiled at them, and they saw him, but did not smile back. They seemed to be worried about the encounter between Sillias and Sterling, but also kept glancing nervously at the trailer that Manuel was piloting.

"We are here for the animals. Toiseean Colony command has told you we are coming, right?" She was being decently polite, but Yolanda spoke quickly with Sillias, not realizing that his vocabulary was having difficulty keeping up.

"Animals?"

She turned and pointed to the north side of the village. Looking that direction, the group that was at the pens was now a bit closer. Seemingly they were coming into town as well, as dust plumes were rising behind them, indicating their speed.

"Yes, we are here for the livestock samples your village agreed to provide." She turned back to Sillias, who still had a very lost look on his face. Sterling dipped her head frustratingly, believing the language barrier to be the problem, but Jesse could tell Sillias simply had no idea what she was referring to. He looked out towards the north side of the town, understanding she was asking for their livestock.

"No, wee needed them. We use and for food."

Sterling sighed heavily, annoyed at the misunderstanding. She shot Jesse a look of annoyance then pulled out her tablet. She started to swipe, looking for something. Jesse took the opportunity to approach Sillias.

"Hello Sillias." He extended his hand.

"Jesse, brother, heelo!" Sillias took it with a large grin. JD Yolanda glared over her tablet as she searched more frantically. She seemed to not like the family reunion she was witnessing. Elena, Florence and Kwame had parked and dismounted by now as well, and they were slowly forming a circle around the meeting. Jesse looked over for Elena's attention, and he gestured for her to come closer.

"Elena, come here." She steadily approached his side, side-eying JD Yolanda who was too busy to notice that she was passing her. "Elena, this is Sillias, the village elder." He turned to Sillias. "Sillias, this is Elena." Sillias' welcome smile caused Elena to relax a little. Jesse had forgotten that she had yet to meet a Jolethite personally, so he moved closer to her side, placing his hand on her back.

"Wife?" Sillias asked, looking at Elena, who looked to Jesse unsure of what to say.

"Almost." Jesse beamed. She grinned back at the old man.

"Hello Sillias." She said.

"Isstar sole di." Sillias said in Joelle, cupping their shake with his off hand.

Jesse patted the satchel on his side, anxiously waiting for a moment to hand the Scriptures to him. He felt Yolanda's occasional gaze and knew he couldn't give Sillias the Bible with her looking on, so he attempted small talk. "Your English is sounding good!"

"I thank you, my brother." Sillias bowed slightly. "Have you... tried the writings? We have learned more –"

Jesse put a quick finger to his mouth, making a shush shape with his lips. "Do you not know why we are here?" He changed the subject. Just then JD Sterling perked up and spun the tablet towards Sillias. He looked at the screen, lost but trying to understand.

"Here! Right here is the communication that was sent to you. You responded at the bottom." Sillias looked over the screen, then shook his head and chuckled, shrugging his shoulders.

"I... I don't... see."

Sillias was sent a message? Jesse was able to see most of the screen as well, and then he followed her instructions to the bottom of the screen. Jesse was confused himself, as how would Sillias have received the communication? They don't even have electricity in the village. Sure enough, as Jesse read further, the acknowledgement on the bottom was not that of Sillias, but of Leader Sherii.

"Yolanda, this says that Sherii accepted this procurement. Not Sillias." Jesse pointed out.

She pulled the tablet back from the face of Sillias and studied it herself. The pit of Jesse's stomach started to unsettle.

"Oh... It does." Sterling was back to feeling unsure of herself again.

"Wait, Sherii? Why...?" He started but then it hit him. Sherii was the Prime Leader of United Joleth. He looked at these villagers of Rue, and the things they possessed, as his to do with as he pleased. Or as he would most likely frame it, 'for what United Joleth deemed necessary or appropriate'.

JD Sterling reasserted herself, shaking off her feelings of inadequacy. "Either way, the order is signed by their Leader. We will be moving forward with the procurement." She turned and started back towards her scout when Manuel stood on his tractor seat and pointed out towards the livestock herds.

"Hey, I think that's Captain Yale!"

Jesse's heart sank. He jogged past Florence and Kwame to peek down the road. Sure enough, Jesse could make out the colors of Tristan Yale's uniform from a distance, deep green with flashes of Venture gold. His time was running out as Yale's entourage was only a couple minutes away. He ran back over to Elena directly and grabbed her shoulders.

"Come with me right now!"

He tugged her forward and she jogged with him towards the Church of the Rock, the village members scuttled away from the door at their approach.

"Jesse! What are you doing?! Where are you going?" Yolanda hollered at him as he graced the doorway. She started to follow after him, as an owner after a loose dog. Kwame and Florence exchanged looks and started to follow behind Yolanda, as did Sillias and Jolean. Manuel was still watching the Captain roll in.

"Ya, I'm pretty sure that's Captain —" He turned to see that everyone he was yelling to was moving quickly inside the building. "Hey, where are y'all goin'?" Manuel jumped down and began to jog after them, where he crested the door as Jesse was encouraging Sillias to step forward with him towards the large, erect stone in the middle of the building.

"Whoa, what IS this place?" Manuel said loudly.

Jesse hollered back, "It's their place of worship! A church." He turned to the group but he was focused mainly on Elena. She was in the front of the colonist bunch, huddled in the middle of the building facing the large Drodd, their eyes tracing the stone to the ceiling. Jesse pointed to the rock behind him. "This is Drodd, it's a symbolic large stone where their Messiah, Isstar, was killed long ago."

Jesse was frazzled. He moved quickly around the podium to the surface of the stone. "Sillias, please come!" He beckoned the old man forward. Sillias, seeming to understand at least that Jesse felt the need was urgent, excused himself past the group of colonists to stand next to Jesse close to the drodd. Elena's worry was growing in her chest. Jesse was acting panicked, as if his time was running out and it disturbed her to see him so bothered.

"Elena, everyone, I need to show you before Captain Yale gets here and forces me to stop."

Jolean whispered to herself, but loud enough for Elena to hear. "Oh my... is that where he got the writings?" Her voice had a hint of awe.

Jesse threw his hands into his satchel, gripping the Bible with one hand and dropping the bag with the other. He threw off the Venture uniform that was hiding the Scriptures and he opened them to a marked page. He pointed to an etched inscription on the lower right side of the stone.

"Sillias, please, what does this say?"

Sillias stepped closer and read it out loud. "Bear with your mouth that Isstar is Lord, and believe in your soul that God raised Him from death, and salvation is yours." He had read it out loud, in perfect English, albeit with a Jolethite accent. Jesse smiled at him, impressed.

"You practiced?"

"I remember our talk." Sillias smiled back.

Kwame snorted. "So, what? What does that mean?"

Jesse pointed down to his Bible, "Listen to this! 'If you confess with your mouth that Jesus is Lord and believe in your heart that God raised Him from the dead, you will be saved!'"

"They match...?" Florence said quietly behind Elena. She turned to face her, and studied the faces of the other colonists with her. Yolanda was angry, Jolean enraptured, Kwame confused, Florence shocked, Manuel nervous and Yale — CAPTAIN YALE! Tristan Yale looked enraged. He stood still, blocking the doorway with Ralph Kitting by his side with folded arms. The Jolethite villagers that were in the building had moved to the corners, away from the scene unfolding before them, unable to leave due to the Toiseean Captain. For the first time that she can remember, Elena also saw that Yale was armed. A pistol was strapped to his side.

Jesse continued in front of them all, crossing to the other side of the stone and pointing at another etched verse. He either hadn't noticed Yale's presence or did not care. Sillias followed and read it aloud.

"I, Isstar, tell you, come my way and live true and live alive forever."

Jesse flipped to another passage of the Scriptures in his hand and read, "Jesus said, I am the way, the truth and the life!" He then pointed to another verse higher than this one. Firelight from the flickering candles danced across the chiseled words as Sillias read again.

"See me, the loving shepherd. The loving shepherd sacrifices himself for his flock."

Jesse paged to another spot in the Bible and responded.

"I am the good shepherd. The good shepherd lays down his life for the sheep."

Kwame shouted, "Jesse, what does all this mean?"

"Yes, Mr. Hearshire, what does all this mean?" Captain Tristan Yale's voice boomed over every niche of the church where the very beams seemed to shudder. Jesse stopped, his excitement and rush gone, his enthused grin dropped but his resolve remained. He looked at Elena, then to the back of the church where Yale stood.

"You have ears don't you? Don't you all?!" Jesse looked around at the lost faces, hesitant to answer out loud. "What else could it mean but that God has sent Jesus to Toisee, just as He sent him to Earth!? Do you not see it?"

Yale started walking straight towards Jesse, expecting the colonists to move aside to allow him to pass, which they did.

"All I see, and all I hear, is a lying fanatic."

"I am not lying!" Jesse protested, feeling angry and starting to feel trapped.

"I explained to you why religion is illegal in the colony, did I not? Is this not exactly what becomes of those who ascribe their foolishness to faith in a false god?" Yale stopped next to Elena, whom he glanced down at. She cowered and lowered her eyes away from him.

"I am proving to you right here that this is true!"

"Because these simpletons wrote some words on a rock? Verses etched in stone mean nothing, Jesse." Yale's voice was calm and dismissive. Jesse could feel his own emotions getting the best of him, so he closed his eyes and lowered his head. What else could he do to show them? They were refusing to listen, refusing to believe. He started to pray a quick and desperate plea for help, and a few beats later, Elena spoke.

"It's not just words though, is it?"

Yale looked down at Elena, and surprisingly, she defiantly started right back. She turned to face the other colonists behind her. Her words were precise and her vocal cords sharp.

"These words by themselves are meaningless. They are just verses etched into stone. But it's not the words that hold power, it's the movement… the action behind them!" She pointed to the stone, then to the sky. "What Jesus, or Isstar, said and did… That is the real power. Don't you see? These words are witness to that messiah. They tell what God has already done!"

"Isstar, li Havori!" "Jesus, my Savior!" "Isstar, li Havori!" "Jesus, my Savior!"

The Isstarleans started chanting from the corners of the church, repeating the words over and over again. All with tenacity. All with fervor. English and Joelle, Jesus and Isstar. Captain Yale wheeled around, and when Elena and Jesse saw his face before it turned, it was furious. Sillias had his hands raised to the ceiling, chanting with his congregation, faces upturned to God.

Jesse talked to the back of Captain Yale's head. "You cannot place regulations and laws on the Holy Spirit. He is going to move no matter what you do. These stones, and this book, " he held aloft the Bible he carried. "Are history's witness to what God has done among his people. You cannot make illegal the God of the Universe!"

"Jesus, my Savior!" "Isstar, li Havori!" "Jesus, my Savior!" "Isstar, li Havori!"

Jesse dropped his arms and opened the Bible more time. This time he moved to the podium and placed it on the altar. He paged to Psalm 19, which had been dropped into his head and declared the verses over the chanting voices.

"The heavens declare the glory of God,
 and the sky above proclaims his handiwork.
Day to day pours out speech,
 and night to night reveals knowledge.
There is no speech, nor are there words,
 whose voice is not heard.
Their voice goes out through all the earth,
 and their words to the end of the universe."

As soon as Jesse had stopped reading, Sillias had lowered his hands and the congregation's chants grew quiet. A tear fell down Elena's face as she radiated a joy that finally understood what Jesse was trying to tell her. She glowed with the brilliance of the Holy Spirit, and Jesse could see it all over her. As with Sillias and his congregants. As with Jolean and Kwame and Florence.

However, there was a tangible darkness in the middle of the church. Jesse could not see this with his eyes, but he could feel it with his heart. Junior Director Kitting and the other colonists, they all held faces of disgust, repulsiveness and mockery. Then a deep laugh began to shake the room. Yale turned around from the congregation to face Jesse again, and he was no longer furious but full of patronistic glibness.

Chuckling still he said, "Oh, Jesse. You say that your faith is built upon history? That all of this", he raised his hands and spun to the right and to the left, "Is based on what that says?" Tristan pointed to the stone behind him.

Jesse lowered his eyes and readied for Yale's reaction. He could feel the tension ready to explode in the room as the captain had shut his ears and was not going to concede.

"Your faith... your 'power' is in that book?" He pointed to the Bible on the podium. "Do you know the wonderful thing about history? It's written by the victors. And if I destroy that, I can mold this colony into exactly what it was intended to be. Godless."

Jesse picked up the Bible off of the podium and backed away. He had nowhere to go, as his back was inches from the drodd behind him. Yale tilted his head back and to the left, towards Ralph Kitting. "Junior Director Kitting, please remove that religious propaganda from Mr. Heartshire."

Without hesitation, Ralph stepped past the captain and quickly towards Jesse. Jesse dodged to the right, placing the podium between himself and Ralph.

"Ralph, don't do this! You've seen and heard!"

"I've seen and heard nothing but regressive dogma whenever you speak!" With his final syllable, Ralph threw his weight against the podium and sent it crashing towards Sillias. He was caught off guard and wrapped his arms around the altar as he fell over backwards, the podium slamming down on top of him. The candles rattled and the flames danced at the aggressive landing. Elena was the closest to him and rushed over to try to help him lift the heavy stand off of himself.

Jesse tried to escape past the grasp of Ralph by darting to the right, but

Kitting was too close and too fast. Ralph thrust his arms against Jesse's chest, where he gripped onto the edges of Jesse's Scriptures and threw his body back, attempting to wrestle the tome from Jesse's arms.

Thorold and Esth were by Elena's side, helping to pull the podium off of Sillias, his head must have a small gash as red blood had trickled onto the wooden floor beneath him. While they struggled, Captain Yale turned to his right, making eye contact with Manuel and Yolanda.

"Arrest Miss Aquino." He ordered them.

Jesse and Ralph were spinning in circles with each other, both clinging tightly to the Bible between them, both slamming into the stone drodd. Ralph threw a punch that grazed Jesse's jaw, but still he clung on. He swung again, impacting above his right eye, splitting his brow.

But still he didn't let go. Jesse was so desperate to hold onto the Scriptures that he didn't even notice Manuel and Yolanda grab either shoulder and arm of Elena, yanking her back and off of the podium. Losing her help on the heavy altar caused Thorold and Esth to put all of their effort into helping Sillias escape its weight.

"No! Let me go! JESSE!!" She yelled out, looking to her fiance for rescue. He heard her cry and focused his strength into his legs. Jesse shouldered Ralph hard and then pushed him away with a heel to the gut. Ralph stumbled backwards, losing his balance but catching himself on one of the front pews.

"Elena!" He cried and started towards the colonists who held her. However, Ralph Kitting recovered faster than he had expected, and threw a hard left swing into Jesse's right cheek. Jesse reeled, wobbling on his legs then falling in a lunge to his left where he slammed into the giant candles illuminating that side of the drodd. He collapsed on top of them as they thudded hard onto the floor. They were so heavy that cracks could be heard from the fall as they splintered parts of the wooden floor, clanging and ringing like bells.

The candles themselves were not wax as Jesse had previously thought, but apparently hollow metal. From their ringing tones that echoed through the church did he discover this, but also from the bruising impact in his left ribs. Out of the tops of the candles flew hot, flammable oil that shot across the back wall of the church. The tallest metal candle had toppled so hard that it had blown a decent sized hole in the church's siding. In an instant, the still burning wicks touched the doused wood and a blaze of fire erupted in the corner of the building.

The congregants that were still towards the front entrance of the building shrieked in terror and anguish as they scuttled and fled for the door. Jesse's side throbbed, and it hurt to breathe, but he had not let go of the Bible. Ralph Kitting, astonished at the mess their tussle had created, hesitated and looked back to Captain Yale.

Manuel and Yolanda had passed their captain and had complete control over the kicking and screaming Elena. Tristan frowned at her as they went by.

"Take her back to command." Yale demanded. The congregants flooded out of the building, standing a good distance away huddled together. Florence, Jolean and Kwame stood by their scout scooters, watching hard into the windows of the church.

Yale took a few steps towards the outside, scanned the colonists through the windows and then realized that Kitting had not exited. He turned back to find his subordinate dumb faced and Bible-less, backlit by the quickly spreading fire.

"What are you waiting for?! Get the book!" Yale screamed at Ralph. This shook Ralph from his stupor, and he stepped carefully, yet determinedly over the fallen giant candles towards Jesse's sprawled form. Jesse could feel the heat of the fire closing in behind him, but when he turned to flee, Ralph was reaching out his hands at his chest, grasping at the Scriptures. Quickly seizing an opportunity, Jesse kicked hard against a tottering candle at his feet, causing its base to swing away from him. The top of the large metal pipe swung back the other way, impacting the backside of Ralph's knees. He cried out in pain and buckled down just inches from Jesse's face.

Jesse then quickly scrambled to his feet. All around him the fire was consuming the Church of the Rock. Jesse could see tongues of flames licking the ceiling as they climbed the walls. This was not the fire of the Holy Spirit that Jesse had seen in this building not long ago. It broke his heart to witness the destruction of the very thing he was longing to preserve. But Yale was still standing at the front of the building, guarding the only means of escape, and now he had his pistol drawn.

"Give me the book, Heartshire. And I'll send you back home. I'll send you to Earth."

This was his mission after all wasn't it? To bring the Good News of Isstar and his people home to earth and the Christians? Could he really trust that Captain Yale would put him on the very flight he was desiring to take? And what about his marriage to Elena? Maybe they could go home together. This could still end in the way that God had intended. The way that Jesse had originally hoped.

Come help us, Jesse.

The voice of the Spirit spoke. The Jolethites from his dream called to him. He wanted to be the one to bring Isstar to the Christians, but God had called him here, to Toisee. In his heart, he knew that his purpose was here. Jesse needed to bring Jesus to the Jolethites.

The peace and calm that Jesse felt upon his soul at this moment was beyond understanding. Everything was suddenly made so crystal clear. Here was the life he was called to. This was where he belonged for now. His mission field was with the Isstarleans. Images of Thorold, Sillias, Esth and many others flooded his mind. Their church was going up in flames, and they needed him. And there were many more Jolethites here that needed to hear the matching message of Jesus.

Jesse looked to Yale and said this realization out loud, not declaring it to

Captain Yale, but declaring it to himself. "This is my home!"

With that, he about-faced and sprinted as fast as he could at the hole that was made in the back of the church building. It was wreathed in flame, the wood looking shrunken and charred from heat. BLAM, BLAM!! Yale took shots at him with his pistol as he fled. His only hope was escape. Jesse prayed that the boards would give way, so he gritted his teeth, closed his eyes and he thrust all of his body against it as hard as he could.

CRRRACK!!

Splinters were sent flying in all directions. Aflame and agitated woodchips with shooting sparks exploded from the back of the church. His shoulders screamed at him in pain and he tumbled forward, landing hard onto his knees. A sharp, stabbing pain shot threw his legs but he was out. Bits of blazing red coals scattered around him, and his face felt singed. Glancing quickly behind him, Jesse rose, grimaced against his suffering knees and sprinted towards the field of tall growing 'wheat bananas' directly in front of him.

Out front, Elena's heart shattered as she feared the worst at the sound of gunshots in the church. But seconds later inside she rejoiced, because although she was held tightly between Manuel and Yolanda, she saw through the tears in her eyes Jesse's back as he disappeared into the tall crops. Moments after Captain Yale supported a limping Ralph Kitting out of the front of the church building. The Church of the Rock was now fully engulfed. She could feel the heat pulsing against her face, which normally would have felt nice and warm against the chill of the day. Jesse seemed to be alive and escaping, but everything she had been hoping for was literally going up in flames. When her eyes grazed upon the disillusioned faces of the Isstarlean villagers as she was pulled away to the scooters, her heart felt nothing. It had left her, and was somewhere running through a crop field, desperately clutching the Word of God.

CHAPTER 21
A STRAND OF THREE CORDS

The lightning was getting brighter, matching with the ever-loudening rolls of thunder. It wasn't raining yet, but the smell of must was heavy in the air. The odor reminded Jesse of his discussion with Junia which seemed like a lifetime ago now, when she enticed him to sniff from her novel, Into the Wild Black Yonder. He was still clutching the Bible, harder than he needed to, but its volume felt like the physical anchor he needed right now. He looked down, brought it to his nose and inhaled. He could smell twinges of oil from Gus' kitchen, traces of rose from his mother's Sweetie Spray, and also just simply the scent of plain paper. That final scent had reminded him of Elena's words in the church, as these might be just words printed on paper, but as she had said, these words reveal the truth of who God is.

Jesse had hidden himself in the field for hours now. He hadn't dared to raise his head above the golden stalks and bunches of 'bananas' for fear of being discovered. But with the approaching storm, he was exposed here in the open. The forest edge on the far side of the village was tempting, but it also put him uncomfortably close to the colony, and he knew he could never go back there again.

He was also ashamed to approach the Isstarleans. It wasn't his fault, but Jesse did blame himself heavily for the destruction of their sanctuary to Isstar. What if he had allowed Yale to take the Bible? It wasn't God, he couldn't take God. Why didn't he just give it to him?

Because I wouldn't let you.

The quiet voice of divine reassurance rested on his heart. He had wept long and hard when he had first stopped running. He had no more tears to cry. But the emptiness of his hollow chest was being filled with more than just the Toiseean air. He could feel the sustaining presence of Jesus with him here. Jesse knew his own guilt was going to beguile him, and his own doubt was going to accuse him of destroying the faith of the villagers. But he also knew in his mind that the truth was that he did exactly what he felt God was leading him to do. And the confidence and comfort growing in his heart from the Holy Spirit was telling him God was proud of his stance against the forces of evil.

So, finally, after another close lighting strike and immediate thunderclap, he stood slowly to his feet. Only when standing fully erect could Jesse see over all of the tall, pale orange, ready to harvest crops of the field. The storm was closing in, and quickly from the east. The rain band looked nearly to envelop the towers of the Toiseean Colony.

Elena... I'm so sorry. Jesse's thoughts ping-ponged back and forth from Jesus to Elena. She was taken by Yale. Her own proclamation of faith was extremely enriching to his soul, but equally as damning as his own in the eyes of command. He detested the notion that she would suffer punishment for the faith he encouraged her to have. Would she be jailed? Exiled? He had no idea. Their marriage was to take place tomorrow. And a sorrowful realization it was for his bitter heart that their union may never actually take place. Jesse swallowed and sighed, clutching the Word of God to his chest, and set off back for the village of Rue.

The smoke was still rising from the smoldering ashes of what was the Church of the Rock. The massive Drodd stone still stood, obviously impervious to the flames that engulfed the rest of the building. But it was black and charred by the heat.

As Jesse emerged from the crop field, he could see the villagers gathered around the well in the middle of town. Many of them held bags or had crude backpacks thrown over their shoulders. Traces, the horse things of Toisee, were strapped to luggage carrying carts. The members seemed to be huddled around in a circle in the center, and as Jesse approached, he could hear Sillias' voice carrying over the rolling thunder.

The crunches of the gravel gave away Jesse's approach, and Thorold spun around suddenly, on alert.

"Jesse!" He yelled, and the other villagers turned to him. Thorold walked towards Jesse determinedly. Jesse stopped at his approach, unsure of his intention as his face was blank and flat.

"I'm so sorry, I didn't —" Jesse had his hand up, palm to Thorold's approach. The young Jolethite pushed Jesse's hand aside and wrapped his arms around his spiritual brother. He squeezed Jesse tightly and said.

"We so happy see you." Thorold said, his voice muffled against Jesse's back and shoulder. He let go and patted Jesse on the arms, his grin happy but pained from the day.

"Thank you, brother." Jesse said, patting Thorold's arm back. They approached the group together, walking side by side. The Isstarleans parted, making space for Jesse to join their circle. Sillias, his head wrapped in a cloth, bowed in welcome to Jesse's presence.

"Welcome, Jesse. Welcome."

"Sillias, I am so sorry for this. For everything."

Sillias looked confusedly at him. "You lose all, and protect God's Words," He pointed to the Bible in Jesse's hand. "And you sorry?"

"For your church." Jesse waved towards the smoking ruins. "And now you have to leave?" He looked around at the crowd of Isstarleans. They looked tired and worn, but they all held content faces. The bright eyes of each of them rested on Jesse, and they looked genuinely happy to see him. He felt safe and welcome in their gaze, and not exposed or judged.

"We follow Isstar. Not wood building." Sillias explained. "And when Isstar say go, we go."

Esth, who was standing a few villagers down from him, left the circle and presented him a few items. Jesse graciously accepted them, trading with her his Bible, which she clutched to her chest, same as he did.

He looked over the items she presented. A mostly ok Venture shirt, his torn and slightly burned satchel bag, and his half-toasted tablet. He tried to activate it, but unsurprisingly it didn't turn on.

"Broken?" She asked.

Jesse nodded, "Yes, but I don't need it anymore."

She looked sympathetic and then produced a slip of paper from her pocket. "Before broken, I copy window." Esth gave Jesse the slip of paper. On it, it appeared she had attempted to write down what was on the screen, guessing that it may be important information that Jesse needed or wanted. He smiled at her effort.

"Aw, thank you Esth. That was kind."

She bowed and motioned towards Sillias with the Bible. Jesse responded that it was alright, and so she walked it over to him. As she moved away, Jesse scanned further down on the paper she had written.

EXCESSIVE HEAT WARNING
Battery life, 74%.
Horticultural Specialist Jesse Heartshire
Urgent Message from Captain Tristan Yale.

Jesse stopped. Apparently before the tablet broke completely, Yale had sent him a message. He dropped his other things on the ground before him and studied her writing carefully.

Urgent Message from Captain Tristan Yale.

Mr. Heartshire. No doubt you are aware of your excommunication and status termination from this colony. I had warned you that insisting upon your own delusions would have dire consequences if they continued outside of your own foolish mind. You will be officially listed as LOST IN THE LINE OF DUTY upon the Venture Colony manifest. If you do resurrect from the dead in my colony, I have given orders to security to execute you on sight. Do not test the resolve of my commitment to the health of this extension of humanity.

You sir, have done enough damage as it is.

I have officially lost two specialists in the defense of this charter, and I will take steps to ensure the plague of your faith is squelched before it spreads any further. As for Miss Elena Aquino, she will be taking the offer you passed on. For her declaration, she is to be removed from this colony and transplanted back to Earth. Obviously, your marriage is officially cancelled from the colony docket, as the chances of either of you meeting again are nil.

Goodbye Mr. Heartshire. I do not expect to see you again. May you and your God perish in the Toiseean wild.

COLONY DIRECTOR TRISTAN YALE

Jesse tore the paper in half and crumpled it between his hands. Then he threw it on the ground, tossing on top of it the Venture uniform shirt and broken tablet. Yale was banishing Elena from the planet as punishment for her declaration of faith. He was proud of her, but at this moment he wished she would have stayed quiet. At least there would be a chance of them seeing each other again if she were still stationed here. Jesse dismissed that wish quickly though, as her remaining in the colony would mean she would be betrothed to someone else.

Sillias looked at Jesse. "Bad news?"

Jesse nodded angrily. "They have… cast me away." Sillias and the others looked curiously at Jesse, trying to understand his speech. Jesse considered another way of showing it, so he picked up the crumpled piece of paper. He held it in one hand and pointed at it, saying, "Me." Then he held his arm up, and pointed at that, saying, "Toiseeans." Then he turned and threw the paper out as far as he could.

"Ahhh." Sillias said, understanding. "No more Toiseean?"

Jesse shook his head. Looking down at the ground. He didn't want to be in the colony anymore, but being homeless on an alien planet wasn't a thrilling prospect either. Sillias approached Jesse, placing his hands gently on his shoulders. Jesse raised his head to meet his friend in the eyes.

"Jesse, you are Isstarlean." He then reached in his pocket, and pulled out a Drodd necklace, hand wrapped in leather. It was singed around the edges a bit, and smelled like smoke. It must have been in the fire at the church and was saved through it, not unlike himself. Sillias put it around Jesse's neck and tied it behind his head.

"You are Isstarlean, brother. You come with family."

"You want me to come with you?"

"I call you, come with us. Help us."

Sillias nodded and smirked. Jesse looked around at the others in the circle. They nodded and smiled at him as well. They were his kin. Brothers and sisters, children of God, just as he was. They didn't just want him along with them. They needed him, as a fellow member of the Body of Christ. Jesse smiled back at them and put his hands on Sillias' shoulders.

Sillias' words were his broken English attempt at saying he was inviting him to come with them to wherever they would travel to next. Jesse knew that. But he also could tell that God had spoken to him through Sillias. It was the confirmation that Jesse needed to hear. That he was exactly where God had intended him to be all along.

His journey wasn't over, and maybe neither was Elena's. They both were now embarking on the next chapter of their lives following after Jesus. He prayed for himself, and for her. Throughout the rest of the day, as the Isstarleans travelled away, attempting to outrun the storm that followed behind them, Jesse asked God for guidance, wisdom, strength and clarity of what was ahead of them both. He asked God earnestly that he could see her again. He asked God that if it was His will, that He would bless their marital union one day. And most of all, he prayed that both of them would somehow grow closer to each other as their faith grew in Christ.

He couldn't be sure, and he hoped it wasn't wishful thinking, but Jesse felt he heard an immediate answer from a still, quiet voice in his heart.

ABOUT THE AUTHOR

Nathan Bressler currently lives in Pottsboro, TX with his wife Melissa and family. He holds a Master of Theological Studies degree from Southwestern Baptist Theological Seminary and teaches at Texoma Christian School in Sherman. Nathan is also a published playwright of the One-Act Easter/Passover production *Behold Our Lamb*.

He can be reached for comment or question at nate.w.bressler@gmail.com.

Made in the USA
Coppell, TX
06 February 2026

70092417R00150